A Do Right Man

A Novel

OMAR TYREE

SIMON & SCHUSTER PAPERBACKS
New York   London   Toronto   Sydney

SIMON & SCHUSTER PAPERBACKS
Rockefeller Center
1230 Avenue of the Americas
New York, NY 10020

First Simon & Schuster paperback edition 2004

SIMON & SCHUSTER PAPERBACKS and colophon are registered trademarks of
Simon & Schuster, Inc.

For information about special discounts for bulk purchses,
please contact Simon & Schuster Special Sales:
1-800-456-6798 or business@simonandschuster.com.

Designed by Deirdre C. Amthor

Manufactured in the United States of America

21 23 25 27 29 30 28 26 24 22

The Library of Congress has cataloged the hardcover
edition as follows:
Tyree, Omar.
A do right man / Omar Tyree.
p. cm.
1. Afro-Americans—Fiction. I. Title.
PS3570.Y59 D6 1997
813'.54—dc20 97-28611
CIP

ISBN 0-684-82929-0
0-684-84803-1 (Pbk)

To my beautiful and driven mother
Renee McLaurin Alston
may your soul rest in peace.

Love
your son
Antyne Eric McLaurin

October 29, 1996

What is love?
> *Something that makes your heart patter.*

Happiness?
> *Something that makes you smile.*

Romance?
> *Flowers, cards, and candy.*

And chemistry?
> *All the right words*
>> *all the right moves*
>>> *and all the right places.*

So, how come you are still single?
> *Oh, now that*
>> *I don't know.*

Q&A
By Omar Tyree

A Metaphor
for My Life

Ever since I received my college degree back in the spring of 1986, my life has been a big roller-coaster ride, filled with climbs, dips, loops, curves, and high-speed free falls. I call it The Bobby Dallas Whirl.

I thought a formal education was supposed to bring a guy job security and some type of stability in life. Maybe if I had been interested in a career other than radio broadcasting, I would have been better off a lot sooner. Then again, with the money I'm making now, maybe the bumpy ride was worth it.

There hasn't been much stability in radio. A real skill like architecture or engineering would have been a more stable profession. But who am I kidding? With those careers, you would actually have to do some *real* work. Not to say I don't do my share of work in radio, or that I haven't paid my dues, because I have. I'm just saying that radio is a hit-or-miss game, like the lottery. You never know what to expect or if you'll even be employed the next day. You could be on top of the world one day and stuffed underneath a trash can the next. Oscar the Grouch from "Sesame Street," who lived inside a garbage pail, comes to mind as the alter ego of any happy-go-lucky radio professional. A lot of us may seem happy while on the air or out in public, but behind closed doors, we're very insecure. That's just the nature of the business we're in. Nevertheless, on good days with good pay, the bottom line is that we love what we do.

Radio is like a game of Russian roulette—you either get a big bang or nothing. The thing is, once you've experienced that bang, no matter what other stuff you have to go through, you're always willing to keep at it. It's like a night-and-day marriage. On some days you love it like a beautiful, spirited woman, and on other days you hate it like a villain who haunts your dreams at night.

My profession is actually the perfect metaphor for my life. After I completed college, I had no idea what the hell I was getting into from one day to the next. I was like a high-caliber shotgun with no safety clip, trying desperately to find a proper target. I've always been a good man and a good person, but that didn't seem to matter. I mean, I've really been through some hectic shit during my postcollege years. I had to reevaluate my life more than a few times. I got a chance to travel and do a lot of soul-searching, though. I haven't been married yet, and I don't have any children, but I'd like to experience those things. I can't say that I didn't have enough opportunities with women either, because I did. Things just never worked out. Half the time, I was simply trying to gain control of my life.

I'm just now beginning to earn the kind of money that would make any parents proud, and beginning to live the way I always imagined living. I just can't handle the emptiness of being alone anymore. I'm thirty-one years old, for God's sake, and I'm still searching for peace of mind and a permanent woman! Honestly, though, after all I've been through in the past decade, sometimes I don't think I'll *ever* settle down. Maybe, though, if I looked at my love life in the same light as I look at my profession in radio, expecting everyday surprises and daily letdowns, and just learned to roll with the punches, just maybe I could make a relationship work. Maybe I could find that peace of mind in a commitment to one special woman. Or, then again . . . maybe not. And maybe I'll be one of those good black men who got away.

In the Beginning

The roller-coaster ride all began in my senior year at Howard University in Washington, D.C. We called it The Mecca, the high ground of black American culture and education. I was surrounded by high-achieving brown students from every state in America, including plenty of students from the Caribbean and from countries in Africa.

As one could imagine, there were many different types of sisters and brothers to choose from to get hitched to. And the first people you were attracted to were usually in your same classes, whether they noticed you or not. However, just because you were there at Howard, surrounded by all of those beautiful black people, it didn't necessarily guarantee you a partner. Some guys had what it took to entice sisters romantically and some guys didn't. I was one of those guys who didn't. I was a nice guy, and a perfect gentleman from Greensboro, North Carolina. You know the type; "He's just a good friend."

There was this sister from New York named Pearl Davis that I'd had the hots for since our freshman year. We were both radio broadcast majors. Pearl was tall, fine, and intelligent, but her attitude was strictly New York. She carried herself like the halls had her name on them. With me being an unglamorous son of the South, Pearl hadn't paid me any mind for three years. I was the dirty tile floor underneath her brand new shoes.

I remember when I first got her attention. It was late September, 1985. I had finally secured a morning DJ spot on WHBC, Howard University's AM radio station. I was wearing a blue silk shirt and had just gotten a fresh fade haircut. Cheap silk shirts were the things to wear back then and all of the guys wore their hair in fades. I was trying my best to keep up with the Joneses. Howard had a long reputation to uphold, which included campus fashion.

Pearl strutted into the studio and asked me, "What's up with all this Trouble Funk and this go-go music shit?" I got off the air at eleven o'clock. Pearl was on after me. She paced impatiently inside the studio lounge area for ten minutes. I watched her.

"It's on the playlist," I told her with hunched shoulders.

"Yeah, but shit, you have to play it twenty damn times a day?" she ranted. "That shit is so *whack,* man! I'm tired of hearing that shit!"

I was thinking, *I wonder if she knows any words other than* shit. "This *is* D.C.," I reminded her. Go-go was their homegrown music.

"So! This is *our* radio station! We should be able to play what we wanna play!" she responded to me. "I know *I* will."

I smiled at her. She knew better than that. "If you do that on a real job, you'll end up fired *real* fast," I told her. Messing with the playlist was a definite no-no in the radio business.

"Yeah, we'll see," she said. Pearl slid her tall, slim frame into the recording room in blue Jordache jeans. She looked damned good! She had a smooth, angular face with rapid roving eyes that caught everything. To tell the truth, I was intimidated by her.

I grabbed my things and headed for my next class. Faye Butler, my sophomore friend, was waiting for me down the hall. Faye was a fellow southerner, from Macon, Georgia. She was a television/film major with the soft, rounded, baby-face features of a good girl. She was the kind of young, good-hearted soul that knowing mothers liked to fix their sons up with. And although Faye was fully developed with all of the right curves, since her freshman year we had only been friends.

"Hey," Pearl Davis yelled down the hall to me, "I like your shirt! That shit is stupid fresh!"

Faye frowned at me and shook her head in disgust. Even graduation-bound New Yorkers spoke with the street slang of the day, no matter how ridiculous it may have sounded to the rest of the world. Nevertheless, it was 1985, so it wasn't that peculiar.

I was an easily pleased sucker from North Carolina. I smiled back at Pearl wider than a circus clown with a painted face. I looked into her caramel-colored mug, viewing her reddish-brown, wavy hair, and was infatuated. "Thanks" was all I could say at the time. After that incident, though, I couldn't get her off my mind. My smile didn't last long. My friend Faye read my gleeful expression with horror.

"You like her?" she asked me. Before I could respond she spat, "I can't stand that girl."

There was nothing I could say to that.

"I don't know who gave her the key to the world, but she needs to check herself," Faye added.

Like the saying goes, two is company, three is a crowd.

•

As fate would have it, since we were seniors, Pearl and I had to show our faces at a lot of the campus events to stay informed for radio. At every event, Pearl would pick with me for the hell of it. I actually felt privileged to finally gain so much attention from her.

"Here, 'Big Bob,' wear my chain. I can't have you in here looking like a country bumpkin," she said to me at an October party. It was rumored that Def Jam's Run DMC would be performing. They never did show.

Pearl wrapped a thick rope chain around my neck. I was too much in awe to resist. She and her New York girlfriends then proceeded to make me their entertainment for the night.

"You call him 'Big Bob,' hunh?" one of her girlfriends asked Pearl with a grin. Pearl liked to make fun of my six-foot-four-inch frame, especially since I wasn't much of a basketball player.

"Yeah, look at his feet," she responded to her friend. "You know what they say about brothers with big feet, y'all."

"Oh, shit, I need to borrow him tonight then, 'cause my man got little feet," another one of her New York girls commented as they laughed at me.

"No you don't," Pearl snapped with a smile. "I found him first."

"Yeah, well, tell me what woods you caught him in, so I can go big-foot huntin', girl."

It's embarrassing to even think of it. I wasn't too good at defending myself back then. Compared to my plain and practical Volkswagen Bug mentality, Pearl Davis was a red Corvette at a car show.

"Where do you live?" she asked me later on that night. It was nearly four o'clock in the morning. We were all leaving out. No one was particularly hurt that the Run DMC thing was only a rumor. It was still a lively party.

"I live in Slowe," I told her. I was a bit nervous about it. *Why is she asking me where I live? Oh my God! What does this mean?* I remember thinking. At that time of night, a where-do-you-live question could have been easily construed as a possible sleepover.

"You still live in the damn dorms? Shit, man, get a life," she told me with a half frown, half grin. Then she had to tell her girlfriends, who were all climbing inside of a black Honda Civic. "Hey y'all, Big Bob still lives in the damn dorms. I told y'all he was country."

I smiled and began to take off her gold chain. I wanted to say, "It's cheaper to live in the dorms," but I kept it to myself. I don't believe I would have won any brownie points with a comment like that one.

"You don't have to take it off," Pearl told me. "I might be coming with you," she teased, or at least I *thought* she was teasing.

My heart leaped into my throat. "Hunh?"

Pearl was loving it. She was absolutely the aggressor. "Hey y'all, should I go over to Big Bob's barn tonight?"

"Yeah, girl, go choke yourself some chickens!" one of her friends yelled out from the laughter.

"Well, I don't have room to take both of y'all. And you're not sitting on that big nigga's lap in my damn car," the owner of the Honda huffed.

"He only live at Slowe. We can *walk* over there," Pearl shot back. We were at Ninth and T Streets Northwest. Slowe Hall was less than ten blocks away on Third Street.

"Well, get to walking," her girlfriend told us. "Nobody gon' mess with y'all, 'cause Big Bob will take out his hunting knife and jack them up. Won't you, Bob?"

I just smiled, shocked that Pearl Davis had actually decided to go to my dorm room with me.

Pearl didn't say much on the way to my dorm. I was doing most of the talking for a change. I didn't know what else to do. The woman of my college dreams was coming to spend the night.

"You got a lot of work to do this weekend?" I asked her.

Pearl smiled and said, "Why, you got any plans for us?"

I hunched my shoulders. "No, not really."

"Well, I don't have nothing on my mind but sleep," she told me with a grin.

That was fine with me. I didn't care if I didn't get any. I was elated that she would even be in my room. I signed her in and led her to my room on the second floor.

"Hmm, neat room you have here," Pearl said. Then she started taking off her clothes.

My jeans grew so tight that it was beginning to hurt. "I have a sleeping bag. I'll sleep on the floor and you can take the bed," I told her.

She looked at me and smiled. "You are a big teddy bear. Do you know that?"

I smiled back at her while clearing out space on the tiny floor to place my sleeping bag. I had to stretch it from the doorway to the edge of the bed, which was basically the length of the room.

"What are you doing with a sleeping bag anyway?" Pearl asked me. She was pulling her bra off from inside of her shirt.

I looked away and answered, "My mother made me take it."

She stared at me and burst into laughter. "Oh my God! You're a momma's boy, too?"

"No I'm not," I snapped. I really wasn't. I had always been closer to my father.

Pearl didn't comment on it. "You got any shorts I can wear? *Clean* shorts?" she asked me. She stood right at my chest, as if she was daring me to touch her.

I maneuvered around her and to my dresser to pull out a pair of gray Russell shorts.

Pearl smiled at me and said, "Can you close your eyes while I take off my panties?"

I felt ready to burst open at the seams. *This isn't happening!* I kept telling myself. I closed my eyes and could hear Pearl giggling while she pulled her jeans and underwear off.

"Okay, you can look now."

I opened my eyes and peeked at her in my shorts. She was actually wearing my shorts! Pearl Davis! Then she climbed into my bed and got under my covers. I stretched out inside my sleeping bag on the floor. Then I heard Pearl sitting up. She was staring around my room in the dark. I looked up at the clock on my desk. It was close to five in the morning.

"Are you tired?" she asked me.

I was, but I wasn't going to tell her if she wasn't. "Why?" I asked, hesitantly.

"Because I'm not."

We sat in silence for a moment. I didn't know what else to say.

"You wanna get up here with me, or you want me to come down there with you?" Pearl asked me.

I was baffled, not believing my ears. "Hunh?"

Pearl sighed and slid out of the bed and onto the floor with me. Then she leveled herself on top of me. I was too paranoid to move a muscle. "Can I go to sleep like this?" she asked.

"I don't know. Can you?" I responded.

She laughed and shook her head. I knew she could feel my hard-on. "Any other guy would have been clawing at my pants as soon as he closed the door," she told me.

"Well, my name is Bobby Dallas. I'm pleased to meet you." It was the first clever remark I had ever said to Pearl.

She chuckled, and her tall, slim body vibrated against mine. "You ever kissed a girl before?" she asked me. She French-kissed me before I could respond. I mean, she pushed her watermelon-flavored, Jolly Rancher tongue all the way inside of my mouth. She and her girlfriends had been eating Jolly Rancher candy all that night.

"Are you afraid of me, Bobby Dallas?" she asked.

"Very," I told her.

Pearl laughed again. I was on a roll.

"Do you have any protection?"

"Yeah. I'll get it," I said, trying to free myself to get up.

Pearl held me down with her hands pressed against my chest. "No. Where is it? I'll get it."

"It's in the closet, toward the back of the shelf."

She smiled as she stood. "That's your little hiding place, hunh?"

I smiled back at her, embarrassed. I said, "I guess."

Pearl reached up onto my closet shelf and came down with two condoms. "Close your eyes again," she told me.

"What are you about to do?" I asked.

"Just close your eyes. Trust me."

I did it. I then felt her tugging at my shorts and drawers to get them down. I pulled my legs out as she took them off.

"Lord have mercy! I was right!" she said. She was pleased, I guess.

I smiled to myself, proud of my genetic information. Pearl ripped open a condom, slid it on me, and rolled it down. Before I could count to four, she was upon me. I was no longer hesitant at that point. I did what I had learned to do.

"O-o-oh shit! Bobby!" Pearl moaned as her hair dangled in my face.

I began to rub my hands into the small of her back and breathe with her as she did what she had learned to do. Our tall bodies were too much for that small room. I was embarrassed at how much thumping we were doing on the floor. I was wondering if whoever lived in the room below me was hearing the early-morning freak show. I wasn't planning on stopping, and neither was Pearl. You don't stop a dream come true, you enjoy it to the fullest. So I held on to Pearl Davis for dear life, as if she would slip away into oblivion if I ever let go. And with every spasm of the feel-good, I told myself, *I'm not dreaming! I'm not dreaming! This is real! This is real! It's Pearl Davis! YES!*

When we were done, Pearl fell out across my chest and began to pant as if she had just run the mile. I was pretty worn out myself. We went at it pretty good.

"You better not have a girlfriend," she breathed into my face, still exhausted.

"Naw. I don't," I breathed back.

Pearl crashed back down to my chest. "Now you do," she informed me.

That was it. I was Pearl's new man, whether I liked it or not. It still amazes me how simple many things were back in those college years. Things would get a lot more complicated after college. But on that night, I was in love like I don't know what. I felt pretty good about being Pearl's new man, right up until the phone rang at seven-thirty that morning.

"Hey, are you ready to go jogging?" It was Faye. I had forgotten all about our Saturday morning run.

I panicked. "Aw, man, ah, I was up a little late last night at this function I had to attend." I hoped that Faye would get the message that I was canceling without having to spell it out to her.

"Oh, so you're gonna have me jog all by myself? Some pervert may snatch me off the street," she joked. If Pearl wasn't stretched out across my chest, I would have laughed along with her.

"That won't happen," I said. I was as steady as a man in a coma. I don't know why I even bothered to answer the phone in that situation.

"Okay, well, when I get back, let's go to breakfast together," Faye suggested.

"All right," I responded quickly. "I'll be up by then."

"I'll see you later then," she said.

As soon as I hung up the phone, Pearl grumbled, "Who was that?"

I was startled by it. "I thought you were asleep," I said.

"I bet you did. Well, who was it?"

"It was just a friend of mine."

Pearl leaned up and looked into my eyes. "Are you sure?"

I hesitated. "Yeah, I'm sure."

"Hmm," she grunted, falling out across my chest again. "You better not be lying to me."

I stared up at the ceiling not believing the predicament I had put myself in. It was the beginning of the end of my peaceful and platonic relationship with Faye. I was afraid to come clean and simply tell her that Pearl was my new lady. Although Faye and I were just friends, on some days it seemed we were just a word or a touch away from being much more.

A Broken Heart

I tried my hardest to keep Faye from finding out about Pearl, but realistically, it was only a matter of time. I continued to go jogging with Faye on those few Saturday mornings when I was not held hostage by Pearl the Friday before, but it was getting harder and harder to keep coming up with creative excuses. Faye then suggested that we jog on Sundays instead. Since we both had late classes to begin the week, I convinced her that we should run on Monday mornings. That idea worked until Pearl began to plan my entire weekends with her. That's when Faye got suspicious. I hadn't been able to spend time with her on the weekends for months. And once we had gotten past the fall semester and were nearing spring break, Faye had had enough of my elusiveness.

"What is going on with you?" she asked me. She knew that I would be graduating soon. We were standing in the hallway on the second floor of the C. B. Powell communications building. We were about to head to our media relations class that I had somehow put off taking until my final semester.

"What are you talking about?" I responded to her. I was stalling. I knew exactly what Faye was asking me.

She stared at me for a moment. "Are you trying to avoid me for some reason?"

"Avoid you? I see you nearly every day," I said to her. The C. B. Powell building wasn't but so big, and Faye and I had several meeting places where we were sure to see each other.

"I'm talking about on the weekends."

I frowned and said, "What, just because I don't go jogging all the time?"

She returned my frown. "No, it's not just that. I mean, we used to go to see movies and do a lot of different things on the weekends. Now all I'm getting is your answering machine."

I looked away from her. I was never good at lying face-to-face, especially to someone I cared about. Some guys are able to do it every day. "Well, you know, it's been hectic with so many events and things going on that I have to cover for the radio station," I told her.

Faye gave me an evil stare that I didn't know she had in her. "You *used* to ask me to go with you," she snapped.

"Yeah, and most of the time you turned me down."

She stormed off for class without me. I followed her into the classroom and took a seat. Faye chose to sit on the other side of the room. I felt guilty as hell, but I figured it would have been worse for me to tell her that Pearl was my girlfriend and that I had been spending my weekends with her. Even the sight of Pearl in the hallways sent Faye into a rage. I never asked her why she felt so strongly about her. Faye acted as if they had some kind of personal beef.

After class, Faye pulled me aside and apologized. "I know I probably seem childish to you."

"No, not at all," I said, cutting her off. She was telling the truth, though. She *was* acting a bit childish.

"Well, it's just that . . . remember that talk we had before about sex?"

I damn near swallowed my tongue, and my heart rate increased. "Ah, yeah, I remember." *Why is she asking me this, and in the middle of the hallway of all places?* I was thinking to myself.

"Well, I know that we're just friends and all, but when some guys find out that I'm not into having sex and everything, they just get turned off and start making up excuses about being with me."

I shook my head. It was a coincidence that Pearl and I had started seeing each other right after Faye confided her virginity to me during a long, late-night phone conversation.

"That has nothing to do with anything," I told her.

"Are you sure?"

"Yeah, I'm sure. I know we're just friends. I wouldn't do that to you. I'm not a sex fiend like that anyway."

Faye tossed her hand on my arm and smiled. "That's good to know."

My stomach cramped up. It felt as if I was about to throw up my lunch. I wasn't a sex fiend before I started seeing Pearl. But Pearl was. That made me guilty by association. She wasn't having sex four and five days out of a week by herself. Pearl was into repetitions and going the distance, and I wasn't exactly turning her down.

"So you don't need sex either?" Faye asked me.

I took a deep breath before I answered her. "I wouldn't exactly say that."

"Are you seeing somebody?"

Oh my God! I thought. "Not right now," I lied, briefly looking away again. *She knows I'm lying,* I told myself. Then again, I was so unassuming back then that maybe she couldn't tell. I mean, it wasn't as if I was the kind of guy that girls suspected of having a reputation. I was more of a bashful loner. I probably could have gotten away with telling Faye I was a virgin myself.

I had my opportunity to come clean with Faye and I blew it. The next thing I knew, she was squeezing my hand and leaning to whisper to me, "Sometimes I think about us. Do you?"

No, no, no! What do I say now? Faye was moving in for the kill and she didn't even realize it. "Everybody *thinks* about it," I said. It was a good answer.

Faye let go of my hand. "Well, hopefully, if you're not too busy, we can go to the movies or something this weekend."

"Yeah, we'll see." I was praying that I didn't sound too committed to the idea. We parted company with Faye smiling at me. As soon as she disappeared into the stairway, Pearl popped out from down the hall with a girlfriend. She was distressed.

"I don't believe this shit. My mom had a damn accident this morning," she told me.

"Down here?" I asked her. I had barely caught my breath from the conversation with Faye.

Pearl looked at me as if I was an idiot. "No, not down here, in New York. In Manhattan. I'm about to go buy a train ticket now. I'll see you when I get back."

Just like that, Pearl was out of sight and on her way to New York. I didn't even get a chance to ask how long she would be staying. I knew that she would at least spend the night. I got to my dorm room and called Faye immediately.

"You want to go out tonight?" she asked me. She was surprised by my urgency.

"Well, the thing is, I can't make any promises about this weekend, but I *do* know that I'm not too busy tonight, so why not?"

"Well . . . okay," she agreed. Knowing Faye, she probably had a million things to do. I figured if we went out that Wednesday while Pearl was in New York, instead of on the weekend, I could grab a bird and dodge a bullet at the same time. I realized that Faye and I would not have time to cover any bases on a weeknight. It was perfect. I could take her out and successfully maintain our platonic friendship.

I forget what movie we went to see, but it was at Tenley Circle on Wisconsin Avenue. I remember a bunch of black teenagers from D.C. acting rowdy in the lines. Wisconsin Avenue was in the white section of the city, almost in Maryland, but that never stopped the inner-city blacks from taking over the theater. The movie was one of those midweek releases, so the line was packed.

"Wow!" Faye said to me. "This must be the night!"

"Yeah," I mumbled to her. I was looking around to make sure none of Pearl's friends were there. They were always where the action was.

"Are you looking for someone?" Faye asked me.

I was startled. "Naw, I'm just seeing who's out here."

"Oh." She looked suspicious, but I paid it no mind because I didn't see anyone I knew who knew Pearl.

I purchased our tickets and headed for the refreshment line. Faye said she was going to the rest room. When she walked back out, some big, husky guy tried to pick her up. He was dark and intimidating. I know I sound like a petrified white boy, but that's what I remember; he was big and black and built like a football player.

"Can I watch the movie with you?"

"I'm with a friend," Faye told him.

He looked around and quickly spotted me. He was as tall as I was and forty pounds heavier. I was sure glad that Faye wasn't my woman. I might have been compelled to act heroic in some way. To say the least, the situation was embarrassing.

Faye walked over and joined me in the refreshment line. The big black guy followed her.

"Y'all don't go together, right?" he asked Faye. "We could go out another time then."

I couldn't believe how forward he was. He cared less about me being with her.

Faye said, "I don't think so," and turned her back to him.

He looked at me and frowned before walking off.

"I hate guys like that," Faye told me. "That was very disrespectful."

"What if I was your brother?" I asked her with a smile. I was attempting to take things lightly.

"It *still* would have been disrespectful. There are certain ways that you approach people, and *that's* not the way."

I thought about what would be the best way to break the news to Faye that I had a girlfriend. *There is no best way,* I told myself. Any and every method would hurt her, especially since it was Pearl. I spent the whole time in the movie contemplating my predicament. That's probably why I don't remember it.

On the bus ride back to campus, Faye fell asleep against my shoulder. It wasn't that late. It was only after nine, and I kept wanting to wake her up because I was beginning to think some rather sexual thoughts, and people were looking at us. But I was afraid to touch her.

Miraculously, Faye woke up a block or two away from our stop on Georgia Avenue. I was really nervous then. One of Pearl's girlfriends could have been anywhere. I had a strong fear of what would happen if Pearl suspected me of cheating on her. I wasn't looking forward to that type of drama in my life. At the time, I was still very much an amiable North Carolina boy.

"Why are we in such a hurry?" Faye asked me, noticing the pep in my step.

"This is a weekday," I reminded her.

She smiled. "I thought you said you didn't have much to do tonight."

I was puzzled. She was right. I did tell her that. "Yeah, I don't, but I bet you do."

"Mmm-hmm," she grumbled, "blame it on me."

We got to the all-girls' Bethune dormitory. I was tempted to say " 'Bye," and keep on walking down Fourth Street toward Slowe, but Faye made me walk her to the door.

Shit! I remember thinking. *This is all I need.*

Faye looked into my eyes as if she was expecting a kiss. "Well, I guess this is good night," she said.

I stood there as stiff as an Egyptian mummy. Then I shoved my hands inside my pockets. I didn't know what else to do with them. "Yeah, I guess so," I responded.

"Well, okay," she said, with one hand extending to the door.

I nodded, ready to head on my way. "All right then. I'll see you tomorrow."

"Bobby?" Faye said. "You're not gonna give me a hug, Mr. Handsome?"

I was apprehensive about it. It doesn't take much to get aroused when you're already thinking things. "Since when did I become *Mr. Handsome?*" I asked her, stalling again. Faye had never called me that before.

She stepped out of the doorway to let people by. "Bobby, I always thought that you were handsome," she told me. "You have one of those perfect faces. Everything is in the right place. And you have the perfect brown complexion, like a new penny, right before it starts to turn old. I only get that pretty color in July and August. You got it all year-round."

I burst out laughing. She put a lot of thought into that. "Well, ah, you look nice, too," I said, still chuckling. Plain guys like me didn't get told that they were handsome much. Faye had caught me off guard with it.

"So, can I have a hug or not?" she pressed me.

I was still hesitant about the hugging thing. "Are you sure you want me to?"

"Why not? We *are* friends, right?"

"Yeah, but if you were a guy I wouldn't hug you," I joked with her.

"But I'm *not* a guy," Faye argued. She was getting impatient with me.

I still didn't like the idea. What if it felt too good for us to break away? I quickly walked over and hugged her up and off of her feet to get it over with.

"Oh, such strong arms you have," she told me.

I put her back down and laughed it off. I was too afraid to comment on it. I didn't want to start another discussion with her. Who knows where that could have led. I didn't want to find out.

"I'll see you around," I said to her, walking away. I had to get myself out of there in a hurry.

As soon as I got back inside of my room, the phone rang.

"Where were you?" Pearl ranted.

"I went to the movies," I told her.

"With who?"

"Me, myself, and I." It was much easier to lie over the phone. I don't know if Pearl believed me or not.

She grunted and said, "Anyway, I won't be back until Sunday night. I decided to stay in New York with my mom for a few days."

"All right," I told her.

"And Bobby?"

"What?"

"Behave yourself. You hear me?"

"Yeah." I hung up the phone with Pearl and was terrified. I doubted I could make it through that weekend without at least *thinking* about sleeping with Faye. Things were getting hot and heavy between us. Fortunately, Faye called and told me that she would be working on some big assignment she had to finish up before spring break. She still wanted to go jogging that Monday morning, though.

Pearl got back from New York that Sunday night and was in heat. After I signed her into the dorm and led her to my room, she dropped her things and went straight for my private parts.

"Mommy's back home and she missed you, Daddy."

She backed me right up into the bed while tugging at my clothes. I admit, I missed her too. I had gotten used to having sex with Pearl. All of the carnal thoughts that had been running through my mind concerning Faye made me more aroused that night than usual. I went at Pearl as if I was plugged up into a socket in a wall. And she liked it, a lot!

Pearl looked at me and said, "Damn, maybe I need to go on more vacations! That shit was *good,* baby! What did you have to eat today? Give me some of that shit!"

If she only knew, I was thinking. I looked at my clock and it was close to midnight. I was wondering if Pearl was going back to her off-campus apartment or staying the night with me.

"You need me to help you with your things tonight?" I hinted.

She took a deep breath and said, "Yeah. I wish I didn't have to leave, but I got shit to take care of. I'm tired as hell." She rubbed my chest and smiled. "Thanks to you," she told me.

I felt good about that. For a regular guy I was sure getting a lot of ego massaging. I smiled and said, "Hey Pearl, do you, ah, think I'm kind of handsome?"

Pearl looked at me with a sideways frown. "What kind of question is that? You look *good,* Bobby, you just don't know it." She laughed at me and said, "You gotta come out of that shell of yours, man. Stop acting like a damn Cinderella. I wouldn't be with you if you didn't have potential, Bobby."

I thought about the three years when she had ignored me, but I decided not to say anything about it. *Why ruin a beautiful future with reference to an ugly past?* I reasoned.

We got dressed and walked over to her apartment. As soon as we arrived, I put her things down and headed for the door. "I'll call you tomorrow," I said.

"Where are you going?" Pearl asked me. She looked shocked.

"I gotta get up early tomorrow."

"I'll just turn my alarm clock on for five-thirty then."

"Now you know we don't get much sleep when we're in bed together," I told her. I really wasn't planning on staying.

Pearl walked over to me and pinched my right cheek with a smile. "Cute. But I really am tired. There won't be any more of that tonight."

It was pretty obvious that she wouldn't allow me to leave. We had been away from each other for four days, and I didn't have a good enough excuse.

I stripped down to my boxers and T-shirt and crashed on Pearl's queen-sized bed. Pearl was busy unpacking. Then she made a few phone calls to find out what she had missed in class. I don't remember when I fell asleep, but when I woke up, it was after seven.

"SHIT! I forgot to put my alarm clock on!" Pearl was screaming.

I jumped right out of bed and started to get dressed.

"I'm sorry, Bobby. That was my fault," Pearl was saying as I dashed for the door. I nearly ran her roommate off the stairs.

"Damn, aren't *we* in a hurry!" she huffed.

By the time I got back to my dorm to check my messages, I was drenched with sweat and it was almost eight. There were no messages on my machine. I called Faye and got no answer. I didn't hear from her until she called me later that day.

"You know, I ended up spending the night over at my girlfriend's apartment last night," she told me. "I'm sorry. I didn't plan to be over there that late, but we were both working on assignments, and then we got to talking about guys and stuff, and it got later and later until I just fell asleep. You're not mad at me, are you?"

"Naw," I told her. I was relieved if anything. I felt for sure that she would have had a hundred questions for why I had missed out on our early morning run again.

"Well, I got good news for you. I'm going to Virginia Beach for spring break after all. Ain't that good news?" she asked me.

Dammit! I was thinking. It wasn't good news for me. I was supposed to go to Virginia Beach with Pearl and her friends. There was no way I could keep our relationship from Faye at the beach. Pearl would be all over me. It was easier to do at school. Faye wasn't into going to parties and she did most of her schoolwork inside the library. Pearl and her friends were never to be found in the library and they were seldom up early on the weekends, so I filled in the times and places between their opposing schedules. Outside of the communications building, I was pretty safe. Pearl and Faye were both too busy to hang out and gossip inside of the hallways. Or maybe I had just been plain lucky. There were a lot of close calls, but the biggest thing going for me was that Pearl wouldn't consider Faye in her league. And I was sure that Faye didn't consider *me* to be Pearl's type of guy. I couldn't believe I was seeing Pearl myself.

"You know what, I don't know if I'm still going," I told Faye. "I haven't seen my parents since Christmas."

"So, *most* of us haven't. Spring break is supposed to be *our* vacation time. That's what made me change *my* plans. There's nothing at home for me. I'll see my parents in May." Faye had a good point.

"Yeah, well, I still haven't made up my mind yet," I told her.

"I was looking forward to being with you, though."

I was speechless. *Just one more month until graduation,* I thought. *This is getting too close for comfort.*

"You know you're graduating soon. This might be the last time we get to be with each other," Faye added. She was reading my mind.

"Naw, I'll come see you after graduation," I assured her.

"What are you doing after graduation? Do you have a job lined up yet?"

Good question, I was thinking. "That's one of the reasons why I want to go home. I want to discuss things with my parents."

"Oh," Faye mumbled. She sounded disappointed. I couldn't blame her. I was really being a coward.

"I promise, we'll be together before it's over. Mark my words," I told her.

Faye sighed. I don't think she believed me. "Okay," she let out.

We just lingered on the phone after that.

"Well, I have some work to do," she told me. I knew that she just wanted to get off the line.

"I'm sorry," I whimpered.

"Yeah, yeah."

As soon as the phone clicked, I felt miserable. Faye was such a beautiful person, inside and out. I felt like ending my relationship with Pearl and being with my true friend. I had never been a friend of Pearl's.

When I talked to Pearl that week about Virginia Beach, I broke the news to her plain and simple. "I'm going home."

"What? Stop trippin', Bobby, we planned this."

"I got some things I wanna straighten out with my parents. I didn't bother you about going home to be with your mother."

"That's because she was in an accident. I wouldn't have gone home if it wasn't for that."

"Even still, like I said, I'm going home to see my folks."

It was the first time I stood up to her. Pearl responded by slamming the phone in my ear. I went home to Greensboro, North Carolina, for spring break and had a good sit-down with my folks.

•

We were inside the kitchen, sitting at the small pinewood table—me, my mother, and my dad. My younger brother, Brad, ironically, had gone to Virginia Beach.

"You know, your brother is going on to grad school at Chapel Hill," my mother informed me. "I think that's a good idea. What do you think about it?"

Brad, a year younger than I, was finishing school at North Carolina

A&T, my parents' alma mater, a year early. He had gone to school straight through summer, so we were both set to graduate from college that same year.

"I'm happy for him," I told my mother. Brad had his way of living and I had mine.

My father chuckled and sipped his coffee. He realized I was avoiding my mother's question. My mother, an alert, disciplinarian schoolteacher, was not to be fooled.

"I'm glad that you're happy for your brother, Bobby, but what do *you* feel about graduate school?" My mom was a tall and straightforward woman who carried herself with importance. She thought the world of higher education, but all of her academic enthusiasm was a definite turn-off for me.

I got up to get myself a refill of lemonade from the refrigerator. "To tell you the truth, I haven't thought about it."

"Well, why not? What's so terrible about it?"

"There's nothing terrible about it, I just haven't given it any thought."

"Well, what are you planning on doing? You're not coming back here," she snapped at me. "It's time you grow up and do something with your life."

It was the same speech my mother had given me before I enrolled at Howard.

"Roberta, I keep tellin' you, Brad and Bobby are two different boys. Bobby'll be all right. He's just like me, a slow, fine wine," my father said in my defense. He was a big man with massive limbs, but he was pretty lighthearted too. I never saw him use his size to get his point across, yet I realized that he could have if he had wanted to.

Mom grunted and marched off to the bathroom.

Dad looked at me and laughed. "The world ain't gonna end tomorrow. You got time. Sometimes, when you move too fast, you fly right past a good opportunity," he said.

I smiled. My father had a good saying for everything. He was a well-known roofer in our community. His business didn't take off, though, until he was thirty-eight. He told me of several of his young friends who had moved too fast and had run out of steam. "As long as you're breathing good air, eating healthy food, and not hanging out with the wrong kind of people, you always have time to do something with your life," he told me.

My dream was to make forty or fifty thousand dollars a year at a radio station. I had always loved hearing those smooth, brother voices over the radio waves. I had never bothered to be a DJ, though. I liked the talk shows instead. However, after doing several internships around D.C., it seemed that only the big-name people were making any real money. Donnie Simpson at WKYS was one of them. In fact, most of the radio personalities making good money had been around for a while. The younger personalities were mostly rambunctious DJs. You had to be talented, hip, and aggressive. Nevertheless, the word around town was that they still didn't make much money. Radio was a profession you simply had to love in order to last.

I didn't know how talented, hip, or aggressive I could be. As far as being rambunctious and loud, I was more of a mellow kind of guy. I had my own ideas about what would be hip for radio, I just needed an opportunity to show my stuff. One thing was for sure, after driving around North Carolina that week in my father's Buick, I wasn't planning on going back home after graduation. Going to school in Washington, D.C., had spoiled me for the big-city life. My hometown had become too damned small and quiet for me.

•

I wasn't sure if Pearl and I still had a relationship when I got back to school, but she squashed those doubts immediately. Pearl couldn't wait to see me, just to tell me off.

"Well, I hope *you* had a good time, because I sure didn't."

"What happened?" I was just walking into the lobby area to sign her in after receiving a page from the front desk.

"First of all, my girlfriend's car broke down on the way there. Then we had to fight with this hotel manager about our room. My other girlfriend lost a hundred and fifty dollars. And after all of that, it kept fucking raining on us."

I felt like laughing but I held it in. Pearl reached out and squeezed my ass on the way up the stairs and asked me if I had missed her.

"Did *you* miss *me?*" I asked her back.

"I asked you first."

"Well, I thought you were still mad at me."

"I was. But after all that shit happened in Virginia, I figured that you had gotten a better deal. I feel like I wasted my damn money."

Pearl stepped into my room and gave me a brown bag out of her rather large pocketbook.

"What is this?" I asked her.

"Look the hell inside and see."

I looked inside and pulled out an eight-by-ten wooden frame. Inside was a photo of Pearl wearing a bright and colorful bikini at Virginia Beach. It reminded me of the *Sports Illustrated* swimsuit issue. Pearl was very much into taking pictures. She had her own portfolio. Sometimes she even talked about modeling professionally.

"Surprise, surprise," she said to me, planting a sloppy kiss on my lips. "I look *good*, don't I?"

I smiled and said, "Hell yeah! Definitely!" It was the kind of picture that would make any man proud.

"That's what you missed," she teased.

"Can you put it back on for me?" I asked her.

She laughed good and hard at me. "Hell no!" she responded. "That's what you get for not going down there with me. Everybody had a man but me."

As soon as she said that, I began thinking of Faye. I wondered if Faye had found someone at Virginia Beach to spend some quality time with. I was feeling guilty again.

"Did you behave yourself?" I figured I'd ask.

"Maybe I did, maybe I didn't. You wanna find out if I'm still snug?"

I couldn't believe that she said that. I had a hard-on quicker than you could strike a match. I forgot all about my guilt for Faye. Pearl and I jumped right back into doing the nasty.

That next day, I got a knock on my door and I answered it without looking through the peephole. To my surprise, Faye walked right into my room.

"How did you get over here?" I asked her.

"I have other friends in Slowe." She stood right next to Pearl's picture on my dresser and hadn't noticed it. I was about to have a heart attack!

"Let's go to the library. I was just about to head over there," I lied. I made a move toward her. Faye quickly eluded me and took a seat on my bed.

"I don't want to go to the library. I came here to have a face-to-face talk with you."

"About what?"

"About what we mean to each other," she answered.

"We know what we mean to each other," I responded. "Come on, let's discuss this in the library, I got stuff to do."

I could feel sweat dripping inside of my armpits. I was tempted to move over to my dresser and stand in front of Pearl's picture, but I was afraid that it might bring attention to it. Maybe I would get lucky and Faye wouldn't notice it.

"Why? What's wrong with discussing it in your room? Are you *expecting* somebody?" she huffed at me. "Or is it that you don't want me in here?"

I was about to explode! I had become too pushy with her, making her more suspicious. And when Faye stood up from my bed and looked toward my dresser, I felt like barging out of the door and making a break for the exit stairway.

"Oh, what do we have here?" she asked me, holding up Pearl's framed picture.

I was ready to duck, thinking that she might throw it at me. What the hell could I say? I just looked at her to watch for her reaction.

Faye gently set the picture back down and headed toward the door. She was crushed.

"I didn't know how to tell you," I said to her as I stepped aside.

"I'm sure you didn't," she said in a cracked voice.

I attempted to reason with her. "I mean, but we're just friends, right?"

"Friends don't lie to each other like this."

I would have felt better about it if Faye had gotten mad and slammed the door or hit me or something, but she didn't do any of that. She just walked out, obviously heartbroken.

I felt like running down the hall after her, but what would I have said once I reached her?

"It's just a picture, Faye," I mumbled to myself. "It doesn't mean anything."

It's funny how you come up with responses after the fact. It wouldn't have worked had I used it. Even if it *was* just a picture, with it being a picture of Pearl, Faye's nemesis, I might as well have been taking candy from the devil.

When I think back to how I treated Faye, I realize that guys make the same mistake a lot of women do; we always go for those people who are more likely to hurt us than to love us. I knew I had some bad karma to deal with after I had broken Faye's heart, but I still had to live my life. All I could do was expect for it to come back around to me in the future.

New York, New York

Faye barely spoke to me after finding Pearl's picture in my room. Our friendship was ruined. I wasn't tactful enough back then to try and mend things. I just left things as they were. I had no idea where Pearl and I were headed, nor what I was going to do after graduation. I didn't even know where I wanted to live. I was just "a mess," a term my mother had often used to refer to me. Then, one day out of the blue, I asked Pearl about New York.

We were just three weeks away from graduation. The underclassmen were all taking finals. Seniors had already finished. Faye mumbled, "Good luck" to me, and that was it. She wasn't even curious about my plans. That hurt, but I doubt if it hurt me as much as I had hurt her.

Anyway, Pearl was excited about finishing school. We hadn't begun discussing our future yet. However, I did know that Pearl wanted to go back to New York.

"Yes, yes, *yes!* I'm out of here!" she raved with balled fists. We were walking back from the administration building after making sure her financial records were clear. I had checked mine the day before.

"I guess they have a lot of radio stations in New York," I commented. It seemed only logical since New York was home to over eight million people.

"Yeah, we do," Pearl said. "In fact, I could get you on many stations in New York."

I hadn't said that I was going. I simply asked about the stations, and that was all Pearl needed to launch herself on a tangent.

"You know, I was thinking about that, but I thought you might wanna go back home to North Carolina," she told me.

"You were thinking about what?" I asked.

"You going to New York with me."

31

Pearl had always talked about "The Big Apple," but that was typical of most New Yorkers who attended Howard. I never knew she was thinking about taking me, though. I felt for sure that I was just her Howard man. I didn't know our relationship had longevity. I thought it was going to be one of those "fun while it lasted" kind of things.

"My aunt has a friend who's renting out a basement apartment in Queens. We could rent a car and go check it out this weekend," she suggested to me.

I was amazed at how quickly Pearl had run with the idea. "Are you asking me to move in with you?"

Pearl looked at me and smiled. "If you want to. And I don't see why you wouldn't."

The thought of living with Pearl Davis in a New York apartment was definitely exciting. It was making me dizzy. I had to stop and gather my thoughts. *Queens, New York!*

I didn't see why I wouldn't be willing to go either. I had nothing better to do after graduation, so we rented a car that Friday morning and drove up to New York. I had never even been there. Before we arrived, Pearl was pulled over for speeding on the New Jersey Turnpike.

"Ain't this some shit!" she screamed. "Just three more exits to go. I was driving faster than this in fuckin' Maryland!"

"That's the breaks," I told her. "They always catch you when you're not expecting it."

A thin white officer walked up to the car. "You're in a hurry?" he asked us through the window. He gave Pearl an extra long look, as if he was pleased with what he saw.

Pearl handed him her license and the rental information. "Not really," she said.

"You were clocked doing sixty-eight miles an hour."

Pearl was fearless. "If I was in a hurry, I would have been doing ninety."

I smiled, but the Jersey trooper kept his straight face. "The speed limit in New Jersey is fifty-five."

"I thought it was sixty-five," I said to him. "It's seventy-five on some roads down south."

He looked at me with a stern face. "This is not the South. We have much more traffic up here," he responded. "Your tags say you're from Virginia. Are you headed for New York?"

"Yes we are," Pearl told him.

"May I ask what for?"

I was used to state troopers asking who, what, when, and why questions down south, but I didn't know they did the same up north.

"We have an appointment with a rental office."

"You're planning on relocating?"

"Yes we are," Pearl repeated. I could tell she was about to lose it. She had her hands on the wheel and was staring straight out the front window, forcing herself to stay composed.

The Jersey trooper nodded and said, "I'm gonna write you guys a warning. You make sure you slow it down on the way back."

Pearl and I nodded to him before he returned to his car.

Pearl was pissed. "This speeding shit gets on my damn nerves. Why do they make cars that go a hundred and fifty miles an hour if you can only do fifty-five?"

"Good question," I said with a grin.

The trooper handed Pearl the warning notice along with her license and the rental information. "Have a nice visit," he told us.

"We were lucky we rented this car in Virginia," I told Pearl as we sped off.

She wasn't up for a discussion. "Yeah, whatever," she snapped.

We got off at the last exit and headed for the Lincoln Tunnel to Manhattan. The line of cars headed for the tunnel was packed like an army of ants at a cookie jar. New York City was the biggest cookie jar you could ever imagine.

"Here we go," I said aloud.

Pearl softened up and laughed at me. "Are you *that* excited? You sound like a big kid."

"So what?" I barked at her. "Are we about twenty minutes away now? I gotta use the bathroom."

"You gotta piss or shit?"

Pearl said anything that came to her mind. "I gotta do number one," I said.

She chuckled to herself. "We're gonna have to pull over and let you run inside of a restaurant or something."

We cruised into the borough of Manhattan, flooded by cars, trucks, people, and plenty of taxis. I looked around at the New York traffic, stopping and going, and decided it was better for me to hold my water. The Manhattan streets were like a stampede, and I didn't wanna get trampled to death.

We arrived in Jamaica, Queens, and I was very impressed. I liked the lively color and the overall feel of the place. It was a lot more peaceful than Manhattan. You could walk around without breaking your neck, searching for the skyline over all of Manhattan's tall buildings. I took a liking to Queens immediately.

"Okay, let me out at this McDonald's so I can use the bathroom," I said to Pearl.

She pulled over into a tiny parking lot. And I do mean *tiny*. There was only room for two cars.

"Hurry up," Pearl told me. "We're already late. I told her we'd be there by two."

I looked at my watch. It was two-thirty.

I hurried inside of the McDonald's to use their bathroom. I took care of my business in a hurry and walked back out. Pearl still had the engine going.

"How far do we have to go now?" I asked her, hopping back inside the car.

"About fifteen, twenty minutes."

I was thinking, *Man, this city really is big!*

Pearl took out a piece of paper with directions on it and started looking for different streets while she drove. When we arrived at Linden Boulevard, she made a right turn and drove down two blocks. We stopped and parked outside of a single home. I was impressed again. I was under the false impression that all of New York was dirty and ragged like in the many movies I had seen.

"Hey, this is a nice area," I said to Pearl.

She got out and shut the door. "What, you thought I was taking you to the ghetto?"

I didn't expect to be heading to such a peaceful environment, that's for sure. The two-story, single homes on Linden Boulevard even had small lawns, although they were nothing compared to what we had in Greensboro. I expected a loud street with music blasting, a hundred rowdy people walking around, graffiti artists "tagging" walls, and police sirens going off at every corner. Boy, was I off!

Pearl rang the front doorbell while I inspected the cement stairway leading to the basement. A black metal gate protected the basement door entrance. It looked pretty clean and secure to me. I felt real good about it.

An older, cream-skinned black woman with light brown hair that had attractive streaks of gray answered the front door. "Hi, Pearl. How are you doing? Was traffic backed up on the roads?"

Pearl stepped inside and took the woman's veiny hand. "Not really, but we did get pulled over for speeding on the turnpike."

"Oh, yeah, they'll get ya when you're trying to get someplace," our hostess said with a nod and a grin.

"This is my friend, Bobby Dallas, from school. He's from Greensboro, North Carolina."

I stepped up and said, "I'm pleased to meet you."

She nodded again while taking my hand. "Greensboro. I've been down to Raleigh and Charlotte, but never to Greensboro."

"Bobby, this is Ms. Petula," Pearl said.

"What's Greensboro like?" Ms. Petula asked me.

"It's smaller than Raleigh and Charlotte. It's less industrial and a lot greener."

She looked to Pearl and asked, "Have you been to Greensboro?"

Pearl smiled at me. "Not yet."

I smiled back. Ms. Petula then led us to a locked door leading to the basement. "I'll only use this key for emergencies." She led us down the beige carpeted stairway. Inside the basement, there was a sunken living room, walk-in closets, a newly built kitchen, and a full bathroom. The walls had wood paneling, and the lighting system had a dimmer. We had a sunken living room in our basement in Greensboro, but none of the other luxuries. It was nice to see it. I was feeling at home already. Everything looked brand new, and they were even giving us a few pieces of furniture.

"Oh, this is fly," Pearl commented.

Ms. Petula smiled, familiar with the New York street vernacular. Pearl would use it on and off, depending on what crowd she was around. I couldn't understand her sometimes when she was around her girlfriends at school.

Ms. Petula led us back to the bedroom door, past the bathroom. "And this is the bedroom," she announced, gently pushing the door open.

It was nice and large. I nodded and said, "We can fit a king-sized bed in here real comfortably."

Ms. Petula chuckled. "My husband designed this basement himself. We own three apartments in Queens, you know. My husband redesigned all of them."

After she told us that, I wondered how long they were planning on living there with us. It sounded to me like they were budding realtors. *Why would you live in a house with your tenants if you can afford not to?* I asked myself. Most realtors like to have their own space.

Pearl elbowed me in the ribs and smiled at me on the way out.

"What did I do?" I asked her.

She shook her head at me and grinned. "I got your *king-sized* bed," she whispered.

Ms. Petula took us around to inspect the rest of the place—the refrigerator, the sink, the bathroom, and the basement entrance from the outside.

"You need two keys to get in," she told us with a demonstration. "The gold key is for the door, and the silver key is for the gate." She unlocked them both and pushed the gate open as we followed her outside. "As you can see, this is a pretty nice area, but just to be safe, always lock *both* doors."

"Okay," Pearl said. "So it's six-fifty a month with utilities included?"

Ms. Petula nodded. "Yes."

"We'll take it," Pearl piped.

I guess it didn't matter what I thought. Don't get me wrong, I liked the place, but I was thinking more on the lines of five hundred a month for rent. Six hundred and fifty dollars was enough rent money for a two-bedroom luxury apartment in a sky-rise building to me.

Ms. Petula said that she'd have the lease for us to sign with an extra set of keys when we were ready to move in, which Pearl said would be that following week, the first of May.

"Six-fifty?" I said to Pearl. We were back inside the car.

Pearl paid me no mind. "You don't know anything about rent prices. You lived in the damn dorms for fours years. Six-fifty is a steal in New York. We wouldn't even have known about this place if it wasn't for my aunt."

She was right, I wasn't familiar with rent prices. I shut my mouth for the rest of the ride. We drove back to Brooklyn to Pearl's mother's house in Fort Greene, the area that Spike Lee would later make famous with his 40 Acres and a Mule production company.

"So, this is Bobby Dallas?" Pearl's mother said, looking me over. I was used to people using my first and last name from being on the radio, but I didn't expect Pearl's mother to follow suit. She looked like she could be from the Islands. She had wavy hair like Pearl's, small eyes, deep brown skin, and a sexy shape. If I was an older man, I would have died for a woman like Pearl's mother.

"How are you doing?" I asked her.

"Well, I'm all right. I can't complain too much." She had an Ace bandage around her left wrist. I presumed it was from her recent auto accident.

Pearl lugged our things up to her room and left me alone with her mother. I didn't know what else to say to her. I felt like telling her that she was a good-looker, but I didn't feel that would have been appropriate. Or maybe I could have said it and was just plain bashful.

"I'm sorry about that accident you were in," I said.

Pearl's mother held up her wrist and said, "Yeah, and I was almost finished paying off on that damned car."

"That's the breaks," I told her. That was one of my favorite sayings back then. I had picked it up from Kurtis Blow's popular rap song some years earlier.

Pearl came rushing down the steps and said, "Mom, we'll see you tomorrow morning. I wanna show Bobby the city."

"Well damn, good-bye to you, too," her mother snapped.

Pearl kissed her on the cheek. "You know I love you, Mom."

We were out the door and headed for the subway to Manhattan.

"Are we staying at a hotel?" I asked Pearl.

"No."

"So why you tell your mother we'll see her tomorrow?"

Pearl looked at me and smiled. "Have you ever heard the saying 'Manhattan never sleeps'?"

"Oh, yeah, something like that. I think it's 'the city that never sleeps,' " I recollected.

"Well, you're about to find out why."

I was eager as a kid for my first ride on the New York subway system. And it was rush hour. The first thing I noticed were the police. I guess I wasn't expecting them to be standing around patrolling subway cars. The next thing I noticed were all the different kinds of people. New York had every nationality you could imagine. It reminded me of a human version of that bar scene in the first *Star Wars* movie. I also realized where Pearl had gotten her tough demeanor. There wasn't much human communication on that train from Brooklyn. It was as if saying "Hi" was against the transit law.

We got off the train in Manhattan and Pearl took us to a dark, cultural restaurant. There were paintings of Africans on the walls with ethnic clothes and pottery spread around the room. A shapely sister with a Kente wraparound dress, sandals, and a white apron seated us at a window-view table.

"This is a nice place," I said to Pearl. I was very much enjoying my first trip to New York.

"This is my favorite spot in Manhattan," she told me.

"What did you tell you mother about me?" I asked. It was eating at me for the entire ride on the train.

Pearl was startled by it. "What?"

"I mean, your mother said my name like you two had conversations about me," I said to her.

Pearl smiled as she looked over a large, one-page menu protected in plastic. "I told her some good things about you," she said.

"What kind of good things?"

Our waitress came and took our orders. I made it easy for her by ordering what Pearl had. I didn't know what most of the meals tasted like anyway. I think it was West African food. Nigerian.

"Why are you so concerned about what I said to my mother?" Pearl asked me.

"I'm not really concerned, I'm just curious."

The waitress brought us two big glasses of water. Pearl took a sip and said, "I told her that you knew how to please me."

I shook my head and grinned. Sometimes I felt like Pearl's sex toy, but I didn't want to admit it. I was caught up in the fantasy that Pearl had learned to really care for me, and I wasn't going to let it go.

"Is your mother still married to your father?" I asked. I didn't remember Pearl ever speaking about him.

"When did I ever say they were married?"

"You never talked about your father to me at all," I admitted.

"Well, there's nothing to say about him."

Pearl had always been the closedmouthed type when it came to discussing something she didn't want to talk about. I guess her father was one of those subjects.

"Does your mother get lonely?" I found myself asking. I wished I could have taken it back. It sounded really personal, but Pearl answered it anyway.

"She has boyfriends."

I was scared to discuss it any further. I told myself I didn't want to know. Pearl's mom was a criminal justice lawyer, she looked good, and she had never married Pearl's father. That was it. I didn't even know her name.

"Is your mother's last name Davis?" I couldn't help myself.

"No, that's my father's name. My mother named me Davis because I was his child."

"So, she's pretty traditional, you know, as far as names go and all?"

Pearl looked irritated by then. "Yeah, I guess," she answered. She looked away from me, and this tall, muscular guy noticed her and headed right for our table.

"Hey, Pearl, what's up?" he said with a deep voice. He damn near knocked over our drinks. He looked like one of those weight-lifting types, or another football player.

Pearl was flat with her response to him. "Hi, Jamey," she said.

I suspected they had been a couple before, and that Pearl had cut him off.

"When did you get back?" he asked her.

"I'm not back, I'm just visiting."

"Did your mother tell you that I called?"

Pearl looked at me with a grimace. I don't know if I looked like a pushover, but it sure seemed that guys were overlooking me. I was getting a bit tired of it. We weren't blatantly rude in Greensboro. I wasn't used to northern confrontations.

"No, she didn't," Pearl told him. "I'm a little busy right now," she hinted.

"Oh, it's like that now, hunh?"

Pearl ignored him. I was just about to say something when Pearl said, "It's been that way for a while."

Jamey looked at me and grunted. "She a freak, ain't she?"

I was at a loss of words. "What?"

Pearl said, "If I'm such a freak, how come you keep calling me, motherfucka? You don't have a woman by now? Why don't you just leave me the hell alone?"

Jamey looked as embarrassed as I was. All eyes were on us.

A tall African strutted over to our table. "Hey, what's the problem?" he asked Jamey. He looked ready for drama. You could tell that he wasn't to be played with. He had one serious-ass look.

Jamey looked him over, frowned, and walked back out of the door.

Pearl nervously started on her drink. "Some motherfuckers just got nerve," she mumbled.

I was tempted to ask her about her relationship with Jamey—how long ago it had ended, and if she had ever eaten there with him—but I decided not to. I didn't want to find myself on her bad side.

We finished our meals quietly and headed out on the Manhattan streets. Pearl didn't seem to think much of the incident, or at least she didn't allow it to sour her plans of showing me New York. I found it very hard to be bored there. Things were going on in every little alleyway, and there was absolutely no dress code. New Yorkers wore everything from leather and spikes to spandex.

I was busy thinking over Jamey's question. *Was Pearl a freak? And how many other guys had she been with?*

Pearl took me to Times Square, where we went on a horse-and-carriage ride. "Why are you so quiet?" she asked me with a nudge. "I know you're not still thinking about that asshole."

I was, but I didn't want her to know. I didn't want to destroy the possibility of a still beautiful evening. "Naw, I'm just soaking up the city. New York, New York," I cheered.

Pearl smiled and dropped her head on my shoulder while squeezing my thigh.

We went to three different nightclubs that evening. We got inside the last two for free. Pearl sure knew a lot of people. That only made me more curious about her past. We caught a taxi back to Brooklyn that Saturday morning, just as Pearl had said.

"Did you have a good time tonight?" she asked me. We were back at her mother's place and inside of Pearl's old room, snuggled up in a small bed.

I was contemplating my move to New York. I wasn't quite sure if I wanted to do it anymore. "Yeah, I had a good time," I answered. I didn't sleep a wink that night. I kept asking myself if I was making the wrong decision.

That next week I was back at the dorms in Washington, D.C. I called home to discuss my plans with my folks. My dad answered the phone.

"I think I want to go to New York after graduation," I told him.

"Okay."

I guess I was expecting my father to say more, you know, to give his opinion on the idea.

"What do you think about New York?" I asked him.

"It's too much for me," he said. "It's a cold, concrete city, from what I hear, a city where nobody cares about each other."

I thought about all of my high school years going back and forth to work at the Food Lion supermarket before I finally made up my mind to go to college. I did manage to save over six thousand dollars while living at home. That was a nice amount of money. But I hadn't tested life at all. I didn't even buy a car like I planned to while freeloading off of my parents' cars. I hadn't gone out to see what I could do in life. My mother was right about that.

"Well, maybe New York could motivate me to do something great," I told my father. "You know how Mom always talked about how lazy I am. Well, maybe she's right. Maybe New York is just what I need."

My father grunted and said, "You know, this is your life, Bobby. You don't have to ask for my permission anymore. You're a grown man. The only thing that I asked of you, since I was paying for it, was for you to finish school. And you've done that. But now, you know I can't speak for your mother," he added with a chuckle.

I told him to put her on the line so I could get it over with. Nothing I had ever done outside of school had ever impressed my mother. My grades were never that great either. I was graduating from Howard University with a 2.8 GPA.

"What are you going to New York for? You wanna be a celebrity? Is that it, Bobby? I didn't raise you to go to New York and become a celebrity. What kind of life is that for a responsible man?"

My mother was doing what she had always done, trying to force her opinions on me with rash assumptions about my lifestyle and my intentions. I didn't have what it took to become a so-called celebrity. I simply wanted to try out something new with my life.

"If that's what he wants to do, then that's what he wants to do," I could hear my father arguing with her.

"Do you agree with this, Clifford?" she asked him. My mother always tried to make my father choose sides, and he never did.

"Bobby is a grown man, and if he chooses to go to New York, for whatever reason, then you should respect his decision. I don't have anything to do with it."

"Well, I think that's a terrible decision, and he's making a big mistake!" my mother snapped.

The phone line ruffled for a second before my father came back on the other line. "Your mother just stormed back off to her study. I guess you see how *she* feels about this," he said with another chuckle. I definitely got my easygoing spirit from my father. You had to have a sense of humor to endure my overbearing mother for twenty-something years.

I made up my mind right then. I had no other plans, and Pearl and I had already secured a nice apartment. "Well, that's what I'm gonna do, Dad. I'm going to New York for a while," I announced. I was convincing myself, as well as my father.

"Well, good luck to you, son. And I'll see you on graduation day."

When graduation day came, my father and Uncle Deon, my mother's brother, were the only family there. My brother, Brad, and my cousin, Sylvia, were both graduating from North Carolina A&T on that same Saturday in May, 1986. My mother and the rest of the family went to their graduation. We were supposed to all meet that night in Greensboro, but I didn't feel up to it.

"Just tell Brad and Sylvia I said congratulations," I told my father. Most of my things had already been transported, via U-Haul, to my new living quarters in Queens, New York.

My father nodded his head and said, "I know exactly how you feel, son. Some roads are meant to be walked alone." He extended his hand to me with a white envelope. "Here's a little something to get you started."

I gave him my diploma to hang on the basement wall.

Uncle D. shook my hand and said, "You show 'em what you're made of up there, Bobby. You go on up there and give 'em an education on the tough spirit of the South."

I smiled and walked them to my father's Lincoln, parked inside of the Fourth Street parking lot.

My father rolled down the window as they drove off and said, "All right, son. I'll see ya when you're ready to come home and visit us."

I didn't even get a chance to introduce them to Pearl and her family. She was too busy running around taking pictures and such. They knew who she was, though, and they liked what they saw.

I started walking back to the front lawn area of the communications building to find Pearl. On the way, I peeped inside of the envelope my father gave me. It was a check for two thousand dollars. Added to the six grand that I had in the bank already, I was in pretty good shape. "New York, here I come," I told myself.

As soon as I found Pearl, she grabbed me to take a picture with her.

"Put your hat back on and zip your gown up," she hissed at me.

I was ready to call it quits, but it looked as if Pearl was just getting started. I got myself ready and embraced her while her mother took aim and snapped the shot. I began to feel really good about moving in with Pearl. I was stepping into a whole new chapter of my life.

Hobnobbing

Who you know is of the utmost importance in New York. Just imagine eight million people handing in résumés with three to five references. If you knew someone really important, then maybe you would have that extra push you needed to get a good job. Pearl was well schooled in the game.

I applied at four very small radio stations to try and get some work. In the meantime, Pearl told me that it would be wise to apply for a position at a post office or something, just to pay the bills while we were both job hunting. She was working at Macy's department store within a week of our arrival in Queens. "It's only temporary," she told me. Yet she had given all of her radio contacts to me. I began to wonder what her career goals were. It couldn't have been in radio. You don't give good contacts away no matter how small the station. Radio is an extremely competitive business.

I wasn't as worried about paying the bills as Pearl was. I had transferred my checking and savings accounts from North Carolina's First Union to Citibank in New York. Pearl didn't know about my finances, and I intended on keeping things that way. My father told me never to mix my checking and savings with a woman. "It only makes them foam at the mouth," he said. And I had been around enough shopaholic women to believe him.

•

"Where are we going now?" I asked Pearl on a late Friday night. We had just gotten back from meeting and greeting at a party in Queens. It was nearly two in the morning. Pearl was busy changing into fresh clothes after taking a shower. She was advising me to do the same. We had been "clubbing," as she called it, ever since we arrived in New York. Pearl lived for the party. And once she got there, she never stopped moving or running her mouth. I still couldn't figure out where she got all of her energy from.

"Paradise Garage," she told me, tugging on an ass-hugging black skirt.

"Is this place that special?" I asked her.

"You'll see."

I didn't think much of it. I was losing my interest in the party crowd. After you've been to five or six different clubs, you begin to notice that the only thing changing is the scenery. Sometimes even the scenery is the same.

We took a bus to the 169th Street station and caught the Queens subway into Manhattan. When we arrived at Paradise Garage, the place was jam-packed and out of this world. It was the crazy, sexy, cultural, and alive New York that I had pictured it to be. You had to know someone to even get in the place. As always, Pearl knew more than a handful of people.

This really popular DJ, Larry Levan, had quite a large following at The Garage. He was one of the first and few DJs in New York to experiment with house music, which moved to a booming drum kick. BOOMP! BOOMP! BOOMP! BOOMP! The crowd loved it!

Pearl got excited as soon as we walked onto the main dance floor. She proceeded to do her usual thing, dancing and mingling with the crowd. I walked around on my own instead of being her sidekick. Pearl was always able to find me when she wanted my presence. Quickly! I don't know how. I guess she had some kind of radar system and would hone in on me like a bat.

I walked around the place and really got into it. I could actually feel the music telling me to dive into the craziness and just grab someone. That's the kind of freaky place that it was. Larry Levan really had something going. The music kept coming right at you, seducing your mind, body, and soul. It was unbelievable! I felt like I was being tempted by some new form of drug. There were all kinds of people there, feeling it. It was just the kind of place that Pearl was seeking to spin her web of association. She really should have been a public relations major.

"Hey, Bobby Dallas!" someone yelled through the music.

I turned and spotted a sexy, dark-haired Latina woman. She was swaying enchantingly with a dance partner and looking right at me, but I didn't recognize her.

"You don't remember me? I'm Doreen," she said, leaning in my direction. "I work at WHCS in Harlem." All the while, her dance partner was getting his kicks off on her twisted, gyrating body. It was a wild scene.

Doreen was a receptionist at the Harlem-based radio station where I had applied for a job. She looked totally different from how I remembered her on the job. She had her hair pulled back into a ponytail and was wearing heavy eye shadow with scandalous clothes. It was just like that Whodini song, "The Freaks Come Out at Night."

"Oh, yeah," I said to her. "I remember you."

She nodded and said something to her partner. He was a thick-built, brown Latino with short-cut hair. Doreen broke away from him and grabbed my hand to dance. Her head barely reached my chest, but she slammed her sexy hips into me anyway.

"I really like your name. You have a radio name. *Bobby Dallas!*" she yelled. I smelled alcohol on her breath, but she was still good-looking. "I hope you get the job," she told me.

"Me too," I said. I looked around to see if I could spot Pearl.

"Who are you here with?" Doreen asked me.

"My roommate." It was the first thing that came to mind. I hadn't gotten used to referring to Pearl as my lady. She called me "a friend," so I figured I'd lessen her importance as well.

Doreen continued with her interrogation. "You're not from New York, are you?"

I shook my head. "No."

"I can tell. You have an accent," she said with a nod. I was in New York. It was her lingual turf.

"Where I'm from, *you* would have the accent," I commented. "This place is something else though." I tried to back away from her a bit. Things were getting sweaty on the dance floor.

"Word, right? The Garage is happenin', man! I'm telling you!"

I was tempted to ask her if she was a regular when I spotted Pearl dancing with some bald-headed guy. He was holding a camera in his right hand with one of those thick, colorful camera straps over his shoulder. Pearl was as close to him as I was to Doreen, but at least I was trying to create some distance. Pearl looked to be the initiator from my view.

"Where do you live?" Doreen asked me.

"Jamaica, Queens." I felt like a proud New Yorker, as if Queens was the most important place in the world. New York pride was contagious.

"Do you two have separate rooms? I love tall men, man. I hope your roommate doesn't mind," Doreen hinted with a wink.

I was at a loss for words. "Well, ah . . ." She was coming on stronger than I could handle.

"How are *we* doing tonight?" Pearl asked out of the blue. She grabbed me from behind and ran her hands down my chest. "Can I talk to you for a minute? Excuse us," she said to Doreen.

"Ah, hopefully, I'll see you at work soon," I said to my new friend as Pearl snatched me away. I assumed that she was ready to give me the third degree, but instead, Pearl smiled at me.

"You're not used to women jumpin' all over you like that, are you?" she asked me.

"Well, who was that guy you were with?" I asked her. "Did he jump all over you?" I was as casual in my tone as a walk in the mall, but I was still jealous, and I sounded quite assertive. I guess I was picking up the New York attitude, too.

"That was Ronald Claire. He's a photographer, my first big contact."

I grimaced. "Big contact for what?"

Larry Levan mixed in the bass line to Michael Jackson's "Billy Jean." The crowd lost it again. Pearl lost it too, as she began to freak me.

"I'll talk to you about it when we get home," she promised me.

When we finally did make it home, it was breakfast time. I toasted two chocolate pop-tarts, poured a glass of milk, and headed for bed.

Pearl brushed her teeth and joined me under the sheets. I felt guilty about not brushing mine since that morning, but hell, after The Garage experience, I was exhausted.

"Now," Pearl said to me, "remember I talked to you before about modeling."

I remembered, but I never took it too seriously. A woman in America saying she would like to model one day is like an American man saying he would like to be rich. At least men have a bit more control over chasing riches. Women have to be selected to model. Mostly, it was a connected group of ritzy white people doing the selecting, and very few of them chose black women. It would have been easier for Pearl to marry a wealthy black athlete than to become a model.

"This is a perfect time for black women in America," she went on to tell me. She jumped out of bed and rushed into the living room. She came back in carrying several of her magazines. She flipped open pages and pages of *Elle* and *Essence*—with other magazines that I can't remember—focusing on all the new black faces. "It used to be just Beverly Johnson and Iman, but now a lot of sisters are getting opportunities to model," she said. "I'd also like to act and be in music videos."

Pearl was all cheery-eyed like a little girl on Christmas.

"Is that why we've been going to all these parties, so you can meet these people?" I asked her.

"You have to. How else are you gonna get in?"

"Don't they have talent agencies and things that these people belong to?"

"And how do you think you get picked up by an agency? What do you think, you just walk in with an application behind a thousand others? It doesn't work that way. You have to know people."

"I thought it was about a pretty face and talent," I joked.

Pearl looked at me as if I was crazy. "Yeah, right. You know better than that. Just look at radio, for instance. There's many people out here with a good, clear voice and talent, but that don't mean shit if you don't have the right connections."

There was no argument about that. I didn't know anybody, and I didn't have a job yet.

Pearl really wanted to become a star. I could see it in her eyes and hear it in her voice. I started thinking about what my mother had said about me wanting to go to New York to become a celebrity. She would have hit the nail right on the head with Pearl.

"Why, is something wrong with what I want to do?" Pearl asked me. I guess she could read the surprise and concern on my face. It wasn't that I doubted her abilities, it was just that I was so far removed from stardom that I couldn't imagine anyone close to me wanting it either.

"Naw, it's just that . . ." I didn't know what to say without sounding negative. "So, you're not interested in radio at all, hunh?"

"College was my mother's idea. I didn't really want to go. I had to major in something," she answered me. "What, you don't think I can make it as a model?"

"No, it's just that you're talking about some hefty goals," I said. "Everybody wants to model and act up here. You ever heard that joke where a guy asks a girl what she does, and she says she's an actor, and then the guy says—"

"Yeah, I know, I know, what restaurant, right?" Pearl was solemn. For the first time in our relationship she seemed vulnerable. "What the hell do they know? I can make it," she snapped.

I finished my milk and pop-tarts and didn't say another word about it. Pearl was grouchy for the rest of that week, cursing Ronald Claire for not getting back to her about a photo shoot. I spent most of my time listening to various New York radio stations. The radio personalities and commercial spots were beyond aggressive in New York. I was thinking that I would be eaten alive. It was about five notches faster than anything I had been doing in Washington. New York radio definitely had an in-your-face style.

I got a call from the station in Harlem where Doreen worked that Thursday morning. They wanted me to come back in that Friday. Although Pearl claimed to have had little interest in radio, I believe that she was jealous of me when she heard my good news. She wouldn't admit it, though.

"They don't really pay shit. That's why I gave that number to you," she hissed.

"So if they were a big-time station, then you wouldn't have given it to me, hunh?"

"What do you think?"

I was all smiles. "I think I'll be happy to finally have a job, if they give it to me."

"Yeah, well, *I* think you still need to look for something that pays more, because we have some serious bills to pay around here."

"Don't worry yourself about my half of the rent. I got it covered," I assured her.

"Oh, really. For how many months?"

I had to watch myself with that question. I didn't want to give her too much information, I just didn't want her to worry. "For a little while," I said with a grin.

Pearl nodded and said, "All right. If you say so. But I don't want to hear no excuses later on."

I thought about commenting on *her* job. I didn't see how Macy's was paying her that much more than what she expected me to make at the radio station. However, she *was* working some long hours. We hardly saw each other.

I dressed in a white shirt, beige slacks, a tie, and dark brown shoes for my second visit to WHCS-AM. When I arrived in Harlem I was more than a half hour early, so I took a walk around the area. I could tell right away that Harlem was an old place by its sturdy and aged buildings. I bet those buildings could tell a million stories. I walked to 125th Street. I could imagine followers of Marcus Garvey marching in a green, black, and red parade, or Joe Louis and Sugar Ray Robinson shadow-boxing in tailored suits after big knockout wins in the ring. Harlem was also the stomping ground of Adam Clayton Powell, breaking down the barriers of urban politics, and Malcolm X giving fired-up speeches about "white devils." The Black Panthers urged New Yorkers to use their right to vote on those streets, and Billie Holiday sang the blues. There was a whole

lot of black history in the streets of Harlem. My mother made sure that I knew every page of it.

I casually walked into the radio station five minutes before I was expected. Doreen was on the phone at the receptionist desk. We smiled at each other while I waited for her to finish her call.

"How can I help you?" she joked, once she cleared the line.

"I have an appointment to see Mr. Payton."

"Oh, you're Bobby Dallas." She reached out her hand to greet me.

I took her hand in mine and chuckled. That Doreen had a sense of humor. She was back to being the mild-mannered receptionist, conservatively dressed with only a touch of makeup and curled hair. She was like a Lois Lane/Party Girl.

"Yeah, that's me," I said to her.

She leaned over her desk and whispered, "Was that your girlfriend at The Garage the other night? I didn't get you in any trouble, did I?"

She was blowing her Party Girl cover. I shook my head and told her, "No."

"Is that a 'No' to question number one, or 'No' to question number two?"

I thought about it with a grimace, trying to remember the order of her questions. "Ah . . ."

"Well, anyway, I don't date guys who work with me," she said, cutting me off. Then she laughed at my confused expression. It was obvious that she was toying with me. I found out later that Doreen was known to flirt, and she had a big, jealous Cuban boyfriend that everyone at the station knew about.

"Mr. Payton's office is the last one on the right," she said, directing me through the station.

I walked down the narrow halls and past the studio booth. Two older black women were discussing child care. Mr. Payton's office door was closed. I listened in and heard him on the phone before I knocked. A well-dressed black man opened the door and gestured for me to have a seat. I sat down and waited for him to finish his call.

"Bobby Dallas," he said, extending his hand. The gray-haired Mr. Payton was trim and energetic. He had the sharp look of a Wall Street stockbroker.

I shook hands with him and nodded. "That's me."

"So you wanna be a radio producer, not a personality?"

"That's right."

"Why?"

I was startled. "Well, I never thought of myself as a radio personality.

I just want to be a part of radio broadcasting. I've always had a lot of good ideas for shows." I had heard that producing was a much easier way to get a job, too. Everyone wanted to be the star of their own radio show, but few people thought about running things from behind the scenes.

"What about selling advertising time?" he asked me.

I shook my head with a grin. "I don't know if I'm that good of a salesman." Selling advertising space is the most tedious job in the world. I *definitely* didn't want to do that.

"Are you familiar with New York? You're from North Carolina, right?"

I nodded. "I'm from Greensboro, but I've been getting around New York a bit."

Mr. Payton chuckled. "Young brother, New York is a big place. Have you been to the Bronx?"

"No, not yet."

"What about Staten Island?"

"No."

"Long Island?"

I shook my head with another grin. "No, I can't say that I have." I was asking myself, *Why don't he ask me about Queens, Brooklyn, or Manhattan?*

Mr. Payton smiled and leaned back in his desk chair. "In all my years in New York, that question always gets the newcomers. You know why?"

I didn't have a clue. "No. Why?"

He smiled and said, "I know you've been to Manhattan. I know you've been to Brooklyn. And your résumé says that you're living in Queens. Am I right?"

"Yeah," I said. "So what's your formula?" I asked him. He struck me as one of those older guys who knew what he knew well.

"If you're driving to New York, then you're gonna come through Manhattan. And that's where most of the clubs and your night life is. Most people then choose to settle down in either Brooklyn or Queens. Nobody's thinking about going to the Bronx unless you have family there. The same goes for Staten Island. And Long Island is just too damn far for most newcomers. If you get a place in Long Island, you may as well have stayed in Jersey."

His point was well taken. "Good point," I told him.

"You know why I'm hiring you, Bobby? I'm assuming that you *do* still want the job."

"Yeah," I responded eagerly.

Mr. Payton opened his palms toward me. "Okay, so why am I hiring you?"

"Because I qualify for the job, you have an opening, and I'm a newcomer," I answered with a nervous grin. I figured he wouldn't be so informed on the habits of newcomers for nothing.

He smiled at me. "What does being a newcomer have to do with anything?"

"Well, if I'm new to the city, then I'm probably more hungry for work."

"Are you hungry?"

"Pretty much."

"Well, go get yourself something to eat then," he said to me. He laughed and said, "No, I'm just joking with you. That's a pretty good answer you gave me. A lot of young guys up here want to be DJs for your more popular stations. They want to be heard by their boys, you know, stylin' and profilin', but this ain't that kind of station. We're more concerned about issues in the black community. We can get up and shake our asses anytime."

I started to chuckle. I was thinking about his incognito receptionist, Doreen. Of course, Mr. Payton probably thought that I was laughing from his comment concerning ass shaking.

"I see that you're a Howard University graduate, referred by Pearl Davis."

"That's correct," I told him.

"She did an internship with us two summers ago. I guess she's moved on to bigger and better things. She's quite an ambitious young lady. She's feisty like a tiger."

I was tempted to ask him what exactly he meant by that, but I decided to let it slide. All he knew was that Pearl had referred me, and that's how I wanted to keep it, but I was getting more curious about her reputation by the minute. How far was Pearl willing to go to get what she wanted?

"She said the pay wouldn't be much," I informed Mr. Payton. I was hoping she was wrong.

He began to fidget in his chair. "Well, it's not. I wish the station had money to hire the best there is, but the fact is, we don't. I use this place more as a training ground for people who want to break into the business. You'll get hands-on experience here that they wouldn't even think about giving you at a larger station. You'd end up getting somebody's coffee and xeroxing shit for a year. But Pearl, she thinks she's supposed to go straight to the top." He shook his head and smiled. "We had a lot of arguments when she was here. I'm surprised that she even referred you to me."

"So, what kind of wage can I expect?" I asked him. I was ready to talk business.

"Minimum."

"How many hours a week?"

"Well, I'm flexible if you are. How many hours are you willing to work? I'll need all the help that I can get, around the clock."

"I'll have to think about it," I told him.

"What's the earliest you think you can get in here on Monday morning?"

"I don't know. I guess I can get up around six and be out the house by six-thirty."

"If you can make it in here by eight o'clock, we can start your paperwork, train you, and get your broadcasting license. Now let me walk you around the place."

Just like that I had my first radio job in Harlem, New York. I felt like I might have been on my way to celebrity status after all. After putting in my dues, I could have gone straight to the top.

I had a message on the answering machine from my mother when I got back to Queens. It was after six. I made the long-distance call home, and my brother, Brad, answered the phone.

"Where's your mother?" I asked him. I didn't feel like talking to him. Brad had always been Mr. Competition. My parents bought him too many boxes of building blocks when he was little. He just wouldn't let it go. I was always happy with what he chose to do, but that didn't mean I had to do the same things or at the same rate. I was pretty satisfied with my own pace.

"How's New York? I saw that picture you sent Mom and Dad of your girlfriend. She's a little thin compared to what I'm used to, but she looks good. That's how they make 'em up there in New York, hunh? If she makes you happy, though, that's all that really counts."

"Okay, now where's Mom?" I asked him again.

"She went out with Dad, grocery shopping."

"Tell her I'll call her back."

"Wait a minute. You can't talk to your brother for a minute, Bobby? What's wrong with you? New York changed you already?"

I felt like hanging up the phone on him. Brad really knew how to make my blood boil. I was in a good mood after securing my new job, so I didn't want to give him an opportunity to ruin it for me.

"New York is great. The buildings are tall. The women are aggressive.

The streets are crazy. And the people are loud sometimes. Now what else do you want to know?"

Brad began to laugh. "You and Dad got that humor thing down pat. I'll give Mom the message when she gets back in," he said.

"Thank you." I hung up the phone, kicked my feet up on the wooden coffee table, and turned on the TV. Pearl had bought some wires from Radio Shack to connect the TV to her stereo. We had a pretty cool place. And since I had finally gotten a job, I felt totally relaxed in it.

Pearl got home after nine and was in a good mood herself. She jumped into my lap on the living room couch and gave me a sloppy kiss on the lips. "I got it, baby," she said.

"You got what?"

"My first photo shoot!"

"When?"

"Tomorrow."

"I thought you had to work tomorrow."

"I did, but I switched with this white girl."

"You can do that?"

"Evidently. I did it."

"This photo shoot is with this guy, Claire?" I asked her.

Pearl shook her head and frowned. "No. Fuck him! This other photographer I know called me at work and said that one of the girls that he was supposed to shoot is going overseas, and he asked me if I could fill in. I was like, 'Hell yeah, man! Are you crazy!'

"I'm happy as shit, Bobby," she said. "You see, you just gotta keep your heart in it and things will start to happen for you."

I was happy for her too.

"Baby, let's celebrate," she said.

"Okay, where do you wanna go?"

Pearl looked at me with a purr and nibbled at my ear. "Nowhere. It's what I wanna *do.*" She unbuckled my belt and ran her hands under my shirt, caressing my chest as she kissed me. "I'll be right back," she said. "And turn all these damn lights off."

I got up and began clicking off the lights with a hard-on. Pearl came out of the bedroom five minutes later, wearing Victoria's Secret lingerie. We got good and raunchy that night and let the phone ring while exploring every inch of our luxurious basement apartment. Pearl's birth control made things a lot easier. We didn't have to stop and go all night to unwrap new condoms. We could have made our own X-rated movie that night called *The Basement.*

That Saturday morning, Pearl was reenergized and out of the house by seven, carrying several bags of things for her first photo shoot. I got up, took a shower, and called my mother back to tell her the news. I made sure that I kept the conversation short, too. I didn't need my mother wearing me out. I was still exhausted from Pearl.

My mother wanted me to call home once a week, I guess to report on my progress. I wasn't up for that either. I made no promises to her. A call once a month would have been more like it.

We said our good-byes and hung up. I planned to relax for the rest of that weekend before starting my new job.

●

One of the last meet-and-greet functions that I went to with Pearl was at this place in lower Manhattan. I hadn't been around the type of black people in that place since leaving Howard University. The supposed cream of the crop, or as Malcolm X would have called them, "The House Niggers," met there.

Pearl was on a mission to keep getting better modeling work. She was pleased with her progress and making more money. She was happier around the apartment and no longer pressed about our bills. I didn't like the people she was beginning to meet in and around the modeling business, though.

I searched through the pompous crowd of this high-society club and spotted Pearl. She was standing and laughing with a tall, chocolate brown sister who had hair flowing halfway down her back.

I walked over to Pearl and said, "I'm ready to go." I had a headache from the place.

Pearl seemed not to hear me. "Oh, Bobby, I was just about to come and get you," she said. "This is my girl, Kiki Monet."

The chocolate sister extended her hand to me. "So, you're the producer. I've always wondered what exactly producers did."

I felt like ignoring her and snatching Pearl by the arm. I was pissed! I was tired of going to parties and meeting people who weren't really interested in me!

"We produce shows," I told her.

"Oh," she responded.

Pearl's smile turned into a frown.

"So you put the whole show together, you mean?" the chocolate sister asked me. Despite my lack of friendliness, she had a very soothing disposition. I could sense that she was a star. I don't think she was used to people not giving her their full attention.

"I'm sorry," I said to her. "We do a lot of things, actually. Are you a model?" I asked. I was wondering whether Kiki Monet was her birth name. I seriously doubted it.

"Yes I am. Why, have you seen any of my work?" She seemed really excited, as if she had no idea that she was beautiful.

"Yeah, I've seen some of it," I lied. I didn't want to disappoint her.

Pearl began to smile again. "Yeah, we've been to a few of the shows you were in," she said. I guess it was obvious to her that I was lying.

This slender brother slipped between us and announced, "Kiki, Dana Rosenbaum is here to see you." He was so swift that you hardly noticed he was being rude.

"Oh, she's here. Where is she?" Pearl and I were forgotten. That's the way it went at all of the functions Pearl had taken me to. I hated it. Kiki looked back to Pearl and said, "Call me." Then she looked to me and waved as she was quickly ushered away from us.

Pearl looked at me with evil intentions. "What the hell is your problem?"

"I'm ready to get the hell out of here. I'm tired of coming to these places."

Pearl sighed and said, "You're such a damn baby. You need to get out and make some friends. Mingle. Meet people. Find a better fuckin' job."

"Look, I'm about to catch a taxi back home. Are you leaving or staying?" I asked her.

"Bobby, I don't believe you're acting like this. This is my big chance. Be happy for me."

"Be *happy* for you? When are you ever happy for me? And when do you ever do anything that I wanna do?"

"Like what, go to the damn movies? Come on now, that shit is so played."

"My family wants you to come down to North Carolina and visit with me before the summer is out," I told her. It was getting close to August.

Pearl calmed down a bit. "Well, we'll make it down there together one day." She didn't seem too committed to the idea. I figured we'd talk about it at another time. I was ready to go.

"Well, are you catching a cab with me or not?" I asked her.

She paused for a second. "I'll see you later on, then. Okay? I'll be home."

I took a deep breath and headed for the door. I was hoping that Pearl was going to run up behind me and say, "All right, I'm coming home with you," but it never happened.

I took a long, expensive taxi ride back to Queens. It seemed like the longest ride of my life. I was sick to my stomach, thinking that Pearl was ready to leave me. It was the first time I realized how attached I felt to her. I never felt that way about a woman before. Could it have been love? If it was, I guess it just snuck up on me. The idea had never even crossed my mind. I began to think, *How can I be involved with, and live with, a woman without ever stopping to think about whether I'm in love with her or not?* Was it to be understood that we were in love? I wasn't sure.

I remember leaving my last girlfriend before going off to Howard. Julia Henderson worked as a waitress at the Waffle House in High Point. She was pretty much attached to me, but the feeling was never mutual. *Could Julia have been in love with me?* She sure didn't want me to go away to school. It was as if she knew that I wouldn't be concerned about keeping things going between us. After my freshman year, I came back home to Greensboro, and Julia had a new boyfriend. Maybe she wasn't in love with me after all.

Anyway, I got back to my basement apartment on Linden Boulevard at nearly two o'clock in the morning and did some serious thinking. I was wondering if Pearl loved me. She obviously wasn't tired of me sexually. I felt a bit relieved by that. Good sex, however, seemed to be the only thing we had going. With all the time we had spent together, I couldn't remember us having any conversations about what we meant to each other. Maybe Pearl didn't know how to express her feelings. She did seem to have a problem with vocalizing her emotions, unless of course she was displeased with something. She surely knew how to vocalize her anger. Maybe her everyday closeness to me was message enough that she did in fact feel for me.

One thing I did know was that I was not impressed by her new set of friends. I wasn't going to any more of Pearl's meet-and-greet parties. And I meant it! I didn't care if we were in love or not.

The Glamorous Life

She wants to lead. Snap! . . . Snap!
The glamorous life!
She don't need. Snap! . . . Snap!
A man to touch!

That Sheila E. song was glued to my head. I couldn't stop humming and singing it with my fingers popping and my feet stomping. Pearl was out there with the wannabe rich and famous, and I had no bait to reel her back in.

She quit her job at Macy's and began hanging out with Kiki Monet regularly. They were traveling from coast to coast and overseas before I knew what was happening. Pearl was definitely on her way up, but she still had not signed with a modeling agency. She was a scraping and clawing outsider, spending good money to keep up with the crowd, leaving me to pay most of our bills.

Pearl no longer wore street clothes. I remembered when she couldn't wait to get home from work to toss on her jeans and a T-shirt, but after hanging out with Kiki, she wore nothing but expensive fashion statements. She was a walking, talking fashion magazine. Her transformation was unreal. Somewhere along the way she picked up the habit of smoking Newport Stripes.

I would get home late from work and flip through the growing portfolio that Pearl began compiling of her new modeling work. I was actually living with a model in New York. What would my mother say?

Even though Pearl and I weren't married, every once in a while I thought about her being unfaithful to me while on her photo shoots and extensive travel. Every time she came home, though, she made love to me like a tigress. I continued to wonder about her. Maybe she just had a strong sexual appetite. I still hadn't bothered to discuss with her the intents of our relationship.

We never did make it down to North Carolina to see my folks that summer. I got a chance to go home for a few days over Christmas, but that was it. My mother became more concerned about how Brad was doing in grad school anyway. I guess she had written me off. I couldn't blame her. I barely called home twice a month. I was just too busy and exhausted half the time to go through the drama with my mother. I usually called home when something special was going on, like a birthday, a wedding, an anniversary, or the holidays. And I don't know where the time went, but before I knew it, I had been in New York for more than a year.

It was late July 1987, and I was still producing at WHCS-AM in Harlem. Things were getting really hectic there. Mr. Payton had me producing for nearly half of the shows, and operating the audio console. It became harder and harder to keep up with what everyone was doing, and a lot of the radio personalities were some real pains in the ass. Mr. Payton was no saint himself. There were a lot of sexual affairs going on, egos flaring up, and inexperience was everywhere. It seemed that many New Yorkers had the "I am a star" syndrome and didn't want to work with anyone. No wonder Mr. Payton sought out newcomers.

I was tired of being cursed out for things that went wrong on different shows. There were just too many issues in New York's black community to find concrete solutions to on an hourlong radio show. I don't think a lot of the listeners got the point of radio. Some of them assumed that the dialogue on our programs was actually the be-all and end-all of solving problems. People were constantly arguing during valuable air time about what was being said or what needed to be said. No matter how many guests or organizational leaders we had on the different shows that aired, I felt that their dialogue was meant to *inform* the community and not be taken as God's word to man.

A lot of our guests, on the other hand, were disappointed with the minute level of support that the station got from serious sponsors. There was nothing we could do about that. We were one small black-owned radio station in a huge broadcasting market.

I thought we had too many on-air arguments myself. I didn't like controversy nor the Ping-Pong matches of opinions, but Mr. Payton thrived on it. "I know it may not be healthy for the community, Bobby, but we get three times as many callers when there's an argument on the show. A little disagreement gets the blood pumping."

My favorite radio personality at the station was this smart young guy named Reggie Hinton. Mr. Payton canned his show because of low ratings. I thought his "Youth Talk" program was one of the best that we had. It covered a large range of issues regarding black youth. However, since the older listeners and advertisers failed to back it, the ratings were dismal. No one seemed to care about what the youth of New York had to say.

Anyway, we started moving "Youth Talk" around, trying to find a time slot that would be best for it. The original show was on Mondays through Fridays from three to four in the afternoon. "Caught in Traffic," a work-related show, followed from four to six. Reggie thought that "Youth Talk" would have been best on the weekends. There was too much competition on the weekends, though. That's when most of the more successful New York stations played long hours of rap music. Reggie would have been slaughtered. Then he came up with a great idea to bring rappers on the show to converse live with young people. I loved the idea, but Mr. Payton said no go.

Mr. Payton never responded well to the youth who came into the station. Then one afternoon, he simply told Reggie we couldn't do the show anymore. Period. End of story. That broke my heart. You learn to live with the canceled shows, though, and that scared me. I stopped caring as much as I used to about things because there was simply too much to care about. One mind could not possibly absorb it all. I really admired politicians in that regard, because they had to cater to a hundred different issues and millions of different people every day.

The best shows I was a part of at WHCS were when we had Reverend Al Sharpton. That guy had people calling in for days. He really got the people out and talking in New York. Whenever Reverend Al was involved in something, he brought out the strongest emotions in people. He got people to move, and I grew to respect his can-do attitude.

So there I was, a good-natured college boy from down south, thrown right in the middle of everything going on in New York. After a while, I fell into a rhythm of flipping through various newspapers to stay abreast of the local news. I read *The Amsterdam News,* the *Daily News, The New York Post, The New York Times, The Big Red,* and *The Village Voice.* The thing I regretted was that I spent so much of my time trying to produce shows that I missed out on a lot that was going on in New York. It's one thing to produce a show about art, politics, people, and the community, but it's another thing to actually participate in what's going on. I spent far too much time at the station and at home organizing shows. Without Pearl there to literally drag me out of the house, I had turned into a workaholic hermit.

I remember asking Mr. Payton for a raise during that second summer at the station. I wasn't asking for much, so I figured I had a good chance of getting that little something extra. I mean, I had been loyal to WHCS-AM to a fault. It was extra hot outside that day, and even with the air-conditioner on full blast, Mr. Payton looked exhausted behind his desk.

"What's bothering you, Bobby?" he asked me, reading my body language. He could always tell when someone had a gripe. I guess that came from being in the business for years.

I closed the door and sat down.

"Uh-oh," my boss responded. He held out his open palms to me and said, "Okay, what is it? You need a week off, or are you leaving us for good?"

I smiled, nervously. "No, it's not that. I thought I'd talk to you about something else."

"And what's that? Somebody's giving you problems again? Who is it? I'll have a talk with them for you."

I began to wonder if a raise had ever even crossed his mind. Mr. Payton was the cheapest boss that I had ever worked for in my life, but it didn't stop him from driving a Cadillac and owning an elaborate wardrobe. Of course, he made it a habit of telling everyone that those were things acquired *before* his ownership of the station.

"Actually, I was thinking more of monetary concerns," I told him.

The boss leaned back in his chair. "I see. So what are you telling me? You want a raise?"

"That would be awfully nice of you," I said with a smile.

He nodded and asked, "How long have you been working here, Bobby?"

"About fourteen months."

"Fourteen months," he said with another nod. "Do you realize that some of the people working here have been here for three and four years?"

"I'm aware of that," I told him. "But none of them have worked half as hard as I've been working since I've been here. A lot of people are here for two or three hours a day. I'm here for ten and twelve hours sometimes, making sure that everything goes right. I'm even here on the weekends." *Hell, I've been practically* running *this station for the past year,* I thought to myself. If anyone deserved a raise at WHCS, it was definitely me.

Mr. Payton grinned. I didn't know if that was good or bad, I just felt that a raise was overdue. "How much of a raise are you asking for?" he asked me.

"A dollar-and-a-half." I had calculated that with the nearly sixty hours I put in each week, a dollar-and-a-half raise would increase my paycheck by close to two hundred dollars.

"I'll tell you what I'll do. Over the next couple of weeks, I'll think about it for you. And if I can't do it . . ." He folded his hands, and I got the message; either I agreed to work without the raise, or he'd break in another hungry newcomer.

I left Mr. Payton's office with a loss of energy. I felt like taking the rest of the day off and going to the movies. I didn't, but that's what I felt like doing. I wanted to see Robert Townsend's *Hollywood Shuffle*. Everyone was talking about how hilarious it was. I had already missed the premiere and the after party at B. Smith's Bistro. It was big news to have an elegant, black-owned restaurant in Manhattan, and a lot of stars showed up there in support of Robert Townsend's film. All I did was read about it.

•

Pearl was back in New York the last weekend before August. She brought Kiki Monet by the apartment with her. We all sat in the living room eating popcorn and watching *She's Gotta Have It* on video. Pearl and I had seen the Spike Lee Joint the summer before at the Cinema Studio in Manhattan, but Kiki had never seen it.

"I am so proud of that brother," Pearl was saying of Spike Lee. "I mean, that's how you make it in America, you see what you want, and you just go after that shit."

I had already heard the speech a year before. Pearl was repeating herself for Kiki's benefit.

Kiki didn't respond, she was too busy laughing at the come-on lines in the introduction. "Oh my God! This reminds me of when we were in Vegas," she said to Pearl with a laugh.

"Vegas?" I asked, confused. "Like in *Las* Vegas?"

They both ignored me, continuing to watch the video. Pearl never told me about going to Las Vegas. *What kind of photo shoot do you do in Vegas?* I thought to myself. For the rest of that evening, all I could think about was asking Pearl about *Vegas*.

After watching the video, Pearl and Kiki watched tapes of fashion shows until late. I retired to the bedroom after awhile. I was still upset about the Vegas thing.

Pearl walked into the bedroom around three in the morning. I had dozed off to sleep with the light on while reading Piri Thomas's memoir, *Down These Mean Streets*. Doreen had told me about it at work. It was one of her favorite books. I must admit, it was pretty good.

"Kiki's spending the night on our couch," Pearl told me.

"Okay. Thanks for asking me," I responded. I already had a bone to pick with Pearl.

"What's wrong with you? I *do* still live here, you know."

"Yeah, you just don't pay bills anymore."

Pearl frowned and began to undress. "I'll take care of it," she said.

"What kind of photo shoot did you have in Las Vegas?" I asked her.

Pearl sighed, meaning she didn't want to talk about it. "I'm a little tired, okay? We went to Vegas, Bobby. So what? I mean, what's the big deal?"

After she put it to me like that, I couldn't see what the big deal was either. I think I was jealous. I wanted to go to Las Vegas, too. "You never told me you were going, that's all."

Pearl clicked the light off and climbed into bed wearing more Victoria's Secret. Thinking about her increasingly expensive wardrobe, I didn't see how she had money left to pay any bills.

Pearl leaned into me and squeezed my ribs. "I'm always thinking about coming back home to you, baby. You should know that by now."

I was wondering if she was telling me the truth. It's easy to say you miss someone after being away. I was wondering if she had ever once had another guy since we were living together. She surely had enough opportunities. I did too, for that matter. I had remained faithful, though.

"Does Kiki have a boyfriend or something?" I thought I'd ask. The thought had never entered my mind before.

I felt Pearl smile against my chest. "Nope. She just has male associates."

I wanted to ask, "And what about you?" but I didn't. I wondered if she still called me her "friend" while on her photo shoots. From what she had told me, she and Kiki had been to Florida, Dallas, Virginia Beach, Chicago, L.A., Paris, and Italy. Kiki had even footed the bill a few times.

I had another sleepless night, filled with insecurities. Most guys would have never put up with the things I was beginning to take from Pearl. I rarely questioned anything she did.

Early that morning, Pearl slid her hand inside my drawers.

"We have company," I whispered, attempting to pull her hand away. I didn't feel up to it.

Pearl was enthused by the idea. "So what? My roommates were home when you used to come over to my apartment down at Howard, and that never stopped us."

"Yeah, but this is different," I said, still resisting.

Pearl wouldn't take no for an answer. "Come on, Bobby. I want it," she said, getting louder.

To make a long story short, Pearl got what she wanted that morning, and she was louder with her moans than usual. I suspected that she was showing off.

"Stop that," I told her, tight-lipped.

"O-o-oh, Bobby!" she moaned to me.

I tried to shut myself down. The freak-show thing was turning me off. Pearl did her usual wildness in bed, and I couldn't help but finish the job with our box springs squeaking.

"Yeeah, yeeah, yeeah!" Pearl let out. She jumped out of bed when we finished and rushed back out into the living room with her robe on.

"Glrrrl, I want some of what you just got!" I heard Kiki howling as they laughed together. I felt like some kind of circus act, a damned sideshow!

Pearl ran the shower water and took a shower. I sat up in bed, angry at her. Things were really getting foul between us. I looked over at the clock, and it was after 10 A.M. I had to be down at the station by noon. When Pearl finally finished with her shower, it was 10:30. I rushed into the bathroom with my things and Kiki clapped her hands for me. I took my shower in disgust and got dressed for work. Pearl and her girlfriend were still tickled by that morning's events as I headed out the door. I remember thinking that I had somehow turned into a plaything. Or had I always been a plaything to Pearl?

It felt like my manhood had been stripped away from me that morning. I tried to rationalize that any other man would have been flattered by the idea of two beautiful models hooting and howling for his sexual favors, but all I could think about was how violated I felt.

I was a zombie at work that day, and I was out of the station by five. When I arrived back in Queens, I wasn't sure if I wanted to go in the house, thinking that Pearl and her friend were still there. I nodded to my neighbor and slowly headed down the cement steps toward the basement gate with my key. Pearl and Kiki had left. I took a seat on the couch and noticed that Pearl had left her Newport Stripes on the coffee table. I took one out and went to light it at the stove. When I was a teenager, my brother Brad and I had experimented with cigarettes, but neither of us had continued smoking. After our mother caught us one day, she made us smoke an entire pack out in our backyard. Brad cried and plotted to call the police on her.

I took my first drag of one of Pearl's Newport Stripes and laughed to myself, remembering the letter that Brad had written informing the county police department of child abuse. He was all of fourteen years old. I was fifteen. It had been his idea to experiment with cigarettes in the first place. Even then, Brad was convinced he could do anything.

I felt like calling Brad and reminiscing with him as I blew out smoke. I thought about telling him what happened that morning with Pearl and her friend Kiki. "You should have done both of 'em," I could imagine my adventurous brother telling me. Brad started having sex before I did. I remember when he told me that he had "bunned" this pretty girl who lived down the street from us. I called him a liar. He barely spoke to the girl. As proof, that next day, Brad brought home a pair of the girl's underwear. I thought that it was disgusting. From that day on, though, he continued to collect the underwear of girls that he slept with. I asked him how he was able to come away with them, and he told me that he asked.

"But what if they say no?" I asked him.

"Then I beg them for 'em."

"And what if they still say no?"

"Then I just take them. And I tell them if they don't let me have them, I'll tell everybody what we did."

A girl's reputation meant everything down south. I felt sorry for those girls. Brad was sick in the head. I don't know where he got it from. He was just born that way, I guess. He was a predator. He and Pearl were chips off the same ugly block.

I finished the cigarette and decided not to call. I misplaced the number my mother had given me for him anyway. I would have had to call her first to get it, and I wasn't that desperate.

The Newport Stripes weren't all that bad. They weren't as strong as the Marlboros my brother and I used to smoke. We chose Marlboro because we liked the masculine advertisements. The Marlboro brand was a macho man's cigarette.

The phone rang and surprised me. I answered it, expecting Pearl to be calling me from Kiki's apartment in Manhattan, but it was Pearl's mother. We talked on the phone frequently whenever Pearl was away. Pearl's mother was named Marianne Tyler. Ms. Tyler was very likable, but you could tell that she was a busy woman. Whenever her line beeped, she was gone, and her phone rang a lot.

"Hi, Bobby. I guess Pearl's out on the town again," she said.

"Yeah, you guessed it."

"Well, I bumped into one of her girlfriends from Howard University. Do you know Shawn?"

"Yeah, I know her."

"Well, I just gave her the phone number over there. It seems Pearl hasn't kept in contact with her old friends."

Tell me about it, I thought to myself. "Okay. No problem."

"How have things been going for you over at the radio station?"

"I asked for a raise," I told her. Ms. Tyler was a lawyer. Maybe she'd understand.

"Oh, you did? And what happened?"

"I'm still waiting."

"Hmm," she grunted. "Well, you've made the first step. Now after that, you start writing down everything that entitles you to that raise." Pearl's mom was straight business, a pure professional.

"Thanks for the support," I told her.

"Like you said, 'No problem.' And you tell that on-the-move daughter of mine to slow her ass down for a minute and call her mother. Okay?"

"Consider it done."

"Okay, Bobby Dallas. I'll talk to ya."

A minute or two later, the phone rang again.

"Hello, can I speak to Pearl Davis, please?"

"She's not in. Is this Shawn?" I asked.

"Yeah, is this Bobby Dallas?" She sounded surprised.

"Yeah."

"Oh my God! You two *live* together?"

"For a year now," I told her.

"Get out of here!"

"Why, is that so hard to believe?" A year ago, I felt the same way. Me living with Pearl was truly amazing.

"Hell yeah!" Shawn admitted. "Pearl used to say she wasn't gonna have time for a man after college. 'I got moves to make,' she used to say."

"Well, she's still making those moves. She didn't let me get in her way."

"I see. Girlfriend making it in all the magazines now," Shawn said. "I guess she too *busy* to get in contact with somebody, hunh?"

"I guess so. She's too busy for me now, too. And I *live* with her."

"Well, give her my number and tell her ass that I called."

I took down Shawn's number and stuck it on the refrigerator door. She told me she had just recently finished school at Howard. I sat back down on the couch and started thinking about Faye. Faye Butler had one more year to go. I wondered if she had the same phone number or lived in the same dorm. I made a note to get in contact with her as soon as September rolled around.

I fell asleep on the couch that night while watching MTV videos. I expected Pearl to walk in the door late that night, but she never did. I was up bright and early and headed for work that next morning. Pearl had not been home all night, and I hadn't received one phone call from her.

When I got back in that Monday night, Kiki was over at the apartment again.

"Hi, Bobby," she said to me.

"Hi," I grumbled. "Where's Pearl?"

"She's in the bathroom."

Pearl walked out of the bathroom straightening her clothes. I wanted to keep my concern private, so I walked over to her and whispered, "Where were you last night?"

Pearl frowned at me and said, "You know where I was. I was over at Kiki's." She was loud enough for her friend to hear. It occurred to me at that moment that I didn't have Kiki's phone number.

"You could have called and left a number or something," I said. "What if there was some kind of emergency? Your mother called here last night, and your friend, Shawn, from Howard, called."

"Shawn called here?" Pearl stopped and asked. "How did she get our number?"

"Your mother gave it to her. I left a message on the refrigerator."

Pearl walked over to the refrigerator and pulled the message from underneath a magnet. "Thank you," she mumbled.

I ignored it and headed for the bedroom. I was tempted to lock the bedroom door and leave Pearl to sleep out on the couch herself. I was just waiting for her to try and pull another freak show. I grabbed Piri Thomas's Spanish Harlem memoir off the long dresser and picked up where I left off. Once I got back into the book, I heard our basement gate closing.

Good! Kiki's not staying over tonight, I told myself. I went on about my business until I realized it was after midnight. It was a little too quiet out in the living room. I walked out to find that Pearl had left with her friend again. I found a note on the door with Kiki's Manhattan phone number. I was beginning to not like Ms. Monet so much. She was becoming a bad influence.

Things were pretty much the same for a couple of weeks. Pearl was coming and going as she pleased. I felt better about being alone when Pearl was traveling. At least then I didn't anticipate her walking in the door so much.

Something told me that things would only get worse between us, and my hunch was right. I walked into work at WHCS one day, and Doreen was reading *The Amsterdam News*. I hadn't had a chance to get a copy yet.

"Hey, Bobby, isn't this your friend, or whatever?" Doreen asked me.

I walked over to her desk where she pointed out Pearl, hugged up with a New York Knick at a charity basketball tournament. I stopped breathing.

Doreen looked up into my face and nodded. "Yeah, man, she's been to a lot of functions lately. She's been getting around." Doreen went to nearly everything. I think that was her main reason for working at WHCS, she loved the perks.

I stormed off to my tiny office area, which I shared with two senior producers. I didn't know what to do with myself. It was September. I hadn't gotten the raise that Mr. Payton had promised to think about, I was tired of spending all of my hours at the station, and Pearl was "buggin' out" on me, a term New Yorkers liked to use when people acted out of the ordinary. I was ready for a nervous breakdown at the tender age of twenty-three.

"What's wrong with you?" Timothy Gaines asked me. He was in his early forties. He produced most of the early morning shows.

"I don't think I'll be able to work today," I told him. I felt nauseous.

"Have you talked to Payton?"

"Not yet. I just walked in."

"Well, go let him know."

I walked down to Mr. Payton's office. As usual, he was on the phone. I took a seat and waited for him to finish his call.

"Yeah, hold on for a second," he told whoever was on the other line. "Bobby, I'm really busy this morning. Is it urgent?" he asked me.

"Well, I'm feeling kind of sick. I don't think I'm gonna be able to make it through the day," I told him.

He nodded his head and showed me out the door. "Okay, Bobby, I'll be right with you. Let me finish up with this call."

I had heard that one before. He'd be in his office for hours sometimes while you were waiting for him to get back to you. I don't think he realized how urgent my situation was that morning. I couldn't think at all. I would have been no good to anyone.

I walked back into the tiny producer's office with Tim.

"Did you talk to Payton?" he asked me. He was packing up his things.

"Not really. He's busy. You know how he gets," I told him.

"Well, you know, hang in there until he gets a chance to talk to you."

I shook my head and got out that day's schedule. "Not today," I told him.

Tim looked over at the schedule and frowned. "You can't just walk out of the station."

I ignored him and headed on my miserable way. Tim followed me out into the hallway but didn't try to stop me. Debbi Willis, our news announcer, was finishing up a morning news brief. I was supposed to produce "Harlem Is Talking" at ten, with host Shannon Conway. Shannon was having a discussion with Doreen when I approached the front door on my way out.

"Hey, Bobby," she said to me.

"Hi," I responded, walking right out the door. Shannon didn't come out after me. She didn't know that I wasn't coming right back. In fact, I was thinking about not returning at all, or at least not that day.

To hell with work! I told myself. *I wanna see New York.* I had a feeling that I wouldn't be staying there much longer.

I remember listening to a group of white kids who were on their way to school. They spoke as if New York was the greatest place to live in the world. It was the same way though with the kids who lived in Washington, D.C. They loved living in the Capital City. Me? I didn't know where I wanted to live, really. The only reason I was in New York was because I was hooked on Pearl with nothing better to do with myself. I could have gotten radio experience anywhere.

I arrived in downtown Manhattan and just walked around, taking in the multitudes of people and the busy morning traffic. I was a walking zombie. There was a science fiction movie around that time called *The Brother from Another Planet,* starring Joe Morton. That's exactly how I felt in downtown New York that day.

By the time I began to snap out of my daze, it was nearly two o'clock. I must have walked over thirty blocks that morning all in a random fashion, up one block, down another, up two blocks, and so on. I doubt if I could have done that in any other city and still been downtown.

Anyway, I stopped in front of this radio and television place. They were playing Sheila E.'s hit song, "Glamorous Life." I had heard the song before, but as I stood there and listened to it, the song made perfect sense to me. Sheila E. was singing about Pearl Davis. I was so moved by it that I walked right in and bought the tape. That was the beginning of my addiction to the song. I had lunch downtown and headed back on my way to Queens to listen to it on Pearl's stereo system.

When I got back in, after three o'clock, Pearl was sitting on the couch eating ice cream and watching TV in her white robe. She turned around and looked at me and then looked away. "What are you doing back here? Don't you have to work today?" she asked me, facing the television set.

I don't know what I was thinking, but seeing Pearl in her bathrobe made me walk back to the bedroom and check the sheets. They were just as I had left them. Instead of walking back into the living room to face Pearl, I grabbed Piri Thomas's book and began reading again. I was nearly finished with it. Pearl walked into the bedroom a few minutes later.

"What the hell is wrong with you?"

"You tell me," I answered.

She grimaced and said, "I don't have time for this," and walked back out.

"I saw your little picture in *The Amsterdam News* this morning," I said.

Pearl walked back into the bedroom and stared at me. "Is that why you're acting all crazy?"

I stared back into my book.

"Bobby, all I was doing was taking pictures. That's part of the business. Now if you're gonna be with me, then you need to get used to it."

I wanted to ask her, "Is that *all* you've been doing?" But I didn't. I didn't say another word. Pearl did the rest of the talking.

"I don't believe you're acting like this, Bobby. You need to grow up!" she shouted at me from the living room.

The fact that I failed to respond was pissing Pearl off. I felt good about it. I planned on ignoring her all day if I had to.

"Bobby? Bobby!" she continued to yell from the living room. "Oh, you're not gonna talk to me now, right? Okay, fuck you then!"

I looked up and closed my book after she said that. I used my thumb as a page marker. I felt all this anger bottled up inside of me, but I didn't know how to get it out. I had been an agreeable man all of my life. My brother, Brad, would have told Pearl where she could go weeks in advance. Brad would have humiliated her in some way and thrown her the hell out, but I wasn't Brad, and I didn't know what to do. I was simply frozen. Sometimes it's more normal to react to things than to sit and think about it. I was sure there were plenty of brothers who would have been at least verbally violent with Pearl. How was I supposed to deal with that kind of woman, being the kind of man that I was? I felt like a wimp.

I decided to take a deep breath, ignore Pearl, and go on back to my reading. Then the telephone rang. I ignored that, too. Pearl answered it. She sounded as if she was having a conversation with an old friend. The next thing I know, she was at the bedroom door with a new cordless phone in her hand.

"Pick up the phone. It's for you," she told me.

"Who is it?" I asked. Who could I know that Pearl would have a detailed conversation with? I started thinking that it was a call from home, either my mom or dad or even my brother.

"It's Mr. Payton," Pearl said.

Damn! I didn't want to talk to him that day. I was definitely not coming back in to work. I picked up the bedroom phone. "Hello."

Pearl hung up her cordless and walked back into the living room.

Mr. Payton said, "Bobby, that's a hell of a way to get a raise, son. If I didn't like you so much, I might have been forced to fire you for that."

I wasn't even thinking about the raise anymore. Mr. Payton went on, "I didn't know you were living with Pearl."

"Yeah, well, it ain't been no ice cream and cake."

He laughed and said, "I know it hasn't. You can't hold on to her kind too long."

"Why do you say that?" I asked him. I wanted to know what he knew. I was tempted to ask if they had been involved before.

"I just know what kind of woman she is. Her kind ain't changed in a million years," Mr. Payton told me. "Now don't get your feelings hurt over there, Bobby, because we need you at the station. We can start you off with that raise we talked about the first thing next week. I'll let you have the rest of the day off, but you come back in tomorrow. And son, please don't try anything like this again. You hear me?"

"Yeah, I hear you," I told him.

"All right then, Bobby. I'll see you tomorrow."

I felt pretty good after that. I closed my book and went to the refrigerator to pour a glass of juice with a smile on my face. I walked out into the living room to rub it in with Pearl. She was filing her toenails over the coffee table.

"What, you got a little raise, and you feel better now?" she said to me with a grin.

"That's right."

"Bobby, so what? It's only an extra hundred dollars. It's not like you got a company car."

"You know what, how come everything *you* do is so important?" I asked her.

Pearl strained to answer me. "Because, Bobby, you're doing little shit. I could see if you were moving your way up at a major station."

I walked away from her, disgusted. She still had not been signed to a major modeling agency, and I wanted to know when she would start paying her part of the bills again. I had dipped into my bank account more than a few times. I stormed right back out into the living room. "Have you seen the bills for this month?"

"No," she snapped at me.

I looked at her sternly and went to the bedroom. We usually kept our bill notices in the top dresser drawer. I looked in there, and every last bill was gone.

"Did you find anything?" Pearl asked me when I walked back out to her.

"No," I said, confused.

"That's because I took care of the shit. Okay? So get off my damn back."

•

Things were fine for the next couple of days. I went back to work, and Pearl was spending more time at home. I no longer had feelings of anxiety about her leaving me. I even had my raise.

I got home that Friday night, and Kiki was back over at the apartment. Pearl greeted me with her good news as soon as I walked in.

"I got signed, Bobby! I finally got signed!" she told me. I forget the name of the modeling agency she was signed to, but she was real happy about it.

She and Kiki wanted to go out and celebrate. Pearl asked me if I wanted to tag along, but I wasn't in the mood for it. That celebrity stuff was not for me. I didn't want to be around Kiki too long anyway. Pearl was on her worst behavior around her.

I decided to stay home and relax that night. I was pleased to know that my little world was still holding together. Before Pearl left, though, she told me that she would be going to Milan, Italy, that next week.

"For how long?" I asked her.

"For a week."

As it turned out, her one week in Italy turned into three weeks of missing in action. My peace of mind was shattered again. I could no longer take Pearl's traveling. I finally broke down and called Ms. Tyler.

"Has Pearl been in contact with you from Italy?" I asked her.

"Italy? She got back from Italy a week and a half ago."

"She did?" I was baffled, still waiting around for her.

"She hasn't been back to Queens yet?" her mother asked me.

"She hasn't even *called* here," I emphasized to her.

"Mmm," Ms. Tyler grunted. Then her other line beeped. "Hold on for a minute," she told me. I knew what that meant. She came back on the line and told me she'd have to call me back. I didn't expect it to be just minutes later.

"Bobby," she said to me, "this is gonna be a hard thing for you to take, but I would advise you not to bother yourself with my daughter. Take my advice, and get on with your life. I don't think she has your best interests in mind. She's only thinking about herself. And, you know, I really have myself to blame for that, being that I was so busy when she was younger. It hasn't been an easy life for her. She can be very selfish sometimes. I'm just telling you this because I like you. You are a very honest and straightforward young man, and I don't want to see you get hurt by her."

I was already hurt. It was only a matter of time before my relationship with Pearl ended. All of the signs were there. I had been counting the days. Pearl hung around that last week just long enough to receive her important phone call from the modeling agency.

I hung up the phone with Ms. Tyler and just stared at the television. It was my television hooked up to Pearl's stereo. Her stereo didn't cost much. She could do without it. Her mother had bought the bed for us, and all of the other household items were things you could easily go out and buy again. Even the few pieces of clothing Pearl had left in the apartment were disposable. I suspected the next time she came back to Queens, it would be to collect her pictures, magazines, and mementos, if she even wanted them.

It was October by then, and New York was cold. I put on a jacket and walked a few blocks to a corner store to buy a pack of Newport Stripes. I smoked one on the way back and lit up another as soon as I got back in. I sat in my usual spot on the couch in front of the TV and thought about how I had hurt Faye during my senior year at Howard. It served me right that Pearl was acting the way she was. I knew I had some bad karma to deal with.

I still hadn't tried to reach Faye in D.C. I felt like picking up the phone, tracking her down, and apologizing to her, but then I decided not to. Faye had probably moved on with her life and found a more appreciative friend. It had been well over a year since I had spoken to her. The last thing she needed was for me to call and resurrect bad memories.

I got up and turned on Pearl's stereo to play Sheila E.'s "Glamorous Life." I just kept rewinding the tape while smoking cigarette after cigarette like a nicotine junkie.

I was feeling pretty down and out when I walked into work the next day. Doreen was sitting at her desk looking nice and innocent like she always looked on the job.

I leaned over her desk and asked, "If I stop working here, will you stop by and visit me for a few hours?" I figured I had nothing to lose, so what the hell.

Doreen looked up at me and smiled. "What about your friend?"

"What about *your* friend?" I asked her back.

Doreen grinned at me and said, "We'll see."

I smiled back and walked away from her. I remember having this big feeling of relief that morning, as if I had been freed from jail. I had never been in jail, but I had been locked in my emotions with Pearl for two years.

I let our radio personalities, guests, and callers argue all they wanted that day. Usually I tried to cut them off and get everyone back on the subject. The big issue that morning was whether or not uniforms would change some of the negative behavior in public high schools and junior high. There had been an increase in student robberies that school year of 1987. I tended to agree with those callers who believed that it was a sign of the times. If students didn't get robbed in school, they'd be robbed after school. There was a growing desire in young people to take other people's property, and guns were becoming more available to youths. That had nothing to do with uniforms. I planned to produce a couple shows on handguns.

"Those were some hot shows we had today, Bobby. I noticed you let them go for it for a while," Mr. Payton said to me with a big smile that night. "I've been trying to get you to do that for a while. Keep up the good work."

I felt pretty good about the shows myself that day. I rode the subway back to Queens feeling uplifted. I got in and discovered that Pearl had been by the apartment to collect the rest of her things. At first I thought she had left without locking the basement gate. Then I found an envelope on the bed with Pearl's house keys inside, along with a one-page letter. It basically said that she was sorry and that she couldn't face me, but she didn't want to be tied down. She wanted to explore all of her dreams without any inhibitions. She ended the letter by saying I was a very sweet person who deserved much better treatment than what she could give me.

"Tell me something I don't know," I told myself. I guess Pearl wasn't as bold as I thought she was. Our breakup was official, though. We had finally ended it. Pearl did decide to leave the stereo with me. I guess she realized how attached I had become to it. I sat down on the couch and popped in that Sheila E. tape. Boy, was I miserable. The whole affair with Pearl Davis had been a big fantasy for me. It was time for me to wake up and smell the coffee.

"I'll survive this," I told myself. "I'm not dead yet."

I took the train back home to North Carolina that Thanksgiving and had a lonely dinner with my parents. Ironically, Brad had gone to Boston to visit the family of a girl that he had fallen in love with. She attended graduate school with him at North Carolina at Chapel Hill.

I asked my father privately that night about lost loves. He said, "Every man has a few women who got away from him. Unless, of course, you got a chance to marry your second or third grade schoolteacher." That was my father for you. He was always the comedian. He did make me feel better, though.

Back in Queens, the lease on the basement apartment was up at the end of the year, so I told myself after Thanksgiving that I had one month left in New York. That first week in December I gave Mr. Payton my two-week notice at WHCS-AM.

"There's absolutely nothing I can do to convince you to stay?" he asked.

I shook my head and said, "I don't think so. New York's just not my kind of place."

He nodded and said, "I understand. Well, good luck in whatever you decide to do."

I asked Doreen about coming over to visit me again. There had been a few other women I could have propositioned before leaving New York, but I felt closer to Doreen. I felt like we were meant to have a roll in the hay together. Maybe it was my exotic memory of her at The Garage. Doreen was the first woman in New York to come on to me.

"Are you serious?" she asked me. "You're gonna stop working here?"

I told her I was. My time in New York was up.

"Why?"

"I don't know. New York just isn't where I wanna be."

"Well, where do you wanna be?"

I hunched my shoulders. "I don't know that either." I still wasn't planning on going back home.

Doreen and I set a date for my place on my last Friday on the job. I thought she was pulling my leg. She was supposedly loyal to her jealous boyfriend. When she showed up at my basement gate after ten at night, I knew that she was serious about sleeping with me.

"You actually came," I said to her.

"Yeah. I wouldn't have said that I was coming if I wasn't. I'm not like that. I do what I say I'm gonna do."

"What about your boyfriend? You don't feel guilty at all?" I was kind of nervous about it once Doreen showed up. I didn't want her boyfriend tracking me down and stabbing me or something. I don't know why I thought of being stabbed instead of shot or just plain beaten. I guess I had fed into the stereotype that Latino men carried switchblades.

"He has other girlfriends," Doreen told me.

"He does?"

"Sure he does."

"But he's still your guy?"

"I mean, we're not married or anything, but yeah, he's still my man."

It was too awkward a situation for me. I just let it go. Doreen took off her coat and I hung it in the half-empty closet. Pearl had twice as many things as I had. When she left, you could easily tell the difference.

Doreen was wearing a black lace outfit, something I would expect her to wear at The Garage. She had a long brown bag in her right hand with her black pocketbook over her shoulder.

"What's in the bag?" I asked her.

She grinned and said, "A little something to get us in the mood."

I didn't mind. I was all for experimentation. I made sure I let Doreen drink first, though. We took a seat on the couch and clicked on the television.

After her taste test, I took a pop of the drink myself. "Hey, this is pretty sweet."

"I know, right? But watch out. It'll sneak up and get you," she told me as she took a longer swallow.

I took a long swallow after her. Before I knew it, my stomach felt warm and my head was a little woozy.

"This is a nice place," Doreen was saying. By that time we were as close as two people can get with their clothes on. The drink inside of the brown bag was almost done.

"Yeah, it is, isn't it?" I told her. I was feeling over her well-curved body on the couch, reaching for her breasts.

"Umm, if you don't have any protection, I have some in my bag," she said to me.

When I tried to answer her, she slid her expert tongue into my mouth. It felt like an explosion went off. I couldn't wait to get inside of her. I never asked her what was in that drink of hers, but the next thing I knew, I had lifted Doreen off the couch and was clumsily heading for my bedroom. I was in such a rush that I accidentally bumped into the doorway.

"Damn, man, don't break me in half," Doreen said with a giggle.

I was too sexually aroused to feel embarrassed by it. We fell into the bed and had some really good sex, for hours. Despite being a little woman, Doreen could hold her own. I was too loaded to remember all of the particulars, though. I guess I could say we made hungry love, because of all the biting and necking that I remember. I don't think it was a Latin thing. Maybe we were both hungry from the alcohol.

"That was great," Doreen told me.

"Yeah, it was," I said, all out of breath. "I wish we would have done this in the beginning."

"So, what happened to your, ah, friend?" Doreen asked me.

I thought about Pearl. "She's gone Hollywood," I said. I tried to laugh it off, but Doreen felt my pain anyway.

"Do you miss her?" she asked me.

Good question, I thought. "To tell you the truth, I don't know yet," I answered. "I mean, if you got a chance to be a star, would you leave everything behind and just go for it?"

"I don't know. It depends on how important those things were to me," she said. "I mean, I would never leave my family."

"What about your man?"

She laughed and said, "Yeah, I probably would leave his ass."

I shook my head with a grin. "Damn! I thought Latinos fell in love and stayed in love. You ever see *West Side Story?*"

Doreen pounded on my chest in her excitement. "Yeah, that's one of my favorite shows of all time," she said.

"Yeah, I liked it, too," I told her. "It was a damn good musical."

Doreen got quiet on me. "I've been in love once," she said. "But he died."

"Mmm," I grunted. Her comment was pretty dramatic. I wasn't expecting it. After that we just lay there naked for a long time without a word, healing each other's pain with our silence.

"Well, life goes on, Bobby Dallas. That's all I can say, you know. You win some and you lose some."

"Yeah, I guess you're right."

"You *know* I'm right," she said to me. Then she leaned over and kissed my lips.

"What was that for?"

"Because I like you. And I hope that you'll always remember me as your Spanish friend in New York."

I laughed and said, "All right."

"You promise?" she asked, leaning over me and staring into my eyes. "Don't lie, man. I can always tell when people lie."

She had the darkest and shiniest eyes in the world. "Yeah, I promise," I said to her.

Doreen turned out to be quite a lighthearted soul, and I will always remember that lust-filled night and the conversation we had shared afterward.

•

After that night with Doreen, I was ready to move on from New York and close that entire chapter of my life's book. I couldn't stay there because I would have been thinking about Pearl too much. I kept wondering that maybe I should have spoken up a lot earlier about how I felt and asked her how she felt about me. I should have stopped her in her tracks instead of letting her take me for granted for so long. Isn't it natural for a guy, or for anyone for that matter, to establish some type of understanding with their partners? It felt like the breakup was all my fault. Maybe I should have been more of a *man* and stood my ground. I should have shown Pearl how I felt. Brad would have done it, with all of his macho.

I thought back to all of my previous relationships with women. It was never that many. And I never had anyone as driven as Pearl. I guess that's what I needed to begin responding more to women. Maybe my hands-off approach to relationships had painted me as an unfeeling man, or someone who was not concerned. Then again, I don't think I *was* too concerned about relationships. I was just going through the motions with women. Maybe I didn't know *how* to care, or at least how to make women feel that I was there with them. My life never revolved around women like Brad's did. My brother had to have a woman at all times, and there was no denying his emotions. Brad wore his emotions on his chest for all to see.

I remember reading *The Bluest Eye,* a book by Toni Morrison, while attending Howard University. In that book she explained what she called a "plain brown girl," a woman who didn't allow real passion to touch her. Toni Morrison referred to the physical and emotional passion of love as "funk." However, these sedate "plain brown girls" controlled their "funk" by seeming to be above it all, above the physical and emotional vulnerability of love. In some respects, I could have been thought of as a "plain brown man."

My ways of abstaining from emotional drama, I guess, had been an early response to my mother's overenthusiasm. It was how I saw my father deal with her, using his offbeat humor to lessen her bite, and it had finally come back to haunt me with Pearl, a woman who needed all of the "funk" in the world. And I gave her nothing.

Return to
Chocolate City

The second week in December, I caught a Greyhound bus to Washington, D.C., to see if I could get back in contact with Faye before she went home for the holidays. I was going to apologize to her whether she liked it or not.

I checked into the Howard Inn on Georgia Avenue for three days. I figured three days was more than enough time to track her down. In the meantime, I planned to check around at the radio stations where I completed internships to see if I could get a job producing radio talk in Washington. The first thing I did, however, was buy a newspaper to check the real estate section. I had to find a new place to live.

I called a place on Thirteenth Street Northwest, that was near Howard University's campus. I didn't think it was the nicest place to live, I just felt comfortable with the area. Pearl used to live in a rented house less than four blocks away.

The rent for the apartment on Thirteenth Street was $475 a month for a one-bedroom. I thought that was pretty steep, but the apartment *was* roomy.

"You want it?" the lease manager asked me. She was a full-figured black woman with a straight-business attitude. "This is *very* spacious for a one-bedroom," she said. "It won't be vacant for long. Sometimes families of four and five move into apartments this big."

The leasing manager wasn't too pressed about renting to me. She had a take-it-or-leave-it approach that was a good one. I felt that I would have missed out on a good deal had I not taken it.

"Can you hold it for me for two days?" I asked her.

She frowned at me and said, "Are you kidding me? No, I can't hold it for you."

"What if I paid a security deposit, just until I checked around a bit? I

79

mean, if this really is a steal, then I shouldn't be able to find anything to top it, right?"

She smiled at me. I could have sworn I had her going, but then she shook her head and said, "It's too much of a hassle. We haven't even checked to see if you would be approved yet."

"We can do that," I told her.

She was hesitant. "Now see, if I go out of my way to hold this place for you, and then . . . ."

To make a long story short, she held it for me—after I paid my security deposit, of course. I had too much else to do that day to run around looking at other apartments. I figured I would check around at a few other places on my second day in D.C.

The next thing I did was call up my contacts at several of the radio stations around town. No one seemed to be hiring, but they all had internships available. I was past that stage. I wasn't interested in providing my services for free. I needed to be paid.

I walked over to WMSC, a small AM station on Fourteenth Street. I had heard about the small station while I was still a student at Howard, but I had never been over to see the place. They weren't hiring either. An older brother overheard me asking about a producing position and pulled me to the side.

"You say you want to produce a show?" he asked me. He had neatly trimmed, graying hair. He was tall, wiry, and dressed like a sports fanatic.

"Yeah," I answered him.

"Have you produced a show before?"

"I produced as many as five different shows at a time at this station in New York."

He raised his brow. "*Five* shows? Man, they were working you to death! What was the name of the station?"

"WHCS."

"WHCS?" he said with a grimace. "AM?"

I nodded.

He shook his head and said, "I've never heard of that. But it's a bunch of stations in New York that I haven't heard of. When you said New York, the first thing I was thinking of was WLIB."

"Everybody thinks of that one."

"My name is Frank Watts. I do a sports talk show in the evenings, from seven to nine," he said, extending his hand.

"Bobby Dallas," I told him.

Frank smiled. "Bobby Dallas, hunh? I like that. Is that your real name?"

"As long as I've been living."

Frank laughed and said, "Well, I do most of my own producing. I got a young girl from Howard that helps me out every once in a while, but she's not getting paid for it." I wondered where he was going with the conversation before he added, "But I'll see what I can do about you. You into sports?"

I didn't watch or participate in sports as much as the average guy did, but I wasn't planning on saying no. "Yeah, I like sports," I said. "Of course."

Frank thought to himself for a minute. "Hold on for a second," he told me. I stood in the lobby awaiting his return. Frank marched back out of the office area with two tickets in his hand. "I usually give these to the girl that helps me out from Howard when I don't use 'em, but she's studying for finals this week. You think you could use these?"

He handed me two tickets to a Washington Bullets game. They were playing the Philadelphia 76ers. I wasn't planning on turning my new friend down. "Yeah, I could definitely use these," I said excitedly. I didn't have the slightest idea where the Bullets played. I mean, it wasn't as if they were a top team in the NBA or anything.

"You know, I graduated from Howard last year. I had a DJ spot on WHBC on Wednesday and Thursday mornings," I finally told him. I didn't brag about Howard too much, but I didn't deny that I was a graduate, I just wasn't one to wear my degree on my chest. I guess I felt that way because my mother made it such a big deal to have a degree. It was no big deal to me.

Frank got really excited. "Oh yeah? Why didn't you say so, brother?"

"I figured you'd find out eventually," I said.

"All right, a young Howard brother!" He seemed really pleased by it. He handed me two of his business cards and told me to make sure I called him that next morning. It wasn't anything definite, but I did feel pretty good about it, I just wasn't so sure how it would affect things with his helper, or "Howard girl," as he called her. I didn't want to end up stepping on her toes. Nevertheless, I needed a job.

After that, I walked back to Howard's campus to Bethune dormitory in search of Faye. I stopped outside of the front entrance and took a few deep breaths while wondering what I would say to her. It was after five in the evening by then, and it was beginning to get dark. I got myself together, walked inside, and stepped up to the front desk. "Faye Butler, please."

"Do you know her extension?" the student working at the desk asked me.

"No I do not."

She proceeded to flip through the residence list and came up empty. "Umm, I have a Tamika Butler," she said to me.

"No, her name is Faye."

"Well, there's no Faye Butler in this building. Are you sure you have the right dorm? Is she a freshman?"

I smirked. "A freshman? I don't know any freshmen here. She's a senior."

"Well, I don't know, I'm just trying to help you," the girl at the desk snapped.

It wasn't her fault that I had lost contact with Faye. "Yeah, I'm sorry," I told her.

"Mmm-hmm," she grumbled, going on about her business.

I walked back out into the cold without a clue of where to begin looking for Faye. Howard University had more than a few dorms, and several of them were off-campus. I figured I would try Slowe Hall, and then call it a night. Maybe Faye decided to move into my old coed dorm.

"Faye Butler," I said, going through the whole process again. She wasn't listed at Slowe either. I walked back over to the hotel on Georgia Avenue wondering if she had moved out of the dorms and found herself a place to live off-campus like Pearl had. I got something to eat at McDonald's and hurried back inside the Howard Inn.

It was getting colder outside by the minute. It was close to seven o'clock. Then I remembered the tickets I had to the Bullets game. The game started at seven-thirty. There was no way that I was going. As it turned out, the game was aired on a local cable station. Too bad I couldn't use the tickets, but at least I could comment on how the game went. The Bullets lost again, 100–79. Charles Barkley from the Philadelphia 'Sixers had 28 points, 16 rebounds, and 4 steals. The man was simply a monster on the court, and too much for the Bullets to handle.

I had a hard time falling asleep that night in my hotel room. I kept wondering what could have happened had I chosen to be with Faye instead of with Pearl. Then again, Faye had not graduated from school yet. What if I had gotten a job somewhere else? She wouldn't have been able to move with me. It would have been one of those long-distance relationships, and I wasn't too good at that.

Even if I had decided to stay in Washington, it might have been a stretch. It seemed like a huge jump from college to postcollege. I didn't know of many undergraduates who lived with their boyfriends. But Faye didn't necessarily have to live with me. Maybe it could have worked out between us after all. I guess the whole idea of living with Pearl had led me to believe that moving in was the only way to go. That assessment, of course, was far from the truth.

•

My second day in Washington, I walked out of the Howard Inn slightly before eight o'clock in the morning. Faye had always been a morning person. I had a hunch that I might bump into her somewhere on campus before eleven, and if that didn't work, I planned on breaking down and asking the communications counselors what classes seniors took in television/film.

First, I planned to check inside the communications building, then I'd walk over to the library. As soon as I walked into the bottom level of the C. B. Powell building, I spotted Faye headed straight in my direction toward the computer room. The computer room entrance was half the distance between our line of vision. I hadn't had a chance to prepare myself yet. Faye was hesitant herself. At first we just stared at each other, awkwardly.

Faye spoke first. "How have you been?"

"Fine. How about you?"

She seemed slightly taller, wearing a black-and-white checked business suit, a white blouse, and black stockings. Her hair was done up in a French twist. Faye was looking damned good! A senior! "I'm hanging in there," she said. "So, what brings you back to Howard?" she asked. I couldn't tell if she was over her disappointment with me or not.

I leveled with her. "Actually, I came back to tell you that I was sorry."

Faye held out a hand and said, "Please, don't patronize me, okay?"

"I'm serious."

She shook her head. "You didn't come all the way back to Howard just to apologize to me. Besides, you have nothing to apologize for. You had your life to live, and I had mine. But I really can't get into this right now because I have things to do."

"Let's talk later on? I'm in town for at least two more days," I told her. I didn't want to go as far as to tell her I was thinking about moving back to D.C. I would have sounded desperate. You can't sound desperate while on the rebound. I learned that lesson a long time ago. Very few people want someone who seems needy. It's a major turn off.

Faye sighed. "I'll have to see," she said.

"How do I get in touch with you?" I asked her.

Faye took out a pen and a piece of paper and wrote her number down.

"I won't be home until after seven. And if I'm not in, I'll probably be in the library."

"Okay," I said.

"See ya," she responded. She seemed cheerful when she walked into the computer room.

I just stood there, stunned for a second. I was wondering if she sounded cheerful because we would be meeting each other later on that night, or was she cheerful because I was leaving?

Anyway, I was anxious for the rest of that day, anticipating talking to her. I wanted to catch up on how she made out over the past year and what she had planned for her future. I wasn't even thinking about her personal life, I was only hoping that we could be buddies again.

I walked down the hall and peeked inside the WHBC office. They were up and at it bright and early, playing Heavy D & the Boyz' song "The Overweight Lover." I waved to the students inside the studio and went on about my day.

I felt really detached as I walked around Howard's campus. I was surprised at how different I felt about the students. Everyone seemed so young, and I had only been away for a year and a half. I guess that's how things go after you've moved on from something. Old things seem worlds apart.

I went back to the hotel to call Frank Watts and kept getting the receptionist. "Just tell him that Bobby Dallas called," I told her. Then I gave her my number in New York.

I thought about checking around at other apartments for rent, but I didn't feel up to it. It was too cold outside to wander around different areas looking at apartments. I figured I would have to deal with what I had for a while. I went to the movies in Georgetown instead.

I called Faye after seven o'clock and got her answering machine. I left the message that I'd look for her inside the undergraduate library at our usual spot on the second sublevel.

Faye had changed her clothes and was hard at work once I caught up to her. She looked up at me and told me to pull up a seat next to her cubicle. "How's life after graduation been treating you?" she asked me without looking away from her work.

I chuckled and said, "I still have my health."

Faye wrote down a few things and responded, "I don't have a boyfriend, but I am seeing someone."

Where did that come from? I wondered. "Oh, I wasn't thinking about that. I just wanted to see you again. I didn't want us to end a friendship on such a sour note."

Faye finally looked into my face. "And how have things been with you and . . . what's-her-name?"

My heart rate jumped like a sprinter's after the starting gun goes off. *Should I just tell her the truth?* I pondered. I decided that I would. I didn't want to get off on the wrong foot again.

"That relationship wasn't meant to be. I was more infatuated than anything else," I said. That was the truth.

"You didn't like her at all?" Faye asked me.

That was an even harder question to answer. I had to admit that I liked Faye's arch rival. "Well, I definitely had an attraction to her," I said.

Faye just stared at me. My answer wasn't complete enough for her. "You didn't like her at all, you were just attracted to her?"

She was baiting me to say the wrong thing. I tried to gather my thoughts before speaking. "I did *grow* to like her, but our relationship wasn't meant to be. We were just too different to be together."

"You couldn't see that before?"

"Well, like I said earlier, I was infatuated. And you know, you don't think right sometimes when you're infatuated." I was rambling. It was already hot inside the library, and it was getting hotter by the second. I felt like stripping down to my T-shirt.

Faye nodded and said, "I see." Then she went back to work.

"Are you still angry with me over that?" I wanted to know. I could tell that she wanted to be. She was still holding back, though. I had been the same way with Pearl. Faye and I were so much alike, but at least she had the courage to let me know how she felt about me. I still had to learn to let more of my feelings out.

Faye stopped what she was doing and took a deep breath. "I *was* upset about it. Yeah. But we were friends, and it doesn't matter anymore anyway."

"So why are you still bitter?"

"Because it happened," she snapped. "You had more than enough opportunities to tell me, but you just let things go on and on between us until I found out on my own. And if I didn't just barge into your room when I did, you probably would have never told me. In fact, you *didn't* tell me, I found out, Bobby."

When she finalized her response with my name, I knew that she was beginning to release some of the tension she had built up toward me. "I was a big coward back then," I told her.

"Hmm," she grunted. "You don't have to tell me."

We were silent for a few minutes before I decided to ask her how she had been.

"Like I said earlier, I'm hanging in there. I had a few internships with television news stations, and I'm looking forward to heading back to Atlanta after graduation. I made some good contacts down there this summer."

I nodded. "Things are really looking up for you then."

"I guess so. How has radio been working out for you?" she asked me.

"Well, I'm finding out that you have to pay heavy dues to get to where you want to go."

"That's in anything you do," Faye responded. "I was talking to my girlfriend about that just last night. That's why more women are starting to get ahead. A lot of men want things to come fast, and it doesn't work that way. Women are much more willing to pay those dues, but a lot of guys would rather quit and complain."

I couldn't argue with that at all. I quit my job in New York just because my relationship with Pearl went sour. I doubt if many women would have moved out of a job position after breaking up with a man. Pearl wouldn't have done it.

"Yeah, you might be right," I told Faye. "A lot of brothers are just too impatient for all this waiting and waiting."

Faye nodded. "I know," she said. "Guys are impatient about a lot of things."

I didn't comment on that. I thought maybe she was hinting about her sexuality. I doubted if she was still a virgin. I was even tempted to ask.

"Well, I do have things to do," she suddenly told me.

"Yeah, I guess I better let you get back to your work," I said. I stood up to leave, but I really wasn't ready to go. I felt empty, as if our brief chat was useless. "Ah, I guess I'll stay in touch with you," I told her.

"Mmm-hmm," Faye hummed. She didn't even look me in my face.

I stood there frozen. *It can't end this way,* I told myself. *It just can't!* I don't know what I wanted to say to her, but it was something to the effect of, *I need your friendship again.*

Faye noticed my hesitancy and finally looked up at me. "What's wrong, Bobby? I mean, you're standing there as if you want me to say something."

"You could say that you accept my apology," I said.

She smiled with a light chuckle. "Okay, I accept your apology. Is that what you want me to say?"

I still wasn't satisfied. She didn't have any feeling in that at all. "You could say it like you mean it."

Faye stopped smiling and shook her head. "Bobby, I don't have time for this. You just picked the wrong time to come back. I'm studying for finals."

"What if I come back again in January?" I said. I was beginning to sound desperate. I couldn't even stop myself.

"For what, Bobby? I told you that I was seeing someone."

"Oh, I didn't mean like that, I meant so we could finish talking about things."

"If you don't mind, I don't want to talk about that anymore."

"Okay, we could talk about anything." I was beginning to sound like a pest, and I had never been a pest before. I had never chased girls aggressively enough to be a pest. In fact, all of the previous women that I had been with were either mutual attractions, or the girl had approached me first.

"I don't believe this," Faye said with a grimace.

I needed Faye's friendship badly. It felt as if my life depended on it. "I mean, are we still friends or what?" I asked.

"Is that what this is all about, you wanting to be my friend?" she asked me. "Bobby, I can't trust you like I used to. I don't feel close to you like that anymore. And I'm wondering if you hadn't broken up with what's-her-face if you would've come back to see me at all. When did you break up with her anyway?"

Oh my God! I panicked. "In the springtime," I lied. "I thought about coming to see you earlier, but I couldn't break away from my hectic work schedule. But now I'm thinking about getting a new job in the D.C. area, and I just wanted to know if we were still cool."

I couldn't believe that I said all of that. It's amazing what you can do when your adrenaline is pumping. However, I believe that I might have said too much too soon. I heard it said before that a lie mixed with the truth is the worst lie of all, and I had done an excellent job of mixing truths with falsehoods. I didn't know I had it in me.

Faye was speechless. She looked at me then looked away and then looked at me again. I had said my piece, and it was her turn. Faye suddenly gathered up her things and stood to leave. "Excuse me, but I have things to do." She looked angry, hurt, and determined, all at the same time.

I gave her time enough to get away, then I headed back to the hotel room.

•

I was at a crossroads. I headed back to New York, still unsure of my next move. I arrived at that familiar basement site on Linden Boulevard and took out my key. It was around six o'clock, and I felt exhausted with a ton of things to do.

I checked my messages and found that I had received two hang-ups and a message from my mother about visiting the family for Christmas. I didn't feel like calling her. She had probably been the one to hang up on my machine, both times. I felt guilty about relocating back to D.C. It would have been all too sudden for her. I hadn't even told them about quitting my radio job.

The last message on my machine was from Frank Watts. He said that he had worked something out for me with the manager at WMSC. It wasn't much, but I was used to not making much anyway. It was better than nothing. I called them back and told them that I would take it. Then I called my landlords at their new home number and told them I would be vacating the premises within the next couple of days.

Ms. Petula asked me about Pearl, and I told her that she had moved out several months ago.

"I knew she wasn't any good for you," she commented to me. "That girl was just too fast. Her type run right past good men all the time. She'll learn her lesson before it's all over. You mark my words."

I felt better about my split with Pearl after talking to the landlady. She made me feel as if Pearl had a payback coming to her like I had.

I began to gather my things at the apartment and made all the necessary phone calls I needed to make before I left New York. I gathered the last of my bills and had my magazines forwarded to my new address in D.C. I ordered a U-Haul truck and then called the phone company to have my phone cut off. I decided that I would write my parents and tell them in a letter what I had been through and where I had gone. I figured my mother couldn't argue with a letter. Then I would contact her after she had calmed down. *Maybe I'll call her from D.C. in a month or two,* I told myself with a grin.

I went out and bought a bunch of large boxes to pack up my things. Then I told my neighbors who had moved in upstairs that if they helped me move, I would make it worth their while. They were four Columbia University students. Two of them, with nothing better to do, agreed.

During my last day in New York, I traveled around the city a bit. I can't say that I thought I would miss The Big Apple, but I knew that I would miss Pearl Davis. I just didn't know how much I would miss her at the time, or how much I would long for Faye Butler while living in D.C.

I thought about calling Doreen for another consoling roll in the hay, but I decided against it. It would only increase my feelings of loneliness. At least Doreen had someone to go back home to.

That last night in my Queens apartment seemed like the longest night of my life. I stretched out on a bare, lumpy mattress inside the bedroom with my hands behind my head, staring up at the ceiling. I reminisced on all the nights I had been there with a woman who was simply too much for me, and how I had let my beautiful soul sister slip away.

"This is ridiculous," I snapped. "There's other fish in the sea," I tried to convince myself. I still didn't get any rest, though. I listened to my clock tick, tick, ticking for the rest of the night, anticipating my one-way U-Haul ride back to D.C.

New Territory

I moved into my new D.C. apartment the week of Christmas, the last of 1987. The six-story apartment complex on Thirteenth Street sat at the top of a hill that allowed a perfect skyline of the city. I hadn't noticed it before, but once I moved in, I was addicted to my third-floor view. I had made a good choice indeed, despite the ruggedness of the area.

I slept in my sleeping bag that first night, and the next morning began a busy day for me. I had to buy a new mattress and several other household items. I had to get my D.C. telephone number, and then I had to meet with Frank Watts and the station manager at WMSC on Fourteenth Street. The small AM radio station was conveniently within five blocks of my apartment.

I met with the station manager, a short, stout man named David Cooper, around three in the afternoon. Mr. Cooper looked to be in his sixties. He was wearing a white, short-sleeve knit shirt that was opened at the top. He was a light brown man with a full head of gray hair brushed to the back. His look reminded me of the great abolitionist Frederick Douglass.

Mr. Cooper was going through some paperwork when I walked in. I took a seat in his small office and waited for him to address me.

"I hear you worked in New York," he finally said to me.

"Yes, sir, at WHCS." Mr. Cooper looked as if he would demand respect, so I gave it to him.

"Why'd you leave?"

"Actually, I just decided to move on," I said. It was a stupid answer.

Mr. Cooper stared at me. "Move on to what?" he asked. He didn't understand my logic. "You just left one of the top radio markets in the country."

"Yeah, but New York wasn't my kind of place."

"So what's your kind of place?"

"I don't know yet," I said with a grin.

Mr. Cooper nodded and said, "But you do know that New York wasn't."

I wasn't sure if it was or not, but I agreed with him anyway.

"How long are you planning on staying in D.C.?" he asked me.

I wasn't sure of that either, but I wanted to say something positive. "Oh, I like D.C. I went to Howard here for four years."

Mr. Cooper was still staring. "Is that so? And you majored in radio?"

"Yes, sir."

I was getting worn out pretty quickly from his questions. I didn't seem to be convincing Mr. Cooper of anything, and Frank Watts was nowhere to be found to help me out. I thought everything was a done deal, but I was finding out differently.

"I used to work at Howard," Mr. Cooper told me. "I worked there for nearly twenty years."

"Oh really? In what capacity?" I asked him.

"Administration," he answered. Then he grunted and said, "Well, at least you got an education. My three kids could have all gone to Howard for free, but only my daughter went."

"When did she get out?" I asked.

"In eighty-four. Then she went to Howard's law school."

"Oh," I said. He had a lot to be proud of. I really wanted to talk about the job, though.

Mr. Cooper shook his head in disgust. "But my two sons," he continued, "one of them went to work in them damn casinos and whatnot in Atlantic City. The oldest boy, Michael, went to Georgetown for one semester and dropped out. He lives in Maryland now, working for some cable television company."

I thought of Faye Butler for a second when Mr. Cooper mentioned cable television. Faye had always said that cable television was the wave of the future.

"You young folks have so much going for you today, and I just don't understand what it is that makes you want to rebel so much," he said. "But a man has to learn to take his licks on his own. I can't tell them what to do anymore. I just think they're wasting their damn time."

Why are you in radio? I wanted to ask him. I didn't see how radio broadcasting was that different from cable television. I understood his angle, though. His generation had worked hard to get us young black folks opportunities in education, but at some point they have to realize that the world is always changing. My mother already thought of me as a lost cause because of my interest in radio, but like it or not, the communication field is the new place to be.

"Is your daughter practicing law in D.C. now?" I asked him.

Mr. Cooper sat up at his desk and said, "Oh, Pamela? Yeah, she works in Mayor Marion Barry's office, but she's planning on branching out soon." He reached into his back pocket and pulled out his wallet to show me a picture of her. "She's real smart," he said while passing it to me. She was real pretty, too. I had to give him his photo back before I became too attracted to her. She had the *Jet* magazine, beauty-of-the-week look. I didn't remember her from Howard. She had graduated two years before me.

Mr. Cooper stood up and said, "All right, let's get you started, Bobby." I guess some of the paperwork he was looking over had my name on it. "I have you down here to produce for 'D.C. Sports Talk' with Frank Watts and 'Community Watch' with Tammy Richards."

I nodded to him. "No problem," I said. It was a good deal to me, and it was just what Frank had told me, two shows.

Before the holiday, I met as many people at the station as I could. I started work that first week in January 1988.

•

In no time at all I was producing radio shows again. My mind was too preoccupied with my radio career to think about my social life or my family. I did, however, get a chance to call my parents over the holidays and inform them that I had moved back to D.C. My mother took it as another growing pain and my father took it with a grain of salt. He explained to my mother that radio was like that, the doors were always turning. My mother responded that that was exactly the kind of career she didn't want me to have.

Anyway, Frank Watts and I had a lot of Washington-area athletes on the show and plenty of freebies to the games. The talk of the town was Doug Williams and the Washington Redskins. Frank was dying to get Doug on the show before the Super Bowl, but Mr. Williams was too focused on the upcoming playoff games to be bothered with every local station trying to interview him. I tried, though, real hard.

"Shit, Bobby, we probably won't get an interview with Doug until after everything is all over," Frank pouted one day. He had an *Essence* magazine in his hands. "I'm telling you, Bobby, Doug's gonna be the first black quarterback to win the Super Bowl."

"You think so?" I asked him with a grin. In my short time at WMSC,

I learned that Frank's predictions, like those of many other sports fanatics, were inconsistent.

"You damn right! Doug almost took Tampa Bay to the Super Bowl in nineteen eighty. They ended up losing to the Los Angeles Rams nine to nothing. This time Doug has plenty of help around him and good coaching. I'm telling you, Bobby, it ain't no stopping him."

"What about John Elway and the Broncos?" I commented.

"Oh, I take nothing away from Elway. That white boy can run and throw his ass off, but he's gonna lose to Doug. Plain and simple.

"Damn, they got some foxes in this thing!" Frank shouted, still looking through *Essence*.

I walked over and took a peek myself. It was a fashion spread of plenty of sisters in Milan, Italy, Pearl Davis and Kiki Monet included. For a second, my heart dropped. I felt so close to her and yet so far away. On the one hand I felt proud of her, and on the other hand, I wanted to rip that magazine into a million pieces. "Yeah, they are pretty nice," I said.

"They're pretty nice?" Frank asked me. "Man, shit, you give me one of these young girls for a couple of hours, and I'll show you what to do wit' 'em."

I forced myself to smile.

"If you could just have one of 'em, which one would you pick?" Frank asked me, adding insult to injury. *If he only knew,* I thought to myself.

I was tempted to tell Frank that I had already been with one, but I doubted he would believe me. Pearl had elevated to that next level where it's amazing to even know her.

"These are just regular girls," I told Frank. "They just seem extra beautiful because they're in this magazine. Brothers usually like more meat on their women anyway."

Frank broke out laughing. "Yeah, you right about that," he said. "You haven't met Mona Freeman yet, have you? She'll be back soon."

"Who's Mona Freeman?" I asked him.

"That's the girl from Howard I was telling you about. She went home for the holidays, but she'll be back. And *man* does she have a body! I have to kick and bite myself to keep my hands off of her every time I see the girl."

I could imagine. Frank had been married once, had a son, got divorced, and had been playing the field ever since.

I wish I hadn't seen Pearl in *Essence*. I walked home from the station that night feeling like the only man on the moon. I had been forcing myself not to call Faye after our incident in the library, but I was losing my strength.

I broke down and called her that night anyway. The phone rang four times. Just as I was ready to hang up, she answered, out of breath. "Hello."

I hesitated. *Why don't I just leave her alone?* I asked myself.

"Hello," she said again.

I punked out and hung up the phone. As soon as I did it I felt like calling her right back. "What the hell did I do that for?" I shouted.

I walked over to the window to have a look at my view. It would have been so romantic to share it with someone. Especially for my birthday. I wondered if Faye even remembered it, January 16. I remembered her August 26 birthday.

I sat there thinking, confused by everything. *How 'bout I just call her back and remind her of my birthday?* I thought. I picked up the phone again but couldn't dial. The next thing I knew, a whole hour had passed and I was still sitting there in the window with the phone in my hand. It was close to midnight, and I was still debating whether I should call Faye or not.

I had it bad, a certified love jones. Faye *was* seeing someone. What if I called and her new man answered the phone? Talk about heartbreak— I would have been shattered. Why couldn't I have chosen Faye Butler in the first place?

"Damn!" I fumed to myself. I had absolutely no one to be with. It was nearly two o'clock in the morning. I walked over to the stereo that I acquired from living with Pearl, and popped in Prince's *Sign O' the Times.* I fast-forwarded it until I got to the last song on side two, "Adore." I must have played that song five times in a row. Whoever said it first was right; music soothes the savage beast.

This is all Pearl's fault, I told myself. I lit up a cigarette and started imagining Pearl Davis walking into that apartment door in something silky and easy to take off. She had done it on countless occasions while we were living in New York together. I couldn't get the thought of her off my mind. The fact that I was still smoking her brand of cigarettes didn't help any.

"Pearrrll Day-vis. What have you been up tooo, girrrl?" I sang to myself. Then I began to laugh like a madman. What a ridiculous life I was leading. I still had no idea where I was headed in my life, but since I'd made my new bed in D.C., I was prepared to lie in it.

•

When I was due to receive my first paycheck from the station, I had to see Mr. Cooper to get it. I knocked on his office door, and he told me to come on in. His daughter, Pamela, was sitting in the chair in front of his desk. I was shocked to see her there. I wasn't sure if I should say "Hi" to her or what. I waited for Mr. Cooper to give me my cue.

"Hey, Bobby," he said, pulling my paycheck from the stack of envelopes that were spread out on his desk.

I made inadvertent eye contact with his daughter and raised my hand to say, "Hi."

She smiled at me and returned the gesture. It was one of those polite smiles that I was used to getting from being raised down south.

"Oh, yeah, Bobby, this is my daughter," Mr. Cooper said, as if it had slipped his mind to introduce us. "Pamela, Bobby graduated from Howard University, too."

Pamela gave me a second look, and that time I knew it was more than just being polite. "Really? You went to Howard?" she asked.

I nodded my head and mumbled, "Yeah." I was embarrassed. She had gone on to become a lawyer. I was just a radio guy. I didn't feel I was her equal. I found myself struggling to look her in the eye. I felt like a roach on the floor, and Pamela Cooper was ready to squash me. All I could do was bow my head and wait for the kill.

"What year did you get out?"

"I got out in eighty-six," I told her.

"So, you just stayed in the area? I mean, you're not from here, are you?" Pamela seemed very mature. I was guessing she was somewhere around twenty-five, but she was addressing me as if she was thirty-five. I figured she would make a hell of a lawyer. It sure felt like she had me on the stand inside of a courtroom. The office walls were caving in on me, and I didn't have enough room to breathe. I thought about loosening my tie, but then I realized I wasn't wearing one.

"Actually, I just moved back here from New York about three weeks ago." I had to throw New York out at her to gain a little self-respect. I noticed that people took note whenever I told them I had been living in New York for a while.

Pamela grimaced. "You don't seem like the New York type."

"That's because I'm not. I'm originally from North Carolina."

She smiled and said, "Now that's more like it."

I could tell that Pamela wasn't into showboats. She was a good, down-to-earth girl. I smiled back at her. "Yeah, I guess you could say that," I said. She sure didn't seem like the D.C. type. She was a hell of a lot warmer than many of the women in D.C. that I had met. "Chocolate City" wasn't like a southern town at all as far as politeness was concerned. A lot of the sisters there were as cold, calculating, and materialistic as many of the sisters in New York.

Mr. Cooper began to chuckle. I had almost forgotten that he was there with us. His daughter was friendlier than what I expected. I was all shook up for nothing.

Pamela Cooper took out a business card and a pen and wrote her number on the back. I just knew she wasn't giving it to me. "Call me," she said, extending the business card. "Maybe I can show you some of the nicer parts of D.C."

I was tempted to look over at Mr. Cooper to see if I had his approval. It was an eerie feeling. I had gone from embarrassment to glee. *We can go out on my birthday,* I thought to myself. It was in two days. "Okay," I told her.

She stood up from the chair and said, "Well, Daddy, I'll see you later."

They embraced and shared a kiss. I almost felt like I was part of the family. I would have married Pamela Cooper at the drop of a dime. She waved to me as she walked out the door.

Mr. Cooper caught my stare. "She's a nice girl, isn't she?" he asked me with a grin.

I was choked up. "Ah, yeah, of course. She's very nice. Friendly, too."

Mr. Cooper chuckled with the mockery that old men have when they know what a young man is thinking. "Go on back to work, Bobby," he said to me.

I walked out of his office and had another problem on my hands, or I should say on my mind, because I couldn't stop thinking about his daughter. I had just met the girl. I was a big mess. My mother was absolutely right about me.

On the "Community Watch" show with Tammy Richards, we had a couple of District government workers who spoke about the restoration of U Street. The District had torn up the street to build a new subway station, and many of the black businesses had suffered. U Street and parts of Georgia Avenue looked like something out of a science fiction movie after World War III. Tammy believed that the businesses on the historical corridor had every right to complain, and I agreed with her. It was a hot show that day.

I got in after Frank's show that night and wasted no time calling Pamela. I felt close to her and was no longer hesitant about her lawyer status. I told her when my birthday was and asked if she was busy that night. She said that she wasn't, and I had a hot date on my hands.

I still hadn't called Faye to remind her of my birthday. After securing a date with Pamela, it wasn't that important anymore, and since it wasn't, I was able to call Faye without feeling so pressed. She wasn't home when I called, so I left a message with my number.

Pamela planned to take me out on the waterfront to Hogate's seafood restaurant in southwest D.C. I had heard about it, but I had never been there before. She picked me up in a gray BMW, 1986. I was immediately spoiled, thinking that she was going to pick up the tab, especially since it was my birthday. I mean, it wasn't as if she couldn't afford it.

We arrived at the restaurant and checked our coats. I noticed that Pamela was casually dressed in black jeans and an off-white sweater with one gold necklace. She looked sophisticated in the simplest clothes. She didn't have to overdo anything. You could tell that she was worth something just by the way she carried herself.

She looked at me with a smirk and said, "You're very quiet, aren't you? I mean, this is your birthday, right? Lighten up a bit."

I laughed it off. I was thinking how unlikely it was to be going out with Mr. Cooper's daughter, a lawyer. I was sure there were plenty of men who were more her speed than I was. It still seemed unbelievable to me, or maybe I didn't give myself as much credit as I deserved. Then again, I couldn't see what I had going for myself. I had no car, a low-paying job, and an apartment in a rugged area, and Pamela was even older than me. I mean, sure, a few women would say that I was handsome, and I've always been tall, but that's about it. I lacked most of the other things that women looked for in men—things like charm, confidence, money, athleticism, and so on.

"I'm just enjoying this," I said. "I'm enjoying everything."

I was wearing an outfit that Pearl had bought me for my birthday a year ago, all midnight blue. While in New York, I bought a pair of blue leather shoes to match, so I did feel pretty confident about my appearance.

"That's a really nice outfit you have on," Pamela confirmed for me. "I like the cologne, too."

"It's Lagerfeld," I told her. Pearl had bought the cologne as well. I never used it much.

Pamela and I gave our orders and began to warm up to each other.

"Are you planning on settling down in D.C.?" she asked me.

"Are you?" I asked her back.

She grinned and said, "I don't know yet."

"Me neither," I told her. "Who knows what may happen tomorrow? I might be offered a job in Los Angeles."

"Would you go?" she asked.

I paused for a moment and thought about something cool to say. "If I had someone special to go with me."

Pamela smiled big-time at that. I was doing pretty well with her. "That always makes it better," she agreed.

"So how do you like working for the District?" I asked her.

She hunched her shoulders. "What can I say? It pays the bills."

"Is that all it does?"

"Right now, yeah. I mean, I'm not looking to work for government for too long."

"Yeah, your father told me."

She raised her brow. "My father told you what?"

"That you wanted to break out and do your own thing."

She smiled and asked, "What else did my father say about me?"

"He said that you were really smart."

She laughed. "Did you believe him?"

"Yeah, I had to believe him. I mean, you're a lawyer at age twenty-five."

"He told you how old I was, too?"

"No, but he said that you graduated from Howard in eighty-four, so I figured that you're turning twenty-six sometime this year."

"Actually, I'll be turning twenty-five in April. I was skipped, way back in the first grade."

"See that? You *are* smart," I told her. "You even got skipped."

"You didn't get skipped with your birthday in January?" she asked me.

"I could have, but my parents decided against it. It can really mess a kid up if they're not ready for it."

"I know that's right," she said.

"Why, you felt out of place?"

She nodded. "I always did. I felt like a little girl everywhere I went. I already had two older brothers."

"Did your father know how you felt?"

She frowned and said, "Shit, you kiddin' me. He was too busy being proud."

Women had a way of unleashing the most personal feelings on me. I guess I had that certain innocence about me. "I'm sorry to hear that," I told her.

"It's okay. I mean, I'm over it now."

Our drinks arrived, and Pamela started on hers with a bang.

"Don't drink that too fast, or else I'll have to drive us home," I joked.

"You can drive if you want to," she told me.

I didn't comment on that. Our food arrived a few minutes later and it was superb! "Well, you sure have good taste," I told Pamela while wiping my mouth with my handkerchief.

"You think so?"

"I know so."

"Why?"

"Because you took me out for my birthday," I answered.

She smiled. "I like to be able to treat guys to dinner for a change, you know? I hate the thought of someone else always having to pay my way. It makes it seem like women are economically powerless. You know, like you're just a burden to a man."

I was impressed. "I never heard of anything like that before," I said. "Economically powerless? I gotta use that one."

Just when things seemed so perfect, Pamela got a page on her beeper. I didn't even know that she was wearing one.

"Excuse me, Bobby, I'll be right back."

I hoped that it was nothing too important. I was having a great time for a change.

Pamela came back to the table and was suddenly ready to leave. I could tell that it was none of my business, so I left it alone. Pamela drove me back to the apartment complex with few words.

"Is everything all right?" I asked her. She seemed really preoccupied after the page.

"Yeah, I'll be all right," she told me. It was more of a brush-off than an answer. I didn't like the way our date ended at all. Whoever paged her had really gotten the best of her.

"I'll call you, okay?" she told me.

I grumbled, "All right," and climbed out of her car. As soon as I walked into my apartment, I checked my phone messages. Faye had called me back to say happy birthday. She also wished me good luck in my future. I guess I really didn't have a shot in hell of making our friendship what it had been again. Faye was making it understood that she wanted to keep me at arm's length.

I fell out across my bed, emotionally exhausted. I was in excellent shape before Pamela got her little page at the restaurant. I actually felt connected to her for a second, as if we could really be a couple, but I had no such luck.

•

Mona Freeman showed up at the radio station that third week. Frank introduced us. Mona, brown and curved like a Hershey's Kiss and a sophomore at Howard, was a heck of a catch. Frank was right about that. I tried as hard as I could not to pay her too much attention, though. I didn't need any more women on my mind.

It was no big deal to Mona that I was producing on Frank's show. She was making some good contacts, getting lots of experience, and enjoying the perks that came with it. In fact, the biggest problem was deciding who would get what tickets to what games.

"So how was your date with little Ms. Cooper last week?" Frank asked me away from Mona.

I was surprised. "You know about that?"

"Come on, Bobby, you think you can get away with something like that around here?"

I grinned. "I guess not."

"So, how did it go?"

"Well, I can't kiss and tell," I told him. I really didn't want to talk about it. Pamela had not called me since that night, and I wasn't sure if I should have called her either considering the way things had ended.

"You kissed her?" Frank asked me. He looked shocked.

I shook my head and said, "No, that was just a figure of speech." I didn't want any false rumors floating around, especially with the station manager's daughter. "We just went out, had dinner, good conversation, and that was basically it," I told him.

Frank nodded with a smile. "Yeah, that sounds more like it."

"Why, you don't think I could have kissed her?" I was curious.

"Shit, from what I've seen around here, you look like you're scared to death of women," he answered with a laugh. "You been avoiding eye contact with Mona all night," he whispered to me.

"That's just because—" I stopped myself in mid-sentence. Frank didn't need to know all of my personal business. "Look, I'm not afraid of women, okay?"

He laughed at me. "Yeah, well, you gotta prove it to me, 'cause I don't believe you."

Frank asked me to walk Mona back to Howard's campus that night. The walk was a good eight to ten blocks in the cold. Frank usually gave her a ride, but he supposedly had something to do that night. I suspected that he did it on purpose, just to see what I would do. I couldn't let her walk home by herself, and she seemed eager for me to walk her, so I went along with the program.

"You seemed really busy tonight," she said to me. I was running around as if the president was coming to the station. Most of my extra energy that night was because of the anxiety of being around her. I needed some sister companionship badly, Mona just didn't know it.

"Yeah, I was, wasn't I?" I responded. I still didn't want to look at her too hard.

She smiled and nodded to me, showing off her double dimples. I had to look away. I didn't want to allow myself to dive into another empty pool of water. If I kept barking at so many different women, I was sure that I was about to grow a tail and shaggy fur.

"What dorm do you live in?" I asked her.

"Bethune," she answered.

It figured. With my luck, she probably lived on the same floor that Faye used to live on. "Oh yeah, what floor?" I asked.

Mona looked at me skeptically. "You're moving a little fast, aren't you? We just met each other a few days ago," she said with a grin.

"Naw, naw, naw, I'm not even thinking about that."

"So what *are* you thinking about?"

"Ah . . . nothin'," I said. I didn't want to tell her that an old friend of mind used to live in Bethune. It didn't feel right to tell Mona that.

"Well, anyway, I live on the fifth floor," she told me. Faye used to live on the fourth.

We reached the entrance of Bethune dormitory and old memories surfaced. I guess Mona could read my dazed expression. "You used to have a friend who lived here?" she asked me.

"What makes you say that?" I was startled.

"From the way you're looking at the door, it's like you're having flashbacks or something. Then you asked me what floor I lived on, like you've been in here before."

"Actually, I was wondering if you were gonna invite me in for a nightcap," I joked, just to throw her off.

Mona smiled and shook her head. "No you weren't. You weren't even thinking about me." She was right. Mona was very perceptive and quick to speak her mind. "Besides, I don't want my business all around at the station," she said. "I got ears, and I hear how Frank talks about women. He's probably trying to see if you can get with me because he's too old for me."

I was speechless. Mona knew that she was telling the truth. "I wouldn't tell a soul," I said to her. All of a sudden I was interested. Maybe it was the intrigue of it all.

"Are you sure?"

I don't know if Mona was serious or just teasing me. She was probably still a teenager, but she damn sure had me going. I wasn't *that* much older than her. I said, "I promise."

Mona burst out laughing. "I'll see you next time, Bobby Dallas. Go on home now."

I stood there for a second as Mona walked inside of her dorm and waved to me. I guess she *was* teasing me. Nevertheless, she had me turned on. I started thinking about who else I could call as I walked away. Faye Butler's was the only number that I knew by heart.

I got to a pay phone and called her up, desperate to see her. Sure enough, just as I had feared, a guy answered the phone.

"Hello."

I hung up on him. "Shit!" I cursed, smashing the phone with a balled fist. I didn't know what else to do. I took out another cigarette from my inside coat pocket and headed home. There were some low-budget hookers who hung out on Thirteenth Street, but I didn't plan to stoop so low as to seek their favors. I wasn't *that* bad off.

If I had learned anything from my relationship with Pearl, it was that I couldn't allow women to get away with taking me for granted. I got inside my apartment after eleven and decided to call Pamela Cooper and give her a piece of my mind. I figured, *How could she take me out for my birthday and have such a good time and then flip out on me after a page?* She never even called me back. I wanted to know what her damn problem was!

"Hello," Pamela answered.

"It's Bobby Dallas from the radio station," I told her.

"Oh, hi, Bobby, I was thinking about you," she said excitedly.

"So how come you didn't call me?"

She sighed and said, "It's just so much that's been going on lately."

"That's no reason not to call somebody and tell them how you've been. I mean, I thought we had a good time. I know *I* did."

"We did have a good time."

"Yeah, if you say so," I snapped at her. "I'm tired of being Mr. Nice Guy and getting walked on," I said. I was pissed off and talking out of my head that night.

Pamela just laughed at me.

"Wait a minute, this isn't funny. What's so funny about this?" I asked her. "I'm tired of being taken for granted, and I'm tired of being a damn doormat. I thought you were a nice person."

"I am a nice person."

"Yeah, well, I can't tell anymore."

Pamela was getting the backlash of all the things I needed to say to Pearl a year ago.

"Well, I'm sorry, Bobby, okay?" she apologized.

"I guess that's supposed to settle everything," I said.

"I mean, what do you want me to do, drive over there and make it up to you?" she joked.

I was tired of being toyed with, too. "Yeah, I want you to drive over here right now," I told her. I basically didn't care anymore. I had reached the end of my rope.

Pamela paused and said, "Okay, I'll be down there in a half hour." She lived in Silver Spring, Maryland. By car it was less than thirty minutes away, but I thought she was pulling my leg.

"Yeah, right," I said.

"You know what, Bobby? I'm dead serious," she responded.

"Well, I'll see you when you get here then."

I hung up the phone and felt like a complete fool. Pamela Cooper was not hardly going to drive her BMW down to Thirteenth Street at close to midnight on a weekday to see me. Only in my dreams would that happen.

I sat back in bed and lit up another cigarette. Just in case Pamela did show, I wanted to make sure that I was awake. I didn't make any preparations though.

Sure enough, after forty-five minutes, my intercom went off.

"Who is it?" I said.

"Hurry up and buzz me in," Pamela responded.

I buzzed her in and began to smile. Even if I didn't get to roll in the hay with her that night, the fact that I had spoken my mind and gotten immediate results was satisfying enough.

She knocked on my door a few minutes later. I had enough time to at least light incense in my bedroom.

She walked in smiling. "You thought I wasn't coming, didn't you?"

"Naw, I didn't think you would come."

She immediately noticed my view out the window. "This is a dynamite view," she said.

I was more viewing her, in a pair of skintight blue jeans. Pamela wore them well, very well. She kicked off her black suede pumps, wearing no socks. Sisters rarely took off their shoes for nothing. I was wondering if she had worn a bra and panties. Pearl didn't when she used to visit me late at night in Slowe Hall.

Pamela sniffed the air and asked me if I smoked.

Usually I smoked privately, so not that many people knew. "Not that much," I lied. "I had one earlier."

"What brand do you smoke? Can I have one?" she asked.

"I didn't know you smoked," I said.

"I didn't know you smoked either," she responded.

I walked over to my coat pocket and pulled out a cigarette for her. I knew I had some explaining to do.

Pamela looked at the long, thin cigarette in her hand and said, "You smoke slims?"

I chuckled. "I figure I can cut down on a little bit of the cancer," I told her.

"Just stop smoking then," she responded.

"Good idea."

Pamela looked around at my hardwood floors and the space I had. "This is pretty big," she commented. "Bigger than my apartment."

I bet she was paying a lot more for hers in Silver Spring, too.

She walked into my bedroom while I followed her. "Oh, am I sup-posed to be in here?" she joked with me. She faced me, looking as sexy as a brown doll.

"You can go anywhere you want to go," I said, moving closer to her. I wondered who was going to make the first move.

"Oh really?" She moved closer to me.

"Really." I leaned over and kissed her lips. Pamela wasn't as short as her father, but she was nowhere near as tall as Pearl, or even as tall as Faye. Pamela was a medium-height dynamo.

"You want me to put this cigarette out?" she asked me.

"Yeah, you do that."

She walked inside the bathroom and ran some water over it before tossing it in the trash. When she came back inside of the bedroom with me, her pants were unbuttoned. She wasn't wearing a belt.

"Can I help you with that?" I asked, pointing to her jeans. I sat on the bed. Pamela walked over to me. When she got close enough, I pulled her zipper down. She wasn't wearing any panties either, and I was ready for take-off.

We both got undressed and Pamela said, "Here, use these," handing me two lambskin condoms. I thought it was rather kinky, but hell, she knew what she wanted.

There was a whole lot of sweat produced that night. I guess it was because I hadn't been sexually active in a while. I was sure active with Pamela, though. And she was very vocal with her instructions to me. She was a take-charge woman in bed, just like I figured a lawyer would be. She really knew how to enjoy herself. I thought that my neighbors were going to complain about her volume a few times. I wasn't sure if it was me, the lambskin, or both that gave her so much pleasure.

We both had cigarettes when we finished. It was nearly three o'clock in the morning.

"You know you work at my father's station," Pamela hinted to me.

"Yeah, I know. You don't have to tell me."

"Thank you," she said. "That would be all I need to add to my problems."

"So who was that paging you on my birthday date?" I had been dying to ask her.

"My former fiancé."

I was shocked. "Shit! Really?"

She nodded and blew out a ring of smoke. "Really."

"What happened?"

"I found out he wasn't as ready to be married as he said he was."

"You caught him cheating?"

She took a draw and nodded. She blew out the smoke and answered, "Yup . . . with his damn secretary."

I smiled and said, "That's right out of the movies."

Pamela chuckled. "Ain't it, though. Now he wants to call me up and bug me all the time about how it was a mistake. It was a mistake all right, a mistake I made to fall for his ass."

I was silent for a few minutes. I thought about myself versus other brothers. It seemed that you were either screwing a woman over, or you were being screwed. Maybe I was just hanging around the wrong damn crowd. "When were you engaged?" I asked Pamela.

"Three months ago," she said. "I didn't even get a chance to show off my ring. My father doesn't even know I was engaged. I was gonna surprise him, but I ended up *getting* surprised."

I was ready to ask her how she found out, but I decided to leave it alone. I wasn't feeling excited about sleeping with her anymore. It felt like I had taken advantage of her when she was vulnerable.

"I'm sorry, I didn't know," I told her.

"And I didn't tell you," she responded. "That's why I never called you back. I still have a lot of thinking to do."

She sure does, I told myself. "Well, I think the best thing for me to do would be to back off and allow you a chance to make the decisions you need to make," I told her.

"Thank you," she said. Then she leaned over and kissed me.

I was being Mr. Nice Guy again. That night turned out to be a onetime thing between Pamela and me. And I never told anyone about it.

The Dating Game

"Pearrrll Day-vis. What have you been up tooo, girrrl?"

Once that little melody began to pop back into my head, I knew that I had to do something about my love life. Faye Butler was out of the question, and Mona Freeman was still teasing me at the station. I guess she was still too young to be serious about my advances, or maybe she was simply having a good time toying with me.

Anyway, I started hanging out on the club scene with members of the Washington Bullets. I didn't expect to find my future wife at these clubs, but after a while, I figured that any woman was better than no woman.

It was just a coincidence that I started hanging out with young Bullets players. I invited several of them on Frank's show, "D.C. Sports Talk," and connected really well with Gary Mitchell, a rookie point guard who had been drafted from the North Carolina Tar Heels. He invited me to a club out in Maryland where a lot of the younger players hung out and entertained basketball groupies. That was the beginning of my association with the Bullets and the women who chased them. Many times, because of my own height, women would mistake me for a ballplayer.

I was dressed for the cold February weather and ready for my ride at twenty minutes to midnight on a Friday. I heard a horn honking outside the window a few minutes later. I walked outside and noticed my new friend Gary Mitchell sitting inside a burgundy 300ZX, dressed like a lady's man. He had on an off-white, all-silk outfit and there was a hooded fur coat in the backseat.

"Nice threads," I told him, climbing inside his flashy sports car.

He brushed my compliment off with a smile. "It's just a little somethin', you know." From a woman's point of view, I wouldn't say that Gary was all that good-looking, but he *was* a wealthy young ballplayer. That counted for a lot more than looks.

Gary's 300ZX had a luxurious gray leather interior. I reclined the seat back and relaxed, listening to the bass boom from his sound system. He was listening to WPGC radio. "PGC" was really going after the urban youth market. They were knocking other Washington-area stations out of the box.

"You like that go-go music they play down here?" Gary asked me.

I nodded. "I think it's cool that D.C. has its own style of music," I told him.

"Yeah, they love that shit here, man. I had this girl in the car last week, and I went to put my tape in while one of them go-go songs was on, and she tried to rip my damn arm off."

We laughed. I could imagine it. D.C. and Maryland women were aggressive like that, especially when it came to their music.

We pulled up to this club called Players in Marlboro Heights, Maryland. I could tell it was a money place by the cars that were parked there. Gary got excited and said, "This place is it! We didn't have anything like this down in North Carolina."

He didn't have to tell me that. We walked inside, had our coats taken, paid ten dollars, and strolled on in. This place definitely had a who's who atmosphere. Everybody was looking around.

"Hey, rookie!" someone yelled out to Gary.

Gary smiled and shook his head. "I'm getting tired of this rookie shit," he told me. A few of the other players came over to greet us. I blended right in with them. Gary and I were about the same height.

"Yeah, this my boy, Bobby Dallas, from the radio station in D.C.," Gary introduced me.

"WPGC?" someone asked me. I didn't know all of their names. The older Bullets were more noticeable, but they didn't hang out in clubs.

"I wish," I responded. "I work at a small station, producing a talk show with Frank Watts called 'D.C. Sports Talk.' "

"Yeah, I listened to that show before," one of the guys said. "How can I get on there?"

"We just invite you on," I told him. Sometimes I hated people approaching me about being on the shows, but that's all a part of being a producer.

"Aw'ight, well invite me on, man. What's your name again?"

"Bobby Dallas," I said. A sexy sister pulled him away to the dance floor. If it wasn't for her, he probably would have tried to force his way on the show. I hate to admit it, but a lot of the younger athletes I met while producing Frank's show were rather obnoxious. I guess I would have been a little cocky too if I had the world at my feet.

"Aren't you Gary Mitchell?" a healthy sister asked my friend. She was at least 180 pounds, and she was tall.

"Yeah," Gary responded.

She was quite assertive, too. "You wanna dance?"

"Naw, honey, not this guy," Gary said with a laugh.

"What, I'm too big for you? You can't handle this?"

Gary seemed shy and was embarrassed. "I don't think I want to," he told her.

The other Bullets began to tease him. "Go ahead, man. She can teach you how to crash the boards for a rebound."

I laughed myself, but it wasn't *that* funny. That sister could have really had her feelings hurt if she wasn't so headstrong.

"I don't think *none* of y'all can handle me," she boasted.

"We damn sure can't!" someone hollered.

"Well, that's all right, baby, 'cause I like more meat on my men anyway. All I see is a bunch of *toothpicks* over here."

"Yeah, I got a big toothpick you can put right in your mouth."

"Take it out then, honey. Let me see what it look like."

It was beginning to get a little too raunchy for me. I slipped away to disassociate myself from the group. I had to use the bathroom anyway. While walking through the club, I noticed plenty of sexy women peeking at me. I had never caught that many stares from women in my life. I could really feel the power of athletic popularity and money. And like I said, I had always been tall and sometimes handsome, so with the addition of popularity and money, I felt like a king.

I walked out of the rest room with a chip on my shoulder, as if I could approach any sister there.

"How you doin'?" a sweet voice called out to me. I looked down and spotted this exotic, caramel sister in a royal blue sequin dress, cut at the knees. She had beaten me to the punch.

"I'm doin' okay. How 'bout you?" I asked her.

She pulled up a chair for me to have a seat. She had two of her girlfriends sitting at the table and looking like hungry vultures.

Oh my God! I thought. I didn't know if I was ready to handle that new type of power yet. I took a seat like a lamb among lions. "My name is Bobby Dallas," I told the sister.

"Kimberly Green," she said, extending her hand. I took it in mine, squeezed it, and let it go. Kimberly raked my fingers as she pulled her hand away. I was wondering exactly what that meant. It sure felt good.

"Those are your friends over there?" one of Kimberly's girlfriends asked. She was looking in the direction of the Bullets. I guess they saw me earlier.

"Yeah, a few of them," I said.

"Well, why don't you introduce me to somebody?"

I hadn't gotten a chance to acquaint myself with Kimberly yet. I pointed to my ride in the off-white silk. "That's Gary Mitchell from the Bullets. Go tell him that I'm over here waiting for him, and he'll walk back with you."

She looked at me and smiled. "I'm sorry, but that's not my style. Why don't you go over there and get him?"

"Do you play, too?" Kimberly asked me.

I decided to ignore her friend and answer Kimberly's question. I thought about saying I played for the Philadelphia 76ers. They were the only team close enough to Washington for me to get away with it, but I decided against it. "I produce a sports radio show, so I meet a lot of these guys," I said.

Kimberly watched me with dreamy eyes. "Oh really?"

"Yeah. We're still trying to get Doug Williams on the show."

She looked confused. "Who's Doug Williams?"

I was shocked she even asked me that. It threw me for a loop.

"He's the quarterback for the Redskins, girl. Where you been?" her second friend said with a nudge. She had been a silent observer up to that point.

Kimberly laughed it off. "Shit, girl, I don't know."

I was pretty disappointed about that. As it turned out, Doug Williams became the first black quarterback to win the Super Bowl. Frank Watts's prediction was right. Doug broke many passing records while leading the Washington Redskins to a victory over John Elway and the Denver Broncos. I felt like everybody should know, especially black people in the D.C. area. I realized that sports trivia wasn't exactly a woman's thing, but Kimberly's lack of knowledge on the subject really turned me off. I wasn't a huge sports guy myself, but it was the whole attitude in which she presented her lack of knowledge. She didn't even care that she was ignorant.

"Yeah, I guess it's not that important to you," I said. "Anyway, what do you do?"

"I'm a secretary at the District government building."

I immediately thought of Pamela Cooper and her former fiancé. I doubted if Kimberly was the one he was cheating with. There had to be at least a thousand secretaries in D.C. The chances were slim, but that didn't mean it was impossible.

Gary joined us at the table without being summoned. "Hey, what's up, man?" he said.

Kimberly's first friend got another chair for him.

"Yeah, Gary, this is, ah—" I didn't know her name.

"Tonya," she filled in. "How you doin'?" she asked him.

Gary sat down and said, "I'm all right. Pleased to meet you."

"The pleasure is all mine."

The second friend got up to excuse herself. "Well, let me go find somebody to dance with."

"What are y'all doin' after this?" Gary asked Tonya and Kimberly.

"Why, is it something else going on tonight?" Kimberly asked him.

"That depends on you and your girl. I mean, nobody has to get up early tomorrow, right?"

No one said anything. Gary wasn't so shy after all. He was moving much faster than what I was thinking. He seemed to have a lot more experience in picking up women than I expected.

"What did you have in mind?" Tanya asked him.

"We could all get a hotel room and order a big breakfast in the morning."

Kimberly looked at Tonya, then back to Gary. "What about our girl-friend?"

Gary hunched his shoulders. "She can come if she wants, but you know, it's only two of us."

Then Kimberly grinned at Tonya. "It's up to you."

All I did was watch and keep score. Gary was going for the quick ally-oop, slam dunk. Tonya was hesitant, but she agreed anyway. I guess she didn't want to be the party pooper.

"Aw'ight then, you wanna dance?" Gary asked her.

Tonya grabbed his hand and said, "Come on."

I looked at Kimberly and grabbed her hand.

We all ended up in a two-bed suite at the Ramada Inn off of I-95. Gary paid for their girlfriend's taxi ride home, so it was two on two and real comfortable. Everyone was loaded with alcohol but me. I was still too busy taking notes. I had never been in that situation before. It was the kind of thing that my brother, Brad, would have been more familiar with.

"Come here," Gary said, stroking Tonya's waist. He was leading her into the bathroom.

"Where we goin'?" she asked. It wasn't as if she was pulling away from him.

"Just come here."

Gary got her inside and shut the door. I sat in the room with Kimberly, not knowing what to do. "I wonder what they're about to do in there," I said to her with a chuckle.

She grinned at me and moved her hips. "Doin' it from the back, doggie style."

You would think that after being with Pearl I would be used to the off-the-wall sexual references some women made, but I wasn't, and Kimberly could tell. She laughed at my bewildered expression, and she was still pretty loaded. I wondered if she was feeling as horny as I was.

"I hope she took her protection in there with her," Kimberly added, digging into her leather bag. She pulled out a roll of condoms and headed for the door. "Hey, girl, are you protected in there?"

"Ah, hold up! Hold up, Kim!" Tonya panted. It was a whole lot of activity going on inside the bathroom. That only increased my hard-on. It was animal instincts.

Kimberly waited at the door and laughed, listening in on them. All of a sudden, I began to think of Pearl and Kiki out in Las Vegas having moaning contests.

"I don't believe you're listening to that," I snapped at Kimberly.

"Aw, what's wrong, you jealous or something?" she said to me with a grin.

I was speechless. I think I *was* jealous.

Kimberly walked over to me and boldly grabbed my crouch. "What do you want to do about it?" she asked me.

It has to be the alcohol talking, I thought. I could smell it all over her breath, but I was in no condition to deny her. I kissed her right in her mouth and grabbed her behind, hard. The next thing I knew, she was pulling at my zipper and trying to shove her hand inside of my fly.

I quickly led her to the closest bed and took one of the condoms from her. Kimberly pulled her shiny blue panties off and stretched out flat on her stomach. I climbed up on the bed behind her. Kimberly lifted herself into me and began grabbing at my legs as I went into action.

"Aw, yeeah!" she moaned.

Right when we began to get into it, Gary and Tonya walked out from the bathroom. I panicked and stopped.

"What are you doin'?" Kimberly said. "Don't stop."

"Oh, my fault. We'll go back in the bathroom until y'all finished out here," Gary responded with a laugh.

I was too far gone to stop completely, so I sped up to get it over with, which only made things more embarrassing for me as Kimberly reacted with louder and more frequent moaning.

"Damn! Don't kill her out there, Bobby!" Gary yelled with another laugh.

"Do that shit, girl!" Tonya cheered. It sounded like she was right behind me. I didn't want to look to find out, still rushing to get it over with.

The spasms took me by surprise when we reached the end of things. It was much stronger than I expected. I hopped up as quickly as I could without injuring myself and slipped inside the bathroom. My heart was racing and I felt light-headed as I grabbed for my chest. I took a couple deep breaths to regain my composure. Kimberly was beating on the door when I finally got my nerves and clothing together.

"What are you doing in there? I need to wash up, too, dammit!" she hollered.

I took my time before opening the door for her. I wasn't sure if I wanted to walk back out into the room with Gary and Tonya, but I did it anyway. Tonya was staring at me in awe. I guess she was impressed.

"Dag, man," she said with a shake of her head.

Gary couldn't seem to wipe the grin off his face. Every few minutes or so he would laugh to himself like a giggling fool. I wanted to go home, but I doubted if anyone wanted to take me. It was after four in the morning.

It took me a long time to fall asleep in that hotel room that night. I kept thinking how crazy a night it was. My mother hadn't raised me to be some kind of a freak. I was ashamed of myself, and I wanted to get away from those people.

In the morning, Gary tapped me on my shoulder. "Hey, man, I gotta go. Let me talk to you in the hallway for a minute," he whispered.

I looked up and saw that it was twenty minutes of nine. Kimberly and Tonya were still knocked out. I walked out into the hallway with Gary, who was all ready to go. He handed me two hundred dollars.

"Pay for the room and stuff, man, and get a taxi back home. I gotta get ready for practice."

"I thought you said nobody had to get up early," I reminded him.

He smiled and said, "That's just what I told *them,* but I got shit to do." He shook my hand and headed for the elevator down the hall. "I'll be in touch with you, man. We go to Denver and L.A. next week, so it'll prob'bly be awhile."

I nodded to him. "All right then, I'll see you around."

Damn! I thought. I didn't feel like walking back into that room. It smelled inside and everything. I took a walk down to the hotel's restaurant and had breakfast instead. I was thinking about paying for the room and leaving extra money in case Kimberly and her friend ordered room service when I saw them walking out. I looked at my watch and it was after ten. I had no idea that I had been downstairs that long. I had hardly finished my breakfast. I guess I had been daydreaming.

"Some more coffee, sir?" a waitress asked me.

"Oh, no, ma'm," I told the older woman.

I paid for the room and took a cab back to Thirteenth Street. I hadn't even given Kimberly my phone number. I guess that was the end of that, and I was glad it was over. I felt so guilty about that Friday night that I called home to my mother. There was no way in hell that I was planning on telling her what I had been through, I just needed to be grounded. Talking to my mother was enough to ground any young man or woman. When I called, though, my brother answered the phone again.

"Back home for a visit?" I asked him.

"Yeah, Mom cooked a big breakfast this morning. We called you, but you wasn't in. Mom said you was probably out all night in sin. I said, naw, you probably went to church early this morning."

It's amazing how right mothers can be without even trying sometimes. "Church on a Saturday, hunh?" I joked with Brad. "Where's Mom at now?"

"She went out riding with Dad. They're checking out new property. They're thinking about moving next year."

"Get out of here!"

My parents had been talking about moving ever since Brad and I shipped off for college.

Brad chuckled and said, "Yeah, they say they're serious this time. But hey, man, I have other news for you, too. I want you to meet Brenda, my fiancée."

Fiancée? Brad? "Wait a minute, you're bullshittin', right?"

"Naw, I ain't bullshittin'. Here she is right here."

He put her on the phone. "Hello, Bobby, I heard a lot about you. How's the radio business?" I still couldn't believe it. *Brad, engaged to be married!* He hadn't finished grad school yet. He wasn't even turning twenty-three until May.

I was kind of shocked. "Oh, ah, things are looking up. Yeah, they're looking up."

"That's good to hear," Brenda said. "I can't wait to meet you. I've seen all of the pictures of you and Brad around the house, but nothing beats the real thing."

I kept thinking that any minute Brad was going to jump on the phone and have a good laugh at me, but it never happened.

"Ah, you're from Boston, right?" I asked Brenda. She seemed really friendly, the kind of woman Brad used to screw over in a heartbeat.

"Yup, I'm a true Bostonian," she said. "Both of my parents were born and raised in Boston, and three of my grandparents."

This is not happening, I told myself. *There is no way in the world.* "Is Brad pulling my leg about this marriage thing? Now you don't seem like a liar, so tell me the truth," I warned her.

She laughed and said, "But it is the truth. We decided on it over the Christmas holiday. Brad took me to the Virgin Islands."

"I didn't know that," I told her. "Well, if *Brad* took you to the Virgin Islands, then he *must* be serious about you."

"He says he is," she joked.

I paused, wanting to hear it from the horse's mouth. "Do you mind if I speak to him?"

"Oh, no, not at all."

Brad got back on the phone. "You believe me now?" he asked me.

"Hey, man, you're not gonna hurt this nice girl's feelings, are you?" I was concerned for Brenda. I thought Brad was making one of those impulsive decisions of his, where he changes his mind at the last minute. He had done that a lot when we were growing up.

"Naw, man, I'm serious. It ain't nothing out there in them streets. So if you find somebody that you really care about, then take her to the altar."

I burst out laughing. I remembered another saying that Brad used to have. "Hey, man, remember that time you said the only way you're getting married any time soon is if a woman cuts your legs off and drags you to the altar?" I reminded him. He sounded like a hypocrite.

"Bobby, that was a long time ago, man. You need to grow up."

"*I* need to grow up?"

"That's what I said, man. I love Brenda. We gave this thing a lot of thought, Bobby. A *lot* of thought."

Ain't this some shit! I thought. Of all the people to be grounded by, I would have never, *ever* thought that it would come from my brother. "You're really serious about this?" I asked him.

"I'm *dead* serious."

There was a long silence on the phone while I tried to think of something else to say. "Well, good luck, man. I'm, ah, proud of you."

Brad sounded excited to hear me say it. "Thanks, man. And you know you're my best man at the wedding, right?"

"Oh yeah?" I was surprised by that, too.

"Yeah, Bobby. You my big brother, man. Who did you think was gon' be my best man?"

"I could name fifty of your friends—"

"Yeah, well, I haven't known any of them as long as I've known you, so that ain't even an argument," he responded, cutting me off. "A lot of them brothers aren't trying to go anywhere near a wedding. To tell you the truth, man, I outgrew a whole lot of them brothers. And I mean, *a lot of 'em!*"

I was thinking Brad had outgrown me, too. I finished the conversation with him and told him I'd probably talk to Mom and Dad that Sunday. I'd had enough news for one day. I needed time to think. They would have been too curious about how I was doing with women. At that point, the only thing I knew about my love life was that I didn't have one.

•

The next thing on my mind was buying myself a car to get around in. If I wanted to meet a nice girl and go to nice places, I needed my own vehicle; that way I wouldn't have to depend on anyone. Washington, D.C., had a Citibank like New York, so I never did have to transfer my bank accounts. The money that I once had took a big dip in the move from New York, though. I was making less at my new job, and I had to pay all of my bills by myself. I figured it was best to get a car before I ran out of money for the down payment.

What I quickly discovered, however, was that I didn't have any credit, so no bank would finance me unless I used half of my savings as a down payment. I couldn't afford to do that. I needed every extra dollar that I could find. I hadn't even been thinking about credit. Pearl had gotten herself a bunch of credit cards while I was in New York, but I had passed on them. I wasn't gung-ho about buying things, especially on credit. If you don't have credit, though, no one wants to give you any. And if you don't make enough money to receive credit, then you lie about your income. Pearl had done it with all of her credit cards. What I ended up doing was putting up my own money to get what they called a secured credit card, which is basically the same as having a bank card that you withdraw from every time you buy something with it.

"Welcome to the real world, youngster," Frank told me with a laugh. I was complaining about the credit situation at the job. "You think you can get everything you want right out of college? I can't get half the shit I want now, and I'm *forty*.

"What you need to do is ask your parents for some money. That's what these young white boys do. They come out of college and get a check from Mom and Dad."

"That's only rich white people," I told him. I had already gotten my check, and I wasn't planning on asking my parents for any money unless it was a real emergency.

"Yeah, well, them broke white folks don't count to me," Frank said. "I'm talking about the ones that make the world go 'round. You come out of college with no money, and it'll take you a good five to ten years to get something, especially with these motherfuckas bugging you about them damn college loans.

"Oh, excuse my language, Mona. I didn't see you come in," Frank said, apologizing.

Mona took off her coat. "You don't have to change for me. Just be yourself."

Frank looked at me and smiled. "They all say that shit, Bobby, but don't you ever believe it. Don't you *ever* believe that."

Mona shook her head and flashed her dimples as Frank walked out of the room. "You had a big date last Friday, hunh?" she asked me.

"*You* didn't?" I asked her back.

"I was at Chicago's."

Chicago's was a popular D.C. club in the Dupont Circle area. A lot of college students partied there.

"Oh yeah. And did you have a good time?"

"Not really. It was a bunch of guys breathing all down my throat, but I wasn't interested. I tried to call somebody up so I could have something better to do, but they wasn't home." She looked at me real hard when she said that.

"Was this *late* Friday night?" I asked her with a grin.

"Umm, I think it was. Yeah," she said.

"And what was gonna happen if this person had been home?"

"I have no idea," she said, and walked out of the room.

Yeah, she's still teasing, I thought with a smile.

•

Frank promised to take me to a car auction in Baltimore to buy a good, inexpensive vehicle with no strings attached. He said the government auctions sold a lot of cars they had confiscated from lawbreakers that sometimes went for just a few thousand dollars. I found that hard to believe, and I was right. You had to have at least twelve thousand dollars in hard cash to buy any of the top-of-the-line cars. It was much cheaper than buying from dealerships, but I didn't have that kind of money.

I ended up buying a 1984 Honda Prelude for twenty-five hundred.

That wasn't too bad. It was black, in good shape, and all I needed was brakes, so they said. On my first date with Mona, my muffler fell off in the middle of the street. We were just cruising and talking on a Saturday afternoon. It was late March by then.

"Oh my God! Where did you say you got this car from again?" Mona asked.

I was embarrassed, but I was glad that it was only Mona. Had it been a new woman, something like that could have been real hard to live down. I stopped the car, picked up the rusted muffler, put it in the trunk, and noisily drove around until we found a nearby repair shop.

"So, Bobby, tell me again how you got a steal on this car," Mona teased me.

I shook my head and grinned. "Where are you from, anyway?" I had never asked before.

"Motown."

"Detroit?"

"That's right."

I knew a few girls from Detroit who went to Howard in my day. They were all city slick and self-assured. Mona fit the mold. "Were you always a comedian?" I asked her.

She smiled. "Well, you know, life is funny sometimes, so I say enjoy it with a laugh."

"Are you ever serious?" We were sitting inside the waiting room at the repair shop.

"I'm serious about my schoolwork."

"Why?" I asked her.

"Why?" Mona looked at me as if I had lost it. I was just asking to see what she would say.

"Yeah, why is your schoolwork so important?"

"Well, I don't wanna waste my parents' money, number one. And number two, how else do you get what you want out of life if you don't work hard for it?"

"You could steal it," I joked with her.

She looked at me and frowned. "Now you trippin'."

"Some things you can work hard for and still never get. Have you ever thought about that?"

"I try not to think about failure," she told me.

"Yeah, well, failure is a reality."

Mona said, "Maybe it's yours, but it's not *my* reality." She was definitely determined and in control of her life. I needed to be more like that.

I smiled and asked, "Why are you such a tease?"

Mona broke out laughing. "I'm not a tease with everybody."

"Well, then, why are you torturing *me?*"

"I'm not torturing you. When I wanted to see you, you were out doing other things."

"What am I supposed to do, just sit around and wait for you to call me?"

"Yeah."

"Okay, now *you're* trippin'," I told her. "I guess you like to call all the shots."

"That's right. I'm a strong sister. I would have been leading the movement back in the day."

I laughed. Mona's self-image was huge. "So, what kind of man do you need?" I asked her.

"Umm, correction. I don't *need* no man," she answered. "Now I would *like* a man who does what he's supposed to do and acts how he's supposed to act."

I thought about it. "And what is that, and how is that?" I asked her.

"If you don't know by now, then you need to go back to school."

I sat back and grinned. "Yeah, that's what I thought."

"What?"

"You don't know what the hell you're talking about. How are *you* gonna tell a man how to *be a man?*" It sounded like a good question to me.

Mona said, "I've been around good men all my life—my father and my brothers."

"And you've *never* had to walk in their shoes," I responded to her.

She smirked. "*I know* what I know," she said.

A greasy dark-haired man backed my Honda into view. "She's ready," he said.

Mona frowned at him. "Shit, I hope he put some plastic inside your car before he sat in it."

"Yeah," I agreed.

I paid $116.73. I don't know if that price was high or low, but I wasn't too happy about it. I was still living on a shoestring budget, especially after buying the car and paying for the insurance.

There were a few other women that I began dating, but none of them were as much fun to be with as Mona. She had a youthful, vibrant, and creative spirit that energized me. Mona made me see just how easy it was for older men to fall for much younger women. We were becoming friends like I had been with Faye, but with that extra sex appeal that Faye and I had not bothered to address until it was too late.

"You know my birthday is next month, Bobby. What are you gonna get me?" Mona said, once we were back on the road.

"Oh, really. What day is it?"

"April the twelfth."

"So you're an Aries then."

"That's right."

I nodded with a big smile. "No wonder you think you know everything. My mother's an Aries. Her birthday is April the sixth."

"Is she tough?"

"Damn right she is."

Mona said, "Yup, we do what we gotta do. And you're a Capricorn, so I know I got you going. It drives you crazy that you can't figure me out."

I laughed. "I see you've been reading them astrology books."

"Yeah, I try to read a little bit of everything. It's good to know a lot."

"Do you talk this much with other people?" I asked her. I had a hunch. "I think you like me, Mona. My mother only talks a lot when she likes somebody."

Mona laughed and got quiet on me.

"Unh-hunh, your silence must mean that I'm right."

"If you think so, Bobby," she hummed to me.

•

I was avoiding Gary Mitchell from the Bullets like the plague. Believe it or not, I didn't want to hang out and sleep with different women every night. That lifestyle wasn't for me, especially after finding out that my brother was engaged.

The other women I began to date off and on weren't really important. A lot of women think they're important to a guy, but after the years go by, a lot of them end up not making your permanent memory banks. Only the unforgettable incidents matter, like that one-night stand I had with Kimberly or the night in New York I spent with Doreen. I would always remember Doreen.

Pamela Cooper could have been important in my life, but she went back to her former fiancé. They were engaged again. Even Mr. Cooper knew about the new engagement. He was bragging about it down at the station. That left me with Mona, an undergraduate student who was still a teenager until her upcoming birthday. No matter how hard I tried, I couldn't shake the thought of sleeping with Mona from my mind, and Frank Watts had instigated it.

"Why did you get me to walk that girl home that night, man?" I asked him at the station. It was a week before Mona's birthday.

"Who are you talking about?"

"Mona."

"Oh, Mona, yeah."

"Yeah, Mona. Why did you get me to walk her home that night? She's been messin' wit' me ever since."

Frank chuckled and said, "She got the whammy on you, hunh?"

"Yeah, man, she does."

"She had it on me for a while," Frank said. "I figured you're younger than me, so maybe I could get it off of me and get it on you, 'cause I don't want to get in no trouble with her. She's a very bright girl, but she's just too sexy for her own damn good. And she *knows* it, too. That's the new black woman for you; smart, sexy, and they know it."

Mona walked into the station minutes later, looking fabulous for the springtime. She had some new curls in her hair and was looking bright and colorful. Frank and I looked at each other and changed the subject.

"Somebody was talking about me in here," Mona said.

Frank and I gave ourselves away by giggling like two oversized kids.

"She got us again, Bobby," Frank said to me. He walked into the recording room as our guests arrived, two Paul Lawrence Dunbar High School basketball players. Dunbar had an excellent basketball program in the District. They had already won several championships and were on their way to another one. Their program was nationally known.

Mona kept teasing me about how good-looking these two high school guys were, and how they would have a lot of women falling for them in college.

"Do you mind, Mona? I'm trying to produce a show here," I pouted.

"Yeah, you're just jealous."

"Jealous of what? These guys aren't stars yet. I've been hanging out with *professional* ballplayers. These guys are good, but they have a long way to go yet."

"How come you have them on the show if they're not stars yet?"

"Because we see their potential," I snapped with a smile.

Mona had on some new perfume that day and was working overtime on my senses.

"Mona, you're gonna have to move away from me a little bit. You're smelling a little too good in here to be so close without me grabbing you," I joked.

"Do what you have to do," she challenged me.

I was about to go crazy. I couldn't wait until the show was over that night. To top things off, one of the Dunbar seniors asked who Mona was.

"Oh, she's my assistant producer," Frank told him.

Mona smiled at them and then at me.

"Can I talk to you for a minute?" the young ballplayer asked her.

"Ah, I think you have to get out of high school first," she told him.

His teammate laughed at him.

"Oh, it's like that?" he asked.

Mona ignored it.

"Come on, man," the teammate said, pulling his friend toward the door.

"I already got a man anyway," Mona said to me with a wink.

"Will he mind if I drive you home again?" I asked. Mona didn't have a man. She loved her freedom like a bird loves to fly.

"To my home or to your home?" she responded.

"To my home," I said.

"Oh, I don't know about that. I mean, why would we go there?"

I had never chased a woman in my life like I was chasing Mona. She was driving me out of my mind. "All right, that's it, Mona. From here on out, I got nothing to say to you anymore."

"What about on my birthday?"

"What about it?"

"I was gonna let you take me out."

"Oh, you was gonna *let* me take you out?"

"Yeah."

I got my things together and followed her out the door. Frank spotted us walking out together and laughed. "Hang in there, youngster," he said to me.

"Mmm-hmm, I knew y'all were talking about me," Mona said.

We climbed into my Prelude, and I had all intentions of taking her right to my Thirteenth Street apartment.

"Have you ever thought that this car was a little too small for you?" she asked as I squeezed in.

"I have to squeeze into any car, unless it's a Cadillac or a Lincoln."

"What if you get in an accident? You won't be able to get out."

"I'm not thinking about any accidents."

"But what if?"

"There is no 'What ifs.' "

I drove up the hill on Thirteenth Street and parked around the corner from my building. You had to be lucky to get a spot right out in front.

Thirteenth Street was a busy rush-hour path, connecting Downtown to northwest D.C.

"This looks like a popular area," Mona said. She hadn't commented on me driving her to my place yet. She even got out of the car with me. I guess she was finally willing to give me a visit.

"It is pretty busy around here," I told her. "And I have an excellent view of the city."

Mona smiled and said, "I bet you do."

We walked around to the front of the building and got on a just-arriving elevator. I was filled with childlike excitement as we rode up to the third floor.

"This place looks old," Mona commented.

"It is," I responded while opening my apartment door.

Mona looked at me and grinned. "This the first time you had me over here. I know you're excited." She was too smart for her own good, just like Frank had said.

"Anyway, this is my place," I told her, changing the subject.

Mona looked around. "Yup, it's just like I thought your place would be, neat and plain."

I hadn't exactly jazzed the place up with artwork and things. I couldn't afford to.

"Maybe when I start making some real money, things'll change around here."

"When you start making some *real* money you need to buy a house," Mona suggested. She walked over to my window and checked out my skyline. "Yeah, this *is* a nice view."

"Buy a house, hunh?" I asked. "What do you know about buying houses?"

"My father owns three houses. We rent two out."

"Oh, so you're a little rich girl," I teased.

"No, we're not rich, but we're not poor either."

With the moonlight outlining Mona's curves in the window, I had a sudden urge to caress her, and I went with the feeling.

"Umm, Bobby, what are you doin'?"

"I'm enjoying the view with you."

"Look, I told you I got a man. Don't set yourself up to be disappointed."

"Come on, stop it, you don't have a man."

"I do so."

She still hadn't pushed me away. She was close enough to kiss, so I bent over and planted one on her lips.

"What would he say about that?" I asked.

"He'd kick your ass."

I laughed. "He'd kick *my* ass? What would he do to you?"

"You kissed me, I didn't kiss you."

"But you allowed me to."

"Oh, like that's gonna hold up in court."

That legal talk scared me. I let her go. "That's it, I'm washing my hands of you," I said.

"What, am I dirty?" she asked me with a smile.

I chuckled. Mona had a comeback line for everything. I looked at her wonderful body again and said, "Why don't you take your clothes off and let me see?"

"In here? You don't even have blinds on your windows. What if it's some Peeping Tom downtown with a telescope?"

"That would have to be a pretty powerful telescope."

"If they can see the moon and stars and shit, Bobby, what makes you think they can't see me in your living room?"

"All right, let's go in my bedroom then. It's harder to see in there."

Mona had me sounding like some perverted teenager, but what the hell, I was enjoying it.

She followed me into the bedroom and stood at the door. "I wanna see if you're dirty, too, 'cause I know I'm not." She kicked off her shoes. That was a positive sign.

I grabbed my belt buckle. "Oh, I'll show you everything you wanna see." I was beginning to sound as fresh as Mona. If you can't beat 'em, join 'em.

Mona started to smile and undid her pants. "All right, let's go piece for piece."

"Pants first," I said.

Mona let her jeans hit the floor. She was wearing lace panties with flower designs on them. They looked pretty expensive. Her legs were perfect. Mona had the kind of legs that a sculptor would die for.

I let my pants hit the floor after hers. It was a good thing I was still limp. I don't know how, but I had a whole lot of control that night. Maybe my body knew not to waste unneeded energy on Mona. She had worn me out many times before, to the point of having blue balls.

"Look at them duck legs," she joked.

My legs weren't that thin, but compared to hers, I would have had to be a sprinter or an NFL running back. "Well, everybody can't be gifted like you," I told her.

Then Mona took off her shirt. Her bra matched her panties.

I laughed. "It looks like you were ready for a show tonight."

"Maybe I was," she responded with a grin.

I took off my shirt.

"Oh my God, you got a bird chest, too!" Mona squealed.

"No I don't." I wasn't going to allow her to get away with that one.

"How much do you weigh?" she asked me.

"Two-ten."

"*Two-ten?* Well, where is all your weight at?"

I looked down and started to laugh.

Mona smiled. "Yeah, right. Let me see then."

"See what?"

"Don't play."

"Let me see you first," I said, embarrassed. Mona was calling my bluff.

"I've been taking off everything first," she responded. She had a point there. I was on the spot. "Come on, don't be shy," she said.

"All right, let's do this at the same time then."

Mona pulled her panties down in a heartbeat and unclipped her bra. I was ready to fall out from shock. There was nothing else to be said. I dropped my drawers, and Mona gave me a good looking over.

"Now was that all that bad?" she asked. Then she walked over and fondled me. My tool immediately stiffened in her hand.

"Damn, Mona, I didn't think you would be this forward," I said.

"Come on, let's get under the covers," she told me.

Fortunately, I had made my bed and cleaned up that day.

"Do you have any protection?" Mona asked me.

I pulled two condoms from my nightstand drawer.

"Convenient spot," she joked.

Rubbing up against her body felt like I had warm satin sheets. I couldn't wait to explore Mona, but wait was exactly what she made me do. We must have kissed, fondled, and held each other for a half hour or so before going to the next phase. Everything was slow and calculated like a scientific experiment. Even the moaning and groaning was in slow motion. Mona knew what she was doing, and she was well worth the wait. I hadn't felt that relaxed with a woman in my entire sexual career. That wasn't saying much at the time, though, since Mona was only the twelfth sister I had been with.

We fell asleep in each other's arms and slept good and hard. Our slow lovemaking that night reminded me of those Calgon commercials for bubble baths. Mona took me away.

Keep on Moving On

My relationship with Mona Freeman became a close friendship with sexual contact. That's about the best way to describe it. Neither one of us was willing to take things further. We were both content with how we dealt with each other as "friends/consenting adults." Those were Mona's words, not mine. The only disparity was that I continued to look for and to court new women, while Mona was pretty satisfied with what she had with me. I was still searching for a woman I could latch on to for the long haul. Mona was more concerned about finishing school and making contacts for her future. Occasionally she needed soothing from the opposite sex—that's where I came in.

My brother's approaching marriage was a problem for me. Believe it or not, I never thought of Brad as my little brother much. He was only a year younger than me, and he had been able to handle himself since we were kids. I never once had to take up for him. Sure, I beat him up a few times, but he got the best of me a few times, too. I would call it a draw. I didn't even mind that Brad graduated from college the same year that I had, nor that he was about to finish graduate school. Yet, Brad getting *married* before I did was unacceptable.

I had always considered myself Mr. Maturity to Brad's Little Wild Man. I would never say that a Little Wild Man couldn't be intelligent, entertaining, progressive, and studious, as long as he was never mature, or at least not as mature as Mr. Maturity. However, with Brad getting married and me hopping from city to city, job to job, and woman to woman, he looked like Mr. Maturity to my Little Wild Man. I had a problem with that, a serious problem. I mean, that bothered me so much that I actually fantasized once or twice about beating Brad to the altar with a woman I had fallen in love with. Those fantasies never incorporated Mona. She was too young. Nevertheless, she was the only woman in my life at that time I would have even thought of asking to marry. Unless, of course, I could have convinced Faye Butler that we were meant to be together.

It was May before I knew it, and Faye was nearing graduation. I had spent plenty of time traveling around D.C. and even going back up to Howard's campus with Mona, yet I hadn't bumped into Faye once.

I decided to call her up and ask her about graduation and the future. If she responded to me with any interest, maybe I'd ask her out. If she went out with me once, maybe I could beg her to do it again. And if we went out on two dates, I'd try my best to force myself back into her life.

I called Faye up with all the hope in the world and got her damn answering machine. I hesitated before deciding to leave a message. "Ah, Faye, this is Bobby Dallas. I wasn't expecting—"

"Hello," she answered, cutting me off.

I chuckled. "You're screening calls, hunh?" She couldn't have been screening for me. I had only called her a few times, and that was months ago. Something was going on. Maybe the guy that she was seeing had messed up.

"Yeah, I've been real busy trying to get ready for graduation and all," she told me.

"Well, congratulations. It seems like just yesterday when I was graduating."

Faye paused and said, "I'm sorry about not making it."

"I understand," I told her. "But I see no reason for me to miss yours."

She paused again. I guess she was still reluctant to communicate with me. "You really want to come?"

"Yeah, I wanna come. What kind of question is that?"

Faye must have had a hell of a lot on her mind, because there was a delay to every one of her responses. "You have a black Honda Prelude?" she asked me.

"Ah, yeah." That question put me on guard. I guess Faye had spotted me somewhere.

"You have somebody you're seeing now?" she asked.

"Nobody more important than you," I told her.

There was more awkward silence. "You want me to send you an invitation?"

You didn't really need invitations to see loved ones graduate from Howard University unless it rained and the ceremony was taken indoors. All you had to do was walk up on campus and find a seat, but I decided to use Faye's question to my advantage.

"Yeah, do you have them already?"

"Not yet."

"Well, when you get them, I'll just come by and get one from you, and maybe we could catch a movie or something for old times' sake."

"You just won't leave it alone, will you?" Faye finally snapped at me.

"Faye, if I could only take the time back, I would have never let you out of my sight." I actually said that to her. It's amazing what a man can think of when he's filled with hope.

"I mean, what do you want me to do, Bobby? I keep telling you, I don't feel how I used to."

"How can that be, Faye? We were like brother and sister at one time. Now you can't tell me—"

"Things change, people change, everything changes, Bobby," she said.

"Well, I haven't changed how I feel about you."

"Okay then, how *do* you feel about me? Because you obviously didn't feel what I felt."

"That's where I made my mistake. I *did* feel the same way, I just had a problem expressing myself back then."

"You didn't have a problem expressing yourself to somebody else."

There was no way I could win the argument. I had too many strikes against me, so I said the first thing that came to my mind. "I love you, Faye."

Faye sighed and said, "I can't go through this right now, okay? I have to go."

"Come on, let's talk about it, Faye. Please." I had come a long way when it came to expressing myself to women. I was pleasantly surprised, but there was still nothing I could say to change Faye's feelings.

"I don't want to hang up on you, Bobby," she warned me.

I was getting nowhere, but I didn't know how to quit. "Well, don't then," I said. "Talk to me."

At that moment, Faye must have dropped the phone down and gone on about her business.

"Faye? . . . Faye, are you there? . . . FAYE, TALK TO ME!" I was screaming into the phone like a lunatic and getting no response. Finally, I gave up and let her go. Painfully, I let her go, and hung up the phone.

"SHIT!" I yelled at the walls. Then I called Mona. "What are you doing?"

"Studying for finals."

"Are you finished?"

"Not hardly."

"Well, I need to see you anyway."

"Not tonight you don't."

"I have to, Mona. Now we're friends, right?" I was stooping low.

"Bobby, I told you not to abuse our friendship like that. That was one of our rules."

I had forgotten all about those things. I think she had five of them. "Look, this is about life, this has nothing to do with breaking the rules," I said.

"What is so important, Bobby?"

"I just have to see you and talk to you. You can do your studying over here."

"Talk to me about what?"

"Come on now, we're wasting time," I complained.

"Okay, Bobby. Damn!"

"I'm on my way," I told her. I grabbed my car keys and headed out the door. When I got to Bethune, Mona was waiting outside for me with her things. She jumped inside the car and didn't say a word. I didn't mind, as long as she was coming with me.

I told Mona the whole story that night of how I chose the wrong girl. I had to tell somebody. Mona was the only person I felt close enough to tell. I had to be close to someone, close to someone who cared about me and someone I cared about.

"Do you feel lonely?" Mona asked.

"Not when I'm with you." I was seriously becoming what they call "hopelessly romantic." I wasn't fake at all. I really meant everything that I said.

Mona held me in bed, but it wasn't a sexual thing. I didn't need her there for that, although I admit that it would have been nice.

"Would you just up and leave a guy like that?" I asked her. I was referring to what Pearl Davis had done to me in New York.

"When I was home last summer, I had a guy who was sorta like my boyfriend—I guess you can call him that. And he was like, 'Don't leave me. I love you, I love you.' But, you know, I had to go back to school. Then when I got down here, he just kept calling and calling. I was like, 'Damn! You're running up a hell of a phone bill!' And every time I wasn't in my room or something, he was thinking that I was playing him. And I wasn't. So after a while, you know, that shit was just too much for me and I had to end it."

"Yeah, I went through something like that, too, but she didn't call me at all. She just let me go."

Mona said, "Well, with this New York girl, from what you told me, you just wasn't strong enough for her at the time, because she just walked all over you."

"Have you ever gotten played like that?" I asked her.

"Nope. When somebody starts acting up on me, I'm gone. This girl gave you a whole lot of signs, you just wasn't reading them."

"Okay, what about the other one?" I was referring to Faye. I didn't tell Mona their names. I didn't think it was important.

"Now, she's harder to figure out. But what happens with a lot of girls, or people in general, is that when you hurt their feelings, sometimes they can't recuperate from it. That's what it seems like with her, she just can't let the pain go. That's why I joke around a lot, because then I take things less seriously. Life can get to you sometimes, man, it really can.

"Can I go to sleep now?" Mona asked me with a grin. I had talked her ears off. Of course, I made it seem as if Faye was last year's news, and that she had moved back to Georgia. I didn't know if Mona had fallen for it at the time. I tied the whole conversation concerning Faye and Pearl into my brother getting married and me feeling left behind.

"Yeah, I guess you can go to sleep now," I told her.

Mona sunk her head into the pillow and said, "By the way, Bobby, don't ask me to marry you. Just because your brother's getting married doesn't mean *you* have to rush out and buy no ring. You hear me?" Then she started to quote a classic song: " 'Momma used to say, Take your time, young man.' "

I burst out laughing. "Wait a minute," I said. "Are you sure you're only twenty years old?"

"Yeah, but I got three older brothers, so I know a lot about guys."

I leaned up and looked at her. "You have *three* older brothers."

"Yup."

I smiled. "Well, I guess you *do* know a lot about guys then," I said. Then I added, "But you still can't tell a man how to *be* a man."

"If you say so," Mona responded.

•

I was still unsure about showing up at Faye's graduation. I never did call her back to discuss it with her. The night before the ceremony I couldn't sleep.

Mona moved into Slowe Hall for the summer. She had an internship at WOL radio, run by Cathy Hughes, a sister who was definitely on the move. Cathy Hughes was a dominant figure in D.C. talk radio. When Cathy talked, people listened. I was proud of Mona. And since she was still in the area, I worried about her wandering on campus and catching me at Faye's graduation.

My final decision, which wasn't made until graduation morning, was that I wouldn't go. Faye was too determined in her rejection of me. There was nothing I could gain by showing up at her graduation. What if her new man was there? I decided to pass on it.

The next big event for me was Brad's wedding in July. I was with Mona the night before taking the long drive home. She told me to make sure I took lots of pictures.

Brad and Brenda were getting married at a large church in Winston-Salem. At first they thought about planning the wedding at a site halfway between Boston and Greensboro, like Philadelphia. That didn't make much sense to me. Everyone would have been forced to pay for hotel rooms. At least if the wedding was in Boston or Greensboro, one family would be on its home turf and could split the costs with the visiting family. Brad and Brenda were planning on staying in the Triad area for a while anyway, so they decided on the church in Winston-Salem, where a lot of my family members lived.

I sped down I-95 South for North Carolina on a Thursday morning. My brother was getting married that Saturday. I wasn't paying too much attention to my speed, though. A Virginia state trooper jumped right behind me flashing blue lights. I looked down at my speedometer. I was doing close to a hundred miles an hour. That Prelude could really fly!

"License and registration."

I handed him my things. The trooper then went back to his car and sat for an extra long time. The next thing I knew, there were two more police cruisers pulling over behind me.

"Could you step out of the car, please?"

I did what I was told. Those three white men didn't look like they were playing with me at all.

"You wouldn't happen to have any illegal substances in the car, wouldja?"

"No I don't," I told the first trooper. I had a lot of things in the car for my three-day trip home, but no "illegal substances." One thing my Prelude *didn't* have was a lot of room. I had to jam my things in wherever they fit.

"You mind if we take a look?" the second trooper asked me.

I did mind, but since I knew there was nothing illegal inside, I agreed to it. The second and third troopers went ahead and ransacked my car. I moved to protest, but the first trooper pulled his gun on me. "Step back away from the car," he said.

"I just wanted to—"

"Step away from the car," he repeated, violently.

People were driving by and watching. I looked like a common criminal. Meanwhile, those two backup troopers were ripping through my things like a tornado and found nothing.

"Is there any reason why you were driving so fast?" the first trooper asked me. He still had his gun out.

"I wasn't paying attention to how fast I was driving," I answered.

"Yeah, well, you *need* to start paying attention. Where are you headed?"

"North Carolina?"

He looked at me. "May I ask what for?"

I felt like saying, "To express my damn freedom to travel!" I said instead, "To be in my brother's wedding."

"Is that right?" He nodded his head and looked over to his backup. "You guys find a black tuxedo anywhere inside there?"

"Yeah," the third trooper told him.

The first trooper looked me over with hate in his eyes. I guess he was disappointed that I was telling the truth. "You watch him. I'll be right back," he said to the others. He walked over to his cruiser and wrote my ticket.

"You're coming from the Washington area, are ya?" the third trooper asked me.

That's what my damn license plates say! I thought. "Yeah," I told him.

"We've had a whole lot of illegal drug traffic from that area," he said.

"So you thought I had some drugs because I was from Washington?"

"We're just doing our jobs," the second trooper said. "If you weren't speeding, you'd still be on your way. You think about that next time, you hear?"

The first trooper returned with my ticket, my license, and my registration. "You make sure you pay attention to your speed next time."

I climbed back inside my car and was pissed. I lost close to an hour of traveling time, and was humiliated. I'm not saying that I was in the right, but I doubted I would have been accused of carrying "illegal substances" if I wasn't a young black man. I was in a sour mood for the rest of my drive. I didn't even feel like listening to any music. I reminded myself if I ever got stopped again and a police officer used the expression "May I do such and such?" I'd reply, "Hell no!" and let that be the end of it. That's when they would probably arrest me and make up a charge for it, like resisting arrest. Any free man would resist arrest if he didn't feel he was being rightfully charged. That was elementary, especially for a black man. Many of our arrests, on the simplest of charges, had turned into horror stories.

•

"I got searched while driving down here on the highway today," I told my father. He was wondering why I had such a sour disposition once I arrived at home.

"Was ya speedin'?"

"What if I was?" I asked him.

"Then you gave 'em the right." It was that plain and simple to him.

"They wouldn't have done that if I was white," I snapped.

My father frowned at me. "Do me a favor and go take a good look in the mirror then, Bobby."

I attempted to walk away from him. He grabbed me by my shoulder and took me to the mirror on our living room wall. It was one of the very few times that my father used his size and strength to get his point across.

I looked away from the mirror and said, "Come on, Dad, this is ridiculous."

"No it ain't, either. I've been waiting for this day to come ever since you went up there to Howard," he told me.

"What's that supposed to mean?" I asked him.

"A lot of them uppity Negroes up there think somethin' changed, and I'm here to tell you that it ain't. They're blind, Bobby, blinded by their own damned ignorance!

"Do you understand that we own more property down here in the South than them uppity Negroes will ever own up there? And you know why? Because we understand how to deal with these white folks; crackers, honkies, rednecks, devils, whatever you want to call 'em."

"How, by ignoring them and acting like racism doesn't exist?" I guess the northern science of complaining about racism had rubbed off on me without my noticing.

My mother walked into the room, overhearing the commotion. "What's the matter?"

"This is, ah, men's talk here now. We're all right. It's just me and Bobby having a face-to-face," my father told her.

My mother looked and walked away. Brad was looking in from the kitchen.

"Now go ahead and look in that mirror, Bobby," my father repeated to me.

"I know that I'm black," I said. I was still resisting.

My father looked deep into my face and said, "Actually, you're brown, Bobby. Now go ahead and look." He started to laugh, and I couldn't help but smile with him.

I finally looked into the mirror at my smooth, medium-brown skin, strong, broad nose, dark eyes, mustache, and sharp-cut kinky hair. I was a tall, handsome black man, and I liked what I saw.

"Okay, I'm looking in the mirror. Now what?" I responded to my father.

"I *like* what I see, Bobby," my father said with a proud nod. "But *they* don't like what I see. So *you* have to say, 'To hell with them!' and always do what's best for *you*, while understanding that *they* don't like to see you get ahead. But you know what, Bobby? You're gonna do it anyway, whether they like it or not.

"Now the key is not to give them any excuses—that they don't already have—to throw your narrow ass in jail, and throw away the key. You hear me? They can't stop you unless *you* stop yourself. 'Cause God don't like ugly, Bobby, I truly believe that. And my two boys ain't ugly. Because if *they* ugly, then that makes *me* ugly, and I *know* I ain't ugly. You hear me?

"If you don't sleep with the pigs, then the pigs can't sleep with you," he added. Then my father grabbed my arms and pulled me into a hug. "Now go on back there and meet your brother's wife," he told me. "I got some things to take care of."

Dad went up the stairs. I smiled and took a walk toward the kitchen, where Brad and Brenda were helping Mom prepare food.

"Aren't you two supposed to be separated until the wedding or something?" I asked them.

"Man, that's old-fashioned. We gon' stay together as long as we want," Brad said.

Brenda said, "Actually, I'll be on my way to join my family at the hotel after I leave here."

"I'm going with you, ain't I?" Brad asked her.

"But you're not *staying*. I like some things old-fashioned," Brenda responded.

Mom said, "That's right. If it ain't broke, then keep it together."

"That ain't how it's supposed to go, Mom," I told her.

"Look, Bobby, I'll say it the way I wanna say it. Now everybody knows what I mean."

I looked at Brad's fiancée. She was definitely marrying material. She wasn't all that thick in the body like Brad had bragged about though.

She reminded me of one of those tall, good-looking black teachers that little boys fall for in second and third grade. Everything about her was neat and pretty. I couldn't even imagine Brenda sweating.

"I'm pleased to finally meet you, Bobby," she said to me.

I held her hand in mine. It felt like I could break it if I squeezed too hard, until she squeezed mine. "Wo, that's some grip you got there," I said.

"Yeah, she ain't no pushover," Brad spoke up. "I can't be marrying no pushover. Brenda's a fighter."

Brenda smiled, too brown and mature to blush.

"What did you get your master's in again?" I asked her.

"Education," she answered.

Just like Mom, I thought with a smile. Brad was a Little Wild Man after all. He was about to marry himself a regal, I-don't-play-that teacher, just like his mommy. I smiled good and hard. Brad had his master's in business management. He had always talked about being a big-shot businessman, "bigger than Dad," he used to tell me. I felt uplifted to see his dreams coming true. I was suddenly real happy for him, and proud, like a big brother should be.

I looked at Mom, but she didn't return me the favor. She knew what I was thinking, I'm sure of it. Her Brad had turned out to be a good little boy after all.

After a while, Brad and I finally got a chance to talk alone outside.

"So how's D.C., Bobby?" He hadn't shaved or gotten a haircut yet. Brad was thicker than me and a few inches shorter. He was slightly browner too, and rougher around the edges. He could get sharp when he needed to, though. I guess he was waiting for the last minute.

"I'm struggling to hold down the fort, but that's good for you sometimes," I told him.

"Without struggle, there is no progress," he responded, quoting Frederick Douglass.

I smiled at him. "So, you went out and married an imitation of Mom, hunh, after all the complaining you used to do? 'I'd never marry no woman like Mom,'" I teased him. Brad had been adamant about that.

He laughed and said, "Ain't that a trip? It was like Brenda knew all the right buttons to push, and which ones to leave alone."

I nodded. "Just like Mom is with Dad."

"Well, hey, man, you know that's what they say. Every boy is looking to marry his mom, and every girl is looking to marry her daddy."

We shared a laugh just as Mom and Brenda walked out the door.

"You ready to go?" Brad asked Brenda.

"Help your brother and his wife carry the food to the car, Bobby. Make yourself useful while you're down here," my mother said.

I shook my head and smiled. That's the kind of thing Brad would have to get used to from his new wife. "They're not married yet, Mom. They still might change their minds," I joked.

Brad looked frozen for a second. "Naw, naw, it ain't gonna be none of that."

"It better not be. Because I'll make you explain it to every one of my family members who flew all the way down here from Boston," Brenda said.

Mom couldn't hold it back. She burst out laughing. It was probably something she would have said.

I helped them carry the food to the car for Brenda's family.

Brad said, "You know the rehearsal is at eleven tomorrow morning, right?"

"Yeah, I know."

"All right, I'm just making sure," he said.

"I'll see you tomorrow, Bobby," Brenda said.

"Okay now, and don't have any nightmares about this. Everything's gonna be all right."

We all laughed as they pulled out of the driveway and hit the road for the hotel.

Before I made it back in, my father stopped me at the door and handed me the phone number of one of Brad's closest friends. "Ivan said to call him about the bachelor party. It's gonna be tomorrow night. They want you to drive Brad over there," he explained with a grin. Maybe he was reminiscing on his own bachelor party, more than twenty years ago.

"So, what do you think about this marriage thing?" I asked him.

"Bobby, marriage is the oldest institution in the book. It's the only thing that keeps chaos from breaking out all over the world."

"There *is* chaos all over the world," I said.

My father looked me in the eyes and responded, "That chaos ain't nothin', Bobby. You let people stop getting married and see what happens."

"You think marriage is that important, hunh?" I was just instigating. I was sure that I wasn't pressed about getting married anymore. Brad was jumping right back into the frying pan. I was suddenly proud of my freedom.

"Look at it this way, son," my father said. "You know how the eggshell holds everything together? Well, without marriage, it would be nothing but yolk and egg white all over the place, a big, sloppy mess."

I laughed with him and headed inside the house. I had forgotten all about being searched on the highway that morning. I guess that wasn't so overwhelming after all. I had more important, positive things to think about. My brother was getting married in two days.

•

At the wedding rehearsal that Friday morning, I looked over at Brenda's bridesmaids. They all looked like distinguished, professional women. I later found out that most of them were Delta sorority members. Then I looked over at Brad's groomsmen. They looked petrified, like turkeys in November. I broke out laughing. I couldn't wait to get back to D.C. and tell Mona. It was no question about it, I was cured of the marriage blues.

"Hey, Bobby, what's so funny, man?" Brad asked me.

"Nothin', I'm all right."

Everyone seemed serious but me. I could see Brad's entire future before my eyes. Brenda would strap him down with two kids and know his day-to-day schedule as if it were her own. I was *not* looking forward to that. What the hell was I thinking about, worrying about marriage?

Brad's friend "Champ" eased over to me a bit later and asked me which of the bridesmaids I thought was the best-looking. Champ had gotten his nickname from hitting three home runs in a Little League baseball championship a full decade earlier. He had been a player ever since, with sports and with women. He just couldn't get enough attention.

"Which one do *you* think looks the best?" I asked him. I was sure that he had checked them all out already.

"The two sisters in the middle," he said with a smile. "Shorty in the front is all right too, but she looks a little thin. I'd have to fatten her up a few pounds."

I laughed. I produced a show in New York discussing the perception of weight in the black community compared to the white, Latino, and Asian communities. You'd never hear a white guy saying he wanted to fatten his woman up a bit. Latinos were similar to black men in that they didn't mind a few pounds on a woman as long as she looked good with it. Asian women all seemed to be about the same size anyway, petite.

"I haven't really thought about it," I told Champ. "But the ones you pointed out do look good. There's no denying that."

He smiled. "Yeah, you know I know how to pick 'em."

"What do you think about Brad's girl?" I asked him.

Champ looked at me and said, "Now *she* scares me. I ain't even gon' lie."

"Why?" I asked him with a grin. I could imagine why. Brenda was very forward and she didn't seem to take any nonsense. Champ was full of nonsense. He had always been that way. Brenda could read him from across a crowded room.

"Shit just seems so tense around her, man." He cringed when he said it, as if Brenda was an ice woman. "Brad always been hooking up with them kind of girls."

"So you'd rather be with an easygoing girl?"

"Yeah. Wouldn't you?"

We quieted back down. Brad was back in the area. He was running around like a drill sergeant getting everyone in order.

"Ivan still ain't here, man. What the hell is he doin'?" Brad asked both of us.

Champ and I looked at each other. Ivan was probably making last-minute arrangements for the bachelor party. We both knew, but we couldn't tell Brad. Fortunately, Ivan walked in within the next five minutes. Brad wasn't going to let him off the hook, though. His good friend was more than an hour late.

"Ivan! Where the hell you been, man? I told everybody eleven o'clock, so we can get it out the way!" Brad screamed at him inside the church. I thought we had done pretty well without Ivan. All he had to do was walk down the aisle with a woman on his arm. How hard could that be? I think Brad was more angry about the principle of Ivan being late.

"See what I mean, man? She got him all tense now," Champ whispered to me.

"Ivan *is* late," I said.

"Yeah, but we both know why."

"Well, he shouldn't have waited until the last minute to take care of things."

Champ looked at me. "That's right, you're his big brother, so of course you'll agree with him."

Me being in agreement with Brad was definitely rare. I smiled at the thought of it as we all got back to rehearsing our steps, positions, and exits.

•

"See what I mean about them guys, man? That's why Ivan's not my best man. I *knew* I couldn't count on him," Brad told me later that night. I was about to take him to the bachelor party that he didn't know about. I'm sure he had a hunch, but I wasn't even sure if he was interested in a bachelor party from the way he was talking. He really did seem a bit tense.

"Ivan been trying to talk me out of this wedding ever since I told him about it," he said.

"Why you think that is?" I asked him.

"Man, I don't know. Maybe he thinks I'm steppin' off on him or something."

"Hey, is Skip Murphy still on the radio down here?" Skip Murphy had a nice following in Greensboro. I used to envy that guy.

"Why, you thinking 'bout working down here?"

"Oh, no, I'm just asking if he's still here."

"Yeah, he's still on the air. You thinking 'bout hosting your own show one day, Bobby?" Brad was smiling at me. I guess he found it comical to envision my mild-mannered self on the radio.

"I thought about it a few times," I said. Actually, Mona had been talking about it and that got me interested. Mona had a radio personality for sure. I still didn't know if I had it. I felt a lot stronger about it than when I first came out of Howard, though. After a few more years around the business, maybe I *would* be ready to step up to the mike.

"Shit, go ahead and do it, man. What's the sense of being in radio if nobody knows you?" Brad said.

I nodded. "Good point," I told him with a grin.

"What would you call your show?" he asked.

"I have no idea."

"How 'bout 'The Bobby Dallas Show'?"

I broke out laughing. "Yeah, that's being real original."

"Yeah, but I mean, you got that kind of name, man. Bobby Dallas. It has symmetry, Bob-bee Dal-las. My name is flat, Brad Dal-las. See, it don't have that same symmetry."

I laughed even harder. Brad joined in with me.

"Yeah, man, Brenda came up with that stuff when I first told her your name and said you were producing radio in New York. But she's right, though. Your name got that symmetry appeal to it. It just sounds good together."

"All right, you made your point," I told him. I shied away from the idea. *"The Bobby Dallas Show"? No way. That makes me sound too important, like a celebrity,* I thought.

"Hey, man, where we goin'?" Brad suddenly asked me.

I had told him to ride with me to buy some juice from the grocery store for his wedding reception, and we had done that already.

"Well, you know, I haven't been down here lately, so I'm just riding around and seeing what's new." I was getting better and better at lying every day.

Brad smiled. "Yeah, okay." I was pretty sure that he knew what was going on. "Hey, man, I heard these Preludes are pretty fast. Let me see what it can do," he said, challenging me.

I smiled and opened it up.

"Yeah, I felt that!" Brad yelled. "Pour it on, baby, pour it on!"

As soon as I gassed it like a fool, a police car jumped out of nowhere and pulled us over. We were just two blocks from the bachelor party.

Brad broke out laughing. "Hey, man, it's my fault. I'll pay for the damn ticket."

A black officer walked up to the window. Brad noticed him and said, "Hey, Tim, how you doin'?"

Tim smiled and shook his head. He was all ready to write out our ticket.

Brad said, "My fault, man. You know I'm getting married tomorrow."

"Oh yeah? No, I didn't know," Tim responded.

"Yeah, in Winston-Salem. This is my older brother, Bobby. He just came down from D.C. yesterday. He produces a couple radio shows up there."

"Oh yeah?" Tim looked at me, and I proceeded to smile at him.

Brad said, "Yeah. He was just trying to rush me to the bachelor party and everything. But I'll pay the ticket, man. How much is it?"

Tim looked at us and grinned. "I'll tell you what, you slow down your speed and get there in one piece, and I never saw you."

"Hey, thanks, man," Brad told him. "We appreciate it."

Tim nodded and said, "Have a good night. And congratulations." Then he walked back to his cruiser.

Brad grinned at me and said, "Lucky it was a brother. I didn't think he was gonna let us off, though."

I got back on the road and told Brad that I was pulled over for speeding in Virginia the day before, and that my car had been searched.

"They caught you doin' a hundred?" he asked me with a smile.

"It wasn't exactly a hundred," I said.

"Shit, it was close enough. You lucky they didn't arrest your ass on the spot."

I guess Dad had schooled my brother well.

"Anyway, how'd you know that we were headed to your bachelor party?" I asked him.

"I mean, where else are we gonna be headed?" He looked at his watch and said, "It's about that time, and I know the boys won't let me down on a bachelor party."

"Is that okay with Brenda?"

"So what if it ain't?" he responded.

"Yeah, right," I told him. "Don't act like you got rank now."

"Aw, hell naw, Bobby! I still climb on top, okay? You remember that."

I just laughed as we pulled up to the bachelor party. Ivan had apparently invited three sisters who still had the hots for Brad. That didn't go over too well. Brad pulled me to the side. "What kind of shit is that, Bobby?"

I was still surprised that they agreed to come, and all three of them were eager for one last swing on the vine. It was unbelievably embarrassing for Brad. They did a mock dating game where Brad was supposed to choose which one to be with later on. They all told us how they met Brad, what his best moves and features were, what they wanted to do to him, and so on. I just couldn't believe it. Brad must have had it better with women than I thought to get that kind of attention on the eve of his wedding day. Had he been interested, I guess finding a woman on the side wouldn't have been a problem for him.

Of course, Brad didn't choose to be with anyone that night. He rode back home with me in near silence. "Well, this is it, man. Tomorrow's the big day," he finally said. It was close to two in the morning.

"So, when you planning on having my first niece or nephew?" I asked.

"Your nephew? Probably in two years."

"No niece, hunh?"

"Naw, not the first one."

"Why not?"

"I need somebody to protect her from the knuckleheads," he told me.

"You mean like Ivan and Champ?" I asked.

"Knuckleheads like me, too," Brad answered. "You believe them three sisters, though, man? I wonder if Ivan *paid* them to do that shit. That was wild."

"It was different, I give 'em that."

Brad shook his head and hummed, "Mmm, mmm, mmm," followed by a hearty laugh. "Life is something else, Bobby. Enjoy it while you can."

•

Everything at the wedding went as planned. It didn't seem that long at all. During the rehearsals, it looked as if things would drag on forever, but once the real event happened, it went by like a flash.

At the reception, the families mingled and got along well. Brenda had a younger sister and brother and plenty of cousins that I met. Champ flirted with one of Brenda's friends that he had his eye on, and Ivan looked like a fish out of water. I guess the whole wedding thing had caught him off guard.

"I guess you can't wait to get the hell out of here, hunh, Ivan?"

Ivan just shook his head. "Man, I can't believe he went and did it . . . at twenty-three."

"How long you plan on waiting?" I asked him.

Ivan took another sip of his drink. I think he had somewhere around four since I had been watching him. "As long as I can get away with it," he said.

I smiled and said, "Amen to that, brother," toasting his drink with my fruit punch.

•

"So how did everything go?" Mona asked me. She called me that Sunday night when I arrived back in D.C.

"Well, they both said, 'I do.' "

"And how did you feel about that?" Mona had concern in her voice.

I smiled, happy about my new opinion on the subject. "Better him than me, right now," I told her.

"Oh, so you're okay now?"

"Yeah, I'm okay. I'm better than okay. I'm not thinking about marriage at all now."

"Good," Mona responded, "now I don't have to dodge you."

"Oh, you were thinking about dodging me?" I asked her.

"I didn't want to, but if you came back talking that marriage stuff . . ."

"Yeah, I understand," I said. I didn't want to harp on the subject for too long. I was thinking about other things. "So, what are you doing tonight? You wanna catch a late movie and celebrate my new state of mind?"

Mona laughed and said, "Come get me."

"I'm on my way."

Same Mistake Twice

Gary Mitchell had finally gotten in touch with me again. It was the off-season in early August, so he had a lot more time on his hands to party. I'm sure that a lot of guys would have loved to have been in his position, having women throwing themselves at you because you're a well-paid ballplayer. However, I wouldn't exactly think of these women as the kind you'd put much trust in. Most of them were here-today-gone-tomorrow money chasers. However, Gary couldn't seem to get enough of them. I still wasn't too thrilled about associating with his fast crowd, but Brad told me to enjoy life while I could, so there I was at another club in suburban Maryland with Gary.

"How do you feel about your rookie season?" I asked him. We were sitting at the bar with drinks in our hands. This place was so incognito that it didn't even have a marquee. Nevertheless, the place was packed with high spenders. I wouldn't say that all of them were spending honest money, either.

"I mean, I wasn't all that happy with it. I figure things'll get better when we start winning more games," Gary responded to me. Then he smiled and said, "You know that them two girls we were with that night still be asking about you, man?"

"Oh yeah?" I mumbled. I wasn't at all concerned about it.

Gary said, "They wanted me to give them your phone number, but I wouldn't do it. I told them I had to ask you first."

Good thinking, I thought. After a while, I separated from Gary to do my own thing. I felt a lot more at ease at the club that night. I was no longer in awe of pretty women. They were all human, just like me. And if they were there, then they were available. That was my new attitude with women. No one was out of my reach anymore; that was the old me.

"Can I buy you a drink?" I asked a sister. She was a one-punch knockout, but no one seemed to be approaching her. I looked over and noticed a bunch of guys all huddled around the bar area. They were drinking and looking, but none of them were conversing with the fine women who surrounded us. I probably would have been one of those guys a few months earlier. They were all gun-shy.

The sister looked at me and said, "Sure. You can buy me a drink."

"What are you having?"

"A sloe gin fizz."

I still didn't know that much about different drinks. You learn these things as you go along. "Is that good?" I asked her. "What does it taste like?"

"Ah, it's sweet, but kind of strong," she answered with a smile. And boy did she have a smile! Her smile made her look like a teenager, fresh out of high school. I realized that she had to be at least twenty-one to get in, but I wondered. Mona had fake IDs.

I ordered two sloe gin fizzes and found us a table.

"Hey, girl, is this where you're gonna be?" a girlfriend asked her.

My new friend looked at me and said, "That's what it looks like."

Her girlfriend looked at us both. Then she gave me her approval with a grin and a nod. "All right then."

I know I asked the sister her name and other general questions, but I don't remember any of her answers. I know that she was from New Jersey and went to school in Virginia, but that's about it. I remember saying some real cool and funny things to her that made her laugh. We ordered more drinks and danced. Then I remember Gary saying how good she looked and asking me if I was going to take her home.

"If she lets me," I told him. I believe that I was at least halfway drunk by then. She did go home with me, but she didn't spend the night. She had her own car and went home before I woke up. I had a big headache that Sunday morning, and then I got a phone call.

"Hi, Bobby Dallas."

"Ah, hi you doin'," I answered. I was still kind of drowsy. It was a first-time caller, so I assumed that it was the woman from the night before, but I didn't remember giving her my number.

"This is Kimberly. We met a couple of months ago at the club. You were with your friend Gary Mitchell from the Bullets. We ended up at the Ramada Inn that night," she said with a giggle. Someone else was on the phone with her.

"Is there someone else on the phone with you?" I asked.

"Yeah, this is Tonya. You met me that night, too." They had me on a three-way phone.

"Where you been at, Bobby? I was thinking about you for a while."

"Me too."

I guess Gary broke down and gave them my number that night or early that morning. "I've been taking care of business," I said. I needed some Tylenol badly.

"Gary told us you got a car now," someone said. I think it was Tonya.

"Yeah, I had to. Taxis can get expensive."

"You been keeping yourself in good shape lately?"

I couldn't tell who was who, but they were both laughing.

"We wanna hook up with you tonight, if you don't mind." That was Tonya. I recognized her forwardness.

"You already let Gary know?" I asked her.

"Who said anything about Gary?"

They were laughing again. I didn't know how to respond, but I was definitely flattered. "I don't know about tonight," I said. I didn't want to make any commitments to them.

"Well, whenever you're free from your busy schedule and all, why don't you call us up?" Kimberly suggested. I was beginning to tell them apart.

"Which one?" I asked.

"It don't matter," Tonya said.

"What's the numbers?"

They ran off their phone numbers to me and we all hung up. I sat in bed and stared up at the ceiling. "I don't believe this," I said with a grin. Then I checked my messages. Mona had called twice about some concert tickets she had. I returned her call.

"Hey, I'm sorry I missed it," I told her.

"You're slippin', Bobby. I ended up going with some guy I didn't know," she told me. "He kept trying to come on to me. I almost had to take a taxi home."

"How did you hook up with him?" I asked her. I know she didn't just pick him up off the street.

"He gave me his phone number a few weeks ago," she said. "He just got lucky by being home when I called, after I called *you, twice.*"

"How come you didn't tell me about the tickets in advance?"

"I had just gotten them myself. This girl that works at WOL with me couldn't go."

"Oh, so don't blame that on me. That was a last-minute thing."

"I'm not blaming it on you, I'm just saying that you blew."

I smiled and shook my head. "All right then, whatever."

"So where did you go last night? You don't have to answer that if you don't want to," she told me.

"You know Gary Mitchell from the Bullets?"

"He was on Frank's show before, with a monkey face?"

I stopped myself and smiled. "Why do you have to talk about him like that?"

"I mean, he does have a monkey face. I'm just being honest about it."

"Stop, Mona, that's very negative," I told her.

"Okay, I take it back then. Gary Mitchell does not have a monkey face."

I couldn't stop myself from grinning. "Some people think that about all black people," I said.

"You mean white people, Bobby?" she asked me. "I don't care what they think. I know the difference between good-looking and ugly. A lot of *white* people look like monkeys."

"Okay, let's get off of this subject," I said. It was beginning to sound ridiculous. I don't think Mona liked Gary Mitchell because she knew that I received extra attention from women when I was around him.

"What are you doing today?" she asked. "I can tell that it's gonna be hot. Let's go to Haines Point, or how 'bout the Baltimore Harbor or something?" she suggested. "Yeah, let's go to the Baltimore Harbor," she repeated excitedly. "Cathy Hughes talks about it a lot."

"You've never been there before?" I asked her. I had been there twice.

"No, but I wanna go, though. So what time are you gonna pick me up?"

Mona was becoming more and more demanding of my time. I don't even think she noticed it. I usually liked her company, but I was extra tired from the night before. I needed to rest.

"That's a forty-five-minute ride," I hinted.

"So?" Mona snapped. "As much as we ride around doing nothing in D.C., you should be *happy* to get away. But if you don't want to take me, Bobby, then just say so. Don't make up no lame excuses. My feelings won't be hurt."

I was beginning to get annoyed. Mona was telling the truth, though, because I was beating around the bush about things. "Remember you said something about not taking our friendship for granted?" I reminded her.

She gave me the silent treatment. "Yeah, you're right," she said. "I'm sorry." She sounded like she hated to admit it.

I felt guilty. I said, "I'll tell you what, I'll cal you back after I've washed up and everything and let you know."

"All right. That sounds fair to me."

Mona wasted no time hanging up. She was pissed off about it, I could tell. It didn't sound fair to her at all. I realized that she was used to getting her way with me, but I was only used to getting my way with her sometimes. It was a lopsided friendship.

Gary called soon after I hung up with Mona. I guess I had the hot line that morning. "Did you do that girl last night, Bobby?" he asked me with a chuckle.

I didn't answer him. I said, "I got a call from Kimberly and Tonya this morning. They woke me up."

He responded, "Yeah, they called me up late last night, buggin' me for your number."

"And so you finally gave it to them."

"Well, when I talked to you at the club last night, you didn't tell me not to."

He had a point, so I backed off. "Yeah, I guess you're right. I didn't."

"So, what's up for today, man? I got these two girls from Fredericksburg that we could hook up with later on. You wit' it?" Gary was originally from Paterson, New Jersey. Maybe that had something to do with his jones for women. Paterson was probably too close to New York's fast-paced streets for comfort.

"I don't think so. I still need some Tylenol from last night's headache," I told him.

"Man, you got all day to get rid of that headache. We can get with these girls like seven, eight o'clock."

I could tell that Gary wasn't prepared to be turned down, but I was going to have to disappoint him. "Naw, man, I'm gonna have to pass until next weekend."

"Aw'ight then, suit yourself."

When we hung up, I prayed that I didn't get any more phone calls, and I didn't. I fell back to sleep and didn't wake up until after two o'clock in the afternoon. I couldn't believe I had slept that long! I must have been in overdrive that Saturday night. I really didn't feel like calling Mona then, but since I told her that I would, I called her anyway.

"I haven't taken a shower or anything yet," I said. "I'll get ready and call you back."

Mona was silent again. That wasn't a good sign. "You know what, Bobby? Don't even worry about it. You don't have to take me to Baltimore."

I still didn't want to go, but I didn't like how Mona was taking things, so I pressed the issue. "No, I'll take you."

"Bobby, don't do me any favors, okay? If you don't want to go, then just say it."

"How are you gonna tell me what I don't want to do?" I protested feebly.

Mona sighed and said, "Go ahead and get your rest, Bobby. I've made other plans already anyway."

•

I was at another crossroad. *Do I get more involved with Mona?* I asked myself. I realized that things were headed that way, and hanging out with Gary again didn't make things any easier. In fact, since Mona knew about it, I believe that it made things worse, she just hadn't spilled it out yet.

I had a lot to think about that afternoon. I didn't want to end what I had with Mona, but I wasn't sure if I wanted to give up my freedom either. I was just starting to feel comfortable with my social life again.

I decided to call my brother. I explained the whole situation to him and how I had made the same mistake before with Faye. Instead of securing a good thing that I had with her, I went after a long shot with Pearl. I didn't want to make the same mistake twice. I wasn't a basketball star, nor could I imagine putting up with the insecurity of Gary's partying lifestyle.

"I don't know what to tell you, man. I mean, this girl at Howard did say that you were friends, but yet she's still fucking you. And sex clouds the mind of a woman, man, I don't care what they tell you.

"You wasn't boning that other girl from Howard, right?"

"Who, Faye? Naw."

"Well, this situation is different then."

"Okay, so what do I do?" I asked him. Brad had been in far more relationships than I had been in. Most brothers find it hard to ask their good friends about relationships, let alone think of asking their younger siblings. Their egos would get in the way. Nevertheless, my younger brother was married and well experienced with women, and I was not.

"You ask her if she still wants you to be single," he said. "You have to cut through the bullshit with this girl and ask her what she wants to do."

I hesitated. Brad didn't understand. Mona and I had made an agreement. "We both agreed that we wouldn't try to force the other into a commitment or anything," I told him.

"Well, it sounds to me like she's not keeping up her end of the bargain, Bobby. It sounds like she wants to have her cake and eat it too."

He was telling the truth. It was a no-win situation for me. I risked giving up the freedom to date whoever I wanted, which I didn't want to do. However, I didn't want to end the sexual friendship that I had with Mona either. I wanted to have my cake and eat it too.

"I guess I can't keep things the way they are, hunh?" I asked Brad with a chuckle.

He laughed. "You knew that before you even called me. Call me back in a couple of days and tell me what happens," he added with another laugh.

When I hung up the phone, I realized that Brad had given me the only sane advice. I hadn't noticed just how much Mona expected from me until it was too late. It was a make-or-break situation, but hadn't I used her in the same way? She broke her rules for me, yet I wasn't willing to do the same for her. I was being a hypocrite.

I called Mona that Sunday night, but she wasn't in and I didn't want to leave a message. I decided to show up at Slowe Hall and have a face-to-face with her after work that Monday night. I thought it would have been much better to talk about things in person.

•

"When we said that we weren't gonna take our friendship for granted, did that include popping up unexpectedly?" Mona asked me once she came down to meet me at Slowe.

"Let's go outside. I have to talk to you," I told her. I was as calm as a monk.

"What if I don't feel like it?"

She sure wasn't *acting* like a friend anymore. It had only been four months since we had started our strange relationship. Faye and I had been friends for over a year before things got too hot. Nevertheless, like Brad mentioned, Faye and I never had sex.

"This is about us," I said.

Mona looked at me and walked out the door. I followed her out and down the street.

"Okay, what do you want to talk about?" she snapped at me.

I calmly asked, "Are we more than friends now? Because you're acting like you have a problem with my availability."

"I've always been there for you. Why can't you do the same for me?"

"I've been there for you," I said.

"Not lately."

I lost my cool. "Look, I was just tired yesterday, that's all."

"Now see, that's what I mean. I was *tired* before. And I had other things to do, but I was *still* there when you needed me."

"Well, I didn't think that *you* needed anybody," I snapped back at her.

Mona stared at me with spiteful eyes. "All I ask for is your company. And I've been giving *you* more than that."

"Oh, don't act like we were having sex just for me. Don't even start that."

"It's not about sex, though, it's about feeling appreciated."

"So is that it, you don't feel appreciated?" I asked her.

"No. No, I don't."

I calmed down again. "So what do you want me to do, Mona?"

"I mean, just . . . I don't know, Bobby, okay? I don't know."

I didn't know if I wanted to say it, but it came out anyway. "I thought you had all the answers."

"Now see, why you gotta get smart with me?" she responded.

"You get smart with me all the time, and that never bothered me. It just seems like you wanna do everything that *you* wanna do now."

"Oh, and *you* don't?"

"Well, at least I'm honest about my feelings for you. You haven't even told me that you liked me. And I know that you don't like me hanging out with Gary, you just haven't said it yet."

"Is that what you wanna hear?"

"I wanna hear something!" I yelled at her.

"Mmm, this is better than the soap operas!" someone hollered from across the street. "Hold on, I'll be right back. I'm goin' in the house to get some popcorn. I live right around the corner, okay? Hold that pose."

Mona and I started to smile. We *were* pretty dramatic, and D.C. was a residential area like Philly, New York, Detroit, and Chicago, with houses packed together like sardines. Anyone in the vicinity could walk to their front porch and hear our argument.

Mona said, "All right, if you want me to say it, I'll say it then. I like you. But it ain't like you don't know already. And no, I don't like you hanging with . . . your friend. Okay?"

I shook my head and grinned. I had to go through all of that just to get Mona to express her feelings to me. "Is it that hard for you to admit that you like somebody?" I asked her. "I mean, you're acting just like guys act. Oh, that's right, I forgot, you *do* have three older brothers."

Mona looked at me and said, "I don't know if I'm ready for a boyfriend. In the beginning, we said that we wouldn't do this to each other."

I chuckled. "Like they say, 'Rules are meant to be broken.' "

Mona paused and thought about it. "So is that what you want?" She was being vulnerable for the first time since I knew her, and it was a bad time for it. Although I hated to admit it, hanging out with Gary had given me a view to new possibilities with women. I still wasn't ready to give up my freedom. I didn't like that boyfriend/girlfriend thing anymore. It seemed so teenaged. We had to figure out something else.

"I don't think so," I answered. "What else could we be?"

Mona grinned. "Partners," she said.

"We've been that already."

"Well, now we can be more committed partners."

"And where does that lead to?" After my brother's wedding everything else seemed like nonsense to me. Either you're married or headed for marriage or you're not.

"Wherever," Mona answered. "Wherever it goes."

She didn't know where we were headed, and neither did I. She was just saying the first thing that came to mind. I felt trapped. Usually a guy feels relieved when a girl finally expresses that she likes him. I think I would have been better off had she not admitted it.

I was finally turning into a real guy, a pain in the ass to women. I knew damn well that I wouldn't be able to pass on those groupies. I was sure that I could pass on some of them, like Kimberly and Tonya, but certainly I wouldn't be able to pass on all of them. Hell, if I was in Africa, and I had the money, I would have made Mona my first wife and moved on to court my next one. I had tasted the addictive power of womanizing and I couldn't stop thinking about stealing to home base with a new woman, even as Mona stood right there in front of me. I was a tortured soul indeed.

SHIT!!

Dodging Bullets

For the next couple of months, I immersed myself in my work, attempting to stay away from both Mona and Gary. It got a lot easier once September and October rolled around. Mona was back in school and Gary was with the team again. It was just those damned weekends in between that were crazy. In fact, on Saturdays, I ended up taking an extra producing job at WMSC just to keep busy. I could use the extra money, too. Things weren't exactly looking up in the economic department. With entertainment, keeping my car running, and paying all of my bills, I had more holes in my pockets than I could handle. I kept having to tap into my savings account to stay afloat.

"You've been hearing them rumors around the station?" Frank asked me in the rest room at work. He was speaking in a low tone.

"What rumors?" I thought he was talking about some social rumors about the guys and gals who worked at WMSC. My nose was pretty clean there, so I knew it was nothing on me. My escapade with Pamela Cooper was a sealed vault.

"I heard the station might be moving to Baltimore next year," Frank said.

"Get out of here! Are you sure?" I knew nothing about it.

"No, I'm not sure. That's why I'm asking you if you heard anything."

"Well, who did you hear it from?"

"From Lyle, on the morning show."

I grimaced and shook my head. Those morning show people always got the news firsthand. "Seems like I'm the last to know everything around here," I commented.

"Tammy didn't say anything to you about it?" Frank asked me.

"She don't talk to me much at all."

He smiled and went back to speaking in low tones. "Yeah, she had an affair with a station manager before and they fired her behind. Now she's strictly business."

"At this station?" I asked, surprised. Tammy Richards didn't seem like the affair type at all.

"Not at this station, but I can't tell you where, that's privileged information. Most people here don't even know about it. But she was having an affair with a white boy thinking that she was gonna move up into a hotter time slot, and it never happened."

I smiled. "So that's why she's so grouchy around here? She's back working with the natives and she don't like it too much," I joked.

"Shit, I'm 'bout to get the hell out of here myself," Frank told me.

My smile turned into a frown. "Are you serious?" No Frank Watts at the station meant problems for me. We were a team, and Frank was my troubleshooter.

"Yeah, I'm serious," he said. "If they're moving to Baltimore, I'm not goin'. Baltimore don't even have a football team anymore."

"They got baseball."

"Man, baseball's been going downhill for years, especially for black people. We don't support baseball that much anymore. We should have never stopped the Negro Leagues. It's basketball that's hot now. If we could ever get them Bullets to win some steady games, you would see. And they need to build a stadium right here inside the city instead of playing out in Maryland. People don't want to go all the way out there. The Redskins just won the Super Bowl, so you know they're hot."

"What would you do if you stopped working here?" I had gotten comfortable with putting my dues in at the place.

"I'd move on to another station," Frank answered. Then he looked at me and smiled. "You haven't figured this business out yet, hunh, Bobby? Once you build a reputation, you can go where you wanna go. It happens all the time. Don't ever get too settled at one place unless you're part owner or something, because things are always changin'. It's best to be ready for it. I take all this in with a grain of salt and a shot of tequila," he said with a laugh.

We finally walked out of the bathroom to air our next show. I invited a couple of D.C. high school football stars on to talk about the upcoming playoffs and the popularity of the Catholic and private league versus the public league. Frank had raised the issue of who got more press coverage from the *Washington Post* sports section, so I produced a few shows on the subject from various different angles. We even had a *Washington Post* sportswriter come in and explain how the decisions concerning story priority were made.

I wanted to ask Frank if he'd take me along with him if he left WMSC, but I decided to wait and see if the station was really moving to Baltimore first. Maybe I could even work something out with Mr. Cooper to see if I could host a show. I could produce it myself and collect both paychecks. I was beginning to think ambitiously, and why not?

Radio was starting to remind me of the lottery, where the little numbered balls scrambled around and eventually popped out at the top, and I had just been watching things. I figured, *What would it take for me to become one of those numbered balls?* Brad seemed to be right—"What's the sense in being in radio if nobody knows you?" You'd just end up being fired and moved out for new shows, new management, and higher ratings.

•

"How do things look jobwise over at WOL?" I asked Mona over the phone that night.

"What, as far as getting a job over there?"

"Yeah, that, and keeping a job."

"Oh, it's *very* competitive. People leave left and right. Either your show brings in the ratings, or you're gone. Cathy Hughes don't play. That's what I like about her," Mona answered. She seemed excited every time we talked about radio. She loved it!

"What if the show is real important to the community?" I commented.

"Every show over there is important to the community. It just depends on what shows the community chooses to listen to. I mean, we learned that at school."

"Yeah, I just didn't realize how serious it was," I told her.

"You gotta be cutthroat like that sometimes to compete with everybody else. Look at PGC, they're taking no prisoners *at all.*"

Shit! What have I gotten myself into? I was thinking. I was getting nervous about the future. Could I really compete against everybody else? I knew that I was a good producer, but I still had to make myself known in the larger radio circles.

"Hey Mona, do you really think you can survive out there?" I asked. I was actually concerned about myself, and I figured maybe some of Mona's confidence could rub off on me.

"Yeah, I'm not even worried about it," she said. "Even Cathy Hughes told me, 'Girl, you got spunk. You're gonna go far. I just hope I'll have enough money to hire you one day.' "

"Cathy Hughes told you that?"

"Yeah, I'm not lying."

I knew that she wasn't. I was excited for her. I wished that I had some big-time radio mover and shaker recognize me. Mona was in the right place at the right time. She still volunteered at WOL whenever she got a chance. Even though she wasn't on salary yet, I was jealous of her.

"Oh, by the way," she said, "did you get the Bullets tickets yet?"

Gary Mitchell was buying me a pair of season tickets. "Oh, so you don't mind using his tickets after you done bad-mouthed him so much, hunh?"

Mona laughed and said, "You didn't tell him, did you?"

"Naw, he don't even know you," I said.

"Well, I don't want to know him either," she responded.

"Yeah, you just wanna use his tickets."

Mona laughed again and said, "They're *your* tickets now."

"Well, I haven't gotten them yet anyway."

"Don't the season start next month?"

"Yeah, but sometimes they wait until the last minute to see who's buying what seats."

Mona said, "If he plays for the team, he should get first choice."

"Are you crazy?" I told her. "The money gets first choice. Just like ratings on the radio."

"Well, you let me know when you get them. But I got work to do."

I hung up with Mona and thought about those tickets. What if I wanted to take someone else to a few of the games? I didn't know how I would manage it. I was doubtful that Mona would be able to go to every game, but which ones would she miss? Mona would most likely be going home over the Christmas break, but what if I wanted to take someone else to a few games before then?

Damn! I thought. *I just can't get a break.* I was still meeting new women, and things had been so far so good, but how long could I really expect to get away with it without Mona finding out?

•

I received the season tickets right before the Bullets' opening game in November. I got a late-night phone call from a female "associate" named Sybil that same week. I hadn't said anything to her about having tickets. It would have been just my luck if she wanted to go to the season opener. I knew I couldn't deny Mona *that* privilege. I would have to turn all other comers down.

"What's going on?" I asked her. It was close to midnight on a Tuesday. The Bullets' opener was that weekend.

"Nothing at all. Are you in bed yet?"

"Nope. Not yet."

"So what are you doing?" she asked me.

"Watching a late show."

"Oh, so I guess you're in for the night." Sybil sounded extremely bored, and I had a strong idea of what she was hinting at. I hadn't exactly tried to jump her bones, so to speak. I had to think real hard before I responded to her. It was the moment I feared, cheating on Mona.

"Maybe, maybe not," I said. If I was gonna finally break my discipline, I wasn't gonna succumb easily. She had to express how strongly she wanted my company.

"I don't have classes until late tomorrow," she told me. She went to Georgetown.

"So what are you saying?" I asked her.

"It would be nice if you could come see me," Sybil answered softly.

I repeated it myself, *It would be nice if you could come see me.* Sometimes the simplest words can have the strongest effect on you. *You damned right it would be nice!* I thought to myself. There was no way to deny the excitement I felt.

Then Sybil added, "My roommate is staying over her friend's house tonight."

I took one deep breath and said, "All right, I'll be over there in less than an hour, unless you want me to take longer than that." I was joking. I had a hard-on already.

"Don't do that," she responded. "You made me wait long enough as it is."

Oh my God! I thought. My zipper was about to break. "Well, let me get on my way then."

I hung up, brushed my teeth, tossed on some cologne, straightened myself up, and was out the door. With the light traffic that night, I made it to Sybil's apartment in Georgetown in eighteen minutes. It was only a hop and a skip from where I lived on Thirteenth Street.

At first I thought about sitting outside of her building and smoking a cigarette to waste a few more minutes. I didn't want to seem too anxious. But then I thought, *For what? I'm a grown man. So what if I got here fast?* She called *me.* Then I thought about Mona. Before I knew it, I had a cigarette in my mouth anyway.

All my life I had been a decent man. I felt that cheating on Mona would cross the line into the unknown, and I just couldn't do it. I turned my engine on and drove off, pissed at myself. Why couldn't I just be an average guy and take the opportunity of a chick on the side? Mona and I weren't married!

I didn't feel like going back home, so I drove downtown. There was an army of hookers marching around on Fourteenth and K Northwest. I counted them and stopped at thirty-four as I drove to Thirteenth, up to L, and across Massachusetts Avenue. That's how sick in the head I was that night. Plenty of other guys were out there, too, honking their horns and looking for a safe spot to pick up the hookers. I just drove on by and kept going. Then I decided to give Mona a surprise visit in the hope of releasing my excess late-night energy.

I called Mona from a nearby pay phone. "Bobby, I am in bed, asleep," she ranted. I opened my mouth to respond and she cut me off before I could even get started. "Call me tomorrow."

I reluctantly agreed and went on about my torturous night. I contemplated driving back over to Georgetown, but by then it was after two in the morning. There was a strong possibility that Sybil was still up, but I couldn't find the devilish drive to do it.

I must have sat inside my car until four in the morning, smoking cigarette after cigarette. I was still a decent, loyal man and I absolutely hated my guts for it.

I called Sybil back the next day and got her answering machine. I told her that I was sorry about the night before, but something else had come up. I never heard from her again.

•

That Saturday afternoon, I took Mona to the Bullets' opener against the Chicago Bulls. It was a sellout, not because of the home team, but because everyone wanted to see Michael Jordan and his gravity-defying dunks. Even Frank Watts was there at the Maryland Cap' Center with a date.

Mona kept jumping up and down and hollering at the players. She acted more like a rowdy football fan than a basketball fan, and we had good seats. I could feel the people around us beginning to fidget in response to Mona's hyperactivity, but no one was willing to say anything.

"Oh my God! Did you see that dunk?" she yelled. Jordan was doing his thing.

"You're a Chicago Bulls fan, are ya?" an older white man asked Mona from behind.

Mona looked at him and said, "No, my team is the Detroit Pistons."

I could tell the guy had something else to say. Mona's answer must have thrown him off. He was probably expecting her to say that she was a Bulls fan.

"Could you calm down some?" I asked her out of courtesy for the other fans.

"For what? This is what you come to the games to do, to release energy. Give Jordan the ball!" she hollered. I just shook my head.

Despite Michael Jordan's 38 points, the Bullets managed to edge out an opening game win 98–94. The legendary but aging Bernard King scored 32 for the Bullets. My friend Gary had a terrible game, with only 8 points and 9 turnovers. He had his hands full with Jordan. I guess anybody would.

"Man, your friend Gary Mitchell was *sorry,*" Mona said during the ride home.

"Give him a break, Mona. I mean, he was up against Jordan, the number one guard in the country."

"So, Isiah Thomas can stick 'em."

"Gary's not Isiah Thomas. Isiah gets a lot of help on defense anyway. Detroit has the best defense in the league." I had been paying much more attention to sports since producing "D.C. Sports Talk." What kind of producer would I have been if I didn't?

"I know that's right," Mona bragged about her hometown team. "I can't wait until they play the Bullets. The Pistons gon' blow 'em out. When is that game?"

"I don't know, I have to look at the schedule."

"Well, you make sure you find out, because I definitely don't want to miss that one."

I started wondering when it would be possible to take someone else to a game, but I couldn't ask Mona when she wouldn't be able to go, of course; she would have gotten suspicious.

"What are you thinking about?" she asked me out of the blue. "You've been acting real quiet around me lately. What's goin' on with you?"

"That's because you've been doing most of the talking lately," I responded. The truth was that I was always preoccupied with my thoughts. I wasn't satisfied with our relationship.

"No, you're acting like you got something else on your mind," Mona correctly assumed.

"What gives you that impression?"

"Bobby, I know when you're thinking shit. Don't play with me. You get all quiet just like you are now."

I just decided to ignore her and drive her home.

"Are you in a hurry to get somewhere?" she asked me. I guess I did accelerate a bit. I wanted to get away from Mona and be alone with my thoughts.

"Yeah, I'm tired," I said.

"You mean you don't want to go to a movie or something with me?"

"Maybe later on, after I've gotten some rest."

Mona smiled. "Dag, I made you that tired last night."

"Yes you did," I told her. She was wearing me out. Even her voice was starting to annoy me. I planned to stay away from her as long as I could. In fact, I ended up hanging out with Gary that night. He was down in the dumps after the game. I guess he needed someone outside of the team to talk to about it.

"Hey, man, that was Michael Jordan. I know you know about his reputation. He was a Tar Heel, too," I said, trying to ease the pain of being humiliated in front of thousands.

Gary had a drink in his hand. I felt like telling him to leave the drinks alone, but I didn't.

"They say you need a short-term memory in this league, man, but I'm not used to losing, and I'm *definitely* not used to playing this bad," he grumbled.

I felt like advising him to stay away from the clubs and women for a while, to dedicate himself to the game, but I didn't do that either. "You just gotta hang in there, man," I told him instead.

Gary smiled and said, "I guess y'all won't have me on the show this year. I'm not the popular rookie anymore."

"You wanna be on the show again?" I asked him. "You gotta be ready to answer all the critics if you do. We could have an 'Ask Gary Mitchell Show' if you think you'd be up to it. But what would the coach say?"

"I don't know."

"Well, think about it for me and I'll see what I can do." It sounded like a good idea to me. I couldn't wait to tell Frank.

•

It was early December before we got Gary on the show. Frank was as excited about the idea as I was. The Washington Bullets' record was 6–10 by then, and Gary hadn't gotten much better in his game.

"You used to shoot the ball more accurately at North Carolina. What happened to that shot of yours?" the first caller asked him.

"I wish I knew," Gary answered with a laugh.

"The defense in the NBA is a whole lot tougher," Frank said to help him out.

"Yeah, that's true," Gary agreed. "Plus, I've been asked to push the ball a lot more than what I'm used to. I have less time out there to find my range."

"Well, you're a pro now. Don't you think you should be finding your range? You've been playing in the NBA for a year," the caller said.

"Yeah, well, maybe he will find it in one of these games," Frank butted in. "He's only in his second year. Next caller, Bobby."

"I've heard that you've been at a lot of the clubs around town, and that you like to party, Gary. You think that's messing up your game?" a brother asked.

I was eager to hear the answer to that question myself.

"Ah, I don't think that has anything to do with it. I mean, I'm young and I'm still in good shape, so I don't—"

"I thought North Carolina had a code of respect and discipline or something down there with Dean Smith," the caller responded, cutting him off.

"They do, but you know, people are people," Gary told him.

"Well, if you stopped partying so much and kept your focus on the game, maybe you'd do a lot better," the caller advised him.

"Okay, thanks for your call," Frank said. "Who's up next, Bobby?"

"This is Louise from southeast D.C., and I'm calling for my girlfriend, Myra. I just wanna ask Gary why he be try'na play people out like toys. My girlfriend really liked you."

Frank and I looked at each other through the studio glass. "Ah, only basketball-related questions on this show, sister," Frank interjected. "Bobby, next caller. If you didn't know, the show is called 'D.C. Sports Talk,' people," he reminded our listeners. It was a good thing for Gary that Frank was player friendly.

I cut the sister off the line and went to the next caller.

"I heard that you didn't want to come to Washington and that you were hoping to be drafted by the New Jersey Nets. Is that true?"

"Well, you know, when you get drafted you don't really have a say-so in who's gonna get you, but you go to whatever team, hoping to help out on the court and to have an impact. So I'm happy to be in Washington, I'm just looking forward to playing better and helping the team win more games."

Good answer, I thought. Gary handled himself pretty well for the rest of the show.

"It wasn't that bad, was it?" Frank asked him once we wrapped things up for the night.

Gary shook his head and sighed. "Man, them questions were coming from everywhere."

"Yeah, my fans do their research. It was a good show," Frank said, shaking Gary's hand.

Mr. Cooper was still at the station that night. He peeked out of his office and said, "Good show." That was rare for him to do. I was hoping that he knew it was my idea.

I walked Gary out to his car. He shook my hand and said, "Hey, thanks, man."

"Yeah, you did good," I told him.

He nodded. "You told me to make sure I was prepared."

"And you were ready. Now you just gotta try and get your game together," I told him.

Gary opened his car door and said, "Aw'ight, I'll call you up, man."

I walked back inside the station with Frank. "So Frank, if you leave, are you taking me with you?" I whispered. We laughed about it, but Frank knew I was serious. We hadn't talked about the rumored move to Baltimore for months, so I assumed there was no validity to it.

"Look, I brought you in here, didn't I? I damn near begged Dave to give you this job," he said. "So you know I gotta take you wit' me when I leave. But hey, how are things with you and Mona goin'?" he suddenly asked me. "I've been seeing her with you at all the games."

"We gettin' along," I lied.

"Oh yeah, so when is the marriage?"

"Are you kidding me? I'm not thinking about marriage with Mona. She sure ain't. She don't even want a boyfriend."

"You can believe that shit if you want to. She just needs somebody to be strong enough with her. She knows what guys she can pull along," he said with a grin.

"What are you saying, I'm weak?"

Frank just laughed at me. "Go on home and get a good night's sleep, Bobby."

I couldn't get Frank's comments off my mind that night. It was already clear to me that Mona was tying me down. Obviously, I was still not able to handle aggressive women. I got paranoid every time Mona asked about my whereabouts, and I hadn't even done anything.

Mona was studying for finals before the Christmas break, but I called her up that night with a bone to pick anyway. Frank had done it to me again.

"What is wrong with you?" she asked me. She could read my tone as soon as I started.

"Look, Mona, I don't think this is gonna work between us."

She was silent for a minute. "I've been thinking the same thing," she said to my surprise. "I don't think I'm ready for this. This relationship is just too damn stressful. I got other things to think about."

She took the words right out of my mouth. "We're still friends though, right?" Boy, did I feel relieved! The Mona situation had been killing me.

"Yeah, we're still cool, but I can't have sex with you anymore."

"Are you sure about that?" I teased.

Mona chuckled. "That's what got us in trouble in the first place. I don't know what I was thinking to try that with you."

"To try what?"

"You know, to be friends with you while having sex. It just doesn't work."

"It was your idea, not mine," I reminded her.

"I know it was. But I've just been thinking lately with finals and stuff coming up that I couldn't even concentrate because I was so worried about us."

"You were? I'm flattered," I said.

"You wasn't thinking about me?" she asked me.

"Yeah, too much."

Mona laughed. "And we said that we wouldn't do this to each other."

"We didn't know any better," I told her.

"Now I see what was up with that other girl you were friends with."

"Who, Faye?" I slipped and said. I had forgotten that I never told Mona her name.

Mona laughed and said, "Yeah, is that her name?"

I chuckled. "Yeah, that's her."

"Well, I know now that it's hard being friends with someone that you could really like. If you were just a stud, I could screw you and be on my merry way, but since I like you as a person it just made things more complicated."

"I know what you mean," I responded. "I didn't want to hurt you either, so I just prolonged things when I knew that we weren't getting along like we used to."

"Yeah, I know. Oh well, it was good while it lasted," she said. "And you can still take me to a couple of them games, too."

I didn't plan to respond to that.

"The Bullets lose all the time anyway," Mona added. "You don't have to take me if you don't want to."

"I'll take you to the Pistons game," I told her. I figured it was the least I could do since she was from Detroit and all.

"Okay, I can deal with that."

"Are you sure you're gonna be all right?" I asked her.

"Man, don't worry about me," Mona said. "I'm the last person you need to worry about. I mean, to be truthful, it was only a matter of time before this happened. I think you would have always worried me because you're just so laid back about everything. No offense, but I need a guy who's more . . . more passionate about things."

You mean a strong man that won't take no shit from you, I thought. Frank was right, but I decided to keep it to myself. I was getting off the hook with Mona, so why add insult to injury?

After hanging up with her I had second thoughts. We could have worked things out between us. We were both giving up without a fight. Then again, every relationship isn't meant to be, no matter how decent and loyal you are. I had new freedom to pursue whoever I wanted, but that didn't mean everything would be peaches and cream in the future. I was learning that most new relationships are unpredictable despite how wonderful they can seem in the beginning. A lasting alliance can only happen when you have two focused and committed partners, and Mona and I didn't have that kind of focus. We were both headed in different directions and at different speeds.

When Everything Is Going Fine . . .

I had ended my more-than-friends relationship with Mona, so I began to date other women regularly. It was nothing serious, though, and I preferred to keep it that way. I wanted a rest from the drama that serious commitments seemed to spark. I decided I didn't need that in my young life. I wanted to focus more on my career instead. I was stealing that page out of Mona's book. She was really focused on her career in radio, and had the straight A's in school and the excellent recommendations to prove it.

I was finally getting name recognition around town as a radio producer. Although I still wasn't making that much money, I felt at peace with my progress. Over the Christmas and New Year's holiday season, I went home to North Carolina and found that Brad and Brenda were expecting. Brenda was three months pregnant, so I would be an uncle to a little niece or nephew once the summer rolled around.

It was January 1989, and I was set to turn twenty-five in a few days. Things were really looking up for me. I was waking up with a smile on my face.

"Did you hear the news about your boy Gary Mitchell?" Frank called early one morning and asked me. It was barely nine o'clock, so I knew it must have been important.

"What news?" I asked him. Judging from Frank's tone, I thought maybe Gary had broken his leg and was out for the rest of the season or something. It didn't sound like any positive news.

"He was charged for rape last night," Frank told me.

My mouth dropped open. "Oh shit! Are you serious?" I already knew that he was. It was only a matter of time before Gary got himself into trouble with a woman. He had been begging for it.

Frank said, "I've been meaning to tell you to watch yourself around

Gary for a while, Bobby, but I guess I don't have to now. I mean, I like women too—God knows—but I learned a long time ago how to pick 'em. You can't be out there trying to fuck every one of 'em, Bobby. That's why I never went nowhere near Mona. I'm not *young enough* or *stupid enough* to make them kind of mistakes. Especially when you're a public figure. And I hope that *you're* not that young or that *stupid,* Bobby! You hear me? You're too good of a man to get mixed up into that shit."

I was speechless. I couldn't wait to talk to Gary to get the full scoop. It took me three days before I could reach him. It was the day before my twenty-fifth birthday.

"Man, the bitch is lying!" he told me. "She did every fuckin' thing on her own, and then she gon' yell rape!"

"She didn't say, 'No' or 'Stop' at any time?" I asked him. That was the big gender argument at the time. If a woman uttered the word "No," then that was supposed to be it.

Gary said, "Man, you know how that shit is. She says, 'No' and 'Stop,' and in the meantime, she's sucking your dick. I figured that was how she got her kicks off or something."

I didn't want to argue the point with Gary, but his case didn't sound good at all. I wasn't even halfway sympathetic. I had argued the same issue with Brad, years ago. Brad was lucky he never got a rape charge. He had this crazy notion that some women had to be convinced that they really want it. I thought it was ridiculous, but more men than not seemed to believe it.

"What did your lawyer say?" I asked Gary.

"Oh, you know she's after some money. These bitches are scandalous nowadays, man. My lawyer said that I was a target before I even touched her."

This is really interesting, I thought. Every woman was a target to Gary. He was finally getting some of his own medicine. Nevertheless, his rape charge soured my birthday date. I went out with another sister I met on the club scene, and I was afraid to lay a hand on her. It wasn't as if I had any money, because I didn't. It was just the principle of the thing. I had been with Gary, the women, the drinks, and had sex at the hotel. That was as close as you could get. I felt guilty by association. I hoped that Gary wouldn't take it too personal, but I wasn't planning on hanging out anymore. I couldn't afford to. I had a future to look forward to that could not sustain that type of negative publicity. Not to mention that I knew it was wrong. Gary knew it, too, he just couldn't help himself. It takes a mature and disciplined man to realize that he can't have every piece of candy in the candy store. I had prided myself on maturity, so it was no doubt the right thing to do.

•

In February I walked into Mr. Cooper's office and shut the door. He wanted to speak to me.

"You've come a long way since you first walked into this office, Bobby," he began. "You seem more self-confident and focused. Did you learn a lot?"

He was just giving me an old-fashioned pat on the back. I was hoping he was thinking about giving me a raise of some sort, or a promotion. "Yeah, I've learned a lot here," I told him.

He nodded and said, "I guess you heard the rumors about the station moving to Baltimore." He looked up at me to make sure I'd heard them.

I nodded back to him and said, "Yeah, I heard about it a while ago."

"Sit down, Bobby," he told me.

I had been standing up, thinking it would be a short chat. I took a seat in the chair in front of his desk and continued to listen.

"A lot of these small urban stations are being bought out by larger stations because they see a lot of money in the urban marketplace now," he explained to me. "This radio business is starting to get really hot."

Tell me something I didn't know, I was thinking.

"That's what's happening to us," he told me. "Nothing's final yet, but I'll be sure to put in a good word for you. I don't think I'm gonna be manager anymore when this thing happens, but I wanna make sure I take care of you."

I nodded again and said, "Thanks, I appreciate that."

"You're a good young man, Bobby, and I want to see you go all the way to the top."

I smiled and thought about the night I spent with his daughter. I wonder if he still would have considered me a good man if he knew about it. It *was* consensual, though.

"Now you're gonna have a lot of jealous people around you, so never let anyone know your next move," he warned me. "You keep as much to yourself as you can. This can be a real cutthroat business sometimes, and you want to be able to protect yourself. You understand me?"

"Yeah, I understand you."

As soon as I walked out of Mr. Cooper's office to prepare for the

"Community Watch" show, Tammy Richards was all over me for information.

"What did he say to you in there?" she asked. Tammy looked like a brown raven, with sharp eyes and nose and a narrow face. She was tall and lanky with a bounce in her step. She never talked to me about anything outside of her show, the station, the ratings, and the weather. I wasn't gonna trust her. After what Frank told me, I figured Tammy was dying to use any angle she could to promote and protect herself. She never cared much about anything I ever tried to do, and I had put together some excellent shows for her. She never once said, "Thank you."

I thought of the safest lie to tell her. I knew I didn't want to tell her that Mr. Cooper had commended me on my work. That would have made her jealous. I didn't need that getting in the way of us putting on a good show. I wanted everything I was a part of to maintain professionalism.

"He asked me about some of the new sponsors we've been working with," I said.

"What did he say about them?"

"He said that the marketing department is doing a good job in helping us out."

Tammy frowned at me. "What does that have to do with you?"

"I guess he just wanted to talk to someone about it."

Tammy stormed off for the recording room. "Is our guest here yet?" she asked with her back turned to me.

"Not yet," I told her. I had successfully given her the runaround.

She looked back and said, "It figures."

Later on that night I told Frank about the incident. "I told you how she is, Bobby. She don't tell you anything, but she wants you to turn around and tell her *everything*? She's crazy! She's one of those power-hungry sisters. I shouldn't even call her a sister, since she slept with the enemy."

"You never slept with the enemy?" I asked. The question just slipped out of my mouth.

"Never," Frank answered proudly. "And I never will. But getting back to business, Bobby. So Cooper said that the station was moving, or not?"

"He said that he didn't know yet."

Frank grimaced. "Mmm-hmm. I see how this is going. It's gonna be one of those last-minute things. You be ready for it, Bobby. This is the kind of shit that I hate about this business. They'll just pack shit up and move on you overnight. That's why it's better to work for union stations."

"Is it that bad?" I asked him. I don't know why, but I felt as if everyone was exaggerating. I guess it's because I hadn't been in the business that long.

Frank smiled and said, "Boy, you got *oceans* behind your ears. You watch and see what happens."

•

Everything remained at peace at the station for a couple of weeks, and Gary Mitchell's rape charge had been thrown out because of unsubstantial evidence. Economically speaking, I had finally gotten some real credit with a spending limit of six hundred dollars. Frank and Mona both told me to buy a couple of small things and pay the money right back. They said that that would look good for my credit ratings. I didn't want to use the thing at all. I figured just having an unsecured card was credit enough, but what did I know? I needed a few new pairs of pants and some shoes anyway, so I decided to take their advice.

When I got outside and walked around to my car, I noticed a woman pulling into the parking spot that I could have sworn I had. "MY CAR!" I yelled. The first thing I thought was that I had gotten towed. I had paid all of my parking tickets, though. I only had a few of them, and they were taken care of months ago. I stood there in the cold for a second, confused about what to do. I took a jog up the block to Fourteenth Street and back around the corner to Thirteenth. I guess I thought I would see my car lying around somewhere. Then I decided to run inside and call the police to report it stolen.

I got back to my apartment to find my phone ringing. I answered it, prepared to tell whoever it was that I would call them back.

"Is this Bobby Dallas?" a white man's voice of authority asked. It had that rigid detective sound to it. Being in the radio business, I was a pro at voices.

"Yeah, this is Bobby Dallas," I answered optimistically.

"You own a black Honda Prelude?"

"Yes I do, and it's missing right now," I told him.

"We have it down here at the station. I'll have an officer pick you up outside your door and bring you down "

"Thanks," I told him. "That was fast," I said to myself after I hung up.

The officer who picked me up from my apartment complex was a brother. He explained to me that my car was stolen by an underaged youth who apparently took it for a joyride. The boy was stopped close to Howard's campus on Georgia Avenue by an officer who thought he looked mighty small to be driving a car.

"What a way to celebrate Black History Month," the brother said as he let me out at the station. It was off of Sixteenth Street, not that far from where I lived.

"Yeah, tell me about it," I told him.

I went inside and asked about my car. I had never been inside a police station before. It was dull and messy like the big-city police stations I saw on TV and in movies.

"Bobby Dallas, I'm Detective Stephens." I recognized the white man's voice as he shook my hand. He was a large man in his forties, wearing a pale blue shirt and a checkered yellow tie. Policemen have never had a reputation for dressing well. I don't think I would have been that concerned about how I looked if my job collected bad news every day either. "We arrested a fourteen-year-old youth, driving your car around Georgia Avenue and Harvard Streets."

That's right at Howard, I thought to myself.

"Would you like to press charges?" Detective Stephens asked me. He was all ready for it.

"Was the car damaged?" I asked him.

"Well, your ignition is all torn up, but we didn't see any other damages to the car. Do you remember locking the door at all?"

"I guess I didn't lock it," I answered. I wasn't sure, and since it had been stolen, I couldn't give myself the benefit of the doubt.

"So you're gonna press charges?" he asked me again.

I began to think it over. The thief was only fourteen, he had not really damaged my car, I assumed that he was black, and it was Black History Month. I shook my head. "Naw, that's all right," I said. "Just let me see him." I wanted to see what this fourteen-year-old looked like.

"You're not pressing charges?" the detective asked me again. He really wanted to book the little guy. That only made my decision stronger.

"No, I'm not pressing charges," I repeated to him.

"If you don't press charges, he's just gonna go out there and do it again," the detective ranted.

I figured I'd let someone else press the charges then. I didn't respond to him. Detective Stephens then led me to the room where the boy was being held. He was a little guy indeed, with the same penny-brown skin as me. He tried to look tough to disguise his fear, but I could tell that it was an act. He couldn't even look me in the eyes.

"Are you sure you don't want to press charges?" I was asked one final time.

I had made my decision and I intended to stick with it. "No, I'm not," I said for the last time.

The little car thief looked up at me for a second. When I caught his eye, I said, "Hey, don't do this again." He let his head droop back down to the big table in front of him. I hoped that he heard me, because the next victim may not be as forgiving.

Detective Stephens, with a deep, noisy sigh, said, "Aw, isn't that sweet," while he led me out of the room. "He's gonna do it again," he insisted.

I felt like asking that white man what made him so sure. "Because he's black!" I wanted to yell. Most likely though, Detective Stephens was right. You just can't change some of the youth. If they want to be criminals, that's what they're gonna be. It's a lot harder to be a doctor or a lawyer than it is to be a criminal. I just wanted to see my car and get out of that place.

My ignition was damaged just like the detective told me.

"There it is," he said. He gave me a demonstration. "Now you just connect these two wires here, and wa-la." I guess he had enough of me. He walked away and went on about his job.

I looked at my ignition ring and wondered how much it would cost to get it fixed. Then I saw a thirty-something black woman rushing for the station. I assumed that she was the boy's mother. I thought about asking her to pay to get my ignition fixed. I imagined the woman telling me how she didn't have any money, how sorry she was, and how Junior's usually such a good boy, while crying and smacking her son upside the head. I guess I knew those police shows well, because I could see the entire scene in my head. I decided to just drive off and get the damned thing fixed myself. I wondered what else could go wrong in the new year. Usually bad news comes in bunches.

Sure enough, at the station that night, Frank told me that he was quitting.

"Shit, Frank, you could have at least given me a warning," I told him.

"I gave you a warning months ago, Bobby."

"I meant like a more recent warning," I said. "What's going on anyway?"

"Man, fuck him!" Frank hollered, referring to Mr. Cooper. They hadn't exactly been getting along over the past couple of months. "They gave that old man an option to keep the station right here, and his senile ass didn't take it. If he didn't want to be manager anymore, then all he had to do was recommend somebody else. I could have been the manager, but I'm not goin' to Baltimore!"

I knew that something was going on at the station when Tammy Richards was acting funny earlier, but since she never told me anything, I didn't really know until Frank came in. It wasn't every day that Mr. Cooper talked to me, Mr. Last-to-Know-Anything.

"So when are you planning on doing this?" I asked Frank. I was hoping that he meant in a week or so, so I could gather my thoughts on what I planned to do.

"I feel like walking out of here tonight," he said.

"You can't do that, Frank. We have guests booked for the rest of this week."

"Bobby, frankly, I don't give a fuck," Frank said with fire in his eyes.

One thing I noticed about older men is that when they're pissed off about something, they are *really* pissed! I couldn't calm Frank down.

"Matter of fact, fuck it! I'm gettin' out of here right now!" Frank grabbed his things and marched for the front door. I felt like grabbing him and getting him to stay, but I realized that if I even made a move in that direction, we probably would have been fighting.

Frank walked out the door, jumped in his car, and took off.

What the hell do I do now? I thought to myself.

Someone went and told Mr. Cooper about it. "Bobby, can I see you for a minute?" he called to me. I walked inside his office, shut the door, and sat down. "You're gonna have to do the sports show by yourself for the rest of the week. I have to figure out what I want to do," he told me.

I was shocked that he had so much confidence in me. "D.C. Sports Talk" was the third-highest-rated show at our station. There was a smaller recording room that would allow a host to work the audio console with guests in the room. I had to talk myself into remaining calm and pulling it off. Then I thought about Frank Watts again and panicked. I was sure that he would be listening. What if he didn't take too kindly to me filling in on his show? I could screw up my relationship with the very man who brought me in. I couldn't do it.

I walked back into Mr. Cooper's office and told him my predicament. Surprisingly, he understood. I thought he was going to tell me some jazz about having to do things that are hard or something. I was thankful that he let me off the hook. He didn't have to do it. He could have forced me to take over the show or walk out with Frank, but instead of doing that, we decided to cancel the shows for the week and run previously taped shows that were classics with our audience.

I called Mona up that night and told her the news.

"I knew that was gonna happen," she said. "That place was never too stable."

"You think I can get a job over at WOL?" I was just shooting in the wind.

"No way," Mona answered me. "They have a waiting list for jobs over there. So unless they're calling you, forget about it."

I hung up with her and thought about other stations in the D.C. area. I wasn't looking forward to being moved up to Baltimore either. There had to be *someplace* I could work. I was hoping that Frank would find something in a couple of days and let me know. We were a team.

My next day on the job, Tammy Richards followed Frank's lead and walked out herself. That didn't shock me at all. She had always complained about WMSC anyway.

•

The station was moved to Baltimore that next week. I couldn't believe how quickly things had happened. Frank wasn't exaggerating after all. I believe that his and Tammy's walkouts had a lot to do with speeding things up, though. I didn't understand why they didn't stay and fight for their positions like I planned to do. It was just my luck that the two people I worked with had the biggest egos. I still hadn't gotten a call from Frank, so I decided to call him up instead of waiting.

Frank seemed undisturbed, as if he was on vacation. "Hey, what's happenin', Bobby?"

"You found anything yet?" I asked him.

"They didn't ask you to go with them?"

"I have a meeting with the new management in Baltimore tomorrow," I told him.

"Well, take whatever they give you, man."

I was confused. "Actually, I wanted to keep working with you if you had something else," I said. I felt attached to Frank. He was my professional blanket.

"Bobby, I need a break for a while, so I'm not going right back into it. You go ahead and make the moves you need to make, and maybe we'll hook up again in the future." Frank seemed like he was in a hurry and rushed me off the phone before I had a chance to respond to him.

"Damn!" I yelled at my apartment walls. My meeting in Baltimore the next day didn't go any better. Once I saw how many white guys they had walking around at the place, I knew what my fate would be.

"Well, we're looking to go in a different direction with the station up here, ah, Bobby," the new manager told me. He was a thirty-something white guy wrapped in excess baby fat. He struck me as the kind of man who would never exercise. He seemed pretty reasonable as a boss, though. Nevertheless, I didn't have a counterargument for him. I was drained from the entire process. It was like being caught up in a hurricane, and I couldn't find my bearings.

I just took my release from the station lying down. In a sense, I expected to be let go. I guess Frank and Tammy already knew that it was more emotionally acceptable to quit than to be told you have no more use. I had to learn that lesson the hard way.

•

I don't know what made me think I could go out on a date that night. I didn't feel too romantic after just losing my job.

"That's the kind of business that you're in," my date said nonchalantly. She was a pretty, cheerful sister named Robin. I met her at the downtown library on Ninth Street, believe it or not. I was doing research on sports books and happened to strike up a conversation with her. She was twenty-seven and worked for the D.C. public school system.

We were just riding around in the Maryland area, aimlessly. I told her some of the things that had happened to me over the past month or so.

"You just have to shake it off and get out and find a new station," Robin was saying.

I was pretty much numb. We had ironically driven out to Greenbelt, the area where WPGC Radio broadcasted from in Maryland.

"Hey, we're near Greenbelt Mall," Robin noticed. "Come on, Bobby, let's go in the mall and window-shop. That always cheers *me* up."

She just didn't get it. When a man no longer has a job, he doesn't go window-shopping! "I don't think I'm in the mood for that right now," I told her as calmly as I could.

Robin looked over at me and said, "Okay, they have movie theaters in there, too. I'll pay for it." She wasn't gonna let it rest until I agreed to do something in the name of cheering myself up.

"Okay, let's go to a movie then," I told her.

"Good. I mean, you'll get another job. This isn't the end of the world. A lot of people lose jobs and move on. That's a fact of life in any profession. I could see if you had a family to support," she said to me with a smile.

Robin had that older woman's maturity about her. However, I was beginning to get upset. Talking about the regularity of losing a job wasn't helping me any. It wasn't a "fact of life" for me. I had never lost a job before.

"Look, could we stop talking about this, please?" I didn't want to hear any more about it.

"Okay," she calmly obliged.

I had gone overboard. I grabbed her hand and told her that I was sorry.

"Mmm-hmm, don't even worry about it," she responded. "It's all a part of being a man. Instead of talking things out, you all wanna keep it to yourselves and have attitudes with people. I understand that perfectly."

Robin was trying her best to be supportive, but it didn't matter. Her sarcasm caught me off guard, and I was in no emotional condition for it.

I stopped walking all of a sudden. Robin stopped and looked back at me. I walked over to her and said, "Look, ah, if you don't mind, I'm not really feeling up for this tonight. So let's just, ah . . . end this date. And I'm sorry for wasting your time."

Robin nodded and said, "Okay."

I felt terrible about it, but what else could I do? If I had gone through with the date, she would have had me on my worst behavior. I just felt that it was safer, for both of us, to end the night before things got ugly.

I drove Robin back home in near silence. She climbed out of the car before I could open the door for her and said, "You have a lot of learning to do about life."

I thought that I had learned a lot already, but she was right. I was only twenty-five, and I expected to live for at least another quarter of a century. There were many things I hadn't experienced yet.

It occurred to me at that moment that I needed more male friends to talk to. There were a few guys from Howard that I knew, but I never hung out with any of them. I was the biggest loner in the world. It seemed like I had been hanging out with only women for years. Brad always said that I was the "friend type" with girls. I attracted lady "friends" like a magnet, but they couldn't help me understand my manly emotions. I needed other men to help me out with that.

I drove back to my apartment and just sat inside the car for a while, smoking another cigarette. Then that little melody jumped in my head again: "Pearrrll Day-vis. What have you been up tooo, girrrl?" I started to laugh, looking at myself in the mirror. I was going out of my damn mind, with no job! I told myself that I would leave women the hell alone for a while, or at least until I got myself together. No woman should settle for an unfulfilled man, and at the time, that's what I was, because that's how I felt.

•

It may sound crazy, but I took a trip to Las Vegas shortly after losing my job to get away from things and clear my head. I got a dynamite deal from a travel agency that had a cancellation on a nonrefundable down payment, so I ended up with a four-day, three-night vacation for an incredible $345. I figured it would be an excellent way to break in my credit card.

So there I was, out in Las Vegas at twenty-five years old with no woman and no job, watching all of that money floating around from big spenders hopping in and out of limos and such, while plenty of poor suckers walked around blowing their life savings with lucky rabbits' feet in their pockets hoping to strike it rich. It was a perfect representation of America's fake dream.

Everything was a lot simpler to me while up in New York with Pearl. I was struggling, but I was satisfied with myself and with what I had. If I could only have had those days back with that simple frame of mind when I was satisfied with so little, I would pay anything. The trip out to Las Vegas only made me see that my days of being satisfied with less were in the past, and that America was forcing me to get ahead or be left behind, because in the decade of the nineties even keeping up with the Joneses would be like swimming upstream.

When everything is going fine, I thought to myself . . . *look out below.*

Out of Limbo

Limbo is defined as a region of lost souls who float around in empty space, ignorant of the path that could lead them to the light. That was me, for the next three years. I floated around from radio station to radio station as a producer and then as a little-known DJ briefly in Baltimore and in Virginia, until finally landing somewhere where I could host a talk show back in D.C. It took six years in the radio business for that to happen, and even then, it was only as a substitute on a small international station broadcasting from the Adams Morgan area. By then it was 1992, and I was twenty-eight years old.

It seemed like everyone had passed me by during those limbo years. Mona Freeman graduated from Howard and went back home to Detroit to squeeze her way onto a hot FM station. Pamela Cooper finally married, passed the bar exam, and was hired by a law firm in Alexandria, Virginia. Frank Watts and Tammy Richards moved on to host shows elsewhere. And back home in North Carolina, my brother and sister-in-law had moved farther south to Charlotte. Brenda was expecting their second child. Their first child was a girl, my niece Aminah.

During my limbo years, Brad and I became as close as when we were kids, and he helped me out financially when I needed it. He worked as a leasing consultant for a suburban mall. He had big plans of buying enough cheap commercial property in Charlotte to open up his own mall one day. Little bro was doing his thing.

As for me, no matter what, I just wouldn't let go of my love for radio. It takes time to break in. I grew to understand that. My parents lost their patience, though. My father was behind me all the way until I had to borrow money to pay rent and other bills while in between jobs. That's when he decided to tell me, "Maybe you need to find something more stable until you can get a break in this radio thing." The smaller stations

175

where newcomers could gain experience and build reputations were being gobbled up by the larger stations all over the country, and that meant limited opportunities for me.

I got desperate enough at one point to call back up to New York. I found that Mr. Payton had sold WHCS in Harlem. The new owners came in, revamped the place, and made it the station that I always thought it could be. I couldn't get a spot on that station once it was under new management if I broke a leg off. They were giving WLIB a run for the money.

I should have never left that place. I kept finding out from other radio professionals that they would have killed to have any job at a station in New York City. I guess I took the experience for granted. It would have taken me a lot less time to make it big if I had stayed in New York for three more years. If I could do it all over again, I would have forced myself to forget about Pearl Davis and moved on with my career in The Big Apple.

Pearl had started me on a blind downward spiral where I spent far too much time worrying about women instead of aggressively focusing on my radio career like I needed to. It was just like my NBA friend Gary Mitchell. His partying took away from his focus on the game. Eventually, the Bullets traded him to Golden State, which was limbo to any up-and-coming basketball star.

Anyway, I met this brother at a conference on Howard University's campus at the Blackburn Center in November 1991. I was there to talk to a few of the lecturers about appearing on a show at the station where I worked in Arlington, Virginia. The brother told me that he could use someone with radio experience to help out on his show a few days a week. Because of many changes in his life, including running a new fabric and design shop he owned on Georgia Avenue, he told me that he didn't always have the time or the energy to host his show as much as he had in the past.

The brother's name was Abu, or that's what he called himself, with no last name. He told me that it was a Swahili name meaning "nobility." He was a big guy dressed in colorful African garb with a matching hat. I asked him about the pay, and he told me that it wasn't a problem. WUCI, "The International Station," was also a union station. Abu said that he could guarantee me two hundred dollars a show if I joined. I told him to put it in writing. I had been promised similar good deals in my struggling radio career that all fell apart.

Abu said that first he wanted to see how sharp I was, so he brought me on the show in December as a guest. The station was located on the third floor of a building on Eighteenth Street Northwest, in the heart of Adams Morgan. I sat down inside the recording room in front of the microphone and was perfectly at ease. I was *more* than ready for my break.

I liked Abu's style as soon as he did his introduction. I could tell from that alone that I would be in good hands.

"This is Brother Abu, bringing information to your ears once again from The International Station, WUCI. And the show is called . . . 'The Awakenings.' "

I smiled and nodded my head, imagining what it sounded like to the audience out there with their radios tuned in. I couldn't wait to be introduced.

Abu said, "I've been asked by people a lot over the years the same question of 'How do you get into the radio business?' Well, today I have a young brother in the studio by the name of Bobby Dallas, who's an aggressive, young radio professional, and he's gonna share his experiences in the business with you so you can see if I was lying to ya.

"How are you doing today, Bobby?"

"I'm starving to get a break. That's what everybody does at the bottom, unless you have an uncle who owns the station," I said. There was no sense in being shy about it. The more straight you were, the more the people seemed to love you.

Brother Abu laughed. "So it's the old who-do-you-know game?" he asked me.

"Yes, sir-ree, and that's in any profession. In fact, I started off at a tiny station in New York, and the only reason I got that job was because I knew somebody who worked there before. And I think she was close with the owner in more than a business way."

Brother Abu had another laugh. "So it's the old sleep-around game, too."

"Whatever works, for some people. But you know what they say, 'Sometimes what gets you there is what keeps you there,' so if you sleep around to get to the top, you might have to keep on sleepin' even when you're not tired anymore."

I was rolling! I was doing it! I was sharp, crisp, and to the point, and Brother Abu just couldn't stop laughing. "So you're saying to watch the way that you break into the business then?" he asked me.

"I would say so, yeah. But that's because I'm a good guy. A lot of bad guys end up with the jobs, though. That's because they'll do anything to get there. They come into the business with sharpened knives, and wait for you to turn your back. But I haven't really tried to associate with those kind of people."

"So you're saying that our business can be vicious?"

"Have you ever seen *The Godfather?*" I joked. "Naw, it's not that bad. You just have to have a whole lot of love for it so you can survive the ups and downs that you're gonna go through, that's all. It's just like any other competitive profession."

"What makes radio so competitive?" Brother Abu was a pro. He didn't need a script in front of him and he never stuttered.

"R-A-T-I-N-G-S. Ratings," I answered him. "That's what everybody's after. If your show has the listeners, then that means you have a certain stature in the radio community and with the advertisers. It's like being a platinum singer, a best-selling author, or a tenured professor at a university. With good ratings you have clout, and clout moves people."

Brother Abu looked at his watch and decided it was time to take our first break. He would play a jazz song or two, announce a sponsor, and then go back on the air. His format was pretty loose. I liked that, too. He didn't have to follow any rigid time schedule.

Brother Abu brought us back on the air with a shocking announcement: "You're listening to The International Station, WUCI. I'm your host, Brother Abu, and this is 'The Awakenings.' Our guest in the studio today is Bobby Dallas, who is soon to be my *co*host on the show, 'The Awakenings,' whenever we can work it out to get him back in here."

I smiled for the rest of the hour.

"That was a very good show, brother. What do you think?" Abu asked me afterward.

I nodded. "Yeah, it was." I was really excited! I hadn't felt that good in a while!

"That's how a show is supposed to go, smooth and informative," he said. "A lot of these other shows may have good ratings, but a lot of times they're airing a bunch of nonsense. A lot of these new talents are acting a fool for the ratings."

"I agree," I told him.

He said, "Never compromise yourself to compete with these other people. If you stay true to yourself and true to the people, then no one can ever stop you from being a success. And you continue to get your commitments on paper. I didn't do that when I first started out sixteen years ago. That's good thinking to have those contracts. Without that, you got nothing but a handshake, and you know what a handshake means in this business—it's next to nothing."

•

I couldn't wait to get home and call Brad with the news. Brad said, "So did you sign a contract this time?"

"Not yet. He's in the process of putting it together. He just wanted to see how I would do on the show first."

Brad sighed. "I don't know what to say, man. I mean, it seems like you're on your way, but we thought that a few times before."

"Yeah, but this time I'm hosting a show instead of being behind the scenes or playing records."

"You never applied for a position at this station before?" Brad asked me of WUCI.

"Actually, I knew of it, but it was mostly a foreign language station, you know, with Ecuadorians and Ethiopians and whatnot."

"And you never heard of this Brother Abu before?"

"Well, I knew there had to be a few brothers or a sister at the station, but I didn't know if I would have fit in with their format. I mean, it was basically foreign music and bilingual talk, and since I wasn't shopping around an idea for my own show, I figured there was nothing over there for me to do. I was tired of being a switchboard operator, and I couldn't even do that if I didn't know the language they were speaking."

Brad laughed and said, "Yeah, I see. Well, go for it then, man. Just make sure you sign a contract."

•

The program director at WUCI was a thirty-something, out-of-the-closet white man named John Sprier. He liked my energy. It was okay by him to have me sub for Brother Abu, so they were able to hammer out a contract for me to sign by late January 1992. I finally found the light at the end of the tunnel, and I wasn't giving up that opportunity for anything or anyone.

My first show without Brother Abu was in February with Sister Niara Vaughn. She had established a private, African-centered pre- and elementary school and was dressed in African garb like Abu wore.

"In a school population that is predominantly black, why is there such a struggle to deny an African-centered or Afrocentric approach?" I asked her. The idea of an educational approach that taught black kids from their own cultural perspective made good sense to me. It seemed like it would make education a lot more relevant to them.

"Well, the educational system of America was not initially set up with black children in mind, so they, meaning those who control the nationwide curriculum, don't see any need to change things," she answered me.

"Now, this is not at all a recent thing, because I had black schoolteachers down in North Carolina who always managed to sneak in something about black culture, but it was never a movement to change the entire system. Where is this new push coming from?" I asked. My mother was a strong supporter of black studies for children, and so was my sister-in-law, Brenda.

"It's coming from everywhere," Sister Niara answered. "The parents, the teachers, the community leaders. What we've been seeing, just in Washington, D.C., over the past five to ten years are increasing numbers of black schoolchildren who have no idea that their ancestors contributed anything positive to this world. That is very false, and very sad. These are the same kids who continue to be dropouts and troublemakers with no sense of self-worth."

"Okay now, what white educators are saying, I guess, is that, 'We're not going to throw out a system that works just because black students lack self-esteem, and then create a system that focuses largely on black achievements just to make you *feel* better,' " I insinuated.

"And that's where they're wrong," Sister Niara responded. "The present educational system continues to perpetuate a false reality of Europeans bringing everything of any significance to this world. And that's false. So by *not* telling the truth, or not focusing in on what *all* people contributed to the world, we have an educational system that is basically a lie. Columbus *did not* discover America."

"So why not add the truth instead of bringing down the walls?" I asked her.

She smiled and said, "Well, you can't add the truth to a lie. That would not be a correct approach to teaching. You have to eradicate the lie and build up the truth. To add the truth to a lie would be like taking half of a bath. If you're only half clean, then that means you're still dirty."

I laughed and said, "But I cleaned my face and my arms, Momma!"

Sister Niara chuckled and responded, "Good. Now you go back in that tub and clean your torso, your legs, your toes, and where the sun don't shine. Then I want you to shampoo your hair and wash behind your ears."

•

"You're doing good work, Bobby. You might be able to take over soon," Brother Abu said to me over the phone that night. He was busy running his fabric shop. He was also trying to open a vegetarian restaurant on Georgia Avenue. I guess the radio business had been good to him.

Brother Abu believed in black ownership like my family did. However, the only thing I owned at the time was a car and my college diploma, and my car was overdue for a trade-in. I was commuting from Arlington, Virginia, and putting a lot of miles on it until I made enough money and felt secure enough to move back into the District. I made that move in July, after my half-year lease was up.

I moved into an apartment complex in the Adams Morgan area right off of the famous Rock Creek Park and near the Washington National Zoo. It was a very convenient location. Rock Creek Park pretty much connected me to the rest of the city, and it was fun to drive through if you liked dangerous curves. Rock Creek Park was like a giant snake.

Things were looking up for me again, but every time it looked good before, something went wrong. I was half expecting my life to go wrong again after a while. When it didn't, I just kept on rolling.

I still hadn't had any serious relationships since Mona. I was preoccupied with survival during my limbo years, so I didn't have much time to think about women. But of course, as soon as things started going well for me again, I began to feel a touch of loneliness. It's funny how when you stay busy you don't mind being alone, but once you have a little free time on your hands, loneliness can kill you. It makes a lot of sense, too. That's why so many cunning brothers with plenty of free time and zeal are the biggest womanizers there are; they don't have anything else to do. Women, therefore, become an interesting challenge to them.

I was still smoking cigarettes. However, I went back to the macho Marlboro brand. I got tired of explaining to people why I was smoking Newport Stripes. I had to let Pearl Davis go anyway. I had to release her from my mind. Of course, that was easier said than done. Every time I saw models on advertisements or sexy women in videos and movies I thought of Pearl again. I needed to stop blaming things on her and move on with my life. Pearl surely wasn't thinking about me.

I was substituting as host for Brother Abu at least two times a week and sometimes three. Then he had me interview a sister from Ohio who was a romance writer. I didn't know it at the time, but she was also trying to break into the radio business.

"This is Bobby Dallas, your host on the show called 'The Awakenings,' on WUCI, The International Station. Our guest today is a sister from Akron, Ohio, romance writer Kathy Teals.

"How are you doing today, sister?"

Kathy said, "Let me see, my feet are hurting, I have jet lag from flying back out here from Oakland, California, I'm hungry, and I could use a massage from a man with big hands."

I was skeptical of her. She struck me as a Tammy Richards type, recklessly out for self. She had the physical frame of a female bodybuilder with short-cut hair and a cute brown face. She would have probably said that I was intimidated by her, and she would have been right. But before I prejudged her too badly, I went on with the show.

"In other words, you've felt a lot better on other days."

"Yeah, but you have to move on anyway, Bobby," she responded. "That's what I write about in a lot of my books, women that could do it on their own, because we're in an era where you can't count on anyone but yourself to survive. So if someone gives you a helping hand in the nineties, without wanting something in return, then that's a plus."

"But isn't a romance book based on a love affair between a man and a woman?" I asked her.

"Yes, but in my books these men are *wants* and not *needs*. Because when you feel that you *need* a man to make your life complete, or need *anything* for that matter, you start losing touch with your internal power. You end up feeling more empty and desperate than anything else. And those are issues that I explore in my books. They're educational as well as entertaining."

I warmed up to Kathy. She wasn't that bad after all. I was all worked up for nothing. "The titles are *Full Moon, Truth and Consequences,* and *One-Night Stand, Forever,*" I read from my notes.

"Interesting titles, right?" she asked me.

"Yeah, you beat me to it," I responded.

"Well, we all know what that full moon can do," she said with a laugh. "One-night stands happen every night in America to somebody, but I wanted to explore a situation where a one-night stand turns into a long-lasting love affair."

"That happens every night, too," I told her.

"Yeah, but this guy is married."

"And?" I asked her with a grin.

"Yeah, I guess you're right, some brothers need a leash."

I didn't like that comment, but it was my fault, I guess, so I had to keep things going. "*Truth and Consequences,* what's the storyline for that one?"

"Well, it's sort of like, you know how we all have skeletons in the closet? Well, what happens when you let those skeletons out *voluntarily* versus someone *finding out* about them?"

"Does it make that much of a difference?" I asked her.

"Yes it does."

"Why?"

"Well, if someone tells you something because they want to be honest with you, then you can gain a certain respect for that person. Now of course, that doesn't mean that you're gonna *like* it. But if you *find out* something that they *didn't* tell you, then that's a whole different story."

"Do you stay with that person if they're honest?"

"That depends on what it is. If a guy tells me he's married with five kids, but he loves me, then I have to tell him, 'Thank you very much, now go on back home to your wife and family.' If he tells me he used to be bisexual, then I have to say, 'Thanks, but no thanks.' "

"So it sounds to me like these guys are better off lying," I responded with a laugh. I was joking, of course.

"Have you ever lied?" she asked me.

"Not about anything major."

"But you *have* lied."

"Sometimes the truth is not worth the consequences," I told her. I was getting myself in deeper trouble.

"See, now I should read you, but I can't because you're being honest," she said with a smile.

"Oh, so I guess the truth is all right after all."

"Yeah, but if you're using truths and lies only to your advantage, then I'd probably have to call you a D-O-G."

"Oh, no, not one of those!" I yelled. I was having a good time with it.

"Yes, get back out in the yard! I'll throw you a bone out the window!" Kathy Teals responded. "Bad doggy!"

Before I knew it, we had gotten totally off the subject. "Ah, getting back to the romance books," I said, redirecting the conversation. I couldn't remember what point we were on. "What were we talking about again?" I asked her.

We both burst out laughing. I had no idea what Brother Abu was thinking about that show. I don't think he would have been too thrilled about it. "The Awakenings" began to sound just like a lot of those other shows with the high ratings and low intellect. John Sprier, the program director, loved it, though.

"You know what?" he said to us after the show. "I think you guys have something. I really like the chemistry here. And you know, relationships are a hot subject in the black community right now. We could produce an entire show around it. We could call it 'Talk with Bobby and Kathy.' "

Author Terry McMillan's third book, *Waiting to Exhale,* was out and selling fast. The black relationship issue was the rave, and John Sprier was ready and willing to capitalize on it. They already had a gay talk show on WUCI.

"That sounds like a plan to me," Kathy told him. She looked at me and said, "We could have the man's versus the woman's point of view on everyday subjects and then have call-ins. I think it would be a hit."

John Sprier looked at me. It was my decision. Things were happening too fast for me. I felt more comfortable with slowing things down and thinking it over. That Kathy Teals was quick on the draw. "But I'm already under contract to substitute for Brother Abu," I responded. I was trying to back down, but John wouldn't let me.

"That's no problem," he said. "I think this show could be a lot hotter for you. We could have a new contract drawn up within a week or two. I really like this, this energy you two have here. I'll be behind it all the way."

That probably meant a competitive time slot to boot. "The Awakenings" aired from one to three in the afternoons, Monday through Friday. Out of curiosity, I asked John what time slot he envisioned for "Talk with Bobby and Kathy."

"I'd push to have it right after rush hour, between seven and nine."

"Monday through Friday?" Kathy asked him.

"Well, maybe we'd try to start it off on Thursdays and Fridays to see how it does. Or maybe even on a Sunday morning."

I thought about black people going to church on Sunday mornings and didn't think it would be a good idea. "Thursdays and Fridays would probably be a lot better to start with. Those are prime nights for dates."

John nodded and said, "Yeah, that's what I figured. Those would be the *best* nights, I think. So, you want to try it out?" he asked me.

I looked at Kathy Teals and asked, "But you don't live here, do you?"

John and Kathy smiled at each other. "Actually, she just moved out here a couple of weeks ago," John told me.

"I didn't know that," I responded. It was beginning to sound like a set-up. Maybe John had plans of trying Kathy out all along, using me to break her in. Program directors do that a lot in the radio business, pairing two people they think had complementary talents.

"Kathy was on a show with Brother Abu last year," he explained to me. "At that time, she ran the idea by me of having a relationship-based talk show similar to the 'Hotline for Men.' With her show, of course, relating to men and women."

He smiled and said, "Well, with Brother Abu being married and an older guy and all, it wasn't his kind of thing. But you, Bobby, you're a lot younger, single, and in tune with the dating game. I figured if I paired you with Kathy, you two guys could pull off that kind of show. Especially now. I mean, with, ah, Terry McMillan's book selling like it is right now, this show would really be a blast."

Kathy nodded and said, "No question."

I was right, it was a set-up. Nevertheless, it could have been a blessing in disguise to get the big break I needed to really secure my name on the air. I had been through enough crazy situations with women to contribute some good dialogue on the subject.

"Let me think it over for a few days," I told them.

"Oh, sure, and in the meantime I'll run the idea past Stacy."

Stacy was the station manager, an enthusiastic white woman in her mid-forties. WUCI was an extremely diverse place to work. The slogan "The International Station" was well deserved.

•

"Bobby, would you like to get something to eat and go see a movie or something? I have nothing else to do for the rest of the day," Kathy said to me. We were walking out of the station together.

I was confused. I thought she was all into the nineties black woman doing her own thing and all. "Would this be like a date?" I responded with a smile.

She smiled back at me. "No, it would be more like two people catching a bite to eat and checking out a movie."

I didn't have anything else to do that day either. "Have you ever eaten at Montego Bay?" I asked her.

"Yeah, good choice," she said.

We walked up Eighteenth Street to the Caribbean restaurant and got a table outside. I had only done that with women I had ulterior motives with. I didn't know what to think of Kathy. I guess in my years of limbo I had fallen out of the friendship thing with women. I either slept with them or I didn't. In any case, I kept moving on.

Kathy took a sip of her drink and looked right at me, "So, how's your love life been?"

I smiled and shook my head. She was a romance writer. What could I say to her that she hadn't already heard or imagined? I didn't consider myself a unique case. I was just a regular guy. "You mean with radio?" I joked. "I've had a lot of ups and downs. Hopefully, I can finally stay on the upside."

Kathy nodded and said, "Yeah, you seem like the jaded type. You just wasn't up for the challenge. This is a long ball game. Most guys don't understand that. They think relationships are first and second halves, and then it's over with."

She shook her head and said, "Nope. Relationships between men and women are like marathons, always have been, always will be. That's why I tell some women to let their men have that piece of ass on the side sometimes, because if you're doing what you need to do, he'll come back. Eventually, all them little chicks on the side will fade away. And it'll be his decision, that's the important thing." She grinned at me as if she was waiting for my response.

Her logic seemed suspect to me. "What if he brings a disease home?" I asked.

"Then you kick his ass and let him go," she responded on beat. I figured she was going to make a hell of a host. "But that's why I tell sisters to never, ever go without protection until your honeymoon."

I grinned and asked, "But what if the brother wants to see what it really feels like before he marries her?"

Kathy chuckled. "Now see, you're one of those insecure brothers. Bobby, you're not marrying what's between the woman's legs, you're marrying the whole woman," she told me in a low tone. The waitress set our food down. "Oh, thank you. And can we have some more water, please?" Kathy asked her. Then she was back to me.

"I hear brothers talking about what kind of sex they had with what woman all the time. And it's all in the mind," she told me. "If you have a sister who loves you, and you know what you're doing, and you love her, then you make it work however you have to do it."

Kathy called for the waitress to get her another drink. I was noticing that she carried herself like a control freak, as if she had strings on her fingers that allowed her to move everything and everyone around her. She sure knew her stuff, though. I figured if I stuck it out with her, I'd go right to the top. All I had to do was hold my own on the show with her.

"How old are you?" I asked her.

She smiled and said, "That's privileged information. I tell nobody that. Especially not my *cohost*. You might slip up on the show and tell everybody."

I swallowed my mouthful and asked, "Why is age such a big deal for women?"

"They get judged by it more," she said before taking another bite of her chicken entree. I had ordered a pasta dish.

"See, an older woman in most societies is either feared, misunderstood, or simply tolerated," she told me. "I don't want to be any of those. I want to be respected. So I don't tell people my age, I just go on about my business."

I thought about my mother and grinned. I feared her, misunderstood her, and I tolerated her all of my life. But I respected her and loved her, too. "You can't be respected *and* loved as an older woman?" I asked Kathy.

"Whenever you're a mother, a grandmother, or an aunt who spoils the nieces and nephews, you're gonna be loved. But respect is much harder to gain from people," she answered. "Most men are respected because of something that they do, but a lot of the things that women do are taken for granted. Therefore, a lot of the respect is lost.

"For instance," she continued, "you weren't too happy about the idea of hosting a relationship show with me. I could read it in your face. A lot of guys don't believe relationships are that important. They call it 'Oprah Winfrey shit.' But relationships are a lot more important than what most men think."

Kathy was coming at me from all angles. I wasn't too thrilled about being pulled into a relationship show. I thought about what my father told me concerning the institution of marriage, though, and I figured Kathy had a point, relationships were important.

"Yeah, well, most guys are more concerned about money, making a living, and how much control they have in the world that they're living in," I said. I was speaking for myself and a whole lot of other guys in the world. "Relationships come after all of that," I added.

"And that's where most men are wrong," Kathy responded. "Do you understand that you have relationships with your employers, with your bankers, your lawyers, your barbers? You have relationships with everyone."

"Yeah, but those are different kinds of relationships," I said. "You don't have to spend that much personal time with them."

"No you don't, but my point is that men who have good relationships with their women also have good relationships with everyone else," she argued. "Now you look around at the successful and happily married men, and you see relationship consistency. But those brothers who are always walking around complaining about 'the man,' and how they can't keep a job, these are the same brothers that are having so many problems with their women, because they haven't mastered what they need to do to keep their relationships intact."

"You could also say that their lack of money takes away their focus on relationships," I told her. I was just arguing to be difficult at that point.

I wanted to see if she had an answer for everything. She made good sense so far.

"Okay, then how do you explain the brother who takes a low-paying job and shows up every day, on time, for twenty years to support his wife and kids, and then ends up sending his kids off to college?" Kathy asked me.

"Well, that's a hell of a man," I said with a laugh.

"See, that's what I'm talking about, brother. You're fighting me now. For all you know, I could be a young-looking forty-year-old woman with a Ph.D. in psychology," she said with a wink. She sure had my respect.

"Are you?" I asked her.

"Not hardly. I'm twenty-two and I just finished undergraduate school at Ohio State." She stared at me for a minute for my response.

"Yeah, right," I said, "and I'm fifty-three with sixteen grandchildren." We shared another laugh and paid our separate bills.

"It's not how old I am that's important, Bobby, it's what I know and the work that I do for the community," Kathy reiterated. "Now, stop your worrying about the show and go ahead and take this man's offer, because we both know that an opportunity like this doesn't come along every day. I've been wanting to get on the radio for years. And if you're not with me, then, brother, I'm gonna have to leave you behind."

I stood up from our table and said, "Just like you focus on in your books, a *want* but not a *need*, hunh?"

"That's right," she answered me. She stood up with me and said, " 'Talk with Bobby and Kathy.' Yeah, the first thing we have to do is change that damn name. We need something that's more . . . catchy."

I got ready to walk off. Kathy grabbed my arm and said, "By the way, a woman should never *allow* a man to cheat. He would lose his respect for her and she would lose her *self*-respect. I just wanted to see how you would respond to it."

I nodded my head and smiled. Kathy Teals was pretty tricky.

●

There was nothing I could do to stop the upward spiral with Kathy Teals. She was set to make things happen. I guess sometimes the most opposite of people end up in situations where they need each other to succeed. Who would have thought that after six years in radio I would finally get my break through a show focusing on relationships? The late-blooming Bobby Dallas on a relationship show? There was no doubt about it, my life was definitely a roller-coaster ride.

Mr. Popular

The deal was that Kathy and I would have until the end of the year to see how the show worked out. In our contracts, we were to receive bonuses if the show did better than expected. If it worked, we both could pull in twenty-six thousand a year, and with bonuses added, we could make up to thirty-one thousand. I couldn't turn down that kind of money. That represented the most money I had made so far in my career. I wondered how much Brother Abu had made while at WUCI. I should have made union stations a priority a long time ago.

I sat down and went over all the salaries I had earned during my six-year stint in radio. In 1986, I made close to sixteen thousand dollars while working plenty of overtime at WHCS in New York, a nonunion station. Once I got my raise, though, I was set to make over twenty-three thousand. That was pretty good money for a radio broadcast major in only his second year out of school. And I was in New York, one of the biggest radio markets in the country! I could have moved up the ladder in no time, but I let my personal problems cloud my logic. If I had been under contract with Mr. Payton, I would have been forced to stay.

"*Damn!*" I felt like kicking myself in the ass for leaving my job in New York. I left it to return to D.C. in 1988 and make only thirteen thousand at WMSC, another nonunion station, while unsuccessfully chasing Faye Butler. From 1989 to 1991, I didn't fare much better, hopping from one makeshift position to another in Baltimore and Virginia. I was basically sleepwalking on the job, but I was finally wide awake after landing at WUCI. There were no more brainless decisions to be made. I called up John Sprier and went in to sign the contract.

"Will I still be able to substitute for Brother Abu during the week?" I asked John in his tiny office after signing. There never seemed to be enough room at any of the small stations where I worked.

John looked at me, confused. "He didn't tell you?" he asked me. "Tell me what?"

"We came to a mutual agreement to cancel 'The Awakenings.' "

I had no idea. I figured that the extra money I made from Brother Abu's show would put me in the forty-thousand-a-year bracket. I guess I was being greedy. "No, I didn't know that," I said.

"Well, the ratings for the show were pretty good for a number of years during the eighties, but with recent competition from other stations like WOL, WPFW, and WDCU, and then the other things going on in Abu's life, his ratings have been declining over the last couple of years," John explained.

"I guess I hooked up with Kathy Teals in perfect timing then," I responded.

"Well, you have Brother Abu to thank for that. It was his idea to get you two together and see what happened."

I was stunned. "Are you kidding?"

"Not at all," John answered. "I didn't want to say anything about it until after I got a chance to see how it could work out. I didn't want to promise you and Kathy anything that I couldn't deliver, but after I heard the energy that you two had on the show, I was behind it one hundred percent."

I was speechless. My career had been dangling on a string again and I didn't even know it. I shook my head and sighed. "Man, this radio business is something else."

John smiled. "If you don't have a strong stomach, then this is definitely the wrong business to be in," he agreed. "By the way," he added, "Kathy wants to sit down and come up with a better name for the show."

"Yeah, she told me. I'll call her up about it tonight."

"Okay, and just run it by me as soon as you guys come up with something good. Don't take forever, though. We start airing the show next week."

•

The first thing I did was drive over to Brother Abu's fabric store on Georgia Avenue to thank him. It was just a few blocks from Howard's campus. It was a small place, but it looked good.

"Hey, Bobby Dallas! How are things going?" he asked me as soon as I walked in.

I gave him a handshake. "Hey, man, I just found out about the show."

He smiled. "I knew this was my last year before I even met you, brother. I just wanted to help somebody else out and bring them on the show before I left. That's how I came on board in nineteen seventy-five. Because if nobody brings you in, it's very hard to get started," he told me.

"I had this other young brother in mind, but he went off and got his own show in Houston. He had family down there. So when I met you up at Howard, it was perfect timing for both of us."

I was very fortunate. Brother Abu was a good man. He hadn't even known me for a year, but he helped me out in my career tremendously. Frank Watts had gotten me into the market in D.C., but he also left me hanging.

"What do you think about this relationship show with Kathy Teals?" I asked.

"Oh, she's a bright sister, Bobby, very bright. She's been shopping that idea around for years, but you know, I wasn't really interested in it. I had other things on my mind. That didn't mean that it wasn't a good idea, though, especially with how we have black men and women carrying on with each other today. Things have gotten really nasty. We could use a show like that in the community.

"Matter of fact," he said, "let me introduce you to my wife." We walked to the back of the store and through a curtain. "Hanifah, this is Bobby Dallas from the show."

His wife was a very handsome woman with the healthiest brown skin I had ever seen in my life. I thought of her as being handsome because she appeared very strong and forward in her African garb and headpiece. She was busy sewing a dress on a large wooden table.

"Oh, how are you doing, brother? I like the shows you put on." She greeted me with a hug.

I wasn't expecting the hug. "Thank you," I said.

"Yeah, he's gonna be doing a show on relationships now with the sister out of Ohio that writes the romance books," Brother Abu informed his wife.

"Oh, Kathy Teals," she filled in. "I read her books. She knows what she's talking about. These children out here today could use a show like that. They're just as mean as they wanna be to each other."

"We weren't all that perfect in our day either," Brother Abu said with a smile.

"Yeah, but we still had a certain respect for each other, sisters and brothers did."

Brother Abu looked at me as if he still had his doubts. I could tell they had a good relationship. The better relationships seemed to always have a healthy trade-off of opinions without friction.

"Well, nice meeting you, brother. And keep up the good work," Hanifah told me. Brother Abu and I walked back out front.

"I wasn't so sure if you liked that show we did last week," I told him.

"Well, I never said you can't have a little fun on the show, as long as you keep the focus," he responded. "Kathy's a good sister and you're a good brother, so I believe you two will be able to do that. There's no question in my mind."

I was relieved. I thought I had let the brother down by settling for lower standards somehow. "I'm glad to hear that from you. I didn't want to disappoint you after bringing me on the show and giving me that opportunity like you did."

He shook his head. "Nah, brother, see you're a different person from me, and I wouldn't expect you to do the same things that I did. What worked for me may not work for you. You're from a new generation. That's what radio is about, constantly moving on to what's new. Bobby Dallas is what's new. And it's just like I said, as long as you keep your focus, nothing can stop you from making the moves that you need to make to keep rising."

"So you think that this is a good decision?" I asked.

"It's a decision that you *have* to make, brother," he answered frankly. "If you want to get in the radio business, you have to get in *first*, establish yourself, and *then* you can say what's what."

I smiled and nodded to him, extending my hand. "Thanks again, brother."

He held my hand and asked, "Were you thinking about not taking it?" He had a lot of concern on his face.

"Well, I signed the contract already, I just wanted to hear your opinion," I responded with a grin.

Brother Abu cracked up laughing. "So you already knew what you were gonna do, you just wanted to see what I would say. All right now, Bobby, you got your head on straight."

"Okay then. I'll stay in touch with you," I said, heading for the door.

"Yeah, you do that. And if you need to ask me about anything, just call me."

I walked outside on Georgia Avenue and felt like a new man. I was tempted to buy another pack of cigarettes and have a celebration smoke, but since I had never smoked around Brother Abu, I decided to wait at least until I got farther away from his store.

•

Kathy came up with the name "His Way/Her Way," for the show. It didn't matter to me, I was just ready to try it out. Kathy had this gimmick that made the show popular in a hurry. If a caller could say the show's title five times in five seconds or less, without messing up, she would give them a choice of one of her three books. As the show progressed, we began to give out movie tickets, dining certificates, and different products. That went over very well with the marketing department.

Most callers could say "His Way/Her Way" the first two times, but by the third and fourth repetition, it came out "His Way/Were Way," or "His Way/Her Ray," and we'd all break out laughing. Once callers started getting the hang of it, we had to change it around and have them say "Her Way/His Way." Depending on how expensive the giveaways were, some people were asked to say the title both ways and interchangeably; that's when things really got humorous.

When we first started out, Kathy and I would simply discuss issues concerning relationships in the black community. Once we started getting regular callers, most of them were women asking questions like, "Why do guys have to have three and four women at a time?"

I joked, "Their mommas told them they better shop around," just to keep the show entertaining. Then I said, "For a lot of guys, if they can't foresee getting married any time soon, then they just can't say no to the overabundance of women there are. I hear in D.C. alone, that it's about seven women to every man."

"First of all, that's a false statement. The term is *marriageable* men versus *marriageable* women," Kathy responded. "Because of the incarceration and unemployment rates of a lot of these brothers, they're considered *undesirable*, and then the so-called *desirable* brothers take advantage of that. It's just plain immaturity. Sister, you need to find some more mature men."

Then we'd continue on the subject for a while.

"On the flip side of that, Kathy, you have some sisters that only like the guys who have other women," I commented. "You know, they like the gigolo types."

"Those sisters are immature, too," Kathy said. "That's like the little girl who wants the chocolate fudge ice cream sundae, knowing that it's gonna mess up her new Sunday dress. Somebody has to tell her, 'No, you can't have that. It's bad for your teeth anyway.' "

We had a bunch of sisters complaining about rap music and the way rappers were degrading women. I couldn't joke about that issue. I didn't agree with a lot of things being said on rap songs of the nineties either.

Kathy said, "A lot of these guys are young, and hanging on the corners with their hands inside their pants, gesturing like they have something monstrous to offer down there. And they get a kick out of bragging to one another about B's and H's when a lot of it is just a front.

"I was out in California recently, and I heard that Ice Cube and Dr. Dre and a lot of these other young rap stars have steady girlfriends and children. So a lot of this stuff is just created to appeal to that young brother hanging on the street corner who likes to lie and fantasize about his sexuality."

"It's kind of like locker room talk, actually," I responded. "I was never into it myself because I wasn't much of an athlete, but I do know the type. And what's happening is that the vulgar talk that boys and men usually have about women behind closed doors is now being said on albums and on Top Forty radio where it shouldn't be."

"It *shouldn't* be in the locker room either!" Kathy snapped.

Kathy and I passed out flyers for our show during Georgia Avenue Day, the Black Family Reunion Day, and of course Adams Morgan Day. Before we knew it, we were already doing better than expected in our ratings share.

I felt like a sword and shield for black men until more brothers began to call in and express their opinions. That didn't happen until months later. One good discussion got started when a brother asked us, "How come it's okay for a brother with money and a good job to have a girlfriend who may not have it going on like that, but a woman who has it going on always pushes the brothers who don't have as much as she has to the side?"

I looked at Kathy and chuckled. "I want to thank you for calling up and asking that question, brother," I responded to him. "We don't get many brothers calling in with questions that they've been thinking about. Thanks a lot."

"Yeah, I was just talking about that subject with my friends last weekend," he said. "It's like, if you don't have more money than what they have, then you can't do nothin' for them. And if we acted the same way, a whole lot of these sisters would be pissed."

Kathy said, "First of all, I'm assuming that the brother on the line is young, and he's dating a lot of women who don't really have any money yet, because I know plenty of *older* women who are willing to pay for a man, buy him clothes and everything else. But a lot of women are used to being pampered and they don't feel that they're supposed to spend their money on a man."

"Now we're talking," I instigated.

"It's hard to break away from that attitude as a woman no matter how much money you make, because that's the way that society has been for so long," Kathy continued. "You have to understand that women having their own money, legally, is relatively a new thing. There were times and places in America where a woman could not legally own property. So now, a lot of men are becoming victims of their own chauvinism.

"Frankly, most men aren't prepared to deal with a woman who has more than them anyway," Kathy added. "They feel intimidated and start acting as if they need to do something extra. These brothers then become insecure and get real physical or mental with these sisters. It's just like that show *Martin* on TV. The brother makes a point to bring his girlfriend down to his level just because she's more educated than he is."

"Well, that's not me," the brother responded. "I don't feel intimidated by them at all. I just wanted to know why I'm always expected to pick them up and to pay for everything."

I added my two cents and said, "I've been with women who made much more than I did who took me out a couple of times, but it was never a consistent thing. So, how do we work toward closing the gap between these two camps?" I asked Kathy.

"It's a lot of sisters who are willing to pick a brother up and pay his way," Kathy answered.

"But it's a lot more who will not. In fact, some sisters would be offended by it," I responded, instigating again.

"That's right," the brother on the line agreed with me.

Kathy smiled and said, "Well, it looks like we're gonna have to have *two* shows for this subject because we're running out of time."

I laughed and responded, "We have time enough to take one more call. Thanks again, brother." I punched in the next caller. "Caller, you're on."

"Yeah, my name is Danyel, and I just wanna say that if the brother can't take the prices in the mall, then he needs to shop somewhere else," she said. She apparently had an audience of girlfriends in the background, cheering her on. Then she immediately hung up on us.

I looked at Kathy and shook my head with a grin. Kathy didn't look too thrilled about that call.

"Now see, we can't be like that as sisters because that turns off a lot of people and it's counterproductive to real relationships," she responded. "We should never judge a guy by how much he has or how much he's willing to spend, because that makes us look like no more than whores."

"Mmm," I grunted. "Do we have time for one more call or what, Kathy?"

"You know what, Bobby, let's just wrap it up for tonight. And I'm going to end the show by saying this; there's gonna be a lot of sisters who will start to make more money than a lot of brothers out there, but what we have to understand is that we're all in this struggle together and it's not about what we have, but how we feel toward each other."

Then Kathy looked at me and said, "Take it away, Bobby."

"Stay tuned for Pablo Garcia and 'Latin Rhymes,' up next from nine until midnight. This has been 'His Way/Her Way' on WUCI, The International Station, with your hosts, Kathy Teals and Bobby Dallas. Until next time, don't ask your girlfriends or the fellas, give us a call."

Pablo walked in with his thumbs up and his head nodding. "Good show, guys."

I chuckled and said, "Thanks, man. Give 'em a party."

"Oh, yeah, I will. I always do," he said with an energetic smile. I liked Pablo. He could have had a lot of women, but he was a dedicated married man, and his wife was a fox.

Kathy looked worn out that night. "What are you doing for the rest of the night, Bobby?" she asked me. We had gone to a lot of movies and functions together to pump our show and the station by then. It was early November. We hadn't been romantically inclined, and I wasn't thinking much of it. Our relationship was strictly professional.

"I don't know yet. Why?" I asked her.

Kathy smiled and said, "I was just wondering if you were starting to get hot dates from the show yet. You know you're getting pretty popular around town."

I chuckled and said, "Get out of here. Nobody knows me."

"I'm serious. You're gonna start getting a lot of women who will want to go out with you," she told me.

We walked out of the station and onto Eighteenth Street. The Adams Morgan area was in full buzz with Friday night traffic.

"I hope not the ones like Danyel," I said.

"You're gonna get all types of them," Kathy assured me.

"What about you?"

"Are you kidding me? A woman talking about relationships? Guys will avoid me like the plague, thinking that I know all of their lines already. And you know what? I do," she said with a smile. "But a *guy* who knows a lot about relationships, oh, the women are gonna *love* you."

"I don't know that much about relationships. You're the one with the Ph.D."

Kathy smirked and said, "You believed that line? I got you goin' good then."

"You sure do, because I *did* believe it. And you act at least thirty-two, to me."

"Well, you'll never know," she said.

"What are *you* doing for the rest of the night?" I asked her.

"Taking off all my clothes and having a long, warm bubble bath," she told me.

A lot of Kathy's comments bordered on flirting, but I usually let it slide. I smiled and said, "All right, have a good Calgon, and I'll see you next week."

Since I lived less than six blocks away, I could walk to work. And on my way, walking back home that night, I actually did think about my popularity with women. I still wasn't dating anyone. In fact, I thought about going out to a club and meeting someone that night. By the time I got home, I decided that I would.

•

I got dressed to impress with a nice tie and splashed on some cologne with plans to catch a jazz set at Takoma Station in Maryland. Brother Abu had often talked about the place. It was supposedly a lot different from the clubs I had been to with Gary Mitchell. It was a more cultural crowd. When I got there, though, they had a long line that stretched down the street. I wasn't planning on waiting in that thing. I walked up to the front of the line where they let people in two and three at a time. The doormen were all wearing black, I guess as a security color.

"Yeah, I'm from WUCI Radio. I'm here to see the jazz set on location," I said. I had gotten used to getting into places over the years from being connected to radio. That was about the only thing that was consistent for me.

The first brother at the door stepped inside to tell another brother, "We got a guy out here from the radio."

The brother inside asked, "What station?"

When the first brother turned back to me, I took the liberty of telling the inside guy myself. "Bobby Dallas from WUCI," I told him. There was no sense in relaying messages back and forth.

"Oh yeah, the relationship guy," the inside brother responded. "We were listening to your show in here earlier. 'His Way/Her Way,' right?"

I nodded and said, "Yeah, that's it." After that, they let me right in.

"You got a lot of fans in here," the inside brother said. "A couple of the waitresses wanted to meet you." He was a cream-colored brother about my height with low-cut hair. He was thicker, though, with the broad shoulders of a football player. He reminded me of a light-skinned Brad.

"Hey, Angel, come here when you get a chance! I got somebody you want to meet!" he yelled, walking me inside. "Yeah, man, my name is Chris."

I shook his hand and looked around. The place was as tight as a can of sardines. No wonder they were letting people in so slowly. "It's pretty crowded in here," I said.

"Yeah, that's how we like it," Chris responded with a smile.

They had a large bar to the left, with a small lounge area that had a television. The main dining area was to the right with a smaller bar. There was a spot for the band in the far right corner. It was a black, educated twenty- and thirty-something crowd.

The waitress named Angel finally made her way over to us. She was a slim sister with a twinkle in her eyes and a cute, smallish face. She had her light brown hair twisted into baby dreadlocks, and she looked familiar to me.

"You used to go to Howard," she said to me with a smile.

I snapped my fingers. "That's where I know you from."

Chris said, "Oh, well, since you two know each other already, let me go on about my business."

Angel said, "Oh my God! *You're* Bobby Dallas?" She wasn't starstruck or anything. She was just surprised to see that I was the same guy she went to school with years ago. "Didn't you go to New York?" she asked me.

"Yeah, I was up there for a while."

Angel had to get back to work. "I'll be back," she told me as she moved to take another order.

Once I found an open seat near the bar, I took it like in a game of musical chairs. I could have been standing for hours if I didn't.

"Are you Bobby Dallas from that 'His Way/Her Way' show?" another waitress asked me. I guess Angel had spread the word.

"That's me," I said.

"That's a nice show. We were listening to it and arguing in here today," she responded with a smile. She was shorter than Angel, browner and just as good-looking.

"Thanks. I'll make sure I tell Kathy that people like it."

"All right, well, keep up the good work."

A sister sitting nearby overheard our conversation and began to eye me. "Excuse me, what show are you on?" she leaned over to ask. She was wearing too much makeup that didn't really match her skin. And she had a lot of brownish-red hair, like a lion's mane.

" 'His Way/Her Way' on WUCI-AM," I told her. "We air on Thursday and Friday nights from seven to nine."

"WUCI?" she asked with a grimace. "Isn't that that Spanish station?"

I nodded and said, "Yeah, that's the one. But it's not just Spanish. We call it The International Station. We broadcast African music, jazz, and we have a lot of different talk shows, too."

"And your show is on Thursday and Friday nights?" she asked again.

"Yeah, from seven to nine," I repeated. Kathy often reminded me to carry flyers everywhere I went, but I always forgot them in my car. I definitely wasn't going back out to get them. It would have been murder getting back in and finding another seat.

Angel made her way back in perfect timing. I didn't want to talk to the makeup and big hair queen for too long. "How long have you been back in this area? You just moved back for the show?" Angel asked me. Her apron was off. I guess she was on a short break. It had to be a short break in that place, unless they stopped taking orders altogether. It was crowded with a lot of people who had the late-night munchies.

"Actually, I've been here since eighty-eight," I answered.

"I graduated that year."

I smiled and said, "I know. You remember Faye Butler."

"Yeah, that's right, you did used to hang out with Faye. She got a job down in Atlanta."

"Yeah, she told me about it before graduation."

Angel pointed at me and said, "Didn't you used to talk to Pearl Davis when she went to Howard?"

"I graduated with her," I said.

"Yeah, you two were in the same year."

"We ended up in New York together until she got famous," I said with a grin.

Angel cringed and said, "Oh." Then she cheered up and added, "But you're about to be famous now."

I smiled and shook my head. "No way."

"I'm serious. That's how it starts," she insisted. "You start off with a good show at a small station, and then the larger stations end up calling you."

"Yeah, well, that'll be a couple years down the road. But I'm doing all right, though. What did you major in?" I asked her.

"Television/film with a minor in drama and the performing arts."

When she said that I held in my smile. I was thinking about the waitress joke again.

Angel smiled at me, reading my mind. "Some things take time," she said.

"Yeah, tell me about it," I agreed. "It took me six years to land this show, and I'm still looking to do other things."

"Oh yeah, like what?"

"To host my own show one day," I told her. I still wasn't too thrilled with being "the relationship guy." There were a whole lot of subjects I wanted to address.

Angel smirked at me and said, "Oh, so you want your *own* thing."

"Yup."

We shared a laugh. Then Angel pulled out her pencil and pad and wrote her number down. "Call me up sometime," she said.

"I thought you'd never ask," I joked with her.

She smiled and went back to work. I was pretty satisfied with that. She wrote her first and last name, Angel Thomas. I didn't have to meet anyone else for the rest of the night. I could have walked out, gone home, and gone to bed right then. But I stayed just long enough to hear a few songs from the band. A group called 2000 Black was performing.

•

For that next Friday's show, Kathy invited on a female stripper named Candy, who flirted with me on the air. I had had my first date with Angel earlier that afternoon. I was certain that she was listening that night, so the stripper situation became very embarrassing for me.

Candy was wearing a black leotard and had a body like an Amazon queen—tall, toned, brown, and curved from D.C. to California. "A lot of people have false ideas about the business," she told us. "Strippers are not hookers. We're dancers. And if you come into a strip club and try to treat us like you can take us home or something, you *will* get your feelings hurt."

"Have you ever been to one of these clubs, Bobby?" Kathy asked me.

"No, I've never been," I answered.

"Why not? It's good clean fun," Candy joked with me.

I laughed and said, "I wouldn't exactly call it that."

"I mean, it's just like going to a movie, it's just rated more than R," she responded.

"It's rated a lot more than R, because it's live action and you get to sit right there in the front row."

Kathy said, "I thought you've never been to these places, Bobby."

"I haven't, but I've seen what these clubs look like in enough movies and on TV shows to know," I responded to her. I felt like they were ganging up on me.

Kathy said, "Okay, we're gonna go to the phone lines and try to get some brothers who frequent these stripper clubs so we can see why they go."

I put my foot in my mouth and said, "It's pretty obvious why they go, Kathy, with women like Candy in there."

"Oh, well, thank you," she responded to me with a smile. "You're pretty sexy yourself, all tall and handsome in here. Some of the girls and I were wondering what you look like when we listened to the show last night.

"He looks *good*, y'all!" she yelled.

I tried not to laugh, but failed.

"Do you, like, pick certain guys out of the audience that you might want to tease?" Kathy asked her.

"*I* do, but everybody else doesn't. You know, I just like to have a little fun when I'm out there."

"Isn't that dangerous, though? You might influence a psycho or something and have him waiting out in the parking lot for you," I said.

"Bobby, you're not a psycho, are you?" she asked me. She was starting to remind me of Mona with her teasing. Candy looked in the age range of twenty-three to twenty-seven.

"No, I'm not talking about me, I'm talking about these guys who frequent your clubs."

"Ah, again, we have a lot of security, but men stalking women is not just for strippers, that's a concern for *any* attractive girl in America. I don't see the difference, really, in me being in a stripper club than in a regular club where men and women dance together. In fact, more women have gotten in trouble after going to regular clubs because they're actually touching, drinking with, and going home with these guys, which we don't do. At all."

Then she smiled at me and added, "Then again, if I saw myself a *Bobby Dallas* in the audience, I probably *would* take him home."

After the show, and with Candy back on her way to work, I told Kathy that although she had embarrassingly flirted with me, the sister seemed pretty intelligent.

Kathy looked offended. "What are you saying, that a woman can't be intelligent because she's a stripper? I don't invite just anyone on the show. I knew she had a head on her shoulders when I talked to her."

Then Kathy smiled and said, "She really liked you, though. That's gonna make you even more popular with women. Bobby Dallas!" she screamed, teasing me.

I tried to brush it off again. "Come on now, cut it out."

"You can't tell me you haven't had women coming on to you because of the show. I mean, I've even had a few guys try and approach me."

I looked at her, surprised that she'd shared that information with me. Kathy could seem extremely private sometimes. "And what happened?" I asked her.

"I took a few numbers," she said with a grin. "I'm not dead yet. I might even have a date tonight."

"You do?"

"Bobby, that's *my* business."

"You ask me if I have any dates."

"And it's your business if you want to tell me or not."

"Oh, so it's like that?" I asked with a smirk.

"Yeah," she responded. "It's like that."

We walked out of the station and onto Eighteenth Street wearing our new wool WUCI jackets. Two college-aged white girls walked past and looked.

"Hey, that's Bobby Dallas!" the blonde said.

"Oh, he *is* tall and sexy," the brunette added with a laugh. They walked off enjoying themselves.

Kathy looked at me and burst out laughing. "What did I tell you? Even these little white girls are screaming for you. We should do a show on that. 'Jungle Fever.' "

One Step at a Time

"His Way/Her Way" was doing great! It had quickly become one of the top-rated shows at WUCI. John Sprier was even thinking about adding an extra day. He was giving us a choice of either Wednesday or Saturday. Kathy and I both said that Wednesdays would be better. Neither of us was willing to give up our weekends, and we reasoned that we were likely to get more callers on a Wednesday night than on a Saturday. People like to go out on the weekends, and while driving to the mall or the movies they would more likely listen to music.

Kathy and I were set to make all of our bonuses. I was prepared to make thirty-one thousand dollars in 1993! I was already starting to build my bank account back up. And I couldn't believe how popular I was becoming in the District. I hadn't received that much attention since hanging out with Gary Mitchell in the clubs.

The weekend before Thanksgiving, I called my parents to tell them I wouldn't be able to make it back down to Greensboro for dinner, but that I would drive down on Saturday and stay until that Monday. My parents still hadn't moved. After all of the planning, they decided that it wasn't worth it. We had too many memories in our house for them to just pack up for a new one.

"Brad and Brenda are leaving that Saturday. You'll miss them. You won't even get to see your nephew," my mother argued. I had a bunch of pictures of him. Anthony looked like his mother to me. Aminah looked more like Brad, but he didn't care, as long as he had his boy.

"Tell them to stay until Sunday then. Charlotte's only an hour drive. I'm driving seven hours."

"So you want them to change around their whole schedule for you?"

I thought about a better idea. "Okay, I'll drive down to Charlotte from Greensboro on Sunday morning and spend a day with them."

My mother got silent. For a minute, it seemed that she disapproved. Maybe she missed her first son after all, and she wanted me to stay home with them. "Are you *sure* you can't get off for Thanksgiving?" she asked me.

"Mom, have you ever heard of a radio station being off for the holidays? We're like TV and newspapers, we're gonna be broadcasting a Thanksgiving Day special." I had told my mother enough about my new job for her to know that I was finally making a nice living, but I didn't go into detail.

"What time will you be getting in on Saturday?" she asked me.

"Sometime after three o'clock," I answered. I was planning to take my sweet time. I hadn't gotten pulled over for speeding again, and I didn't plan to.

I hung up with my mother and decided to call Brad myself. Brenda answered the phone with an earful of the baby. "What's wrong with my nephew?" I asked her.

"Oh, hi, Bobby. He's just fussy. I'm trying to get his bottle together," she said. "You wanna talk to your uncle Bobby?" she asked the little complainer. That only made him scream louder. Brenda sighed and told me to hold on. I didn't remember Aminah having such tirades. "Brad, Bobby's on the phone!"

Brad picked up the line. "I got it!"

"We'll see you on Thanksgiving, Bobby," Brenda said.

"All right," I told her. I figured Brad would give her the news after I talked to him.

"Hey, so how are things going, man?" he asked me.

"So good that I won't be home for Thanksgiving," I answered.

"Yeah, I figured that."

"What I wanted to do, though, was spend next Sunday with you and your family in Charlotte."

"Hey, come on down, man. The pad is dynamite now." Brad had done a lot of renovations to their house. Dad helped him out on many of the particulars.

"I already called Mom and told her, so I guess I'll just see you next week," I said, ready to hang up. I had a movie date with Angel that I wanted to get ready for. "I gotta hop in the shower, though, Brad. I got a movie date," I told him.

"The same-o same-o?" he asked me. I had been updating him over the years on my up-and-down and basically nowhere love life. Brad was ready for nieces and nephews of his own.

"Hey, man, I just don't look forward to much anymore," I responded.

"You're getting old, Bobby. You *and* Ivan."

"Yeah, well, I'm still not in a rush to get married. I'm just getting on my feet with my career."

"So you think this new gig will work for a while?"

"Yup. I'm set for at least another year."

"I hope so, man, because that big three-oh is right around the corner for you."

"Thanks for reminding me."

"Don't mention it."

I hung up with Brad and jumped in the shower. He had me thinking about my future with women again. I admit, I didn't have my hopes too high with Angel. I had been in countless short-term relationships with women, especially during my three years of limbo. I had no reason to think that Angel and I would work. Then again, maybe my job stability had more impact on my relationships than I gave it credit for. If that was the case, maybe something *could* work out with Angel.

•

"Are you going back home for the holidays?" Angel asked me. We were on Wisconsin Avenue on our way to the theater in Bethesda, Maryland.

"Yeah, but not until after the holidays," I answered. I was wondering what my parents would have thought about Angel's eccentric style of hair. My mother shied away from anything considered out of the ordinary. Educators are some of the most conservative people in the country. Even my father felt that blacks in America need not draw any extra attention to themselves. I don't know, maybe it was just a southern thing, but sometimes I felt trapped in the middle.

I liked Angel's baby dreadlocks. She kept them neat, and she trimmed the excess hair from her face and neck, making the dreads look stylish. I wondered, though, if she didn't have curly hair, whether I would have liked it as much. Her light brown curls gave her dreadlocks an extra bounce and a glow to it. I felt terrible for thinking that, but that's how I thought about it. I heard it said once that blacks with curly hair could grow the tallest, most elaborate afros back in the sixties and seventies.

"How long have you had your hair like that?" I finally asked Angel. "I like it." I figured if I got lucky, I'd probably get a chance to mess it all up one night.

She gently ran her right hand over it and smiled. "Since the summer. I can't keep them too long. They just fall out after a while. My hair isn't thick enough to hold them."

"It looks pretty thick to me."

"No, it's not. You wanna touch it?"

I looked at her, surprised. I thought it was some sacred code against touching dreadlocks of any kind. Maybe that was because I didn't know anyone personally who wore them. I thought that if you touched someone's dreadlocks, he or she would turn around and cut your damn arms off.

"You mean I can actually touch it?" I asked Angel to make sure.

"Yeah, I don't mind."

I reached over and held three or four of her small dreads in my hand. They felt as soft as my niece's hair. "Wow, the wind could blow these things out. They're really soft."

"I told you."

"I'm still surprised that you let me touch them."

Angel looked at me and said, "You know, it seems like everybody has some stigma about dreadlocks. Either they're dying to touch them or they're afraid to touch them for some reason."

I laughed. "Yeah, that's the truth," I admitted.

"I mean, but why?"

"Well, it draws a lot of attention, so you feel like you wanna touch it, but then a lot of people who wear dreadlocks look serious and mean."

Angel laughed. "Well, let's put it this way, Bobby; if you just got a new haircut, would you want strangers walking up and touching your hair just because it looked different?"

I smiled. "Probably not."

"All right then. But that doesn't mean you won't let people you know touch it."

"Yeah, you're right."

We parked inside a parking lot around the corner from the theater and walked around. My hand accidentally touched Angel's on the way. She looked at me and smiled. "Are you afraid to touch my hand, too?"

Angel and I were just starting to get to know each other, and since she knew both Faye and Pearl, I was rather hesitant to start anything with her. "I guess you can tell," I said with a chuckle.

"I won't bite you, Bobby."

"Oh, I'm not worried about *you,* I'm more worried about *me.*"

Angel smirked at me. "What does that mean?"

I had not exactly been a good boy with women over the last few years. My body count had risen to nearly thirty women. At least a dozen of them were one- or two-night stands. Angel was playing with fire. "You don't wanna know," I told her.

"I'm a big girl, I can handle it."

"Yeah, but I don't think that *I* can."

We walked inside the theater and Angel asked me if I wanted her to pay.

I smiled. "Does that mean that I owe you anything afterward?"

She laughed real hard at that. Once she calmed down she said, "That's up to you."

She was pouring kerosene on the fire.

We walked in to see whatever movie it was with popcorn, soda, and candy that we went dutch on. Somewhere in the middle of that boring movie, Angel leaned her head against my shoulder. It was some kind of an artsy movie about a thief and a love affair. I remember thinking that I couldn't wait for Spike Lee's *Malcolm X* to come out.

Anyway, once Angel's head met my shoulder, I figured she was intentionally trying to burn the house down with the fire that she had already lit. It was a classic move by women who felt comfortable with their date. Guys generally went for the arm-around-the-chair move.

We left the theater around five-thirty, right before the sun went down, and went to get two Boston Chicken meals.

"Do you want to eat here or take it with us?" I asked.

Angel smiled and said, "Take it with us. But where are we going?"

Good question, I thought. "Well, I live closer than you." Angel lived in Mt. Rainier, Maryland, right outside of northeast D.C. However, Bethesda, Maryland, was on the northwest side of the District, and much closer to where I lived.

"Let's go to your place then," Angel agreed.

We went to my apartment off Rock Creek Park, and Angel loved the place. "Aw, man, I would love to live here! It's so scenic!" she said.

"Yeah, it is, isn't it?" I bragged. For a while, I had lived with nothing but bare necessities because I was relocating so much. After landing the "His Way/Her Way" show on WUCI, though, I finally accessorized my living quarters. I did away with Pearl's old stereo and bought a Kenwood surround-sound system with a multiple CD changer. I had built up a nice collection of freebies from working at different radio stations. I had everything from Luther Campbell to Hiroshima.

"How much is the rent here?" Angel asked me.

"Enough to need a roommate," I told her.

"Really?"

"Well, you know, you're paying for the location."

She nodded and said, "Yeah, that's true. But I guess you can afford it," she added with a smile.

I didn't comment on that. We sat down at my small kitchen table and ate our food.

"I like what you've done in here," Angel said, looking around at my place. I guess I could say that my apartment had an artsy mood to it. I bought plenty of cheap cultural items from the shops in Adams Morgan, including an East Indian rug, Native American clothes, African sculpture, and Asian ornaments. "It kind of reminds me of the seventies," Angel told me.

"What do *you* know about the seventies?" I joked with her. I was just a kid for the majority of the seventies myself, and Angel was two years younger than me.

"Are you kidding me? I loved the seventies. I have aunts and uncles, you know. And they took me places. I always wished I could trade places with them!"

Suddenly Angel's dreadlocks made a lot of sense. Maybe she would have been a big Jimi Hendrix, Bob Marley, and George Clinton fan. "I got some Bob Marley if you want to listen," I said.

Angel nearly snapped her neck off when she nodded and said, "Yeah, I love his music! We have reggae at Takoma Station every Sunday night!"

I chuckled and said, "I guess that means 'Yes.' " I put on Bob Marley's *Legend*.

Angel walked into my living room where she began to dance. "Do you know how to dance to reggae?" she asked me.

"Not at all," I told her. "I'm more like a jazz fan. I don't really like to dance, I just like to listen to the mood and the message of the music."

"You mean you can't *feel* this?" Reggae dancing always reminded me of an X-rated show with clothes on. The way that Angel twisted, turned, and gyrated her body would have been considered a sin in some countries.

"Yeah, I *feel* it, I just don't feel it the way you do," I answered her.

"So, you listen to music like a white man then," she said, still dancing suggestively.

"What is that supposed to mean?"

She ignored me as she got even more animated with her dance, winding and twirling and lifting herself into the air. I guess that it could have been considered spiritual in a way, but she was only making me horny.

"Every culture except for white people has exotic dances that just allow you to express what the body is. And the body is beautiful," she finally answered. "Most white dances are too planned and organized. It's just like jazz. The white man could have never created the improvisations of jazz, because jazz is a free form of music unconcerned with the time."

She sounded like a jazz poet.

"Do you write poetry?" I asked her.

She nodded. "I write a little bit of everything: short stories, screenplays, music."

"What about novels?"

"What about them?"

"Could you write one of those?" I was beginning to think about Kathy and her writing.

"I could if I wanted to. But novels are too . . . too . . . what's the word I want to use? Formulaic. Yeah, formulaic," she said. "After you read enough of them, you already know what's gonna happen. Frankly the shit bores me. And some of them are too damn long.

"Girl loves boy. Boy leaves girl and breaks her heart. Girl then searches for a new boy, finds him, loves him, and they live happily ever after."

I broke out laughing. Angel and Kathy would have had a good discussion on that subject. Kathy was proud of what she did. "So that's all it is, hunh?"

"Basically."

"Have you read any of Kathy Teals's books?"

"Truth and Consequences."

"Did you like it?"

"Yeah, it was different. It was more like a mystery than a romance, though, because you didn't know what was gonna happen next."

"Well, you could do something like that," I told her.

"I would have to." Angel was still dancing as the songs kept changing over, one to the next. She would express the mood of each song. My strong physical attraction to her toned down once she started to express herself mentally. I was just having a conversation with her as she danced.

"Movies are formulaic, too," I said. "They're more formulaic than books are."

"Yeah, but it's the interpretation that you have for your part. Like, one of my favorite movies was *Deep Cover*. Now you can't get more predictable than an undercover cop movie, but Larry Fishburne tore that role up! I mean, he was the *bomb* in that movie!"

I smiled. I liked that movie, too. "All right, I see your point," I told her.

Angel took a peek at her watch. "When are you gonna be back from the holiday?" she asked me. It was getting late and she had to be back to work at Takoma Station. She also worked on and off as a waitress at a restaurant downtown on Pennsylvania Avenue.

"Next Monday night," I answered.

"Okay, well, I'll hook up with you then. Can you drive me to work?"

I was ready to ask her about the in-between time. I wouldn't be leaving for a week, but I guess she had other plans. I decided not to rush things. If I waited until I got back, I'd have something to look forward to.

•

Our topic for the Thanksgiving Day show was "Why Love at All?" I really felt out of my league on that subject. I had a lot of doubts about love after all that I had been through. Even the anticipation of what would happen with Angel was nerve-racking for me. I felt like calling her every night of that week to tell her how cool it was to just talk and listen to music. But since she wanted to wait until I got back from North Carolina for some reason, I felt that I might have worn out my welcome if I called her. It was back to high school jitters and second-guessing all over again. "Why Love at All?" was a good damn question!

Kathy began the show by saying that love is life: "Love is nine months of waiting and then delivering," she said. "But once you deliver, does the love stop there? No. It continues for thirty, forty, fifty, sixty years. And not even death can stop love."

I said, "That's a different kind of love that you're talking about, Kathy. That's mother love."

"And *mother love* is the greatest love that there is," she responded. "What we need more of is father love. But what we have is too many scared young men who are so afraid to give it because their egos are so fragile. And after one or two girls don't return their phone calls, they are just so ready to throw that emotion out the window and let a truck run over it in the street."

While sitting in front of the microphone that night, I felt defensive, as if Kathy was talking about me. "So they're just supposed to keep doing it—keep putting their emotions on the line?" I asked her.

"Bobby, every day you put your clothes on and they just get dirty again. So are you gonna stop getting dressed?"

I chuckled. "Well, I don't think I'm gonna stop dressing, no. But aren't you oversimplifying things a bit?"

"Brothers oversimplify things. You know what you do? Men say, 'Oh, that's just the way I am.' Like that's supposed to answer everything," she said. "If you were hungry and somebody said, 'Look, man, I'm gonna help you get something to eat.' Are you gonna turn around and say, 'Naw, man, that's just the way I am. I'm hungry.' Hell no, you're not gonna say that! You're gonna get up and get that food!"

I cracked up laughing. Then Kathy apologized to our listeners.

"I'm sorry for my language out there, but I'm just getting a little sick of these brothers making all kinds of petty excuses to avoid love."

I calmed down and said, "Kathy, you *have* to eat." That only got her excited again.

"Thank you, Bobby Dallas! Thank you so *very* much for saying that!" she shouted. "Just like you *need* to eat, you *need* to love! That's what's wrong with a lot of these brothers out here today. They think that love is an option, and they go through their life saying, 'No, I don't want none of that love stuff.' But I'm here to tell you, Bobby, that you can't live without loving *something!* Even homeless people *love* to wake up and smell fresh air every day."

"Wait a minute, Kathy, there *are* things that men *do* love," I said. I couldn't let her have a one-way show on Thanksgiving. I had to get my sword and shield out for the brothers again.

"What, the Dallas Cowboys? The Chicago Bulls? Tell me what they love, Bobby!" Kathy yelled at me.

I felt like crawling under a rock, but I couldn't because I was on the air and the brothers would be counting on my answer. I was even wondering if Brother Abu was listening that night.

"We love just as much and just as hard as women do, but it's not as unconditional," I told her. "Men have breaking points that are a lot more delicate than women's. And we get punished very severely, even by women, when we *do* break. So since we *know* this, there is always a protective shield to guard from that type of emotional breakdown. Because, see, women will come to each other's rescue and all that when times get hard, but when a man breaks, he's broke for real. And it'll be fewer people there to help him get up.

"Humpty-Dumpty fell off the wall, and Humpty was most definitely a man, because it took all the king's horses and all the king's men to put poor Humpty together again," I added. "And that's what we have to deal with *every day.*" Before my very ears I was sounding just like my father. If he could have heard me on that Thanksgiving Day show, he would have been home yelling, "Amen to that, Bobby! Amen!"

Kathy couldn't help but laugh. "Well, then, Bobby, we need to start a love group for men. That's just all there is to it."

"Yeah, if you can get them to come," I joked. Nevertheless, I was serious. Men would avoid anything concerning love like black people in a haunted house. They would haul ass after the first scary noise they heard in that place without ever having to see anything.

"So now, I guess it's just to be *understood* that men love, right, Bobby?"

"Basically, yes," I answered with a smile.

"Yeah, because that's what they always say, 'It's understood,' " Kathy said. "So, in other words, if I dropped a bowling ball on your foot, Bobby, you're not supposed to jump up and down and call me all kinds of names, because it's just *understood* that you're in pain."

I laughed. "You came out with your turkey knife ready tonight, didn't you?" I joked again. It was Thanksgiving, so I was trying to keep things as lighthearted as I could.

Kathy was really pumped that night, as if she had been storing up for that Thanksgiving Day show since we began. "That's right, because I'm planning on cutting up some *turkeys* tonight!" she responded. "The football games are over, so I expect to have *many* brothers and sisters sitting in front of their radios and listening to 'His Way/Her Way' on— what station are we on again?"

"The International Station, WUCI-AM," I answered. Kathy would do that every once in a while when she wanted to really pump the show.

"And when do we come on?"

"Every Thursday and Friday night, and soon, we may be including Wednesdays."

"And what time do we air again?"

"From seven to nine, after rush hour and before the party."

"That's right, because we have a lot of work to do on black love. As a matter of fact, Bobby, we probably won't get to any callers tonight, because we have too much ground to cover. So if you're listening, we'll do a full show of responses tomorrow night."

"That's from seven to nine, after rush hour and before the party," I repeated.

"Now, getting back to what I was saying, Bobby, this *understood* thing that men throw around, that just has to go," Kathy started up again. "You have to *reaffirm* your love for someone *every day*. My daddy always told me that he loved me."

"My daddy did, too," I told her. "But it's just a very hard thing for brothers to say, because they know that once you say it, you can't take it back. And if things don't work out, then that woman's walking around saying, 'He told me that he loved me,' and you're sitting around feeling silly about it."

"Mmm, mmm, mmm, the male ego," Kathy grunted. "What are we women gonna do about you brothers? I know what *I'm* gonna do.

"Harold, I hope you're listening because I asked you to and you said that you would, so here it goes. Baby, since you were man enough to tell me that you loved me and asked for my hand in marriage, and since I'm not afraid to say that I love you, and show it, yes, baby, I will marry you.

"Yes, yes, yes, yes, yes!"

I was shocked! "Are you serious?" I asked Kathy. I had no idea what she was doing.

"I am very serious."

What else could I say? "Well, congratulations," I told her. I wondered if anyone else at the station knew that she was going to respond to a marriage proposal on the air. I didn't even know that she was serious about anyone. After the show, I asked her about it.

"I told John that it might be a possibility, but I really didn't expect to do it, it just jumped out at me as the right thing to do, you know, to actually show brothers that it's okay to tell a woman that you love her."

"I didn't even know you were involved with anyone," I said. I still couldn't believe it.

"Harold and I have been on and off for years," she responded. "I knew I was gonna marry him when I moved back to D.C. I met him here about seven years ago. But that's just how some things happen, Bobby. You have to take things one step at a time. As for you not knowing about him, you know I don't spread my business too thin."

"You did tonight," I reminded her.

"Yeah, but that was for all of the people that I really want to help out there, Bobby. I mean, I know it's gonna take time for brothers to express that love that they hide so much, but I'm serious about making a difference, and now *everybody* knows."

"You got that right," I told her. "Or at least the people that listen to our show."

Kathy grimaced. "We are eating up the market, Bobby. Just give us a few more months." She sounded like a ratings-hungry tyrant for a second there.

John Sprier called the station and praised us so much about the show that I could hear him without even being on the phone.

Kathy told her fiancé to meet her outside so they could go to a late dinner. I felt ten times lonely that night. I wanted to tell anyone that I loved them and all I had was Angel. It wouldn't have been appropriate to call her and say that I loved her. Although we had gone to Howard together, I was just beginning to know her. We had only been hanging out for a couple of weeks.

Before I walked home in the cold, Kathy pulled me aside and said,

"Bobby, you just have to believe that it's gonna happen for you. Can I let you in on a little secret?"

"Yeah, sure," I said. I guess she could tell that I was kind of glum after the show that night. I wanted to go anywhere outside of my empty apartment. I had nowhere else to go, though. I hadn't been invited anywhere for dinner but home. Brother Abu and his family didn't even celebrate American holidays.

Kathy said, "Bobby, I'm thirty-four years old and I was married once when I was twenty-one, straight out of college. It was the worst mistake of my life. I was abused, I had a miscarriage, I gained weight, and I went through everything that you can imagine, right on down to having an affair.

"But then I got divorced and decided to get myself together. I went back to school, got myself a master's degree, traveled, wrote my books, got the books published, traveled some more, started giving speeches, and then I finally decided to come back to D.C. and get married. I also wanted this show, which I couldn't have done without you."

I was speechless, just standing there in the cold.

Kathy touched my face and said, "I know what I'm talking about, Bobby. I've been there, and I know that love is real. By the way, my marriage to Harold is a *want,* not a *need,* because if I learned anything else in my thirty-four years of life, it's how to love myself, *first.*"

●

I was still feeling glum when I arrived at my brother's house in Charlotte that Sunday morning.

"What's wrong with you, man?" Brad asked me. "Dad said you was walking around at the house looking miserable. What's the problem now? I thought you were finally on your feet and feeling good and all."

Brenda was out at the grocery store with Aminah to pick up a few last-minute things. She left Anthony home with Brad. We were standing over his cradle as he slept.

"You think he's gonna be more like me or like you?" I asked Brad.

Brad said, "He's gonna be himself, man. What the hell are you talking about?" My brother looked more mature every time I saw him, not really older, just more focused and determined. He always saw things as cut and dried, just like Dad. Either you love her or you don't. Either you'll marry her or you won't. It was just that simple to him. On the other hand, *I* always had to go into deep thought about everything. That's probably why I liked talk radio so much, they were always discussing things. I could never do a show with Brad. Brad would say everything that he had on his mind in one month and that would be the end of it.

I sighed and walked out of the baby's room. "I'm tired, man," I said.

Brad followed me out. "You're tired already? You just started that show this summer, right?"

"I'm not just talking about the show, man. I'm talking about life in general."

Brad looked at me and said, "Bobby, you're not thinking suicide, are you? Please don't tell me that. You're my only brother, man. Don't do it, Bobby!" He was turning it into a joke.

"I'm serious, man. It's not even funny."

Brad turned into that razor-sharp edge again. "Bobby, you're not even twenty-nine yet. I know, because you're only a year older than me and I turned twenty-seven this year."

I looked around the living room at recently framed photos of Brad, Brenda, and the two kids. The renovated house was so altogether thorough that it could have been featured in a real estate magazine. I can't even begin to describe it. It was too perfect to talk about. It was simply a dream house that you would have to take in with your own eyes.

"Damn! Twenty-seven, and you have all of this," I said.

Brad raised his hands to his temples. "Bobby, you're starting to depress me, man, and you *know* I don't like that shit."

I looked out the large front window. Brenda was pulling up the driveway from the grocery store. I walked out to help her with the bags.

"Thanks, Bobby."

"I'm just trying to be helpful around here," I told her.

Brad was right behind me.

"Where's my son?" Brenda asked him.

"He's sleeping."

"I told you about leaving him in the house by himself."

"Well, you better hurry up and get in there with him then," Brad said with a grin.

Brenda stopped and stared at him. "Bobby, your *little* brother is showing off for you," she said with a smile. It was all too perfect for me. Brenda had picked up just the right amount of weight, like Dad had joked about Pearl. Hearing Brenda call Brad my *little* brother didn't help much. I was beginning to try and convince myself that he was a distant cousin who was a few years older than me.

Brad forced me to take a cruise around Charlotte with him in his Ford

Bronco jeep. He was showing me commercial property that he planned to buy. He had it all mapped out.

"This is gonna be a hot area, Bobby. People keep talking about Atlanta, but watch Charlotte surprise everybody. And I'm gonna be here first."

I nodded to him, inspecting the scenery.

"I could have gotten a luxury car, man, but after we had Aminah first, I had to convince myself that I was still a rugged man, you know?"

I looked at him and grinned. I guess it was satisfying in my jealous little way to hear that Brad wasn't flawless. "You believe that old tale about real men having boys?"

"Damn right! We carry the Y chromosomes, don't we?"

"It's just a matter of chance, man. You see you got a boy now."

"So maybe I can sell this and get that luxury car now. What should I get, Bobby, a Lexus? They're the hottest new thing on the market right now."

"Get whatever pleases you." I looked out the window at all the open space in Charlotte. I had gotten used to being around the densely populated northern cities for ten years. It seemed really peaceful in Charlotte after being in New York, D.C., and Baltimore.

"You know Dad is dying to help you out when you get ready to make a move, man," Brad reminded me. I knew that already. I didn't want to waste my father's money like an irresponsible rich man's son just because he was able to do it, though. I wasn't ready for any "moves" anyway.

"Would *you* give me a loan for a house?" I asked my brother sarcastically.

He looked at me seriously at first, then he smiled and said, "Hell naw, you're out here thinking about suicide."

I laughed with him that time. "Yeah," I said, "I wouldn't do it either. Besides, Dad ain't rich. I don't want to have to depend on him like that. I'm making my own money anyway."

"So what's the damn problem, man? I just don't get it. Make me understand."

I nodded. "Yeah, I wish I didn't get it either," I told him. "I got all these crazy thoughts that run through my head and get in the way of me doing the things that you're doing." I took out my Marlboro cigarettes. "Remember Mom made us smoke a whole pack of these?" I asked Brad with a grin.

He tried to hold in his laugh but couldn't. "I wonder if the police ever got that letter I sent them."

"Yeah, they got it. They just didn't respond to your ass," I told him.

Brad pulled the jeep over and put it in park. "Seriously though, man, what's going on?" He really wanted me to explain things to him.

I thought of Kathy Teals and said, "I wanna learn how to fall in love and get married and be happy."

Brad broke out laughing. "You gotta be fuckin' kidding me! Is that what all this is about? You lovesick or something, man?"

"Naw, not *love-sick*, I'm more like *love-less*."

Brad calmed down and sighed. "You were always too damn laid back about everything, man. Now you're finding out that people don't really respond to that shit. People respond to me because I *make* 'em respond. And if they don't like me, fuck 'em. I got other things to worry about. But you, man, you seem like you wanna please everybody. That's why women always liked your ass as a friend. To hell with that friend shit unless you already got a woman."

"I've been more verbal and assertive about my feelings, and that didn't work either," I said.

I offered Brad a cigarette, but he turned me down. "I don't smoke that shit no more, man," he snapped, pushing the box away. "Look, Bobby, you wasn't all that excited about me getting married when I first told you about it, but now all of a sudden you're telling me about this shit."

"I was jealous that you were getting married before me, I just didn't say anything about it," I told him. "I always thought that *I* would be the married one."

"Well, that's just how life works sometimes, man. You'll get out of this thing. You just have to take it one step at a time."

I looked at him with wide eyes and laughed.

"What's so damn funny?" he asked me. He finally pulled back onto the road.

"Somebody told me the exact same thing on Thanksgiving night."

"It's the truth, man. Everyone doesn't run the hundred in ten flat. Some people run a twelve-four and whatnot. But eventually, most of us will cross the finish line. So you're just a slow-runnin' motherfucka."

I chuckled and said, "Thanks a lot, I feel a lot better now. I'm still in the race, I'm just a little slow."

"Yeah, but you're not running the hundred," Brad said with a grin. "Your ass is out here running a mile."

•

I got back to my apartment in D.C. that Monday night and found that I had received plenty of messages while I was away. Most of them were in reference to the show. One of those messages was from Angel.

"Hi, Bobby, this is Angel. I was out of town for Thanksgiving but somebody at the job taped the show. I laughed so hard I cried. Your show is really getting good. Anyway, I look forward to seeing you again when you get back, if you're not too busy for me. I hope you had a nice holiday. I'll be working until late Monday night, but call me Tuesday morning. 'Bye."

Too busy? What, are you crazy? I thought with a smile. I was once again counting my chickens before they hatched, so I calmed myself down. "Okay, I have to take this thing one step at a time," I told myself. Then I listened to her message again.

"Hi, Bobby, this is Angel. I was out of town for Thanksgiving but somebody at the job taped the show. I laughed so hard I cried. Your show is really getting good. Anyway, I look forward to seeing you again when you get back, if you're not too busy for me. I hope you had a nice holiday. I'll be working until late Monday night, but call me Tuesday morning. 'Bye."

"Hi, Bobby, this is Angel. I was out of town for Thanksgiving but somebody at the job taped the show. I laughed so hard I cried. . . ."

No Guarantees

"What's so wrong with giving people a happy ending? Isn't that what everybody wants anyway?" I was with Angel at my apartment again, discussing her outlook on novels. I didn't see what was so wrong with having your dreams come true like in a fictional book. I know I sure wanted a happy ending in my life. I figured I deserved it.

"Because it's not realistic," Angel told me. "Novels give people a false perception of the world."

"What about your acting stuff? That's not realistic," I responded.

"I know it isn't, but my real life is not about a role, it's about interaction with an unpredictable world, unpredictable people, and unpredictable circumstances. I mean, the reality of the situation is that I may never get a major role in a movie, and I accept that."

"So what do you do in the meantime?"

"I work toward it. I've been in plays and I've tried out for major roles, I just haven't gotten any breaks yet. I've even been an extra in a few commercials."

"Would you be satisfied if you never got to play a major role?"

She thought about it and smiled at me. "I probably wouldn't, but I accept that as my reality."

I thought about Mona. "I knew a sister that went to Howard who told me that failure wasn't a part of her reality, and now she's on FM radio in Detroit, straight out of school."

Angel nodded. "Some people get lucky."

"I wouldn't call it luck. I would call it willpower."

"Did willpower get you the show that you're on now?"

I grinned. "No, that was more like luck. But I *did* work hard to get there."

"Like I said, some people get lucky," Angel insisted. "You can work hard all your life and still never get a break."

The phone rang right after she finished her sentence. It was Frank Watts. He had been calling and trying to hook up with me for a couple of weeks.

"All right, then. Where are you gonna be?" I asked him. He wanted us to meet that night in a bar in Southeast. He said that it was a spot I needed to get familiar with on Eighth Street. It was Tuesday and Angel had to be at work soon. She was already looking at her watch while I was on the phone. I didn't have any plans after that, so I agreed to meet with Frank. "Okay, I got it, but I gotta go now. I got company," I told him after he gave me the address.

"I wish you didn't have to go to work tonight," I told Angel once I hung up.

"Well, if it was fiction, I could find some way to stay, but it's not, and I got bills to pay."

I smiled. "Hey, that rhymed," I told her.

"It wasn't done intentionally, but sometimes the poet in me jumps out unexpectedly."

I smiled again. "You don't say."

Angel burst out laughing and said, "That was a coincidence. I wasn't trying to do that."

"Yeah, sure you weren't," I joked.

I drove Angel to work at Takoma Station and thought about things after dropping her off. We were becoming good friends. It wasn't like the friendship I grew into with Mona, though. Mona started off as a tease, so there was a lot of sex appeal between us. The sex appeal with Angel, however, took a backseat to philosophical discussions. Angel was a "deep" sister.

Anyway, it seemed to me that the willful and determined people were the ones getting things done in life; Pearl, Brad, Faye, Mona, Pamela, Frank, Brother Abu, and even Tammy Richards had climbed back out of her hole. She was doing a hot morning show in Virginia. Like Brad said, I was being bounced around like a pinball because I didn't have enough personal drive. In fact, if it wasn't for Kathy Teals and *her* ambition, I could have been unemployed again.

"I have to start taking more control of my life," I told myself. I lived passively, without the passion that Mona had mentioned, and it just didn't work. Had I been more driven earlier, maybe I wouldn't have been forced into stepping over so many stones. I was still just letting things happen to me. I was a counterpuncher with no knockout punch.

I was on my way to meet Frank at this bar he was bragging about called Scotty's. I found the place on Eighth Street and walked in. It was pretty much incognito from the outside. It didn't have any flashing lights or a crowd. Inside was nothing to brag about either. It looked like a regular small bar that you could find in any residential neighborhood. *What the hell was Frank so excited about this place for?* I wondered.

I looked around and didn't see him. I leaned over the small bar to ask the bartender. "You know Frank Watts, the brother who does the sports show?"

The bartender jabbed his thumb into the air. "Upstairs," he said, pointing to a stairway.

I looked to a dark stairway in the corner of the bar and said, "Thanks." I walked up the steps and was pleasantly surprised. The upstairs section was much bigger than downstairs, and much more lively.

"Bobby Dallas!" Frank yelled to me through the jazz music playing in the background. Upstairs and downstairs were night and day.

I walked over to the bar where Frank sat on a stool next to a young, bald-headed friend. I shook Frank's hand and looked for a seat.

"Bobby, I want you to meet Mark Bishop. He did most of the paintings you see on the walls up here."

I nodded to the brother and shook his hand. His oil paintings of the different jazz greats were nice; Miles, Coltrane, Bird, and Dizzy.

I was just about to compliment him on his work when he looked at me and said, "So, you're the relationship guy." It was a statement I was beginning to hear more often, and it was nagging the hell out of me.

"And you're the painter guy," I snapped back at him. I couldn't help it. I felt maybe I had to start carrying myself with more authority.

Frank chuckled. "He didn't mean anything by that, Bobby."

"The Painter Guy" was smiling and bowing his head. "No, he's right. I know just what he means. Sometimes people get so much into my art that they forget about me. I stand corrected, brother. No offense intended."

I nodded to him. His apology was good enough for me. "Okay, no offense taken then. And I like your work," I told him.

Mark Bishop reached out his hand and I shook it again, starting over fresh. "Thanks," he said, standing up. "Well, sorry I can't stay. I'll see you around, Bobby. All right then, Frank."

Frank nodded to him as Mark headed for the stairway. "You done scared the boy off, Bobby," he joked to me.

"Yeah, he *was* kind of short. Maybe he was intimidated by me."

Frank laughed. "Let me introduce you to Big Bill, he owns the place."

I was expecting us to get up and walk off to an office somewhere, but Frank was calling to the heavy, gray-haired bartender. "Hey, Bill, this is Bobby Dallas over here. He used to work with me at WMSC."

Big Bill wiped his hands and was smiling when he walked over to meet me. He reminded me of a fifty-year-old Fat Albert. "Hey, I heard of you. You're that relationship guy."

Frank burst out laughing. At least I knew that the show was making its way around town. "Now, you don't want to get smart with him, Bobby. Big Bill will throw your ass out," he warned me. He was still grinning.

Big Bill looked at Frank for an explanation.

"He don't like being called 'The Relationship Guy,' Bill. I guess it's like somebody calling you 'The Bar Guy' or calling me 'The Sports Guy.' "

Bill looked at me and frowned. "How'd you get on that show?" he asked.

"It was more like my program director's idea."

"Does it pay good money?"

I nodded. "I'm pretty satisfied with it, yeah."

"Well, what are you complainin' about?" he asked. "You gotta take the good with the bad. At least I heard of your show before. That's a good thing."

"Yeah, you're right," I told him. "I gotta take the bitter with the sweet."

"What are you having?" he asked me.

I still wasn't too familiar with drinks. I threw up my hands and said, "Whatever's good."

Big Bill looked at Frank. Frank laughed and said, "Give him a rum and Coke."

Bill didn't say anything to me for the rest of that night. I guess he had washed his hands of me altogether. I wasn't worth his conversation. Hell, I even felt like apologizing to the man, and I didn't know what for.

"So how you like working with this broad?" Frank asked me. It was just me and him. It was as if we were isolated from the rest of the people in the room. Frank was right in my face, alcohol breath and all. He was wearing a plain beige suit with no tie.

"She's pretty wild," I told him. "It's fun."

Frank just stared at me. "Don't get too attached to her."

I began to dislike his tone. "You mean how I got attached to you before you left me out to dry?" I snapped at him.

Frank responded, "That was good for you, Bobby. If you're gonna learn the business, then learn the business. You can't latch on to some-body and expect things to work out. We would have *both* starved. I couldn't carry you."

Selfish or not, Frank did make sense. Paying for a host *and* a producer could put a dent in anyone's wallet. "Yeah, well, we have a joint con-tract," I told him of my business relationship with Kathy Teals. "By the way, her name is Kathy. Kathy Teals. And she's a good sister."

Frank looked at me, shook his head, and started to laugh. "Boy, you're ripe for picking, Bobby, *good* and ripe," he said. "Where are you from again, Alabama some-damn-where?"

"Greensboro, North Carolina," I reminded him. I'm sure he knew it already.

Frank looked into my eyes and said, "Bobby, you have to start doing what's best for Bobby Dallas. You understand me, son? Look out for yourself, *first.*"

"Like you did with me?" I asked him. I was ready to flee from that place. It wasn't my kind of place anyway. I finished off my drink and stood up to leave.

Frank said, "Sit back down, Bobby. Let me talk to you about this."

"Talk to me about what?"

"Your show is getting too big, too fast," he said. "You know what that means, big fish swallow little fish. I'm just telling you to make sure you're protected, that's all. Just make sure you know what you're getting into."

"You think we got a chance to be major?" I asked him. I was curious. I sat back down.

Frank said, "But the broad runs the show, that makes you expend-able."

I thought about it. "But without me she wouldn't have that spontane-ous trade-off of energy," I responded.

Frank leaned back on his stool and laughed. I thought he was about to slip off and bust his behind on the floor. I moved to catch him and break his fall.

"Shit, I'm all right. It's you that needs saving," he said, pushing me away. "Bobby, that woman can get any fool to sit next to her and respond. You gotta make that show work more for you."

I shook my head. "It ain't my kind of show. I'd rather talk about everything."

"Well, do it then."

I frowned. "Then I'll sound like I'm getting off track," I told him. "That's not good to do."

Frank said, "What the hell you think Howard Stern does? He'll talk about anything that comes to his damn mind."

I shook my head. "I don't want to be like Howard Stern."

"Well, who do you want to be?" he asked me.

"Bobby Dallas."

"And who the hell is that, 'The Relationship Guy' who sits next to Kathy Teals on the 'Her Way' show? Because that's what it is. You think she named it 'His Way/Her Way' by accident? She knows she gets the last word. That broad knows exactly what she's doing. I listened to that Thanksgiving Day show and was screaming, 'Goddammit, she's playing Bobby like a damn flute!' My woman thought I was crazy, screaming at the radio like that."

I had nothing to say. I kind of slipped into a daze. My enthusiasm for radio was really wearing thin. Nothing ever seemed secure for me. The contract I had with Kathy at WUCI was up for renewal at the end of the year. What if Kathy did have her own plans?

"In this business, Bobby, these stations have one boss, the ratings. The people that work for the station end up with one boss, the money. The more money they give you means that they respect you more. So if they're not willing to pay for you, you take your show somewhere else. If they don't have the money, then you ain't supposed to be there no way. And if you don't believe me, then ask Donnie Simpson. He left WKYS, and now he's like the million-dollar man at WPGC," Frank said.

"It used to be that you could produce a show for the benefit of the community and just have a good time, but in the nineties, Bobby, that affirmative action shit is over. Either your station is making money or it's losing money. And if they're losing money, they're not gonna be around long. It's just too much other shit going on. They've even been cutting back public radio. Soon you'll have these new computer networks starting to compete with us. You ever heard of that on-line computer shit?" Frank asked me.

I don't remember responding. The rest of that night at Scotty's was a blur. I had a few more drinks and ended up driving back to Takoma Station. It was close to one o'clock when I got there. They told me that Angel was sick and had gone home early.

I called her from a pay phone. "What's the matter? I heard you got sick."

"Yeah, I don't know what I ate, but I had a terrible stomachache and then I had a headache."

Everything she said started to rhyme to me. Anyway, I said, "How are you feeling now?" I was actually about to ask her if she wanted company.

I was back to being needy. At least in my years of limbo I could accept being at the bottom. As soon as you start to climb the ladder of success, even a little setback can be devastating.

"I took some Tylenol," Angel answered. "I'm in bed trying to get some rest. Where are you?"

"Up the street from your job," I told her.

"You came back to see me?" she asked. She seemed surprised.

"Yeah, I guess I did," I answered.

"That was sweet," she responded. "I told you people were unpredictable. Look at you."

I guess I hadn't been trying too hard to pursue her. She owed my return to her job to Frank. His chat about the business side of radio had depressed me. I had been in the business long enough to know, but still, I didn't need to be continuously reminded of its downside. I needed Angel to cheer me back up.

"Yeah, I just wish you wasn't sick," I said.

"Well, that's life, Bobby. Shit happens."

I thought about that: *Shit happens. She's right.* "When are me and you gonna happen?" I asked her out of the blue. Maybe it was the alcohol talking.

Angel chuckled and said, "I don't know. Maybe tomorrow, or maybe never."

Her theory of randomness compounded by Frank's talk of radio backstabbing had worked me into a frenzy. "Goddammit, you're telling me that we don't have control over *anything?!* Is that what you're telling me?!!" I was out in the cold, hollering into a pay phone. I could have easily been mistaken for crazy that night.

Angel's voice went soft. She said, "Bobby, are you okay?"

"No, I'm not okay!" I snapped.

"What's wrong?"

"I'm tired of not knowing what's going on! I want to know what I'm gonna be doing tomorrow! I wanna know if my job is secure! I wanna know that I can come home to somebody! Let me know *something,* please!"

"Bobby, do me a favor." Angel was speaking to me slowly and softly like a shrink. "I want you to go home and get some rest. I'll be over there to see you as early as I can, okay? Now just go home and go to bed."

Surprisingly, it worked. "Okay, you'll see me in the morning?" I asked her, just like a crazy man would.

"As soon as I can make it over there," she said.

"All right. I'm going home now."

I don't remember thinking anything on my way home. Angel had calmed me down. She said she would be coming to see me in the morning. That was the thought I went to bed with that night.

•

My phone rang early in the morning. I grabbed it before it did more damage to my head. My head was aching! I don't know how many drinks I had at Scotty's, but it was definitely over my small limit.

"Hello," I answered.

"Bobby, this is Angel. I'm on my way, okay? I'm at the Metro station. I should be over there in forty-five minutes."

I tried to clear my head to respond. "Ah, okay," I mumbled to her.

"Are you up yet?" she asked me.

"I'll be up."

She laughed and said, "Okay. I'll see you soon."

I looked over at the clock and it was just turning nine. It wasn't all that early, but it may as well have been five in the morning to me. I didn't feel like getting up at all.

I looked myself over and realized I had on the same clothes from the night before. "Damn! I gotta take a shower and get dressed," I told myself. First, I brushed my teeth.

The shower did the trick that morning. I just stood in the warm water and let it pound into my head for a good half hour. Then I toweled off, got dressed, and put on some hot water for tea. I didn't even have any Tylenol. I rarely needed any, but I made a note to buy myself some that day.

Before I could stir the sugar in my tea, Angel had arrived at my complex. I was embarrassed by my actions the night before, so I had a problem looking her in the eye that morning. When you first start to get to know someone, you don't know how they're gonna respond to your eccentricities. I was in that predicament with Angel. What if she thought I was a nut case? I planned to stay busy while she was there. It was a trick that I learned from my mother. We could always tell when she was disturbed about something, but eventually she'd let us know about it anyway.

"I was just making tea in the kitchen," I told Angel. "You want some?"

"Yeah, I'll take some."

I began to make her a cup of tea. Angel sat down at my medium-sized kitchen table.

"Are you feeling okay this morning?" I asked her.

"Yeah, I'm okay. I was more worried about you," she told me.

I stirred sugar in her tea and placed it in front of her. Then I walked over to my window. "It looks pretty cold outside," I said.

"It *is* cold," Angel responded. "Bobby, come sit down with me."

I didn't get a chance to avoid her long at all. "Well, usually, in the mornings I like to get my energy up. I don't sit down too much in the mornings," I lied to her.

"Okay, I'll stand up with you then," she responded.

I got really nervous. I just didn't know what to do with myself. I needed more time to recuperate before seeing anyone. I was glad that Angel wasn't at work when I drove back over to Takoma Station from Scotty's. I probably would have made a fool of myself in front of everyone at her job.

"Here, I bought these for you," Angel said, handing me a small brown bag.

"What's this?" I asked.

"Tylenol," she answered with a smile.

I grinned and looked away from her.

Angel said, "You know, I had an older cousin named Manny, and every time something was bothering him, he'd get real antisocial with everybody, like he didn't want anyone around him. He was having problems on the job with white people, problems with his girlfriend, just a bunch of stuff. This was years ago when I was still in high school.

"Anyway, he ended up crashing his car into a tree and died. They say it was a case of drunk driving, but my aunt thought that it was suicide. I thought it was suicide, too."

I looked Angel in the face and asked, "So what are you saying?"

"I felt really bad about my cousin because he really needed someone to understand what he was going through. So, I guess what I'm trying to say is that I want to help you if you need someone."

I smiled and shook my head. Brad had made the same crazy assumption. "You think that I would commit suicide?" I asked Angel.

She said, "It's not about that, it's about getting help when you need it so it never gets to that point. It's just like on your show, when you talked about the Humpty-Dumpty thing. I'm just trying to stop you from falling, Bobby, that's all. I wanna be your support."

"You know, I don't really need help like that," I responded, on the defensive. "That was just last night. I had a few extra drinks at Scotty's, and this guy Frank, who I used to work with, was telling me some disturbing things about the business. I drove back to Takoma Station hoping that I could take you home with me and forget about it, but it didn't work out that way. Now you're coming over here talking to me like I'm crazy. And I'm sorry about your cousin, but I'm not suicidal and I'm *not* crazy."

"You don't have to be suicidal or crazy to need help, Bobby," Angel responded to me.

I don't know what got into me that morning, but I was getting more and more angry as she continued to try and help me. I had to use a lot of self-restraint to calm myself down. "Look," I said, "let's just forget about this before I say some things . . . and then we end up . . ."

I turned away from her and looked out the window again. The next thing I knew, Angel was working her fingers into my lower back, like in a massage.

"What are you doing?" I turned and asked her.

She looked at me all doe-eyed and innocent. "You don't want me to touch you?"

I thought about it for a second. I was pretty pissed off at Angel for insinuating that I was crazy, but that didn't mean I didn't want her to touch me. I smiled and said, "I don't know if I can let you do that without touching you back. I got a whole lot of tension built up in me right now."

Angel laughed.

"I'm dead serious," I told her.

"I know you are," she said. Then she looked at me and walked closer. "You wanna kiss me?"

Even though I wouldn't have minded, I shook my head and backed away. "Not if this is for sympathy, because I'm not crazy."

"I know you're not crazy, Bobby," she responded with a smile. Then she looked at me seriously. "You're intelligent, thoughtful, caring, honest, and you're very handsome."

If I was a white girl, I would have looked like Santa Claus with the rosy cheeks after all of that. I was a young black man in need of someone to stroke his ego and make him feel like he was still worth something. It felt ten times better coming from an attractive black woman who wanted to know if I desired to kiss her. Usually, ego stroking comes from people you can't touch in an intimate way. That only disqualifies a lot of its potential weight.

I looked at Angel and said, "Is that how you feel about *me,* or is that a blanket statement because you love black men?" It was a damn good question.

Angel looked into my eyes and answered, "I do love black men, but what I just said was for you."

"What makes *me* so special?"

"Bobby, because that's the way I really feel about you, okay! Stop fighting me."

I was making things more complicated than they needed to be, but I didn't want any mercy sex, I wanted the passionate stuff. "Why do you feel so strongly about me?" I asked her.

Angel shook her head and grimaced. I think I might have been turning her off. "Would you rather I not be here? Isn't it obvious that I like you? I mean, I can *feel* you, Bobby, and I like that. Okay? Is it something wrong with that?"

I was confused. "You can *feel* me?" *What the hell is she talking about?* I wondered. *She hasn't felt me yet. We haven't even done anything.*

"Okay, let me explain it to you," she said.

"Please do," I told her.

"Usually, guys show you about two emotions, lust and anger. They either wanna fuck you, or they wanna fuck somebody up."

I laughed. "Damn, such rough language so early in the morning," I said to her.

"I'm just being real about it. A lot of women get used to that. So when a brother shows them that he can be confused in life, or that he can be nervous, embarrassed, scared, or unsure of himself sometimes, a lot of women take that as being weak and whatnot, because they don't equate that with being a real man or whatever. But I see it as being *more* of a man, because you do have all of those feelings, just like women do. So that's what I mean when I say I *feel* you, because you show me all of those emotions. I mean, you're the kind of guy that women usually turn into a friend."

I started grinning. "And you want to make me more than a friend?"

"Oh, from the first time that I was with you it crossed my mind," she answered. "I mean, I've been with a lot of guys—not sexually—who acted like they were all that or whatever, and I know that most of them were putting up fronts, so I wouldn't go out with them again. And they were all wondering why I stopped calling. They all thought that I was going for a guy that had more money than them, or was bigger than them, or more good-looking, and it wasn't even like that. I just couldn't *feel* anything for them. I mean, I don't care about a guy's *car,* I can get my own car. You know what I mean?

"When I went out with you, though, I could tell that it was a first date, because you acted the way a normal person would on a first date, and you weren't out to impress me or show me someone that you're not. So I liked you immediately. I even leaned my head against you during the movie on purpose, just to see what you would do. And you were a perfect gentleman about it. You didn't even try to take advantage of the situation when I came back to your apartment that night. I just felt comfortable with you."

"Well, you know, I'm from the South," I joked with her.

"Being from the South doesn't make that much difference. I met plenty of guys from down South that were just as bad as guys from New York or Compton, so don't even try it."

I felt a lot better after she explained things to me, even without kissing her and taking her to bed. I felt I owed her an apology, too. I said, "I'm sorry for blowing up at you like I did. It was just that, you know—"

She cut me off. "Actually, I'm glad that you did. Sometimes guys who are generally nice feel that they're not supposed to blow up, and that's as fake as guys who act like they can't be afraid of something. I mean, if you're upset about something, let people know. Don't hold it in, that's not natural. Whatever you're upset about is not gonna go away without getting it out in the open, so you might as well get it out there."

We ended up not having sex that morning. I was hungry, so Angel made me a bacon and cheese omelette. I didn't have any green peppers and onions like she wanted to use. She said she would bring some next time. After that, we ended up taking a spur-of-the-moment drive to the Baltimore Harbor, like Mona had suggested years ago. It was cold out, but what the hell, I needed to clear my mind with some good, fresh air.

Angel said, "Bobby, if you *ever* need somebody to talk to about something, *anything,* just call me, all right?"

"What about if it's four o'clock in the morning?" I joked.

"It doesn't matter. As long as I can help you."

"What about when *you* need help?"

"I'll call you then."

I shivered in my stance and my teeth chattered. "Damn, it's cold out here!" I said.

Angel smiled at me and squeezed me real hard. "That's what you have me for, to warm you up."

I chuckled and said, "Like a blanket, hunh?"

She laughed and said, "Yeah, like Linus from *Peanuts.*"

•

I walked into the station that night at WUCI with some show ideas of my own. It was our first Wednesday broadcast. I had come up with plenty of topics for the show before, but I planned to be more assertive about having a say in what we talked about with three shows a week.

As soon as Kathy walked in, I ran my ideas past her. I thought of three ideas while I was out with Angel, including; "Anxiety: Should I Buy Her Something for Christmas?," "The Just a Friend Disease," and "How Much Does His Money Matter?"

Kathy looked at them, nodded her head, and said, "Good work. They sound good to me."

I didn't know if I should be happy or upset about it. That "good work" statement didn't settle too well with me. She made it sound as if I was working *for* her rather than *with* her. *What does "good work" mean for a cohost?* I thought. *Why couldn't she just say, "Good idea. We can use these"?*

The conversation with Frank had messed up my perception of things. For that night's show, we were discussing spousal abuse. I had a bad taste in my mouth about that subject. It seemed like one of those one-sided discussions. Of course, I didn't agree with hitting women, but . . . it just seemed like a lot of battered women went after those type of guys.

Sure enough, Kathy started off the show by saying, "No man should ever, ever, *ever* even *think* about putting his hands on a woman! If he feels that upset about something, then he needs to take it to a boxing gym."

I joked and said, "Okay, that's the end of this show. Next topic."

"I'm serious, Bobby. This is a very serious issue," Kathy responded.

I admit, I didn't see the point in the show myself. "Well, after the big fire that went off when *The Blackman's Guide to Understanding The Blackwoman* came out a few years ago, didn't we discuss that spouse abuse thing enough?" I asked. Shahrazad Ali's self-published book made big-time news all over the country. Many sisters, however, were concerned with one page in the book that discussed an open-hand slap in the mouth when they became unruly.

Kathy said, "Evidently not, because it's still a lot of brothers out there doing it. The numbers are increasing every year."

"I thought that sexual harassment was the new issue," I responded.

"We can get to that on another day, Bobby. Right now we're talking about spousal abuse." I could tell that I was getting to Kathy by her early grimaces. She didn't usually do that until we neared the end of our shows.

"There are a lot of circumstances that lead up to some men hitting their women," I said. "Frankly, I've been around some women who seem to ask for it. And if their men don't respond to them in an aggressive way, then these particular women will continue to push for a confrontation of some sort.

"Now, I believe that some of these women need social or psychological help, because they keep going back to these abusive guys and getting themselves into trouble with them."

Kathy had explained her past abusive relationship to me, but I felt she had done the right thing by leaving the marriage and strengthening herself so that it would never happen again. If she had started the show on the angle of helping sisters *and* brothers to understand themselves more in troubling relationships, I would have been more receptive. But I was getting tired of Kathy downgrading brothers without even trying to be objective about it.

"Bobby, I'm gonna ask you something and I want you to give me an honest answer," she said.

Kathy was ready to put me on the spot, and I was two steps ahead of her. "No, I have *never* hit a woman and I probably *never* will, but I can't speak for every other man out there."

Kathy and I went at it like cats and dogs that night. I stood my ground on every point she made. I wasn't making any excuses for brothers who abused women, because they were wrong. But I also wasn't letting sisters who sought out these abusive brothers off the hook. It takes two to tangle, and after a sister gets burned, in my opinion, she should know to be careful of fires next time. And every brother wasn't abusive!

At the end of the night, Kathy was steamed. "Bobby, the next time you have a problem with one of my topics, you keep it off the air, okay? You had good enough time to say something about it before we went on," she told me as she gathered her things and hurried for the door. She didn't even give me a chance to respond to her.

That night, I walked home in the cold feeling guilty. I guess I owed it all to Frank. Nevertheless, I think that Kathy had gotten used to a complaisant Bobby Dallas who just went along with her program.

As soon as I got in, I called Brother Abu at his home to see if he heard the show. I should have called him right after talking to Frank anyway. What the hell was I thinking listening to Frank?

Brother Abu said, "Partnerships are always harder to do. When they work, they can work really well, but when they don't, it could be for many different reasons."

"Did it sound like I had an attitude on the show tonight?"

"Not at all. She just didn't like what you had to say. I think you made some good points myself, but what do I know? I'm just a man."

"Yeah, exactly, that's what I'm saying. It just seems that sometimes her views can be a little lopsided."

"Well, that's the kind of show that you're on, Bobby. As a journalist, you try to have good, objective discussions, but she's out to do more than that. Kathy has a real passion about what she believes in, and you can tell. But whenever *you* get just as passionate on the other side of the coin, she has to be able to accept that, just like you accept her views.

"Now, just because you two disagree doesn't mean that it wasn't a good show, and it doesn't mean that you can't work together. It just means that you disagree.

"If you've been listening to talk radio half as much as I have, you'll see that most people seem to *disagree* a lot more than they *agree* on things, so I wouldn't even let that be a concern. A lot of times that just makes the ratings hotter."

It's funny how you can learn a lot of things and end up having to hear them over and over again before you finally take it to heart. That was the case with my radio career. Ratings meant everything, but I just kept forgetting the fact. It didn't matter whether or not your show was excellent as long as people listened. What I was concerned about, though, was that Kathy was pissed off with me.

"What happens, though, if she's really mad at me?" I asked. I felt wimpy about it, but Brother Abu struck me as the kind of man who could handle the full range of my emotions without belittling me like Frank Watts would.

"Bobby, you go out and buy her a nice card and tell her that you're sorry but she might as well get used to you saying what you're gonna say. It's simply the nature of human life. You're not gonna agree on every little thing, but you shouldn't allow that to ruin a good show or a good business relationship. You have to respect each other's opinions."

"Hey, thanks, man," I told him. "Thanks a lot."

"Bobby, I told you to give me a call whenever you needed to, and I meant it. Now hang in there, because you're doing good. You're doing *damn* good!"

I hung up with Brother Abu and felt much better about things. It seemed like every other week I needed someone to talk to and straighten out a different concern I had. I was an excellent case study. If people could have walked around with me for a month, they would never let me on a talk show. Then again, the crazier your lifestyle is, the more experiences you have to relate to different discussions. I had been through a little bit of everything.

As it turned out, Kathy and I made up and had smooth sailing right up until the last week of the year. It was time to renew our contract for 1993. When I walked into the office ready to read and sign the new contract, the program director, John Sprier, looked at me with apprehension.

"What's wrong?" I asked him.

"Have you, ah, talked to Kathy?"

"Not since last Friday. Why?"

"Well, it seems that she has other ideas about what she wants to do for next year. I don't think she wants to come back."

I just shook my head and laughed. At that point, I wasn't going to let it get to me. "Okay, so, do we get someone new, or do we try a new show with just me?" I figured I had shown WUCI-AM what I was worth, and I saw it as an opportunity to finally branch out on my own.

"Well, we were kind of hoping that you could talk to her and see if you could bring her back," John told me. "They're even willing to, ah, make it worth your while."

I got real excited. They were willing to give us even more money. I was looking forward to the thirty-one thousand. Anything more than that was icing on the cake. "You told her that already?" I asked.

John looked behind him as if he was watching his back. He whispered, "Bobby, I'm not supposed to tell you this, but they offered her something close to sixty thousand dollars, and she turned them down. I think she was just trying to see what she was worth."

I really appreciated him for leveling with me like he did. To this day, I believe that John's being gay allowed him to be sensitive to just how unfair the situation was. If he was a straight white man, I don't believe he would have cared.

"Let me talk to Stacy," I said.

John shook his head. "Ah, that's not a good idea," he told me. "Kathy and Stacy had a catfight that was something fierce this morning. I wasn't in the office, but I did hear your name come up a few times. Afterward, Stacy told me to let you know she didn't want to see you unless Kathy was with you."

I just sat there in a daze. We weren't supposed to meet about the contracts until two that afternoon, but apparently Kathy had shown up at ten in the morning. I was willing to bet that she took WUCI's offer and used it to get a better deal somewhere else. I couldn't imagine getting her back there with me. Kathy wanted to be on FM from day one, and she had gotten a chance to negotiate with "them," whoever "they" were who owned WUCI. I barely got a chance to speak to Stacy half the time, let alone negotiate with WUCI's owners. Angel was right, it was an unpredictable world, with unpredictable people and a lot of unpredictable shit going on!

I got home and called Kathy, ready to let her have it. Her fiancé, Harold, answered the phone. I believed she had him there to answer her phone on purpose. She had to know damn well that I would be calling her! Harold told me to hold on and handed the phone over to Kathy.

"Bobby, I expect you to be very mature and professional about this," she started. I could tell already she had no plans of working with me again. I figured, why waste my time arguing?

I cut her off and said, "Kathy, I just called you to say good luck with your future. May God bless you." I was working under the "Wish for others what you would love to have for yourself" philosophy, and I hoped and prayed that it would work.

Kathy was silent. She said, "Thank you, Bobby. I'll always remember how civil you were."

•

I walked into Scotty's on Eighth Street that night and the place was jam-packed with the spirit of the coming new year. People were getting themselves loaded and having a jolly good time.

I walked up to Big Bill at the bar and said, "How you doin'? Can 'The Relationship Guy' have a gin and tonic?"

He laughed. "Sure, Bobby. You can have anything you want."

"Yeah, I wish everybody told me that," I responded to him.

Big Bill slid my drink over the counter. "Frank told you to meet him here?"

"Naw, I came on my own."

He nodded. "Oh, 'cause I thought that Frank was going out of town this morning. So, what brings you back to this area?"

"I wanted to tell Frank that he was right about my cohost, Kathy Teals," I answered. It wasn't any sense in being hush-hush about it. People would know soon enough. I figured they might as well get it from me rather than from someone else. At least that way I could control some of the rumors. "She was just out to get a bigger paycheck. I knew I never trusted her. I had bad vibes from her the first time she sat beside me," I said.

Big Bill chuckled and said, "Well, don't take it out on that glass. You got a three-drink limit in here tonight. I don't want to see you drowning your pride over some woman."

I smiled and enjoyed the rest of the merry crowd, dancing on a small floor and talking loud. It was like a pre–New Year's Eve celebration. Scotty's was erupting with energy! I guess Frank was right again, it was a place I needed to become more familiar with.

I found myself without a job in radio for about the seventh time in only six years, but with a smile on my face. I didn't plan to wallow in self-pity. I wasn't even planning on staying at Scotty's long. I wanted to pick Angel up from work and finally have sex with her. I was going to melt bodies with her until the sun came up if she let me. Hell, I felt good about not having a job for a change. I was just going to enjoy the coming New Year without all of the added stress.

"Hey, Bobby, how you doin'?" It was Mark Bishop, "The Painter Guy." He looked pretty excited.

I shook his hand and said, "Long time no see. What's been going on with you?"

"I just came from the Kwanzaa Expo at the D.C. Armory." He leaned into me and whispered, "I just sold sixty-two hundred dollars' worth of art. That's the best that I've ever done at one show."

I nodded and said, "Oh yeah? So how many women you got now?" I was joking of course.

Mark grinned. "Oh, I just got one woman . . . when she wants to be."

I laughed. "That's how it is, hunh? That's just how I feel about my career in radio. I got one career, when she wants to be."

"What happened to your show?" he asked me. He was just one of several people I would confide in that night.

"The same thing that happened to your artwork today," I told him. "It got sold. The only difference is, I didn't get paid for it."

"Damn, I didn't know that they could sell a show."

"Yeah they can. And evidently my cohost *was* the show. She just walked away with it and put it in her pocket to sell to a higher bidder."

Mark stared at me and said, "Damn! That's too bad."

"Yeah, so why don't you buy me a drink and help me get over it?" I joked with him again.

Mark smiled at me and said, "All right. I can do that. It's good to be able to help out a brother in need."

I was on a roll. I said, "Oh yeah? Well, if you feel that way then find me another job, too."

Mark just smiled at me and shook his head.

My Angel

I didn't leave Scotty's that night until late, and Mark Bishop had to drive me home. I was tore up! Angel found out and was upset with me for a couple of weeks. She kept reminding me every chance she got that I could call and talk to her about anything. "The last thing in this world that I want you to do is get yourself drunk," she told me.

WUCI-AM put Latino programming in the time slot that Kathy and I used to have. "Now I know how white people felt when blacks started taking over their jobs during the affirmative action years," I joked to myself. Latinos were the new hot minority market in the District. Black people in Washington were yesterday's news. I figured Pablo Garcia would become a high-profile DJ soon.

I had my twenty-ninth birthday coming up in a week. Fortunately, I had enough money in the bank to last a few months without a job. I learned to always pad my bank account just in case another radio opportunity fell apart. In the nineties, building a nice savings account was a good idea for any professional. It seemed like everybody was losing jobs, particularly skilled people who received higher pay. Even the D.C. government—with new leadership from the first lady mayor, Sharon Pratt Kelly—was cutting back thousands of government jobs and programs to save the District money. Many of the established major cities in America were going bankrupt for some reason, while other cities were cropping up. As the cliché goes, the rich were getting richer and the poor were getting poorer. All those in between were getting moved up or moved down.

I had a lot of time to read and keep up on the news. I was becoming much sharper politically. I didn't feel like looking for a new job, yet, but just because I didn't have one didn't mean that I could begin to slack off. I was no "slacker," and I was no "generation X" kid, I simply lacked a job and motivation for the moment.

I was sitting in my living room, casually dressed, reading newspapers and magazines and watching television news on another weekday morning while waiting for Angel to come over. It was just like my old times with Faye, where I hung out with a woman with no sex involved.

When Angel finally arrived, she was in much better spirits with me than she had been over the past couple of weeks. She walked in and said, "Bobby, you gotta get off your ass and live again. Don't do this to yourself." She was really excited that day, like a motivational speaker.

I smiled and said, "Can I have some of what you had for breakfast? That'll do the trick."

Angel shook her head. "You're still not going to look for a new job yet?"

"That's right. I plan to enjoy my unemployment for a while, or at least until after my birthday."

Angel smiled and said, "Okay then. I'm gonna take you home with me for a couple of days. That'll be your birthday present from me."

I grinned. "You mean I'm gonna meet your family?"

"Yeah, why not? You need to get away."

It occurred to me that I didn't know where Angel Thomas was from. I assumed that she was from the metropolitan area—D.C., Maryland, or northern Virginia.

"So how long of a drive is it?" I asked her. I assumed that I would be driving. Angel said that she didn't like to drive unless it was absolutely necessary.

First she looked at me and frowned. Then she grinned and said, "It would take two or three days to drive."

"Two or three days? Where are you from, California?" I was joking.

Angel looked at me and said, "Yeah."

Then I was shocked. "You're from California?" I asked her seriously.

"San Jose," she answered.

I couldn't believe it! That explained Angel's whole live-and-let-live philosophy. She was a California girl! "You mean to tell me that we've been hanging out for two months and I'm just finding out that you're from California?"

"I stopped telling people."

"Why, are you ashamed of it?"

"No, but people take it different ways. Like, when I told you that a lot of guys I went out with before were trying so hard to impress me, I think the fact that I was from California had a lot to do with it. They like to stereotype you."

I just burst out laughing. I had no idea that I was so close to a California girl. That changed everything for me. No wonder Angel seemed so left-minded. It all began to make sense.

"See, that's why I didn't tell you," she said to me.

"What?" I asked her through my laughs.

"What are you thinking about me now?" she asked. She was serious. I had to wipe the smile off my face.

"Well, you're still my Angel," I told her. Then I started to laugh again. I don't know why I was acting so silly about it. I think I needed a good laugh and I couldn't help but cut loose on her, especially since she had deliberately hidden her California roots from me.

"Do you wanna go or what?" she snapped at me.

California? I thought. *That sounds expensive!* "I don't know if I can afford that right now," I told her. I needed more time to think on it.

"I told you already, it's my birthday gift to you."

I looked at her trim body and said, "I thought that *you* were gonna be my birthday present." Although we had never indulged, Angel and I had talked about sex a few times, just like Faye and I used to do.

Angel smirked at me. "I'm serious, Bobby, I'll take care of your flight tickets," she said. She didn't respond to my birthday wish.

I was still unsure about a trip to California. Angel had just sprung the idea on me. "I don't know, that sounds like a pretty expensive birthday present. Where am I gonna stay?"

"I have frequent-flyer discounts from my auditions in New York and L.A. And you can stay in my house," she told me. "We have a guest room. Bobby, I can get the tickets right now." She walked over and picked up my phone.

"What about your job?"

"I already told them I was taking a week off. I worked straight through the holiday season."

I had run out of excuses not to go. "You're really serious about this, hunh?"

Angel frowned at me and started dialing. "Yes, can I have the number for American Airlines?" She got the number and ordered round-trip tickets to California for the end of that week.

I thought about it and decided to let go of my inhibitions. *California, here I come!* I thought. I was glad to know Angel. A trip to California was just what the doctor ordered.

•

There was plenty of open space in San Jose. Angel told me that most of the housing developments there were new. Just like in the Adams Morgan area of D.C., San Jose had plenty of Latinos. In fact, they looked to be the majority out there.

When we got to her house, I was impressed. Angel didn't carry herself like a spoiled child, but looking at her five-bedroom, California-style home, she easily could have been. They had a lot of large windows with plenty of sunlight and a huge deck that I couldn't wait to stand on.

"So this is California," I said with a smile. We arrived at her house a little after four. Her younger sister was just getting in from school. She was a senior in high school.

"Sabrina, this is Bobby Dallas, my good friend from D.C.," Angel told her.

"Hi," Sabrina said with a smile. She was penny brown like me and cute as she could be. She reminded me of an old girlfriend of Brad's that I had a secret crush on in North Carolina. Marla Dupree.

Anyway, Angel showed me to the guest room. It was as big as the bedroom in my apartment.

"This is a nice-sized guest room. I thought it would be a small chair and a bed."

Sabrina was in the vicinity and started to laugh.

Angel shook her head and smiled. "It's just an extra room that we use for guests."

"We never had one in my family home. If you came over our house as a guest, you got to sleep in the basement."

Sabrina was eavesdropping and said, "The basement?" as if it was something horrible.

"Their basements are fully carpeted, furnished, and nice," Angel told her. "It's not like a small, dusty attic or anything."

"Oh," Sabrina said.

"We don't really have basements in California," Angel explained to me.

I got the full tour of the house. I looked around at all of the Thomas family pictures. Angel was the oldest of three children. Her younger brother was a junior at the University of California, Berkeley. Her mother worked at the local newspaper as a senior copyeditor, and her father was a corporate lawyer. It was a well-established household.

I sat out on that huge deck of theirs and was at total peace with myself. It was 67 degrees, the sun was out, and I didn't have a care in the world. Some environments can do that to you. I couldn't remember feeling as peaceful as I felt at Angel's house in California in my entire life. It was similar to being at an empty beach, and watching the tide come in. It was just me and nature.

"Is it cold in Washington?" Angel's sister Sabrina asked me.

She snapped me out of paradise. "Oh, yeah, of course. It's freezing in Washington right now."

"I hate the cold," she told me. "My father wants me to go to Howard, but I don't wanna go there."

I could tell Sabrina wasn't half as thoughtful as Angel was. Sabrina was more of the spoiled type.

"Yeah, you probably don't want to leave your boyfriend behind for that cold East Coast weather anyway," I joked.

"I don't care about him. Once I'm out of high school, that's over with," she told me.

I grimaced, "Wow! Does he know this?" I asked her. She was pretty straightforward about it.

"Yeah, I told him. He knows."

"And what did he say?"

"He says he's gonna visit me no matter where I go."

"Where do you want to go?"

"To Berkeley with my brother. Or maybe UCLA, or Southern Cal."

"Did you send applications to all of these schools?"

"Not UCLA and Southern Cal, but I plan to."

"So I figure your father wants to send an application to Howard," I said.

Sabrina sucked her teeth. "They already did. Angel sent it in after Thanksgiving."

Angel walked out of the house from cooking and caught the tail end of the conversation. "Angel did what?" she asked.

"Angel saw her way inside the conversation when it was only between A and B," Sabrina said to her.

I started to laugh.

Angel said, "You're not cute, Sabrina. Okay?" She spoke it like a true big sister.

Sabrina responded, "I'm cuter than you, especially with your hair like that."

I didn't laugh at that. Younger sister was getting too personal.

Angel said, "Stop showing off, okay? You're getting too old for that." Then she walked back inside to finish her preparations for dinner.

"Anyway," Sabrina said to me, "I went to Howard's homecoming when I was in the tenth grade, and it was all these guys trying to talk to me. I said, 'I'm not even out of high school yet.' " She shook her head and repeated, "I don't wanna go there. Howard is just a big party school."

I was getting a little sick and tired of people calling Howard University a party school, especially if the only time they'd ever been there was during homecoming. "Let me ask you a question," I responded to Sabrina. "Do you think that those white kids have parties at UCLA and Southern Cal, and especially Berkeley?"

She thought about it and saw my point immediately. "But they don't party *all* the time," she argued.

"And neither does Howard." Sabrina had a whole lot of growing up to do from what I could see. Inner-city youth on the East Coast were light-years ahead of her on street smarts, but on the flip side, I was willing to bet that Sabrina was light-years ahead of them on standardized test taking.

Except for Angel's brother, the Thomas family were all seated by six-thirty at the large dinner table for the stuffed cabbage meal that Angel prepared. I was sitting in the guest's chair, I suppose.

Her mother began the questioning session. I knew I wouldn't be able to escape that.

"So, Angel tells us that you're in the radio business. Do you like it?"

"Yeah, I like it. I'm just having a hard time getting *it* to like *me.*"

The Thomas family all laughed. I felt good about that. I was breaking the ice with a sledgehammer.

"Yeah, I hear it's really competitive," Angel's mother responded. She had short-cut hair and was wearing a business suit. She looked like an official corporate-card sister.

"Radio is so competitive that it's like ten elephants all trying to squeeze into your bathtub."

Angel broke in and said, "Mom, he's exaggerating now. He was just on a top-rated show in D.C. He'll be back on top in no time."

"I'm glad *you* think so," I responded to her.

"Bob-bee Dallas," Sabrina said out of the blue. I guess she caught on to the name symmetry thing. "You should call yourself Bobby D.," she suggested.

I smiled at her. "Maybe if I was a DJ spinning hip-hop records I would."

"That's where the money is," she responded.

"That's only in a few markets," I told her.

"So, you're more into talk radio?" Mr. Thomas asked me. He was pretty quiet until he got me alone inside the family room. That's when he asked me his set of questions.

"You ever thought about owning a station?" he asked me.

Owning a station? I couldn't even imagine it. "I'm having a hard enough time just trying to stay in the station," I answered him.

He laughed and said, "Oh yeah? Well, you're pretty personable. You're funny, polite, witty. That's all the things that you need for radio. And you're still pretty young. You'll get your break. No question."

"Actually, I learned how to be more outspoken through dealing with the downside of the business," I leveled with him. "If you would have met me six years ago when I was just starting out, I would have been the shiest guy that you could meet. What I need now is some loyalty, you know, somebody to look after me," I said.

"You mean like a lawyer?" Mr. Thomas asked me with a grin.

I had never thought of the idea of having a lawyer on my side before. "Sure, that would probably help a lot."

"All right then. I'm an Alpha. I have a lot of brothers in Washington. I'll call out there and see what I can do for you." He extended his hand and said, "The Howard family has to stick together."

I took his hand and responded, "Well, all right! It looks like I chose the right school and the right sister to be friends with!"

•

Without knowing it, my experiences in radio were building my character. I was becoming a lot more loose with people. I was able to joke more about life's shortcomings, and that was a good thing to be able to do in radio, because everyone could relate to going through some kind of hell to get to where they want to go. It was good to be able to laugh at things and keep on striving. I should have learned that from Mona a long time ago.

I wasn't actually counting on anything to happen with Angel's father and the lawyer business. I was just being a good ham. I figured I might as well have a good time while I was out in California, and I *was* having a good time. I rested in the guest room at the end of that first night, planning on having a damn good sleep for a change. Angel slipped inside before I dozed off.

"My father likes you," she said with a grin. She took a seat at the foot of the bed.

I sat up in the dark with her. "That's nice. So does that mean I can marry you now?" I joked with her.

She smiled. "I didn't know you wanted to marry me."

"What if I did?"

Angel stared into space. "I don't know."

"Anyway, what are you doing in here? You came to give me my birthday gift?" I asked her, changing the subject. It was obvious she had other things on her mind. I was only joking with her about the marriage thing anyway. I didn't want her to take it too seriously. Her being pleased with her father's liking me led me to believe it would be a requirement to become her husband and the father of her kids.

"I wanted to talk to you," she said.

"And it can't wait until the morning?"

"No it can't."

"What if you get caught in here with me?" I asked her with a smile. I figured it would have been embarrassing, to say the least.

"Bobby, we're grown. What's wrong with you?"

"Well, it looked like you were sneaking in here to me."

"That's because I didn't want Sabrina to see me."

I nodded. I could imagine what Sabrina would have thought and said. "Yeah, you're right. This is none of her business."

"Anyway, my father told me that he was going to call a few of his frat brothers to see what he could do for you in D.C."

"What else did he tell you?"

"He just said that you seemed like a sharp brother. A good brother."

I grinned. I wondered if I could have gotten Mr. Thomas to write a reference letter addressed to my mother. "What did your mother say?" I asked.

"Oh, she just said that you were funny."

I frowned and said, "That's all? I thought she liked me, too."

Angel said, "I had this boyfriend a few years ago that she really liked, and ever since then, she's been less than cordial to any other guy that I've introduced her to, even if they were just friends. In fact, she talked to *you* a lot. That was a good thing."

"Oh," I said. "So what are we planning on doing while we're out here?" I asked her.

"Enjoying California. We can drive up to Oakland, San Francisco, Berkeley. You name it."

"They're all that close together?"

"Yeah."

"What about L.A.?"

Angel shook her head. "Now you're talking about a six-to-eight-hour drive, depending on the traffic. We fly to L.A. In fact, I have to call out there tomorrow to see about this commercial campaign I tried out for over Thanksgiving."

"So you came back home during Thanksgiving?"

She grinned and said, "Yeah."

Angel was wearing one of those long baseball shirts as a nightgown. I was wondering what she had on underneath it. I had never seen her in so few clothes.

She looked at me and asked, "What are you thinking about?"

"I'm just wondering what you have on under that shirt," I admitted.

"Nothing," she told me with a grin.

I was shocked. "You mean nothing, like in, 'Nothing at all'?" I was wearing shorts over my drawers and a gray T-shirt.

"Mmm-hmm," Angel hummed, still smiling at me.

"Ah, what were we talking about again?" I asked. I wanted to prevent my mind from sending my body the wrong message. Of course, it was a natural message, but I didn't want to get my body excited for a letdown. I figured having sex with Angel would have been highly unlikely that night.

Angel chuckled and stood up. "I'll see you in the morning, Bobby. Good night." Just like that, she walked out of the room and was gone. I was about to go crazy. I wish she hadn't come inside the room at all, especially with next to nothing on. My sleep was ruined. I had a hard on for the rest of that night, tossing and turning and thinking about tapping on Angel's bedroom door.

I got up in the middle of the night to use the bathroom and saw that the door was closed with the light on. Thinking that it was Angel, I waited to get in, hoping to see her. Sabrina walked out instead, wearing the same style of long baseball shirt that Angel wore. Sabrina was more busty than her older sister. We made eye contact, and before I could turn away, she grinned at me.

"Hi," she said in a low tone.

I nodded at her, afraid to speak. As I stepped into the bathroom I took another glance. Apparently, Sabrina wanted to take another peek at me as well, and she didn't appear to be looking at my face, either. Talk about embarrassing turn-ons, I couldn't even use the bathroom for a few minutes, afraid that I would miss and spray the walls.

Once I was finished, I hurried back to that guest room as quickly as I could. I was ready to fly back to my apartment in Washington immediately. My nice stay out in California had turned into sexual torture.

"Dammit, what is wrong with me?" I mumbled to myself. I knew that it was wrong to be thinking about Angel's little sister like I was, but I couldn't get my mind off of her. The more you tell your mind not to think about something, the more you end up thinking about it anyway. I was wondering if Sabrina was thinking about me. I was afraid to even go to sleep, terrified that I might have a sinful dream about her.

I looked over at the digital clock on the dresser. It read 3:48. I swear, that first night was taking forever. I looked at that clock every ten minutes or so. It felt like I could hear every sound in that house.

"Shit!" I mumbled at 4:52. I stood up and squeezed my temples with both hands. "I gotta get some damn rest," I told myself. I had a headache the length of California. I figured I could use it as an excuse to knock on Angel's door, but I forced myself to rest instead.

•

Angel woke me up at 11:08 that morning. "I got good news, Bobby." She was sitting at the foot of the bed again with a big smile on her face. She was dressed in loose-fitting jeans and a bright orange blouse, ready to go.

It still felt like I had a headache, but at least the torture was over with. I didn't remember falling asleep, but I was glad that I had. "What, you got a role in a movie?" I asked Angel. I remembered her telling me she had to call L.A. that morning.

She grinned and said, "Not yet, but I did get a callback for the ad campaign."

"Oh yeah? When do they want you back out there?" I asked her.

"Tomorrow," she answered. That posed a problem for me.

"So, what am I gonna do?"

Angel sighed. "Well, you can stay out here and wait for me if you want, or . . ."

"I can fly back to D.C. tomorrow," I answered for her. Angel didn't want to say it, but it was the only logical answer. I didn't mind. At least I hadn't paid for anything. Angel didn't know that she was getting a callback, or did she? Anyway, I was happy for her.

"Well, it looks like everybody's making moves but me," I told her, sitting up to get out of bed.

"That's not true, Bobby. I mean, it's only a callback. I haven't gotten the campaign yet. They could have called back five different girls."

I knew better than that. It may not have been certain, but callbacks generally involved no more than two people in any business. "Well, California was fun while it lasted," I told her with a grin. "I need some Tylenol right now, though."

Angel looked concerned. "You didn't get a good night's sleep? I have breakfast downstairs for you, but I didn't want to wake you too early."

"You got breakfast ready for me? Thanks."

I never did answer her question about the "good night's sleep." I took two Tylenols with some orange juice and microwaved the omelette that Angel made for me. Then I hit the shower and got dressed. I passed on the tour of northern California. I told Angel to save her energy and prepare herself for her appointment in L.A. instead. By four o'clock that afternoon, her father called the house with some good news for me.

"There's a brother in D.C. named Gene Carlton who wants to produce a politically conservative talk show for black men. I don't know if you're interested, but he told me to give you his number so you two could meet once you got back to Washington. He said he heard you before on a show you were doing with a young sister," Mr. Thomas told me.

I figured I had nothing to lose by it. "Okay, I'll meet with him and see what it's about," I responded with a smile. As I continued to smile, Sabrina walked into the house with two of her girlfriends, a Latina and an Asian. All eyes were discreetly on me. I could tell that she had been talking about me by the grins they were all displaying.

"I'll call him right back and let him know then," Sabrina's father told me.

"Okay," I said. I got the guy's number in D.C. and hung up.

"Hey, Bobby D.," Sabrina called out to me. Her friends broke out laughing.

Angel was standing nearby. She frowned and shook her head. "Well, what did he say?" she asked me, blocking out her sister and her friends.

"He said he has a guy back in the District that I could hook up with."

Angel jumped up and hugged me. "All right! See that? I told you it was just a matter of time."

"Yeah, but it's only a meeting. He may have five other guys he wants to meet," I responded sarcastically.

The next thing I knew, Sabrina was asking me what size shoe I wore. Her girlfriends broke out laughing again.

Angel glared at her and said, "Sabrina, stop it! Okay? Just stop it." Then she walked me out onto the deck. "I am really worried about her," she told me. "She acts so damned *childish*, but then she thinks she *knows* so much."

"It's a sign of the times," I told Angel. "A lot of teenagers are that way now." *They're a lot bigger and bolder nowadays too,* I thought to myself.

"Well, I don't like it!" Angel snapped. "I mean, I wasn't *anything* like her, Bobby!"

I smiled and said, "Yeah, and your name ain't Sabrina, either."

"But we have the same parents and the same upbringing," she argued.

"Come on now, you know people better than that. She's not you. She's her own person."

Angel sighed and said, "Yeah, you're right, but she just pisses me off sometimes."

"Maturity, Angel, that's all it is. I hope she goes to Howard, though, because she needs to be around more black people."

Angel grimaced and said, "Definitely."

I had a lot of anxiety as nighttime fell on my second day in Cali. As it turned out, I would be back in D.C. on my birthday instead of being out there with Angel. She walked into the guest room with me as I retired for bed and started talking about seeing me when she got back to D.C. For some reason, I didn't think it would be any time soon.

"What about your job at Takoma Station?" I asked her.

"I mean, I love that place and all, but come on. If New York offered you a job in radio, would you take it?"

I grinned. "Actually, I already had a job in New York."

"Well, you know what I mean, the chance of a lifetime."

"Yeah, I understand. My big chance came too early for me. I wasn't really prepared for it."

Angel grabbed my arm and shook me. "It's about to come again, Bobby, and you're ready now."

I fell silent and didn't know what else to say to her. I wanted to sleep with Angel so badly that second night that I was ready to catch a red-eye flight to the Washington National Airport rather than accept that we were only friends. A second night of torture was not ideal to me.

"I guess I won't be with you for my birthday now," I said. There was nothing else I wanted to say.

Angel looked into my eyes. I was sure she could tell what I was thinking. She placed her right hand on my chest and said, "I'll be back. Okay?"

I was already resigned to my fate. I would probably never make love to Angel. "Only if you want to," I told her.

I went to sleep much quicker that night. I pictured myself in New York again with the infamous Pearl Davis, enjoying my naïveté in our Queens apartment. Pearl was waking me up from my sleep again, ready to give me more of her aggressive lovemaking. But when I opened my eyes, it was a naked Angel with me.

"I thought you had forgotten about me," I told her. It was after two in the morning.

Angel raised her index finger to my lips. "Sshhh. Don't say anything," she whispered. Then she kissed me and slid her hands under my T-shirt to lift it off. She even had protection handy with her. I thought I was dreaming the whole time.

Angel was a toucher. With every move I made she touched me just the right way and with just the right amount of pressure to my arms, my back, my neck, my shoulders, my ribs, and my slow-thrusting behind. It felt like I was making love to a masseuse.

Not wanting to bring attention to ourselves, we concentrated every muscle and energy into the singular act of one man, one woman in uninterrupted passion. When the inevitable happened, we squeezed each other so tightly that we became human boa constrictors, devouring the prey.

Angel relaxed and whispered, "Bobby . . . that was *so* beautiful."

I smiled and whispered back to her, "Yeah . . . I know."

Thinking back to that night and to the many other nights and the women I had been intimate with, people might have concluded I was a pretty good batter. Yet I was never allowed to take any of the women home with me to keep. It was similar to being addicted to drugs, riding the ups and downs of the high and never being able to keep it. So you do it again, and again, and again and only succeed in wasting more of your soul away.

I thought about that on my flight back east. I wondered if I would have a chance to be with Angel or any other sister forever. Even if Angel came back to me, how long would it last?

God, I felt empty! I didn't even have a pack of cigarettes to pacify myself. I just stared out the window at the fluffy white clouds, forcing myself to think of other things, like radio. What was this Gene Carlton guy about? What exactly was a politically conservative talk show for black men? And how much would it be worth to me to host it?

Back on Track

I met Mr. Gene Carlton on my new turf at Scotty's. He was a business-looking brother with steady, dark eyes and a beer belly, wearing a stuffy dark gray suit. His bright red, striped tie was the only thing that told me he was alive, until he opened his mouth. He spoke very directly. I mean, this guy had the kind of voice that made anyone in the vicinity turn and look as if he was speaking to them. We sat down at a booth and had a couple of drinks.

"Bobby, how old are you?" he asked me.

"I turned twenty-nine last week."

"Perfect," he said. "Are you living the kind of life you want to live yet?"

I smiled. "Not hardly. What about you?"

"I've been there. Now I'm looking to do something else. And you know what that is, Bobby?"

"That's what I'm here to find out," I answered him.

"I want to produce a black radio talk show that can become syndicated in twenty markets," he said. "You ever heard of Tom Joyner?" he asked me.

"Yeah, I've heard of him. He's in the Dallas and Chicago areas, right?"

Gene nodded. "Now he's about to be everywhere. Syndicated. That brother's a pioneer, Bobby. And since he's ready to knock down the door, we want to be able to walk in right behind him. That's how things work, somebody does it first, and then *everybody* does it. We want to be next in line.

"How would you like to be syndicated, Bobby?"

Gene reminded me of a professional salesman. I said, "Asking me how I would like to be syndicated is like asking a teenager, 'How would you like to play in the NBA?' " He had me hooked already, but how hard is it to hook a hungry, jobless man who is more than willing to work again?

Gene smiled. "So you'd be pretty excited about it?"

"Damn right!" I responded. "But how do we get there? I'm having problems trying to stay in one market." I was game for any strategy, any that would work.

"Oh, you don't have to worry about that, as long as you understand one important thing."

"Oh yeah? What's that?"

He clasped his hands together and said, "The market is hot right now for conservative black views."

"What exactly are conservative black views?" I asked him.

"It could be rap music and Spike Lee with the right angle to it," he told me.

I looked at him like he had just given me the cure to sarcoidosis. I had no idea what he was talking about. I frowned and said, "Rap music and Spike Lee? Where are you getting conservative views from them? You mean more like Shelby Steele and Judge Clarence Thomas, don't you?"

"Yeah, them, too."

I shook my head and grimaced. "I'm not following you," I told him.

"Okay, look at it this way," he said. "These young rappers understand that the bottom line in America is money. Spike Lee understands that, Shelby Steele, *and* Judge Clarence Thomas.

"Family is important in America, whether it's a gang, a fraternity, blood brothers, sisters, cousins, a political party, you name it, these are all families.

"Job security is important, protection of your environment, education, good health, freedom of speech, and all of the Bill of Rights."

"Okay, so you're saying that conservative views are made up of the common denominators of society," I said to him.

He looked at me with surprise. "Bobby, I like you already. That's *exactly* what I'm saying, common denominators." He took a sip of his drink and asked, "How'd you get on that show with Kathy Teals?" I was wondering when he was going to inquire about my background. Usually people do that first. Gene Carlton was doing things backward.

"The program director over at WUCI liked our energy together after I interviewed her on her romance books," I told him. I took a sip of my drink. "Anyway, that's what he told me. I found out later on that they were already planning to try to get Kathy on the air; they just used me as a guinea pig cohost. But it worked out for me, too, because now people know me. I just have to rebound and do my own thing."

Gene nodded his head and said, "I hear she's working out a deal with DC Cablevision now for a local television talk show called, ah, 'Washington Love Life.' "

I raised my brow. "Are you serious?"

"That's what I heard," he told me.

I grinned. "She made the big move to TV, hunh?"

"That's where everybody's trying to go nowadays."

I shook my head and took another sip of my drink. "Not me. I'm gonna make this radio thing work for me. I've been through too much shit to quit now."

Gene smiled. "I like that attitude. Everybody has ups and downs, but you have to stick it out."

"You're a lawyer, right?" I asked him.

"Yes I am."

"So, why the interest in producing radio?"

"Good question," he said. "Remember all the media coverage the Clarence Thomas hearing received?"

"Yeah. It made me sick."

"It made a lot of people popular," he responded. "Anybody black that had any importance got a chance to say something about it. Well, during that time, I was one of them.

"I did this radio program on this white show, and I was amazed at how many people were listening all over the country. The guy was syndicated. So I got this idea to have a brother that could talk about black conservative views, the common denominators, on a regular basis and have it syndicated just like this white boy's show."

"Why use the term 'conservative,' though?"

"Because it's popular. And it ain't nothin' but a word. You can say any damn thing you want and call yourself conservative and you'll get everybody to listen. You know why?"

I finished my drink and asked, "Why is that?"

"Because the average black man wants to find out what the hell a conservative black man is, and so do white people. I say it's no such thing. It's just a damn word, unless it means 'the common denominator.' That's the only way I can figure it out. But the shit works, because everybody sits up and listens.

"Now if you call yourself a 'radical black man' in the nineties, ain't nobody listening but the unemployed and the incarcerated, because that radical shit won't get you anywhere. 'The Conservative Black Man' is the new title of the day."

"Is that what you want to call the show, 'The Conservative Black Man'?"

"Would you consider yourself conservative?" he asked me.

I thought about it. I was a college graduate. I was from the South.

My father owned his own business and worked with his hands. My mother was a schoolteacher. My brother was married with two kids and a big new house. And I needed a damn job!

I nodded my head and said, "You know, I think I'm more conservative than I thought I was."

We both broke out laughing. Gene said, "We'll come up with a name, but we could just use 'a conservative black man of the nineties' as your sign-off."

"Have you talked to anyone else about this show idea?" I asked him. I was curious about why he wanted to use me. It all seemed too easy. Maybe I'd be too young to be considered a conservative.

He sighed and said, "I kicked the idea around to a few people, but they weren't really thinking on the same lines of what I wanted to do with the show."

"And I do?"

"Well, the first thing, Bobby, is getting past the word *conservative*. Most of the people I kicked the idea around to couldn't see past that word. They thought of it as a slap in the face to progressive black people. But I don't see it that way. We used to be conservative before integration started up, and look what we have now: teachers that don't care about our children, broken families, a lack of jobs, a lack of black ownership in the communities, discipline problems, you name it.

"Shit, Bobby, we need to go back to being conservative and taking care of ourselves instead of depending on the damned government and white folks so much!"

The irony of Gene Carlton's statements was that we would eventually end up broadcasting from a white-owned radio station in the District and being picked up by other white stations around the country where black *and* white listeners would tune in. In a word, it was integration, a nonconservative philosophy. I didn't care, though, as long as it worked.

I called up Brother Abu the next day and got his opinion on it. He chuckled at the idea. "It would probably work," he said. "This guy's pretty smart. I would listen to find out what a 'conservative black man' is too, and since I know you, I know it can't be all that bad.

"You should put your own tag on it, though. Call it 'The Bobby Dallas Show.' That way people will identify with you instead of just the conservative idea. Put a face on this thing, especially if you're looking to go syndicated."

"You think that would be wise to do?" I asked him. "I mean, I know *I* understood what Gene's talking about, and I know that *you* understood, but what about all the listeners?"

"That's your job, Bobby. You *make* them understand."

"But don't you think I'm a little too young for this? I figure the demographics will be anywhere from thirty-five to seventy. I'm only twenty-nine. I feel like I should be at least *thirty-nine* or something."

"Well, again, that's up to you. They don't know how old you are. A lot of times older guys act younger to reach the youth markets. You never came across to me as that type. You've always been mature for your age, Bobby. You just keep that in mind when you're on the air.

"Did you two talk about money?" Brother Abu asked me.

"Not yet, but I'm not taking anything less than I was making at WUCI," I answered. I wanted thirty-five thousand.

"Good. Just try to keep moving forward, and get as much control as you can."

A few minutes after I had hung up with Brother Abu, I got a call from Angel in California.

"I got the commercial job," she told me excitedly.

I smiled. "I knew that you would. So how long are you gonna be out there?"

"At least for another two weeks. How are things going with you? Did you meet my father's friend?"

"Yeah, I met him."

"Well, what happened?"

"We're just talking right now. We don't even have a station, just an idea."

"What are you gonna call it?"

I smiled again. " 'The Bobby Dallas Show.' "

"Really?" Angel sounded as surprised as I was.

"If I can, yeah."

"Well, congratulations!" she yelled. "I told you, I told you, I told you!"

I held the phone away from my ear and shook my head for a moment. "Nothing is set yet, Angel. You're jumping the gun."

"Well, I wish you the best of luck, and I can't wait to see you," she said.

I thought about our night in the guest room. "Yeah, me neither. And I wish you luck out there."

"Thanks. I need it."

"Don't we all. Hey, send me a postcard or something if you get a chance," I told her.

"Okay, I can do that. Well, I'll see you real soon, hopefully."

"Yeah. Same here."

I wanted to say something else to Angel, something important to me, but I didn't get a chance to. What if the feeling wasn't mutual? I decided to wait until I saw her face-to-face again, so I could see the look in her eyes. I'd heard that the eyes never lie, and I wanted the truth.

I hung up the phone and stretched out on my long sofa. " 'The Bobby Dallas Show,' " I said to myself with a grin. It seemed so long ago that I had graduated from Howard. It was only seven years ago, but it seemed like twenty because I had been through so many changes.

I hadn't talked to my family in North Carolina since the New Year. They all sent me cards for my birthday, but I figured I would feel better about talking to them once I knew something definite concerning a new job. I hadn't told them about the contractual dispute with Kathy Teals and WUCI. They had heard enough of my bad news over the years. I vowed to share nothing but good news with them for the rest of my career.

●

Gene Carlton called me that next week with the news. "I got an offer from an FM station, WLRG," he said. "The format is educational and cultural. I put together a group of dynamite sponsors for the show. And get this, the managers at the station are willing to give us a time slot right after their morning news guy from ten to twelve. They just lost a good show due to a guy relocating to Florida, so I talked them into trying you out in his slot."

I wasn't even prepared to respond. "Oh yeah?" The first thing I thought of was the money. "How much are they offering me?"

"I want to hammer out a one-year deal for twenty-five thousand with incentives and bonuses to pull you to thirty."

"I was making more than that at WUCI," I told him.

"Bobby, you have to make this show work first. WUCI made a commitment to you based on what you had already done with them. This here is a brand new deal. They like your tapes, though. I gave them nothing but the best. Think about it, Bobby, they're giving you a ten-to-twelve slot. That's radio prime time."

In my talks with Gene, organizing how we would do things, he expressed to me that he loved the shows I had done with Kathy where I got excited. Usually, when I got excited, I reverted back to saying something my father would have said. I guess those views *would* be considered conservative. I considered a lot of them defensive, though. Kathy had put me on the spot more than a few times.

"That's the Bobby Dallas that will take you straight to the top," Gene assured me. "Have you thought about a name yet?" he asked me.

" 'The Bobby Dallas Show,' " I answered.

Gene chuckled and said, "Good choice. I was figuring you would do that. Have you ever heard of Petey Green?" he asked me.

"Yeah," I told him. Petey Green was a legend in the District. He had a television talk show where he did and said whatever he wanted. His stuff was classic. He was like a real-life Fred Sanford with a suit and a haircut, uncensored and telling it like it was. Petey Green and Redd Foxx would have made an excellent team.

"Well, I'm not saying to be like him, but you want to give yourself an edge. You want to fire people up and get them listening to you."

I was wondering if Gene was planning on producing on a daily basis or if he was thinking about developing a team of producers with the station. I had no idea how to produce a show of conservative views. I was counting on him for guidance.

"Are you gonna produce?" I asked him.

"Damn right," he said. "This is my baby, and I brought the sponsors in, but it's up to you to pull it off. I can only invite people in and give you ideas. It's up to you to captivate the audience. And if you come up with any ideas of your own, just let me know."

I had already brainstormed a little, but I wanted to call him back when my ideas were more concrete. "When do we meet with the station?" I asked.

"Tomorrow."

"Tomorrow?" It was definitely short notice.

"I can call them back and confirm it now. We got two weeks before we air."

What if I wanted to get a haircut or something? I thought. I looked at my clock and it wasn't too late yet, so I told Gene to go ahead and make the call. I told him I'd call him back with some ideas later on that night. Then I went to get my haircut on Fourteenth Street, close to where I used to live on Thirteenth. The guys inside the shop were talking about being pulled over by police on the highway.

"They really pull you over up there near Baltimore," one barber was saying to a customer. They were both older men in their early fifties.

"Yeah, that's a main strip of highway. They got all that traffic going to New York and Philly out of Baltimore and D.C. Then they got the Baltimore Tunnel traffic and whatnot. You gotta make sure you slow the traffic down before you go in that thing," another barber said. He was the owner of the shop. The younger barbers were just listening.

"I got pulled over up there last week," one of the younger guys finally said.

"How fast were you going?" he was asked.

"I was only doing seventy-one. They gave me a ticket for a hundred dollars."

"Seventy-one? You're only supposed to be doing fifty-five on that road leading up to the tunnel."

I sat there and thought about so many things that happen in the black community that we didn't seem to have any solutions for. I snapped my fingers and said, "Solutions." *That could be the name of a weekly show*, I thought to myself. I would be doing five shows a week, two hours a day. I needed good ideas to fill up all of that space.

When I realized it, the guys in the shop were staring at me.

"What you say, *solutions?*" the owner asked me.

I smiled. "Oh, I was just thinking of ideas for a talk show," I said.

"A talk show?" the other older barber asked me.

"What's your name?" one of the younger barbers asked. Suddenly, all eyes were on me.

"Bobby Dallas," I told them. I usually kept my mouth shut and got my haircut unnoticed.

"Yeah, you was on that show with Kathy Teals!" one of the barbers said. He was really excited about it. "I wanted to call up on that show a couple of times, man, to help you out."

I laughed and said, "Thanks. She *was* pretty tough."

"Yeah, man, that show don't come on no more, hunh?" he asked me. "I ain't heard it in a while. They got like some Spanish people on there now."

"Yeah, we had creative disputes. I'm about to have my own show now," I told him.

The owner asked me, "What are you planning on talking about?"

"Conservative views and news from the black community."

The barbers all looked around at one another with smiles. "Hell, we do that in here every day. You ever thought about having a barbershop talk show?" the owner asked me.

"Yeah, call in at the shop and get our views on things," one of the younger barbers suggested.

I didn't see anything wrong with it. If any institution was old enough to be considered conservative in the black community, it was the barbershops. "I'll have to see about that," I told them. I didn't want to make any promises that I couldn't keep.

By the time I got back to my apartment that night, I had a skeleton format for my new show. I called Gene and said, "On Mondays, we could just talk about what went on over the weekend, and call it 'Monday Morning Views on the Weekend News.' On Tuesdays we schedule as many interviews as we can, including phone interviews. On Wednesdays we could have a 'Trouble in the Kitchen' show where we talk about relationships. Then on Thursdays we got 'Barbershop Talk.' And we wrap it up on Fridays with 'Solutions,' where we take the best letters concerning issues we discussed recently on our shows and read them back to the audience."

"Damn!" Gene responded to me. "When did you come up with all of this?"

"I had a few ideas in my head already, and then everything just came together for me while I was at the barbershop."

"Yeah, well, our meeting is not until three o'clock tomorrow, so we have a little time to sit down and think this thing out," he said. "We still have plenty of time, so we might even come up with some other ideas before the show airs. What you gave me is a good start, though."

"All right then. Where do you want to meet and at what time?"

We met and had breakfast at ten o'clock in the morning at a restaurant on Pennsylvania Avenue in Capitol Hill. The station, WLRG, was within walking distance. I was freshly dressed in a dark suit, with a haircut and a shave, ready to meet with my future bosses.

"I feel really good about this, Bobby," Gene was saying. He was pumped.

I was more reserved. I had been through all the ups and downs of the radio business before. I told myself not to get too excited until after we had signed a second contract for a guaranteed number of years, creative control, and plenty of money.

To stay in line with the conservative scope of the show, Gene threw in "Bootstraps," where I would talk about black business developments within the national community, "Ugly Jim Crow," where I would talk about events going on around the country that remind black people of slavery, and "Uprisings," where I would talk about black politics and politicians.

"We definitely have a good mix of ideas. And what I'm gonna do is gather a list of good contacts to call up all around the country. I got a lot of friends in the NABJ. That'll definitely help us to go syndicated."

The National Association of Black Journalists was a good idea. I had never joined myself, but it was smart to be connected to them. I smiled and said, "You really did your homework for this thing."

Gene frowned at me. "Bobby, I'm a lawyer, and I'm not walking into this thing unprepared. I've been thinking about this day and night for almost two years now. I was setting up the networks and the game plan, and I just needed the right person to pull it off."

"Well, shit, I wish I had met you earlier," I told him.

Gene shook his head. "Naw, naw, Bobby, everything happens in time for a reason. As far as the salary situation goes, don't worry about that right now. We just want to set the groundwork, and then we'll be able to take this show to the highest bidder."

Gene Carlton was a salesman indeed. A great salesman!

"Everything sounds pretty good to me," I told him. I finished up my orange juice and was ready to go over and make the deal right then. It was only lunchtime, though, so Gene and I took a walk over to Union Station to waste another two and a half hours.

"Are you going out with Angel Thomas?" Gene asked me as we strolled through D.C.'s elaborate train station.

"No, we're just good friends," I told him. He didn't need to know more than that.

He nodded and said, "She's a good girl. Smart. I just don't see why she wants to be an actress."

"Different strokes for different folks," I responded.

"I got a daughter at Georgetown. She wants to be like her daddy," he said with a smile.

"Is she smart, too?" I joked with him.

"Of course."

I wondered what she looked like. The next thing I knew, Gene was pulling out his family pictures and showing me his wife, daughter, and two sons. Only the younger son looked like Gene. The other two kids looked more like their mother.

"She looks determined," I told him of his daughter. She had the look of a serious woman, with intensity in her face.

"Yeah, she fell for this ballplayer her freshman year, and I had to straighten her out. She missed a lot of classes and sleep over this guy. You know how young men like to play on two and three courts sometimes. She wasn't ready for that. I told her to keep her heart in her chest until she's ready. And keep them damn skirts up."

"Hell, I *need* to buy her some pants," he said.

I wanted to laugh but I held it in. I remembered how predatory Gary Mitchell was with sisters. I hadn't exactly been a saint back then myself.

"You got any sisters, Bobby?" Gene asked me.

"Nope. I got one brother."

"He's your age?"

"A year younger. Married, and two kids down in Charlotte."

"North Carolina?"

I nodded.

Gene said, "It's always a good idea to get married. It keeps you focused when everything else goes crazy."

I couldn't comment on that. I had never been married, but I figured that it was true because I felt the most secure when I had a steady woman.

Before we knew it, it was time to rush over to our meeting at WLRG. It was a new white building with a lot of glass doors. It wasn't that many brown faces there either. I felt like a token black. Gene was still pretty confident and secure. I guess he was used to being around that many professional white folks. For the majority of my radio career, I had been around blacks.

They showed us to a large conference room where Gene went over the entire idea of "The Bobby Dallas Show" with the program director and the station manager. He included how he would bring in sponsors, local and national.

"That sounds really big," the station manager, Gordon Dates, said. He was a slender guy with a head of gray hair. He liked to slide down in his chair and make himself look shorter. He didn't look pleased or disappointed. He was simply listening.

The program director, Michael Hines, was a lot younger and sharper, with dark hair. He had the spunk of a recent college graduate. "If we could pull all of that together, I think it could turn into a heck of a show." He looked at me and said, "From what I've heard so far, I really like what you have to offer, Bobby."

"Thanks," I told him. "I'm just ready to move on to bigger and better things."

Dates slowly nodded his head. "One year, and we'll see how it does."

Hines grinned at me and pushed his thumb in the air. The two of them reminded me of a good cop/bad cop routine. I read over the contract with Gene and signed on the dotted line. Everyone in the room was all smiles and shaking hands.

Dates said, "Well, I guess we'll meet with you guys again in a couple of weeks."

"No problem," Gene said.

We walked out of the conference room and Dates went back to his office. Hines proceeded to show us around the building, introducing us to the staff and some of the hosts. I hadn't worked with that many white people since leaving Food Lion in Greensboro. WLRG reminded me of the station that cut me loose in Baltimore after buying out WMSC. It was going to be a new experience for me. Nevertheless, it was FM and I had my own show. I planned to make the best of it.

Gene and I walked out of the station sometime after five that evening.

Gene said, "Well, Bobby, we're in. You wanna go celebrate?"

I smiled and responded, "Yeah. Let's go on over to Scotty's and get a drink."

"The Bobby Dallas Show"

"You know, I just can't believe it! I'm sitting here looking at my 'Ugly Jim Crow' reports, and I'm finding out that we're still having firsts. Every week we have new firsts.

"Ah, *The New York Times* just hired their first black columnist, a brother by the name of Bob Herbert, forty-eight. And in Baltimore recently, we had the first black man to be named as the head of the American Society of Newspaper Editors. William A. Hillard.

"That's just unbelievable, people! Of course, we owe these two brothers a congratulations, but this is *nineteen ninety-three!*

"If the establishment won't let you in the door, then build your own house and invite your own guests in, people. That's what we're talking about, bootstrapping.

"Okay, now we're gonna call up The Barbershop. . . . Hey, Mr. Joe, this is Bobby Dallas. You guys been listening to the show this morning?"

"Yeah, we been listening. And there's always gonna be a first in this country for black people, Bobby. Do you know how many skilled jobs and positions we have in this country that black people don't even think about? Thousands of them! I'd even be interested to see how many black folks are plumbers, or carpenters. I know we got plenty of trash men and security guards. Yet we got all these young men running around and killing each other, talking about it ain't no jobs out there. Half of these guys wouldn't know a job if it walked up and smacked them in the face.

"And I hope that new black drug czar that Clinton named don't take it easy on these young brothers selling drugs, because it ain't no reason in hell for them to be killing their own people with all these honest professions that they could have."

"So, you're saying that we're not using all of our resources to find jobs?"

"We're not. A lot of us don't want to learn the skills to get these jobs," Mr. Joe said.

"Bobby, I used to have a job posting board in my barbershop years ago, and at first it was a good idea. We had brothers who loved to look up on that board. But over the last five to ten years, it seems like less and less of these brothers are interested, and it's because they don't want to learn what they need to learn and put in the time to move up the ranks. Even to be a barber, you have to go to barber school or become an apprentice to get a license, Bobby."

"You know, some black people say that those licenses were put in effect just to hold us *back* from getting a lot of these skilled jobs."

"And you know what, Bobby? That's exactly what's happening. We're letting some damn license hold us back. These white boys have to get the same licenses that we have to get, and a lot of them start out just as poor. If you wanna be white collar, Bobby, just like the bootstrap philosophy says, sometimes you have to start off blue collar first."

I laughed. "That's what they say, don't they? The good old-fashioned bootstrap philosophy."

"That's the only philosophy that works. You can't walk around expecting somebody to feed you. You have to learn to grow food and feed yourself. That's why I own my own barbershop."

"You know, I would hate to think of what would happen to black barbershops if white barbers learned how to cut, ah, Negro hair," I said with another laugh.

"We'd go out of business," Mr. Joe responded. "The white man's clippers are sharper than ours. And he gives them candy."

You could hear people laughing inside the shop. I loved "The Barbershop" routine. It was one of my favorite parts of the show. Mr. Joe was always sharp with his comments.

"Well, thanks again for your input at The Barbershop, Mr. Joe."

"All right then, Bobby, we'll talk to you next time. I'm starting to mess this boy's hair up, and you know black folks only get one chance. If you don't do it right the first time, and with a big smile on your face, you can forget about getting any more chances."

I laughed again and said, "You ain't never lied, Mr. Joe. That's why I'm gonna do this show right. Because I want the people out there to keep tuning in."

"Well, hang on in there, because I like talking to you, son. 'The Bobby Dallas Show' should go straight to the top."

We hung up and I got back into the program after a few commercials. Gene did a hell of a job with our sponsors. He worked out a deal where he would produce the show *and* bring in a lot of the ads. I wondered how much *he* was making. I knew it had to be more than I was. I just kept telling myself to do the best show I could to hold up my end of the bargain. Syndication was our goal, and we had an excellent format. "The black syndication market is wide open. And it's right around the corner for us," Gene repeated to me as often as he could. I figured that he was right, because our show was dynamite!

"This has been 'The Bobby Dallas Show,' for the new conservative black man of the nineties, on WLRG-FM. Stay tuned for 'Lunch Hour' with your host, Becky Shaw."

I got off the air and Gene was all smiles. "You're getting there," he told me outside the studio booth. It was May, and I had been working my tail off for months.

"What didn't I do right this time?" I asked Gene.

"Bobby, it's not about right or wrong. You're a good professional. I'm just trying to get you to continue to push yourself," he said with a hand on my shoulder.

"Yeah, well, don't have me pushing myself over the edge," I joked.

It was hard work staying on top of my own show. Gene had turned out to be an excellent producer, but since I was a solo host, I was the one sweating over most of the material. My family was fairly satisfied with my progress, though. I sent them all tapes, and it was pretty clear to them that the conservative thing was not my idea. As long as it was working, I still didn't care. In fact, Angel Thomas had the biggest problem with it.

"You're not being yourself with this 'conservative black man' thing," she told me.

"Well, why am I so good at it?" I joked.

"You're probably getting that stuff from your father," she argued. I had talked to her enough about my family members for her to know.

"*Your* father likes the show, too," I told her.

Angel sighed. "Bobby, a lot of older men are conservative, but you're not even thirty yet." She was calling from her home in San Jose. She was commuting back and forth from Washington to L.A. with the use of frequent-flyer tickets. We hadn't been able to spend three days at a time together, and most of the time, Angel was out in L.A. She was starting to get plenty of work on the West Coast, and her baby dreadlocks were long gone, replaced by whatever hairstyle was required for the new job. Most of her roles were local commercials, so she sent or brought me tapes to watch.

"Do you like all of the things you say or represent in *your* work?" I asked her. There were a few commercials she showed me that were on the goofy side.

"I'm playing different roles and we're not using my real name or identity," she responded. "I mean, Bobby, you're using your actual name and pieces of your personal life. I don't do that."

"It's only to get people to listen to good dialogue," I said. "It's not like I'm trying to push the conservative view down anyone's throat. If they don't like what I'm saying, then all they have to do is turn their dial to something else."

Angel was silent for a moment. "You know what? You're starting to sound just like one of those people who rationalize everything."

"And you don't rationalize your acting?" I was becoming very defensive in my personal life. It seemed that once I really got into my show, I was always finding room to disagree with someone.

"Do you have a problem with my acting? I notice you're always coming back to that."

Maybe I did have a problem with it. Maybe I wanted to be more than friends. We still had not been intimate since that night in the guest room. I thought it was *so* beautiful to her.

"Where do you see our relationship going?" I finally asked.

"What do you mean?"

"Well, are we just friends, or are we gonna be more than friends somewhere down the line?"

"Bobby, I told you, I don't know what's gonna happen," she said. "Do you realize we've only been seeing each other for seven months? I've known plenty of guys for longer than that."

"What is that supposed to mean?"

Angel got quiet again. "This is something we need to talk about face-to-face," she said.

"Okay, so when are you flying back out here to Washington?"

She sighed and said, "I'll have to see."

Her answer didn't sound like any time soon to me. "Yeah, well, send me a Christmas card," I snapped at her. I felt a crazy urge to hang up the phone, but I didn't.

Angel calmly said, "Bobby, are you trying to push me away?"

I think that was exactly what I was doing. It was driving me crazy that I had so much pressure from my job and no steady woman. I didn't even want to get involved with another woman because I was so hopeful of having Angel. I guess I wasn't patient enough.

"Is that what you think I'm doing?" I asked her. I wanted to apologize but the words wouldn't form in my mouth. I wanted to tell Angel that I wanted to be with her. I wanted to tell her that she was the first woman I cared anything about in three years. Every time I was with her during her cross-country visits, I had been patient. But I was running out of patience. I was running out of patience for everything. Things were happening in my life, but they were all happening in slow motion.

"It sounds to me like you need another break," Angel told me.

"A break from what?" I asked.

"Everything."

I knew damn well that she was right. Angel was almost always right. I calmed down and thought about smoking a cigarette and getting a drink at Scotty's. I looked at the clock and it was seven-thirty.

"Bobby, you need to stop smoking and drinking. I did notice that the last time I was out there with you."

I broke out laughing. Angel Thomas knew me like a book, and in a short time, too. That was a tribute to how much soul-searching we had done together. But without her with me on a more consistent basis, I was falling apart.

"Maybe you can help me with that when you get back out here," I said.

Angel said, "Bobby, I need you to do me a favor."

"Oh yeah? What's that?"

"I want you to promise me that you won't go to your favorite bar tonight."

I smiled. *I can't promise you that,* I thought to myself.

"Can you promise me that, Bobby?" Angel pressed me.

That was a rough one. I took a deep breath and said, "I don't know." She just didn't get it. I had to have *something*. She wasn't there with me. I felt like I would slip into insanity if I didn't get out and go *somewhere*.

"Why don't you go to a movie or something?" Angel suggested to me.

I chuckled and responded, "What do you have, ESP or something?"

"No, I just know you, Bobby. You love to go to the movies. The movies is like being at the beach for you."

I said, "Okay, I'll go to the movies then."

"I mean it."

"I mean it, too. I'm going to the movies."

Angel sighed and said, "Please pull yourself together. Things are really starting to go well for you; for both of us."

"Yeah, I just hoped that we could be together," I told her softly.

She chuckled and said, "Soon, Bobby, real, real soon. Just like the Blue Notes."

"Yeah, and those Blue Notes fell apart, didn't they?"

Angel never really responded to me. She said some other things about what she had to do and we said our good-byes. To be frank about it, I blocked the rest of her comments out. I just wanted to get out of my apartment.

I went to the K-B Foundry theater in Georgetown. I don't know why. I guess I just wanted a change of scenery. I never really liked Georgetown. Adams Morgan was more cultural, but they didn't have any theaters. I couldn't even sit through the movie. I got up halfway through and drove down Pennsylvania Avenue all the way back to Capitol Hill. I was really desperate to get back to Scotty's. That place was becoming my home away from home. *How would Angel find out anyway?* I asked myself.

"Hey, Bobby Dallas?" someone yelled. There were a lot of people who knew me at Scotty's by then, and they all knew that I had my own radio talk show. I felt like Norm Peterson from the TV show "Cheers." It was one of my all-time favorite shows.

I said "Hi" to everyone and sat down on a stool at the bar.

"The usual?" Big Bill asked me. I was drinking rum and Coke like it was milk.

"Yeah," I answered him. He was already mixing my drink.

"You're doing a good job on that show," Big Bill told me. "Even Frank said it. He said once you gain a little confidence to do what *you* want on the show, you'll be untouchable."

I took a sip of my drink. "Frank really said that about me?"

Bill looked at me as if I was crazy. "All the time. He sounds like he really admires you."

I frowned. *Admires me for what?* I thought. I wasn't getting it at all. I didn't feel like I was doing anything special. That damn show was hard work, and I wasn't being paid top dollar yet. We were just beginning to inch our way up the market. I guess Frank admired my potential. But like I said, things weren't happening fast enough for me anymore. I was still driving around in that damn Prelude that had over 150,000 miles on it!

Mark Bishop, the painter, walked in. He was heading straight toward us.

"Here comes Smiley," I said to Bill. Mark seemed to have a sunny disposition even when he *wasn't* making money. "Hey, Smiley," I joked with him.

He continued to grin. He was wearing a tweed cap and a smooth outfit that made him look like a New Age jazz musician.

"What's with the hip outfit, man? You got a hot date at a jazz club tonight?"

Mark shook his head and took a seat on the empty stool next to mine. "Nah, I just felt like putting on something different today," he said.

"You just get in those moods, hunh?"

"Yeah. I'm an artist," he answered. "And I love your show, man. I really love what you're doing."

I thought about his artistic mood. He was the happiest male artist I had ever met. I bumped into a lot of artists in New York. Women artists seemed to be more capable of handling their different mood swings. Maybe it was a biological thing.

"Would you consider me an artist?" I asked Mark.

Big Bill had gone on about his business. You didn't get a long time to talk to him. I asked him once why he wanted to fill drinks instead of chill out in an office somewhere, and he told me that he loved to be around drunk black people. He said that was why he named the place Scotty's. "Some of the people here needed to be beamed up into space sometimes." Big Bill had to throw someone out at least three times a week, and he loved it.

Anyway, Mark looked at me and answered, "I guess you could be considered an artist."

I nodded and took another sip of my drink. "I feel like I am. I'm not making enough money, I don't have a steady woman, I'm a chain smoker now, and my emotions run hot and cold. I was even ready to hang up on the only woman I have tonight." I chuckled and said, "She thinks I'm at the movies right now." Then I thought better of it. "On second thought, she *knows* where I am."

Mark looked at me and said, "Don't mess up with Angel, man. She's a blessing from God."

I brought Angel to Scotty's once, and it wasn't her kind of place. It wasn't my kind of place when I first went there either. It grew on me. Mark met Angel that night, and he was obviously impressed with her.

"What the hell? Are you painting pictures of her at night or something?" I joked.

"She's just a nice young lady, Bobby. I would strongly advise you to hold on to her."

I got snappish with him. "Hey, man, how can you hold on to something that you don't have?" I looked at him intently for his response. It seemed like no one ever understood what I was going through. Angel wasn't my damn lady, I just wanted her to be! I was like a mad admirer.

Mark smiled at me and said, "I know the feeling, Bobby, that's why I paint."

I was in a daze. I thought real hard about what Mark said. His response to me was simple and yet it was deep. I said, "Hey Mark, you wanna come on my show sometime? I could invite you on for a Wednesday, my 'Trouble in the Kitchen' day."

"Are you serious?" he asked me. His face lit up.

I was dead serious. I had some good ideas for a show with Mark. "As long as you don't freeze up on me," I told him.

"Oh, I won't. So you want me to talk about relationships, hunh?"

"Yeah, from an artistic point of view." Actually, I wanted to see how similar Mark's love life was to mine. I thought it would be interesting to find out on the air. Unpredictable shows were the best ones to have, and I had a hunch that Mark had just as many love stories to tell as I had. Mark was a few years younger than me, but most of my war stories were from before I turned twenty-six.

It took a month before I could convince Gene that it would be a good idea to let me interview Mark for my "Trouble in the Kitchen" show. Gene didn't like Wednesdays altogether, but I saw it as a necessary evil to keep women interested. Women seemed addicted to relationship issues like men were addicted to sports.

"Women listen to 'The Bobby Dallas Show' too, and I know that they would love this one. I can feel it."

Gene grumbled about it. "Mmm-hmm."

I felt I *needed* to have Mark on the show with me. I needed to talk about the game of love with a brother and share it with everyone. It was something that men rarely did, but I was desperate for understanding.

Angel hadn't had a chance to make it back to Washington. I told her she may as well get out of her lease agreement and stay with me whenever she came back, because she was wasting her money. She wouldn't do it, though, and I had nearly given up hope on her. Things just weren't going anywhere between us, and maybe that's how she wanted it, at a standstill. So I needed someone to talk to to understand things more, someone like Mark Bishop.

•

"It's Wednesday, people! And for the brothers and sisters out there who are regulars to 'The Bobby Dallas Show,' you know that we talk about relationship issues, 'Trouble in the Kitchen,' on Wednesdays. Well, before I introduce you to my guest, a young brother who's an artist in the

D.C. area, I want to share a letter with you that I received at the studio concerning the title. It was a long, angry letter so I'm not gonna read it or anything, but the sister was basically saying that 'Trouble in the Kitchen' sounds chauvinistic. What if a woman's *not* in the kitchen? Is my idea of a woman a cooking, cleaning, barefoot and pregnant woman? And the list goes on.

"I mean, the sister made some really off-the-wall assumptions about me, and I just wanted to say that 'Trouble in the Kitchen' is just a title. I got that title from remembering when my parents used to argue. A lot of the time, for whatever reason, they ended up being in the kitchen.

"Now, I'll have you know that my mother was nowhere near being a cooking, cleaning, barefoot and pregnant woman. So I just want to clear that up with the audience, because I'm not gonna change the name of my Wednesday show. I happen to like that title. Okay? So I hope that the sister—she knows who she is if she's listening—doesn't take it personally.

"Okay, now that we have that out of the way, I want to introduce you to my guest, twenty-five-year-old Mark Bishop. He's a painter and he's been selling his work for four years, and dating women, I guess, for eight years.

"Now I know that a lot of you out there are wondering what such a young man would know about women, but since Mark is an artist, I figured that we could get an interesting view from him.

"So, Mark, how are you doing today?"

Mark was perfectly comfortable. "I'm fine. Things are going pretty well for me. And I've been dating for basically nine years. My first serious girlfriend was when I was sixteen."

"Are you dating someone now?"

"I'm always dating someone," he answered with a laugh. "I meet women constantly. Women are my main customers."

"They're your main customers? Why is that? Do you paint a lot of sexual art?"

"Not really. If I painted more sexual art, maybe I would attract more men."

"Yeah, like a black *Penthouse* magazine. Men would buy that."

Mark laughed. "Actually, I think men like to look more than they like to buy. I've even had women who bought a lot of my art for their husbands. But then you do have men who are collectors, and those brothers buy a lot of art. But a lot of times they get all into the first editions, the originals and all that kind of stuff."

"So, men are a lot more technical about what they're buying?"

"Oh, definitely."

"Now, when you meet a lot of these women who buy your art, do they just give you their phone numbers?"

"Sometimes they do."

"And you just call them up and make a date?"

"It depends on whether we had good conversation or not."

"What would be good conversation?"

"You know, if the sister seems like she has a good head on her shoulders and all the chemistry is right."

"You mean, how she looks doesn't have anything to do with it?" Mark laughed.

"Now you said that you would be honest with me, Mark," I reminded him. "It's not good to lie to my audience. I won't let you do it."

"Yes, I did," he said. "Well, of course looks count."

"How much does it count?"

"Well, again the chemistry is important. I'm not gonna just go out with a woman because she's good-looking."

"Please, brother, don't give me that. You mean to tell me you never went home with a fox's number in your pocket and couldn't wait to call her?"

"Only if the chemistry was right," Mark insisted.

"Okay, well, you're not married, right?" I asked him. "Oh, by the way, for those of you who are late, and for the rest of you who were with us, my guest, Mark Bishop, is a painter. He has a sandy brown complexion, he's about five foot eight, and he wears his hair very low and sometimes bald. If I was a woman I'd probably say that he was nice-looking, but I'm not."

"I'm not married, no," Mark answered with a grin.

"Have you thought about getting married?"

"Actually, with a few women, I have."

"And what happened?"

"Well, you know, we were both young and all and I was concerned about my career, they were concerned about theirs, and it just wouldn't work."

"So you're no longer seeing these women?"

"We're still friends."

"Would you like to be more than friends?"

"Sometimes I do, sometimes I don't."

"You know you're gonna have to explain that to us," I told him.

"Well, some women are more into your program than others."

"So, you're saying that some women get the boot and others get the golden key?"

"I wouldn't say that I give women the boot. It's just like, you know, short-term and long-term memory. Everything is not on the same level of importance to you. Women do the same thing with men."

"Do you just forget about them?" I had forgotten about plenty of women.

"You don't forget *everything*, but you wanna keep moving on."

"Do you think that you get more women because you're an artist?"

"I believe that I could if I wanted to, because I have a conversation piece."

"You mean, through your art?"

"Yeah. It's not like I have to scream, 'Hey, baby, come here!' They just walk up to my table."

"Was that why you started painting things, you know, to get the attention?"

"Well, you have to have inspiration for whatever you do."

"Answer the question, Mark."

He laughed. "I was good at it and people noticed, so yeah, I liked getting that attention. I could also sell it."

"Now, you know what people say about artists, you're kind of quiet, eccentric, and sex-crazed. How would you respond to that?"

"It's a stereotype. It's not true for all artists. I know some guys who are really outgoing and talkative."

"What about you?"

"Well, I'm more low-key."

"Do you have many friends?"

"I have a lot of women friends, actually."

"What about male friends?"

"I have a few."

"Why do you think that is?"

"Ah, I wasn't too much into sports when I was younger."

"Did you play with Barbie dolls or jump rope or something? How did you end up with more women friends than guys? You never hung out with the guys, making noise on the D.C. street corners?"

"No, I did not play with Barbie dolls or jump rope, I just clicked well with women. I was an only child, and I had a lot of girl cousins, so you know, I guess I learned how to deal with women better."

"Were you in a lot of situations where a woman you really liked only saw you as a friend?" I thought of Angel Thomas.

"I think that happens to every guy."

"No, it doesn't either," I told him. I thought of Brad, Gary, Ivan, Champ, and plenty of other players. "I know men who—if they weren't getting busy—they were out the door. They had no time for female friends."

"Well, I'm not that kind of man."

"What kind of man are you then?"

"I would like to think that I'm very thoughtful. I can appreciate a woman for other things besides her physique."

"Were there different types of women who considered you a friend as compared to others?"

"Ah, basically, it just depended on the woman and what her particular situation was. Some of them had boyfriends already."

"Yeah, I've been through that too," I told him. Pamela Cooper came to mind. "You know, I was on another talk show before, where I discussed this friend thing, and it seemed that most of your aggressive women wanted those football, basketball macho types, no matter how good your chemistry may have been with them as a friend."

"Well, that makes sense, doesn't it? If they're really that aggressive, then they want someone else who's aggressive," Mark said.

"I guess it does. They need a man who can carry them up the stairs and toss them in the bed." I was thinking about Mona Freeman.

"I'm not a weak man, brother. I'm just short," Mark said.

"I never said that you were weak, but a lot of women were turned off as soon as you said that you were five eight."

"I didn't say I was five eight, *you* did."

"Okay, yeah, you're right. But you do have some women who don't like short men." Pearl Davis hated short men.

"And then you have women who do," Mark said.

"Another thing they say about black male artists is that you go for white women a lot more frequently than other brothers do. And Mark, I'm gonna let you respond to that as soon as we get back on the air.

"This is 'The Bobby Dallas Show,' on WLRG-FM, the new conservative black man. Stay tuned, and we'll be right back with 'Trouble in the Kitchen.'"

As soon as we got off the air for our commercials, Mark asked, "Hey, man, what are you doing?"

"Well, I told you not to freeze up, and you're doing great!" I told him. I had to keep him pumped.

"I didn't know it was gonna be like this, though, Bobby," he complained.

"Have you listened to my show before?" I asked him.

"Yeah. I listen to it a lot, you know that."

"You know I like to keep things moving then. I'm just keeping a rhythm, like a boxing match, that's all."

"Yeah, I just didn't know you wanted to kick my ass."

"I don't, man. We have a lot in common, actually. That's why I invited you on the show, Mark. This interview can heal a lot of people like us."

"I didn't know that I needed healing," Mark responded. He was right. I was the one who needed the healing.

"Okay, just keep doing what you're doing," I told him as I got ready to go back on the air.

"You're listening to 'The Bobby Dallas Show,' on WLRG-FM, for the new conservative black man. My guest for today is Mark Bishop. He's a young artist, he's in the kitchen, and he's in trouble this morning.

"So Mark, tell us about the black male artists and these white women."

Mark said, "Well, art in general is mainly supported by a lot of charitable white people. Rich white people. And a lot of brothers get used to the hand that feeds them, so to speak, and end up going out with these white girls they meet at various art shows. But my art is black art, supported by black people, so I don't run into that many white girls, nor do I depend on white charity to survive."

"These white girls have money then?"

"Oh, some of 'em. No doubt about it, and plenty of it!" he answered. "Then you look at the economic lifestyles of a lot of artists, and you find that many of them are not too money conscious. Most *sisters* aren't willing to put up with that, nor with the artistic ego.

"Artists can be very particular about the things they like, how they feel, and how they want people to respond to them. And a lot of sisters aren't used to dealing with all of the changes that artists go through and the constant support that they need on a lot of levels.

"Sisters expect you to have a job that pays the bills regularly, and they expect you to act and think like an average brother without taking into consideration that you're *not* the average brother. You're probably used to thinking in ways and doing things that are not normal to them."

"Are white women more able to accept all of that?" I asked.

"Basically, yes. Black women can be very limited in how they think of a man. But if you're a brother dating a white woman, she already knows that it's going to be a special relationship, and so she puts that extra energy in it to make it work, where most sisters won't."

Mark was digging himself into a hole. I wanted to get off of the subject before the sisters banned him for life! I don't think he realized just how many people were listening.

"Have you ever been heartbroken, Mark? A lot of singers are heart-broken. That's where they get the inspiration for many of their songs. I think Keith Sweat had his heart broken a bunch of times."

We both burst out laughing.

"Yeah, I've been heartbroken a couple of times," Mark answered.

"Hey, don't feel bad, man. I've been smashed up against the wall a couple of times too. That's why I'm so familiar with Keith's music. But it's funny how we tend to forget the people who *we* hurt. Have you ever broken a woman's heart?" I was thinking about Faye Butler.

"Well, it was never intentional."

I chuckled. "You're sounding like a woman, Mark, with that 'not intentional' stuff."

"It's the truth, though."

"So, you've never told a woman, 'Look, you're just not pretty enough for me. It's just not gonna work'?"

Mark laughed. "Naw, man, I wouldn't do that to a sister. Have you ever done something like that?"

I said, "It does run through your mind, but I'm asking the questions here, Mark." Of course, I hadn't done it before. I was too much of a nice guy who respected people's feelings.

"Have you ever painted a woman you've dated?" I asked, redirecting the discussion.

"Ah, I try not to."

"It gets too personal? Or is that part of an artist's code of ethics as something never to do?"

"Yeah, it's both. Some women want you to paint them, but you can't paint everybody. You would end up painting every woman who knows what you do, and they're all special in their own way, so you can't turn them down. But that's like letting every woman that *you* date on 'The Bobby Dallas Show.' "

"Yeah, you're right, that wouldn't work at all. I'd be an on-air gigolo if I did that. I don't think the women would like it much either, at least not in America. I could probably get away with it in Saudi Arabia. I'd have 'The Bobby Dallas Harem Show.' "

We burst out laughing again.

Mark said, "Well, that's the same thing for an artist. You don't want to get yourself in the habit of painting everybody."

"What if they have an awesome body, and while you're being intimate with them, you look down and say, 'Wow, I need to paint her'? That's never happened before?"

Mona Freeman! I thought.

Mark chuckled and said, "I would *definitely* be lying if I said that it's never crossed my mind with a few sisters, but that's part of the code of ethics again. Some painters would break that rule, though, in a heart-beat."

"So, Mark, how long do you think it will take for you to become a millionaire? You can get any woman that you want then, right?"

Mark laughed and said, "I don't know. I don't think I'll ever be a *millionaire*. And just because you're rich like that, that doesn't always mean that you'll get the woman that you want."

"You don't think so?"

"Well, let me get rich first, Bobby, and then I'll be able to tell you."

We laughed as the time wound down for another commercial break.

"Okay, it's commercial time again, and you're listening to 'The Bobby Dallas Show,' on WLRG-FM, the new conservative black man. Stay tuned, and we'll be right back with 'Trouble in the Kitchen.' "

•

I talked to Mark Bishop for over an hour about women, money, and art. We must have had over thirty phone calls from angry sisters, but Gene only allowed a few of them on the air. I really enjoyed myself, though. I just needed to get it all out of my system, the whole dating thing. It took us another month to clear up all of the angry baggage I caused, but D.C. was definitely listening. Our ratings points were jumping like crazy! I really started to open things up after that show. I just had to accept things as they were. If Angel wanted to be friends and see me every blue moon, then so be it. The time wasn't right for me to be driving myself insane over women. I had other things to do. I began to concentrate all of my energy on making my show the best that it could be. The word even got around to Kathy Teals.

Kathy called me up one night to congratulate me and to caution me on my methods. "You really have people talking, brother, but don't get off track. You could really hurt the community more than you help it by doing and saying the wrong things."

I told Kathy that I was sorry about her TV show not making it, and that was about it. I didn't have much to say to her. Her television talk show had flopped in a matter of months. It was just too much national competition out there for her. I mean, how many different shows can you have about relationships? Every daytime talk show host in America catered to women with relationship problems. I only discussed it one day out of the week, and after the show with Mark, Gene was trying to get me to drop the "Trouble in the Kitchen" idea. The program director, Michael Hines, argued against it, though. He felt that even though I had pissed off a lot of women on that one particular day, they were still willing to listen to my next "Trouble in the Kitchen." He explained that they were simply hoping I wouldn't go off the deep end again, but I was pretty sure that the men liked it. Gene just shook his head about the whole fiasco.

"What would your mother say about a show like that, Bobby?" he asked me.

"She's never agreed with anything that I've done anyway, so it wouldn't really make a difference," I responded. I definitely wasn't planning on sending the tape home to find out.

Gene shook his head again and walked away. I guess I wasn't as conservative as he thought I could be, but he was pleased with the ratings.

We were still trying to go syndicated, and I was moving right up the ladder in show popularity. We had a perfect time slot. The morning shows were off before my show came on, so I didn't have to go head to head with people like Donnie Simpson and Cathy Hughes.

We got our big break when the National Black Caucus came to D.C. in September. I got to interview five congressmen. Gene made some really strong contacts that week, to go along with the contacts that he had already made. I made sure to keep everything in line that week, all in the name of syndication. A lot of those Black Caucus people were as conservative as you could get, a bunch of stuffy black men in penguin suits with their expensive wives.

I think Gene had the Black Caucus event in mind when he first came up with the "new conservative black man" idea, and it went over like a charm. There were black officials and media people there from all over the country. After taking the ratings in Washington by storm, everyone was talking about "The Bobby Dallas Show," so we followed up with a bunch of phone calls to the other strong black markets around the country who would take us. All we had to do was sell Gordon Dates, and we were off and running for syndication.

I was also due for a new contract. I received all of my bonuses, and I wasn't planning on being bought so cheaply the next time around. If WLRG wanted to keep me, I told Gene to ask for nothing less than seventy-five thousand a year, plus I would collect a big percentage of the syndication money. That was the deal. I wanted to be a six-figure man or I was leaving. I had enough good tapes to get another radio job in *any* market, including New York, if I really wanted to be there again.

Gene said, "You're going big-time now."

"Don't ask them for anything less, Gene," I warned him over the phone. I was dead serious.

"I'm gonna ask them for more," Gene told me. "Let's double it, Bobby. How does one hundred fifty thousand sound to you?"

"You think they have that much to offer me?"

Gene said, "You damn right they do! Washington, D.C., is a major radio market and WLRG has over thirty-four affiliates."

I said, "Well, let's do it then."

Gene said, "I need to get a cut of the syndication money, though, Bobby. I mean, I *did* set a lot of this stuff up."

"How much do you want?" I asked him.

"Twenty percent."

"Twenty percent of my take?" It sounded fair to me.

Gene said, "Bobby, when I first sat down with you, I told you that we were gonna go syndicated, didn't I?"

"Yeah," I answered him.

"I told you that you just had to be patient."

"Yeah, you told me."

"And now we're about to do it after only one year on the air."

I paused. "Okay, so what are you getting at?" Since Gene Carlton was already a lawyer, and he had done extensive research in the radio field before hooking up with me, I decided that I could also use him as my agent.

"I think it's only fair that I get twenty percent of the whole pie, Bobby."

"That would be fifty percent of *my* money," I protested.

"Bobby, when this show goes into syndication, let's say WLRG collects around four thousand dollars a month for it. Your forty percent of that would be sixteen hundred. Sixteen hundred over twelve months would be close to twenty thousand dollars a year, Bobby. And that's just for beginners. You could make up to a hundred thousand dollars a year just off of the syndication rights alone once this thing starts rolling."

"Well, you're making money through the marketing department," I argued. I wasn't willing to give up half of my syndication money, I worked too hard for it. But since Gene had made me a believer in the first place, I had to give him something. "Okay, here's the deal. If you get me over a hundred thousand dollars on salary, I'll negotiate with you on the syndication percentage."

Gene paused. "All right. We'll do it your way then. I've created a monster," he told me with a chuckle.

I hung up with him and thought about things. During the last couple of months of 1993, I wanted to keep the show as clean and family-oriented as possible. I didn't want to rock the boat with Gordon Dates before my new contract was drawn up. One of the more interesting shows I had during those last few months was with moviemaker Haile Gerima, who made an independent film called *Sankofa*. We had such a good dialogue about black film on that show that I decided to make a whole week out of it called "Black Film Week." We talked about black films and stars like Paul Robeson and Sidney Poitier. I even did phone interviews with John Singleton and the Hughes brothers.

I sat back on my couch and lit a cigarette. I felt damn good about things! The first thing I wanted to do with my money was buy a new car, just like a black man would in America. Hell, I needed a new car anyway! As far as women were concerned, I just tried to block them out of my mind again. Like all the women before her, Angel had faded into the background. I sent her father a nice card to thank him for hooking men up with Gene. Some things happen for a reason. I wasn't supposed to be with Angel Thomas, her father was just supposed to help me to get my own show.

"The Lord works in mysterious ways, people," I said to myself. "The Lord works in mysterious ways indeed."

Radioman

I sat at the table inside the large conference room at WLRG-FM and was ready to become a six-figure-income black man before turning thirty. With the additional revenue from the syndication rights, I would be worth at least one hundred twenty-five thousand a year, for three years. That was the deal that was on the table. The station manager, Gordon Dates, could not believe that "The Bobby Dallas Show" had become that popular so fast.

"I just can't believe that you guys are ready to go into syndication after less than a year," he said, shaking his gray-haired head. "It takes some people *years* before they become syndicated."

Gene said, "It takes some people five and six years to pass the bar exam while others pass it right out of law school." He winked his eye at me. Gene had told me before the meeting that we were able to go into syndication so fast because we didn't have much national competition for the black news/talk market. Black news/talk was wide open in a lot of the smaller areas around the country, and many markets that did have black shows had very weak signals, so few people could receive them with the clarity that it takes to maintain a strong radio audience.

"Well, I thought from the beginning that the show would be a hit if we could pull everything off, and Bobby's been able to do that," the program director, Michael Hines, responded to Dates. He had been supportive of us all along.

I sat quietly, biding my time. I couldn't wait to sign that contract.

"You realize that we have exclusive rights to the show in all of the greater Washington area?" Dates said. "And that includes Baltimore."

"Oh, of course," Gene told him.

"All right then, we'll have the syndication paperwork ready for you to sign next week sometime," Dates told us. He didn't seem to be overjoyed about how fast we moved up, but business was business, and we were suddenly one of the highest-rated shows at the station. Only one other show was syndicated at WLRG-FM, a government-funded educational program called "Get Smart" that aired before the afternoon rush hour.

I read over my new contract and signed on the dotted line. My new salary wouldn't be in effect until my old contractual agreement was up in February 1994. I walked out of the conference room feeling light-headed and I was walking on air. I had saved enough money to comfortably put eight thousand dollars down on a new car. I planned to buy myself a convertible BMW or a Mercedes-Benz as soon as the January car sales began.

•

I had missed another Thanksgiving Day dinner with my family, but I was able to make it down to Brad's house in Charlotte for a Christmas dinner. Anthony was eighteen months and wild like most boys are. Aminah was pretty civil and looking even more like Brad. She was five.

I was in much better spirits compared to the last time I saw Brad and his family. I was able to play with my niece and nephew. I was feeling a lot more uninhibited and was able to enjoy things.

"I hear that things are going really well for you now, Bobby. We've all heard your tapes," Brenda said as I wrestled with the kids on their blue-carpeted floor. My mother and father were out taking a walk through the area. Brad was getting dishes out from the kitchen.

"Oh yeah? Did you like them?" I stopped and asked Brenda.

"Yeah, the kids love them," she answered.

My niece, Aminah, looked up and said, "In our bootstrap news for t'day, reports show dat more black women are goin' into business for themselves than any other my-nar-rity group. But I don't like that word my-nar-rity, so we'll just say non-ma-jority group."

Of course, she didn't have a perfect flow yet, but she did memorize it.

Anthony joined in a hot second later and started chanting, "Bootstraps! Bootstraps!" and was grabbing at my shoelaces. I was shocked. They were both learning just as fast as I figured they would. The kids knew some of my funnier lines from the shows by heart. It's something else how kids pick up on things.

"Uncle Bobby, we have your tapes right over here!" Aminah said, dragging me over to their stereo. Anthony followed his sister's lead. "Mommy, can we put it on?!" Aminah yelled.

Brenda shook her head and grinned. "Not right now, maybe later on, okay?" She said, "They want to listen to your tapes every time they hear your name."

I felt honored. "You two like my voice that much, hunh?" I looked down and asked them.

Aminah nodded and answered, "Yes." Just like a kid brother, Anthony followed her lead again.

We all sat down to eat dinner around four that afternoon. Even though I had no family of my own yet, I felt like I was Brad's equal again for the first time in years.

"The kids seem to really love you, Bobby," my mother mentioned at the table. My niece and nephew felt that it was imperative that I sit next to them.

"Why wouldn't they?" Brad asked her.

"Because they don't see him much," Mom answered him.

Brenda said, "They get enough chances to listen to him, though."

"On 'The Bobby Dallas Show,' " Aminah mumbled with a full mouth. "That's *my* last name."

"Chew your food before you speak, girl," Brad snapped at her.

I looked over at him and grinned. "You're not gonna be extra tough on her because she's a girl, are you?"

My father started to chuckle. He hadn't said much all day. I could tell he had something on his mind. It was only a matter of time before he pulled me aside again.

"What, you think I'm gonna be like Mr. Smith?" Brad asked me, smiling with food in his own mouth. Mr. Smith lived around the corner from us in Greensboro, and his toughness with his three daughters didn't stop them from losing their virginity early. Brad had collected panties from the twins, and I almost slept with the oldest girl, but I let the opportunity slip away. I didn't want to do anything in my parents' car with her that night or any other night. However, Brad would have.

"Now what kind of example is that to set for your daughter?" Brenda said. "You can talk with your mouth full, but she can't?"

Brad grinned and said, "I'm grown."

"What about Mr. Smith and his daughters?" my mom asked Brad.

I started to chuckle to myself. Mom was Johnny-on-the-spot. She always had her suspicions about us and the Smith girls.

Brad said, "He was just strict on them, that's all, Mom."

I think my mother let it slide out of respect for Brenda. She did give us the eye, though. "Well, Bobby, I'm so glad to see that this radio thing is finally working out for you," she loosened up and said to me.

I could tell that Dad really wanted to talk to me then. He gave me a look that I knew too well, and before the night was over, Dad found a way to get his two boys outside to talk.

"Ah, Bobby, I've been listening to them tapes of yours, and I know that children are representations of their parents, but when I listen to some of the things that you're saying up there in Washington, on the one hand I'm proud, because a lot of the things are what I would have thought and said, but on the other hand, I think that maybe I didn't allow you two to express enough of your own personalities."

"Aw, Dad, Bobby's just doing that on the show. He don't believe half of that stuff he says. He's just trying to get ratings," Brad spoke up for me. "We do have our own personalities. Bobby is *nothin'* like me."

Dad waited for my response. I was actually stunned that he told me that. I guess those tapes really threw my father's philosophies right back in his face. I didn't see anything wrong with some of his conservative views myself, but he did have a point. It just wasn't me.

I smiled. "So you think I should stop using that line, 'the new conservative black man'?"

"Bobby, if you were really conservative, you wouldn't have taken half of the chances that you've taken to get to where you are now. If you were really conservative, you would have found yourself another career years ago. I just want to tell you to be yourself. You've proven to me that you can make this radio career succeed. And son, I'm proud of you," he said with a hug and a smile. Then he looked to Brad. "Come on in here and get some of this, number two. I'm just as proud of you. And I love the both of you boys."

●

I couldn't sleep that night. I was dying to get back on the air at WLRG. Gene would be pissed off about it, but we didn't really need the conservative phrase anymore anyway. It was getting old and tired. Most of my listeners were tuning in because of my personality. I was Bobby Dallas, the radio man, and the people loved to hear me. They weren't into that conservative talk, they just liked the cool spin that I put on things. However, just because I wasn't conservative, that didn't mean that I would agree with everything either. I wanted to keep my show edgy and provocative. The only way to do that was to keep in mind what Mr. Payton was trying to get across to me years ago at WHCS in Harlem—"a little disagreement gets the blood pumping."

I had more than a few new ideas when I got back to D.C. I brainstormed for the full eight hours that it took me to drive back from Charlotte. Instead of calling black business "Bootstraps," I could use "TCB Reports," taking care of business. It was catchy and more contemporary. Instead of using "Uprisings" for political news, I would use "I Betcha Didn't Know," because a lot of black people didn't know a damn thing about politics. Instead of using "Ugly Jim Crow Reports," which was definitely dated, I would use "Back of the Bus Rides." Last but not least, instead of saying "the new conservative black man," I would call myself "The Radioman," like a superhero. I even thought of using my niece, Aminah's, voice for an introduction by saying, "Mommy, Mommy, it's the Radioman!"

I had some wild thoughts to jazz up my show during my drive back, but Gene wasn't too thrilled when I told him about my new ideas. I wanted to change everything that he implemented on the show. But what the hell, *I* was the host!

"Bobby, you can't go syndicated and then change your whole format," he argued.

"I'm not changing the whole format, I'm just giving the show a more contemporary feel. I'm making it more exciting."

"You're making it sound silly if you ask me. You're starting to sound like a damn disc jockey. These young people don't listen to talk radio."

"How do you know? They probably don't listen because it's so damn boring to them. I'm trying to create a show that *everyone* will want to listen to."

"I wouldn't want to listen to that," Gene responded. "Bobby, just stick to the format that we have already. I have a whole lot of people investing in this show who don't want to hear these new bright ideas that you're talking about, okay? Now you're a professional, Bobby, so act like it."

I said, "Gene, that conservative thing wasn't my idea, but I made it work anyway. Trust me, if you ask most black people why they listen to the show, they'll tell you because it's different, not because it's conservative. We just have a great damn format, Gene! I'm not changing the format, I'm just brightening things up a little, like old silverware that needs a new finish.

"I'm 'The Radioman,' Gene! That's what I always believed in. I loved radio because of the personalities. That's what people get into. You could have all the issues in the world on your show, but if it's boring, it's boring. And I don't want to be boring."

I couldn't even tell if Gene was breathing. I guess it was a hell of a shock to him for me to come back with such a different perspective on my show. I saw it as just a matter of time, though. I couldn't keep playing some conservative guy. That idea was just making my nights longer.

Gene said, "Bobby, you're about to fuck up a good thing, and I don't want to be a part of it."

"So, what do you mean, you're quitting on me?" I asked him. My heart was pumping like crazy. I thought I had screwed everything up in my rare temper tantrum. I was getting worse and worse with my flare-ups, like a real celebrity would. But I was tired of riding in the passenger seat of my life. I wanted to drive for a change.

"*You* quit on me, Bobby," Gene said. "I'm tired of trying to convince you that the conservative idea will work."

"Yeah, it *has* worked, but for how long?" I asked him.

Gene sighed and said, "Yeah, maybe you're right, Bobby, you were too young for this." The next thing I knew, he had hung up on me.

"SHIT!" I screamed, slamming my phone down. Gene was an excellent producer and marketing strategist. I thought of calling him back and telling him that I had made a mistake and I would go back to the conservative thing, but that would have been ridiculous. I believed in what I was capable of doing just like he believed in what he was capable of doing. I had newfound confidence, which was something I lacked for years.

I sat down and thought hard about it and realized that there were plenty of people who could produce informative shows. It was up to me, though, to continue to bring my own crazy energy and humor to the airwaves.

I called up Brother Abu and explained the entire situation to him. He said, "I know plenty of people who could help you in the direction that you want to go in. This idea sounds more up your alley, too. That conservative black man approach was definitely restrictive and something that an older man would come up with.

"Anyone who knows you could tell that you weren't in control of that show, but I had to let you go through with the experience because it's all a part of learning the business," he told me. "But now you've really arrived, Bobby. This is your baby, and you'll succeed or fail on your own. It's all up to you now."

•

I met that next morning with the program director, Michael Hines, and told him my new ideas and what had happened with Gene. Surprisingly,

Michael was more excited about my ideas than I thought he would be. He said the conservative thing would die out fast, especially with black people, because there was always something new going on. I told him that I thought the exact same thing. I felt awkward agreeing with Michael, though, when it was Gene who brought me into the station and pushed the show toward being syndicated from day one. I had no idea what would happen with Gene. He didn't strike me as the kind of man who would give up on an opportunity to make money. Maybe he really believed I didn't have a chance in hell to pull it off.

As it turned out, Gene had a clause in his contract that tied him to my syndication rights whether he produced the show or not. The station manager, Gordon Dates, allowed the clause because I had already agreed to share my revenues.

Like I said before, Gene was a professional salesman. We all agreed that he was to receive no more than twenty-five percent of my take, and that it would only apply to the initial eight markets that we had on board and would not extend to any new markets. Gene argued that the entire syndication progress was like a domino effect, and that he had already set off the lead dominoes, which were the hardest. He was set to go to court over it, and he was a lawyer. Since it wouldn't affect the station's take of the syndication money, Dates went along with Gene rather than take the matter to court. I didn't get too upset about it. I figured it was the least I could do since Gene and I would no longer work together. To help produce the show, I met with a few people that Brother Abu had referred to me, and a few people I knew.

Instead of choosing one or two producers, I went with a team of producers to create the type of well-rounded and informative show that I believed would continue to increase my ratings share locally as well as nationally. I did the last of the conservative stuff and announced to my listeners that "The Radioman" would appear that next week. I was set to start 1994 the way *I* wanted to. I was finally in control of my own destiny.

•

After my last broadcast as Mr. Conservative, I went to Scotty's to do my usual thing on Friday night.

"What's this 'Radioman' thing you're talking about, Bobby? It sounds like some kiddie shit," Big Bill said to me.

I didn't really feel like talking about it. A lot of people are skeptical of new things before you pull it off. "You'll see next week," I told him.

Frank Watts walked in and headed straight for me. I hadn't seen him for a while because he worked afternoons and nights while I worked during the mornings. But we were both able to hear each other's shows.

Frank walked over and just stared at me.

"Are you off tonight, Frank?" I asked him.

He was still staring at me. "What the hell did you go and do, Bobby? I talked to Gene Carlton and he told me you went home for Christmas and lost your damn mind. I turned on the show this morning, and you're talking about some 'Radioman' shit. Every motherfucker on the radio is a 'Radioman,' Bobby. You're not doing anything new. Now that conservative shit had a plan to it."

"I guess you came down here to be my savior then, right?" I snapped at him.

"Somebody gotta save your ass. I mean, you get all the way to the top and then you go and do some dumb shit."

I started to walk out. I didn't need to hear his doubts. Listening to Frank had gotten me into trouble before.

"Where are you going, Bobby?" he asked me.

"I'm going home to kill myself," I answered him.

Mark Bishop walked in with a lady on his arm and bumped into me as I reached the stairway. "Speak of the devil," he said. "We were just talking about you, man. What's with this 'Radioman' thing?"

I smiled and shook my head. At least the whole town knew about it. All I had to do was make the thing work. "You'll find out next week," I told Mark and his lady friend.

After saying "Hi" to everyone who called out my name, I finally made it back outside to my Prelude. My Honda didn't have much longer to be with me. I hopped in and Frank caught up with me before I could drive off for home.

"Bobby! Are you sure you know what you're doing?" he asked me through the window. It was cold outside, too. Frank had frost on his breath.

I looked into his face and said, "I guess we'll find out, won't we?"

He shook his head and walked back off for Scotty's.

I pulled out of my parking spot and headed home to my apartment. Over that weekend, I even got a call from Angel Thomas.

"What's been going on with you out there, Bobby?" She decided to give up her residence in Mt. Ranier, Maryland, months ago, and I hadn't seen her since September. I could tell that she had heard something. I thought immediately about calling up her father to thank him again and to apologize to him for breaking off relations with his contact.

"I'm still getting over you," I lied to Angel. I had decided that it was me against the world. I tried as much as I could to block Angel and every other woman out of my mind in order to become the completely focused and syndicated "Radioman."

"Bobby, it seems like we've really drifted apart. I didn't think that time and space could do that to us. I thought that we were really close at one time."

I thought of Faye Butler again. We had been close, too, and then we had nothing. But at least I knew how Faye felt. She felt deserted, as if she wasn't good enough for me. She was good enough to be my friend, but not good enough to be my lifetime companion in a more committed form. We find ways to sacrifice for what we care about in life, but I had sacrificed nothing to be with Faye, and Angel was not sacrificing anything to be with me.

I felt cold toward her and said, "I don't really know what to say to you anymore. I mean, good luck in Hollywood, but I got my own life to live over here, and I can't continue to allow myself to be tortured."

"Is that how you want our friendship to end, 'Good luck in Hollywood'?"

"What else can I say?" I responded. "At one point I was ready to tell you that I loved you, but then I found out that it would have been premature, because you didn't feel the same way. I mean, why are you even calling me?"

"Because I was thinking about you, obviously."

"Why, because it's the new year? You had a lot of time to call me before now."

"And you couldn't call me?" she asked.

"I was busy just like you were busy, Angel."

"Yeah, I heard," she said.

"Is that why you're calling me, because you heard that I broke off with Gene Carlton?"

Angel didn't respond to it. "So, I guess the only thing I can do for you is wish you good luck, too, then," she said.

At that point, I just wanted to get off the phone with her. What was the use? Unless she wanted to come back into my life for good, I couldn't be bothered with her. "Whenever you're in town again, call me up and maybe we can go back to Takoma Station for old times' sake. But I have to be able to see you to really get into this, otherwise we're just talking to be talking."

"Okay," Angel told me. "I'll do that then."

We said our good-byes and hung up. I thought ahead to my big day on Monday. I couldn't allow the letdown with Angel to get to me. I just blocked her out of my mind again.

•

We began our first "Radioman" broadcast with wind blowing over the airwaves. It was pretty intriguing. Then I came on and asked, "Is it that windy outside today? I'm not in Chicago, am I? I thought WLRG-FM was in Washington, D.C. It's Monday morning, right? And I'm Bobby Dallas, the host of 'The Bobby Dallas Show.' "

I had a bunch of employees who worked at WLRG inside the studio booth with me. On cue, I got them all to chant, "We want Radioman! We want Radioman!" At the end of the chant, I had one guy yell, "YEAAAHH, RADIOMAN LIVES! HE'S ALIIIVE!"

I said, "What in the world is going on here?"

"We're all looking for Radioman, dude," I had one guy say like a seventies hippie.

"Yeah, have you seen him around?" I had the others join in.

"Ah, I think you guys have the wrong show," I said. "I don't know of any 'Radioman.' "

"Are you absolutely sure, dude? We heard that he was around here somewhere," I had the hippie guy respond.

"No, he's not around here. You guys have the wrong station," I said.

"Yeah, all right then. But if you see him around anywhere, you'll let us know, right, buddy?"

"Yeah, sure," I told him. They all walked out and shut the studio door behind them. Then I addressed my listeners. "Ah, sorry about that, people. This is Monday morning on WLRG-FM, I'm your host, Bobby Dallas, and this is my show, 'The Bobby Dallas Show.' "

On that first week, to introduce "The Radioman," I had a lot of interruptions of the show, and they were all timed perfectly. I had put together a great production team and we were working it! All of my years of radio experience were finally paying off. I knew a lot more about listeners than I thought I did. People love surprises and comedy, but I made sure that we mixed every show with strong news events in the black community like any other talk show would.

My concept was very similar to a Krs-One rap album titled *EDU-TAINMENT*. I wanted to EDUcate with news and enterTAIN with my skits and comedy, but it all had to be cool because I wanted to maintain that soulful feeling that black people love so much.

I invited Brother Abu on the show to interview me about the interruptions that first Friday of my new concept. I was going to use that as an official introduction of "The Radioman."

"I want to introduce my listeners out there to a brother who was very monumental in helping me get started as a host in talk radio a few years ago.

"I was in radio limbo before I met this brother. I was just floating around in empty space, trying to grab on to something that could anchor my boat. That's how it is for a lot of people in radio. That's how it is for a lot of people in life, in general. I mean, I still don't have a steady woman yet. I am taking applications, though, in case any women are interested."

I laughed and said, "Anyway, this brother has been on the air for sixteen years, educating the black community on current news and black art, while playing a backdrop of jazz tunes. A few years back, realizing that he had other dreams he wanted to pursue, he allowed me to host his show called 'The Awakenings.' The brother liked my style of talk and my positive energy. and his show, 'The Awakenings,' became the catalyst for me to gain the confidence I needed to later develop 'The Bobby Dallas Show.'

"His name is Brother Abu, a Swahili word meaning 'nobility.' I'm glad to have you on the show today, brother," I said.

"Indeed, indeed, Bobby, I'm glad to see that you've been respecting your elders," Brother Abu responded. It was all a part of the script.

"Yeah, I learned a lot of lessons from the brothers and sisters who came before me," I told him. "Respect is due."

Brother Abu said, "I didn't know that you were a *conservative* man, though."

"Yeah, well, I am from the South."

Brother Abu chuckled. "The South hasn't changed that much over the years, hunh?"

"Some things have, some things haven't," I said. "I still think we need to get rid of Jesse Helms as a representative of my home state of North Carolina, but I guess the other voters don't see it that way."

"Some people have to learn to accept change," Brother Abu responded. "But Bobby, I've been listening to your show all this week, and it sounded like a whole lot of craziness was going on over here. I mean, who in the world is this 'Radioman'?"

"I don't know the answer to that myself, brother. Maybe we just need better security over here," I said, playing along. It was working perfectly.

"Why are these people only bothering you?" Brother Abu asked me.

"I don't know. It wasn't happening to me before."

I had one of my producers, a sister named Tamika Hill, barge inside the studio and holler, "I heard 'The Radioman' was in here! Have you seen him, have you seen him?"

My other producer, Yusef Green, played a security guard. "Let's go, lady!" he shouted.

Brother Abu said, "What the . . ."

Tamika hollered, "NO-O! HE'S HERE! HE'S HERE! I KNOW HE IS!"

"NO HE'S NOT!" Yusef yelled, dragging Tamika out of the studio and shutting the door.

Brother Abu said, "Bobby, I have never seen anything like that in my entire life! What is going on over here? This is one of the top-rated shows in D.C.!"

I said, "You know, brother, I've been trying to hide it for years now."

"Hide what?" Brother Abu asked me.

"Ever since I got my first radio—I think I was around seven—I would sit and listen to these voices that came over the air. And I loved it. I mean, I loved these voices more than I loved the music. My parents thought that I was crazy. I would actually sit around and wait for the voices to come back on, especially if they were funny. And I learned a lot from these guys."

"So what are you trying to tell me, Bobby?"

"Well, I started having these dreams."

"Dreams?"

"Yeah, but they weren't really dreams, they were more like visions."

"Visions of what?"

"Actually, they were visions of me being able to float over the radio waves and go anywhere I wanted to go." I laughed. "It's kind of silly, right? But that's the kind of things that you think of when you're a kid."

Brother Abu said, "Bobby, what does that have to do with this 'Radioman' thing?"

"Well, that's what I'm trying to tell you. These visions that I used to have as a kid, I never stopped having them."

"Well, that's fine. It's nothing wrong with that. Everyone has visions of doing something they always wished they could do in life."

"See, that's just it, though, brother. I'm tired of wishing and hoping and waiting. I'm ready for it to happen," I said.

"Ready for what to happen?"

"The transformation."

"What transformation? Bobby, I'm not following you," Brother Abu said.

We were working it!

I said, "Brother, I want to be able to touch people through the airwaves and make them laugh. I want to let them know what's going on with the people from California to Africa, and even in Japan. I want them to count on me to brighten up their day, brother. I don't wanna be conservative anymore!" I whined. "I don't wanna be conservative anymore!"

"Bobby, we're still on the air, you're embarrassing yourself," Brother Abu said. "Get yourself together, man. You don't have to be conservative if you don't want to be. Just be yourself."

"But that's just it, brother. Will they accept me as myself? Will they accept me as 'The Radioman'?"

"So you *are* 'The Radioman'?" Brother Abu said. He was trying his hardest not to laugh.

"Yes, that's what I've been trying to tell you, brother! IT'S ME! I'M THE RADIOMAN! THEY'VE FOUND OUT! THEY ALL KNOW! THEY ALL KNOW!"

"Calm down, Bobby! Calm down! You're gonna blow their speakers out!" Brother Abu shouted at me. "So what if they know?! If that's who you are, then that's who you have to be!

"You have to walk in here and get on the air next Monday morning, Bobby, and give it to the people straight! You're 'The Radioman'!"

I calmed down and said, "But do you think I can really pull it off?"

"That's up to you, Bobby. If the people like you, then they like you. But if they don't, then I guess 'The Radioman' will have to go back to being just a vision. But I got faith in you, brother. You can do it. I *know* you can. That's why I chose you."

•

We had everyone waiting for Monday morning's show. Over the weekend, I got together with the jazz band called 2000 Black that I saw perform at Takoma Station. I got them to do a soundtrack for my new introduction using a bass line and kick drum groove with backup singers and an African shekere instrument. I planned to go all-out for the show.

We started off using the wind sound again. Then we dropped in the shekere, which sounds like a shaker, followed by the bass line, the drum kick, and the snare drum.

> *Boomp . . . Snap!*
> *Boommm, boomp . . . boomp*

Boomp . . . Snap!
Boommm . . .
"Ray-di-yo-maaann!"
Boomp . . . Snap!
Boommm, boomp . . . boomp
Boomp . . . Snap!
"It's the Radi-yo-maaann!"

It was the coolest introduction I had ever heard! The groove had enough space where I could easily fill in my radio history at a nice slow pace like performance poetry. My coproducer, Yusef Green, did me the honors:

> *The Radioman started off a long time ago*
> *and at first he was just a dream*
> *waiting*
> *in hibernation*
> *but once my man*
> *Bobby Dallas*
> *got closer to the people*
> *he realized that*
> *the Radioman he envisioned*
> *could become a reality*

It was the coolest thing ever! I can't even put it into words. I guess the best way to describe it would be to imagine black people in a dark room with Afros and sunshades, bobbing their heads and snapping their fingers to the God called Rhythm. It was like George Clinton and Parliament, and I was "The Mothership."

"Yeah, this is Bobby Dallas, your host, on WLRG-FM, and this is my show, 'The Bobby Dallas Show.' For the next two hours, I'm gonna give you the news and the views and hopefully get rid of your blues as I do things my way from Monday to Friday."

I was in love with my show and having a damn good time with it! After most of the commercial breaks, I used my niece, Aminah's, chant, "Mommy, Mommy, it's The Radioman!" before coming back on air. I had taped her over the phone and got the sound man to clear it up so that we could use it.

We played my introduction on Mondays only, and at the beginning of each week my listeners couldn't wait to hear it. I used my new ideas, "Who's TCB," "Back of the Bus Rides," and "I Betcha Didn't Know," to give the national black news reports. Before I knew it, everyone seemed to be using my sayings. I still used "Trouble in the Kitchen" on Wednesdays, "Barbershop Talk" on Thursdays, and "Solutions" on Fridays. I tried to reserve as much space as I could for interviews at the beginning of the week. I used any- and everything to keep the show as lively and informative as I could. Sometimes that included making minor changes to keep up with the times. I started reading "Love Letters" and "Letters from Jail" that people sent in. I began interviewing regular blue-collar workers about their struggles on the job, and at the end of every show, I used Aminah's voice saying, "Aw, Mommy, he's gone again" as the wind blew and faded out in the background.

My show used the cool energy of a disc jockey, the information of a journalist, the edge of a comedian, and sometimes the compassion of a friend. The ratings continued to grow tremendously, and more stations were picking up "The Bobby Dallas Show" for syndication. I had proven myself to everyone! I was willing to take risks, and I had succeeded in making myself one of the hottest rising radio stars in the country. The most important thing was that I was finally able to make the crucial decisions that would rule my life. I felt like Janet Jackson, in total control at last.

The Big Payback

Frank Watts had to admit that I pulled it off, as well as Big Bill, Mark Bishop, Kathy Teals, and in particular, Gene Carlton, but we weren't on speaking terms anymore. With the sweet deal Gene had secured with WLRG-FM concerning my syndication rights, he could have been a private fan, or even my number one fan. But I had no way of really knowing if he was listening.

Anyway, I bet the people at WUCI-AM were kicking themselves in the ass for not trying to work out a deal to keep me there. However, I don't think I would have been ready to do "Radioman" then anyway. The experience that I gained by playing a young conservative guy was beneficial to my overall balance as a journalist and my outlook on listeners as a whole. The conservative black man idea really gave me an opportunity to form my own opinions and assessments of what people liked to listen to. It was through that experience that I knew "Radioman" would work.

I got a bunch of phone calls at the station from people who wanted to congratulate me on putting together such a great show. A lot of them had worked with me during my years in limbo in Baltimore and Virginia. Mr. Cooper even called to congratulate me.

"I knew all along that you could be special, Bobby, you just needed more drive and focus," he said.

"Yeah, well, I definitely have drive and focus now," I told him.

"Yeah, so maybe you can go back to New York when you get ready and finish what you started up there," he suggested to me.

"I don't know if I want to do that. I like it better down here in Washington," I said. "I'm pretty satisfied with where I am right now."

When I hung up with Mr. Cooper, I thought about Pearl Davis again. I wondered what she was up to. I hadn't seen her modeling work in any magazines in years. I wondered if her career was over already, while mine was just starting to blossom. I still didn't have a steady woman or anything. I started to meet plenty of women because of the popularity of my show, but a funny thing happened once I acquired my new wealth, I didn't trust many women. I thought all the time about different sisters trying to get me to the altar for their own economic security, so I began to keep relationships as noncommittal as I could. That only made me seem distant and conceited to a lot of women, but I wasn't, I just didn't know what to think of them.

Angel Thomas and I came to an agreement and suspended our communication for a while. I thought it was the right decision. I needed to clear my head from the thought of being more to her than she was ready for me to be. Her career was taking off as fast as mine was. Her local commercials in California had turned into national commercials and she was auditioning for major parts in a couple of television sitcoms that were in development. That's how things work when you're involved with smart and driven people, things start happening all around you.

I was pretty much "TCB" in my own right for 1994. I was thirty, economically secure, and I was basically my own boss. As long as my ratings were high, I didn't have too many problems with management over at WLRG. Every once in a while, things got a little bit out of hand on the show, but we were usually able to work things out.

In a word, things were *great!* I was known throughout the entire Washington area. All I had to do was say my name and people responded, "Oh, you're Bobby Dallas! The Radioman! I love your show! It's good to meet you!"

Imagine going through that nearly every time you went to pay for something with a credit card, or had to identify yourself for some reason. I joked on the show once that I wished the state troopers in Maryland would recognize me and let me slide the next time I was pulled over for speeding. It seems my new black BMW was too fast for my own good. I got three speeding tickets in Maryland all in one month. My car even got searched again, so I did a show about speed limits, fast cars, black and white drivers, and how different state troopers treated people around the country. The production team did an excellent job pulling together all of the information. It was an excellent show. I just couldn't be more elated about the progress that I was making.

•

Big Bill laughed from behind his bar at Scotty's and said, "Mark probably don't know how to dance anyway," before walking off.

It was another Friday. I was telling Mark Bishop that I was invited as a VIP guest to a Marc Barnes party. Marc Barnes had been throwing popular parties in D.C. for years. I wanted to take Mark Bishop along with me, but he said he had to see what his lady was doing first.

"How long have you been going out with this one?" I asked him. Mark never had any hard feelings toward me about the show I did with him. In fact, it made him more popular. He was invited on a couple of other shows after mine, where he got a chance to talk more specifically about his work and the rising popularity of black art in the community.

He smiled and answered, "Since last year. I met her about a week after I was on your show."

"Did she hear you on the show?" I asked him with a grin.

"Yeah, we talked about it."

I shook my head. "That doesn't make any sense, man. You've been on my show *once* and you end up with a steady woman. I'm on my show *five days a week* and I still don't have one."

"That's because you have too many to choose from. Sometimes that can ruin a guy," Mark responded.

"Yeah, you're telling me. I'm going over to this Marc Barnes party to meet some more women I probably won't be steady with."

We laughed as I finished my drink.

"All right then, what are you waiting for, man? Go call her and see," I said.

Mark was stalling. I don't think he wanted to go to the party with me. When he finally went to use the pay phone, I watched him frown and walk back over to me.

"No dice, man. She wants to go to the movies."

Big Bill overheard him. He looked at Mark and asked, "Did you know about this movie thing earlier?" It was nearly nine o'clock.

"Yeah, are you going to the ten o'clock show?" I wanted to know myself.

Mark grinned and answered, "That's what it looks like."

Bill cracked, "Boy, you might as well go and stick some feathers up your ass. You're still a young man, Mark. What are you doing being henpecked?"

I laughed so hard my ribs started to hurt. Bill rarely talked about *his* wife and family. He had three kids and six grandchildren. He was a long way from the dating game.

"Laugh if you want to, Bobby, but at least I know whose bed I'm gonna end up in tonight," Mark cracked at me.

I felt slighted. "Hey, man, *I* didn't call you henpecked," I argued. Big Bill had gone on about his business again, like a hit-and-run driver.

"You didn't have to say it. I know you're thinking it, that's why you laughed so hard," Mark said. "Well, have a good time with the hoochies at the party," he added before he left.

I was a little pissed off by it, and I needed someone to talk to, so I called up my young coproducer, Yusef Green, to go to the party with me. Yusef was a sharp young brother I met while working in Baltimore. He was still in school and doing an internship then, while I was a hard-at-work DJ. Yusef always had some good ideas, so when I had an opening for my producer spot, I contacted him. Actually, I thought I would be in for a fight at WLRG to get my people hired with the limited experience some of them had, but Michael Hines smoothed everything out again. I tell you, that white guy was a blessing in disguise.

•

Yusef was brown like a pair of fine leather shoes, smooth and even. He was a tad shorter than me, maybe six foot two like Brad. He kept a haircut of medium height, a clean face, trimmed mustache, and wore dressy clothes. The women had their eyes on him like he was a singer. Even a few of the white women at WLRG-FM gave him that special look with an extra "Hi." He could easily play hoops with a lot of women if he chose not to settle down too early.

"I don't mean to get in your business and all, but do you have a steady girl, Yusef?" We were in my BMW heading to a club called Quigley's, right below the Dupont Circle area.

Yusef smiled and said, "I'm leaning that way with this one girl."

"Does *she* know that?" I asked him.

"She's been the one hinting at it for a while now."

"And you're not ready for that?"

"Not yet. You know, I'm still trying to make a living."

"What, you want me to get you a raise already?" It was September, and Yusef had only been working with me for eight months.

He shook his head. "No, I'm not saying that. I mean, it *would* be nice, but I realize that you have to pay your dues before you can make the kind of money that you really want to make. Actually, I'm glad you even gave me an opportunity to work with you."

It occurred to me at that moment that I was an older statesman. I mean, I wasn't *that* old, but Yusef was definitely looking up to me. I had the power. I was able to help him like Frank Watts, Brother Abu, and Gene Carlton were able to help me.

I asked, "Has an older guy ever told you to settle down with a good woman as soon as you find one?"

Yusef laughed. "My father and my uncles told me that," he answered. "But it's a different time that we're living in today. A lot of women aren't ready to get married yet either. I wouldn't get married before I was set in my career anyway. Women my age are holding out for their careers, too.

"Frances Cress Welsing says that young black people shouldn't get married until they're like twenty-eight to thirty," he told me. Frances Cress Welsing was a big-name sister in black psychiatry in the District. She wrote a book called *Isis Papers* that ripped the white man's symbolisms of power to pieces.

"How old are you again?" I asked Yusef.

"Twenty-four," he said.

He was light-years ahead of where I was at twenty-four. I was still having a good time ordering pizza and watching videos when I was his age. I was so wet behind the ears after graduating from college that I should have learned sign language, because I damn sure couldn't hear anything that anyone tried to tell me.

"Where are you trying to go in your career?" I asked.

"Man, I got ideas in television, film, music. You just called me with the radio thing first, so I took it to gain the experience."

"Shit, so you're trying to do everything," I said.

"You got to nowadays. You never know what might happen."

I felt petty asking Yusef about relationships after that. If he was as focused with women as he was with making career moves, I didn't think they would have posed a problem for him. I just listened to my car stereo and kept my mouth shut for the rest of the ride.

I parked the car two blocks away from the club and we hopped out and took a walk down to Quigley's on I Street. I had never been to the place before. When we got there, there was a long line with plenty of young folks in it. I already knew that I didn't want to stay too long, but I had brought Yusef with me and he looked thrilled by the sight of the young ladies who were waiting in line.

I walked up front and said, "I'm Bobby Dallas and this is my producer, Yusef Green, from WLRG-FM."

The brother looked me in my face and responded, "Radioman! Come on in."

We slid inside, past the people waiting at the door. It was like a miniature maze to get downstairs to the small, square-shaped dance floor. It had a cement column right smack in the middle. The DJ booth was tiny, and the bar wasn't half as big as the one I was used to at Scotty's. I felt claustrophobic. It was the kind of small place that you could easily walk through twenty times in a night if the traffic allowed. But again, Yusef seemed to be enjoying it.

"This place looks right up your alley," I said to him. "If you're all right, I'm gonna go and get a drink at the bar."

Yusef nodded. "Yeah, I'm all right."

I went over to the bar and got myself a drink. I looked around at the carefree twenty-somethings filling up the club and thought about my age. *I'm actually thirty years old now!* I told myself. Whenever you keep yourself busy like I had, time flies by and you don't even realize it.

I noticed a small area that was sectioned off from the rest of the activity—the VIP section. Since I was a VIP, I decided to head over there and had to stop myself short. I damn near dropped my drink! I calmed myself down after she noticed me, though. I smiled and walked over to her table where she sat with a friend.

"Pearl Davis," I greeted her. "Long time no see."

"Bobby! Oh my God! How have you been?" she asked me. Pearl looked as bored as I was. She was wearing a lime green two-piece suit that fit kind of loose on her. Her hair was curled, and she looked a little heavier and more mature. In fact, she stood up and gently hugged me. "Jackie, this is an old friend of mine from Howard."

Her friend Jackie, a fair-skinned, long-haired sister with legs like a giraffe, nodded to me and smiled. She was wearing a tight royal blue dress that stopped far above her beautiful knees.

Anyway, I pulled over a chair to sit and drink with them. "So, how is your career going?" I asked Pearl. "In fact, what are you doing down here in Washington?"

She was drinking what appeared to be straight orange juice. "Jackie's from Maryland, so we were just visiting after flying in from Britain," she answered.

"Britain? I guess your career is still going well then." It's never been cheap to fly overseas. Pearl still had some money.

"Yeah, pretty much," she told me. "But it's not like it used to be."

She seemed a hell of a lot more subdued than when I was with her, but that was seven years ago. I looked at her friend and asked, "What part of Maryland are you from?"

She looked too cool to answer me. "Gaithersburg," she said with a pause.

"Oh yeah? Have you ever heard of 'The Bobby Dallas Show'?" I figured she might have heard of my show if her folks lived that close.

She shook her head. "No." She looked around twenty-three, and was snobbish. I'd advise Yusef not to bother with her type, especially if Pearl was her mentor.

"You mean you have your own little show now, Bobby?" Pearl asked me. She looked surprised. I didn't like that word, *little,* that she used either.

"Yeah, in fact, I need to get you two on the air. We could talk about black models and whatnot. I haven't had any models on the show yet," I said.

"We're not staying in town that long," Jackie responded.

"No problem. We could do a phone interview from New York."

"Yeah, I'll do it," Pearl said. "It'll be fun."

Jackie looked shocked for a minute, but then she went along with it. "Okay." She had a lot of learning to do about the entertainment industry. You don't ever turn media people down unless you *really* believe you're gonna be the hottest thing walking. I had never seen Jackie's work before, but what did I know? Jackie could have been the next Tyra Banks.

I handed both women my business card, and Pearl gave me one of hers. I asked Jackie if she had one, just for the hell of it. I wanted to see if she was as stuck on herself as I thought she was.

"You can contact me through Pearl," she said.

Yup, I told myself. Excuse my expression, but I thought of her as a bitch in training. "What are you, a modeling agent now, Pearl? Congratulations on stepping up to the next level," I cracked.

Pearl just smiled. She knew what I was getting at. I guess that being highly selective was a part of the business. You couldn't give any Joe Blow your number. I had to screen some people myself.

"Whatever happened to Kiki Monet?" I asked Pearl.

She cringed and shook her head. "Mmm, I don't even want to go there."

"That bad, hunh?"

Pearl looked to Jackie and then back to me. "Look, it's even worse than that, okay?"

I figured that whatever it was, they both deserved it. However, Pearl seemed so calm and personable with me that I took the thought back. Then Yusef walked into the room to catch back up to me. I was curious to see how the two models would respond to him, especially Miss Jackie.

"Oh, yeah, this is one of my coproducers, Yusef Green," I told them.

Yusef looked them over. "Hi y'all doin'?" He didn't seem pressed about it at all.

"Yeah, this is Pearl Davis, and this is Jackie something," I told him.

Yusef shook their hands. Jackie tried to raise her nose again, but I could tell that she was impressed with him. She stared in his face too long not to be.

"I invited them on the show," I told him. "Coordinate a date for us to get them on."

Yusef nodded. I could tell he wanted to talk to me in private. He had that lingering stance that people have when they're trying not to be rude.

"Excuse me for a minute," I said to Pearl and her friend. I stood up and walked back into the club area with Yusef.

"Remember the girl I was telling you about earlier?" he asked me with a grin.

"The one that's getting serious about you?"

"Yeah."

"Okay, what about her?"

Yusef smiled and said, "She's here."

"Did she catch you doing something?" I asked him.

"No, she just walked in and spotted me. She said she called me earlier but I wasn't in. She left a message, but you called me about this party as soon as I got in. I didn't check my messages yet."

Apparently I had more influence on Yusef than I thought. "So what did she say to you?"

"She said that she didn't want to be here, but since *I'm* here, now it's cool with her."

"Who did she come with?"

"Three of her girlfriends. But she said that she was ready to leave whenever I was."

I couldn't believe my ears. "She told you that?"

Yusef smiled. "Yeah."

"Damn! Is this girl fine, too?"

"Yeah," Yusef said without hesitating.

I remembered when Pearl Davis would send me home in a cab before ever leaving her girlfriends. I grabbed Yusef by his shoulder and said, "Look here, man, take it from me, that's a good girl. Don't let her get away."

He grinned. "All right then. I might have to take a cab home, because I don't want to impose on you like that," he told me.

"No problem, man. I'm ready to get out of here myself. I'll wait for Marc Barnes to throw an over-twenty-five party," I joked. Then I pulled out a twenty and slid it in Yusef's palm. "That's for your taxi ride."

"Oh, thanks, man. Thanks a lot," he told me.

"Yeah, and we'll work on that raise for you next year."

He smiled and said, "Okay," before heading back through the crowd to find his dedicated lady. I was tempted to follow him to see what this young, strong-willed sister looked like. If she was willing to up and leave her girlfriends, then she was definitely into him.

I walked back over to the VIP section. Pearl and her friend were packing up to leave.

"That's just what I was thinking," I told them. "I'm ready to go home and listen to my *own* music. I'll be in contact with you for the show, though."

Pearl nodded. "All right then, Bobby. It's good seeing you again."

I got home with a smile on my face and couldn't wait to humiliate Pearl Davis on my show. I bet she thought that I was still the mild-mannered Bobby Dallas that she used to know, but I had news for her. I was going to sock it to her hard, her *and* her trainee! I admit that it seemed childish, but a lot of people could learn from the experience. Someone had to let the snobbish women of America know that they can't always get away with their better-than-thou attitudes without re-percussions. Women surely had enough opportunities to let men know that they were dogs. I figured that after Pearl had dumped a good black man in New York and left him to rot and die, she deserved a payback.

•

It took Yusef three weeks before securing a Monday when we could get Pearl and Jackie on the show, via telephone from New York. I wanted to make it Monday so I could tape it and send Pearl a copy of my cooler-than-cool introduction. But as it got closer and closer to our interview with them, I began to have second thoughts.

A lot of people loved "The Bobby Dallas Show," including all my close and extended family members. My show had been picked up by stations in Greensboro and Charlotte. I had made sure of it. Brenda even had her family listening to my show in the Boston area, especially since her daughter's voice was becoming famous. I had few controversies, and "The Radioman" was basically a good guy.

I started thinking about letting bygones be bygones and doing an interview as if I had never met Pearl. I got so troubled over the whole thing that I called my good friend Brother Abu a week before the show to ask him about it.

He said, "Bobby, I know you like being Mr. Good Guy and being liked by everyone, but you have to do your job, too. You don't have to get foul with this sister, but I think you have a lot of points to make here."

Brother Abu always made a point to be objective about things, but sometimes I just wanted his gut feeling. "Would you do it?" I asked him.

He hesitated. "Well, what I would *try* to do is turn the situation around and make it beneficial to the community."

"Yeah, that's what *I* want to do," I told him.

"So then, what's the problem?" he responded. "I admit, I had to get nasty a few times on my own show. I couldn't take the ignorance sometimes, and from what you told me, this girl represents a lot of ignorance."

"But wouldn't I seem ignorant, too, if I went overboard with it?"

"Well, don't go overboard then. Keep your emotions intact, and know your boundaries."

I don't know why, but I called Frank Watts to get his opinion on it. I guess I just wanted to see the other side of the coin. I told him a little bit about the history I shared with Pearl Davis the model, and he spent the first fifteen minutes asking me about it.

"How come you never told me you had been with her before?" he asked me.

"Would you have believed me?"

He laughed and said, "Hell no! I would have thought that your scary ass was lying. But shit, Bobby, I'd light her ass up if I got her on my show after all of that. You could have gone crazy up there in New York. I can't blame you for leaving."

"Or, I could have simply found a new girlfriend and moved on," I argued. In the name of being objective, I was trying my hardest not to blame Pearl for my misfortunes.

"Well, you're gonna do what you're gonna do, Bobby, but if it was me . . ."

•

I was still undecided about how I would handle the interview with Pearl, so I decided to call her up in New York and do a preinterview five days before the show. I wanted to get a feel for where she was in life and how she thought. When I called, though, a brother answered the phone.

I stuttered and asked, "Ah, is Pearl Davis there?" I wasn't expecting a guy to answer.

"Who's calling?" he asked me.

"Bobby Dallas from WLRG-FM in Washington, D.C."

"Hold on," he said.

When he came back on the line, I asked, "Are you her manager?" I was curious.

"Yeah, you could say that. Is this a business call?"

"Yeah," I answered him. Before I got a chance to ask him anything else, he handed the phone to Pearl. A manager wouldn't have done that, especially if the call concerned business. That made me even more curious.

"Hi, Bobby, I thought the interview was for Monday," Pearl said.

"It is, I just wanted to get a feel for where you were in your career to make it a real informative show," I told her.

"Oh, well, I've slowed down a lot. I get calls every once in a while, but I'm really looking forward to doing something else in my life now. I was going to talk about my past experiences in modeling and let you talk more to Jackie. I'm trying to help her along in any way that I can, you know, like a big sister."

"So your career is winding down?" I asked her.

"Yeah, Bobby, but I've had a good time with it. I'm just looking forward to other things, like March fourteenth, nineteen ninety-five."

"What's that?" I asked her.

"My due date."

I was speechless. I thought about Pearl's extra weight, her loose-fitting outfit, and her orange juice at the club. She hadn't even smoked a cigarette while she was there.

"You're pregnant?" I finally asked her.

"Yup. I mean, it's about time. I did want to have a kid before I wrinkled up and died," she said with a laugh. It was a totally different Pearl. I felt sick to my stomach for what I was thinking about doing to her. Boy, was I glad that I had called her first!

"Did the father just answer the phone?" I asked her. I had a lump in my throat. I believe I was jealous. I would have wanted Pearl to have *my* child.

She hesitated. "Yeah." Then she said in a lower tone, "Bobby, I'm really sorry about how things happened. That was a long time ago. I didn't know any better."

Dammit! I was thinking. I didn't want to touch a show with Pearl after that. I wanted to cancel it right then and there. I said, "I understand. That situation strengthened me in many ways. I've learned that all the unfortunate things that happen in life are only hurdles to make us stronger."

Pearl said, "If I could do it all again . . ."

"Don't even think about it," I told her. "I'm doing real well now. My show is syndicated, I'm my own boss, and I'm having a real good time with it."

"Yeah, I heard," she responded. "Your producer told me. I'm really happy for you, Bobby."

"Yeah, and you got me that first job with Mr. Payton at WHCS," I told her.

"No, *you* did that. I only gave you the contact," she told me. Then she laughed and said, "You still don't give yourself enough credit, after all these years. Mr. Cinderella."

I chuckled. "Yeah, I've been through a lot of rocky storms, and I'm still swimming to shore."

"That's because you're a strong black man," Pearl said.

I was highly skeptical of her praise. I remembered when she used to scream at me to grow up and whatnot. *Could she have matured that much?* I asked myself.

Pearl read my silence. "I've learned a lot over the years, Bobby."

"Yeah, you're telling me," I responded to her.

"I broke off with Kiki Monet years ago," she said. "Kiki did and said some things about me that I never would have done to her. She was really pressed to get this shoot for *Sports Illustrated*. It was for the nineteen eighty-nine swimsuit issue. And neither one of us ended up getting it. I knew I had to cut her ass loose after that shit. I was *pissed!*"

"Yeah, I could imagine," I told her. Then I thought about Marianne Tyler, Pearl's mom. She had always liked me. "How's your mother doing?"

"Oh, she's still practicing. She loves what she does. And she can't *wait* to be a grandmother!"

I felt miserable. I finished my small talk with Pearl and thought about calling in sick on Monday to avoid doing a show with her. I didn't know what I was going to do, but I knew that I couldn't bring myself to sock it to her. Pearl had actually turned into a decent woman. She even hinted to me that the father-to-be had proposed to her and that she would probably take him up on his offer. I was numb for the rest of that week.

•

That Friday afternoon, Yusef called me at home. I was still feeling paranoid about that coming Monday. He said, "Pearl Davis called and said she had to cancel the show for Monday. She said something else had come up. But she got in contact with Beverly Johnson to see if she could do it instead."

"Beverly Johnson?" I asked him. Yusef wasn't usually the joking type, but I wasn't sure. It would have been a good one if he was, but he wasn't.

"Yeah, she's supposed to be working on a book that's coming out soon," he told me.

"Okay. Did you set it up?" I was excited in two ways. First, I wouldn't have to interview Pearl, and second, I would interview Beverly Johnson, the black American *queen* of modeling!

"I'm in the process of doing that now," Yusef said.

It all seemed too good to be true. I wondered if Pearl had canceled on purpose. I called her back to find out and got her answering machine.

I said, "I'm sorry about not being able to do the show with you, but we thank you for contacting Beverly Johnson for us. That was real nice of you to do. And congratulations on your upcoming motherhood."

We went ahead and got Beverly Johnson on the line with us that Monday morning. She talked about her life in modeling, good health, good genes, and her beautiful teenaged daughter, who had already been in *Essence*. It turned out to be a wonderful and informative show.

When I got back in that day, I had a message on my phone from Pearl.

"Bobby, I knew that it would have been awkward for you to interview me after all we had been through. I decided that it would be best not to do it. Plus, Jackie was on a photo shoot in Jamaica, and instead of her rushing back to New York, I just told her to stay down there and enjoy herself. That's why I went ahead and hooked you up with Beverly. I met her a few times and we liked each other, so I knew that she would be the perfect one to talk to.

"I really like your show, too. They have it on a station in Jersey. 'Mommy, Mommy, it's The Radioman!' " she chanted, imitating my niece. "That was really *cute*. You've come a long way, Bobby. I am really proud of you.

"Well, I can't take the time back, but I *do* hope that you'll forgive me one day. Peace out, and good luck in the future."

I smiled for a few minutes after listening to her message a couple of times. "Life is a long journey," I mumbled. I was happy for Pearl. She had probably been through as many changes as I had, yet *she* had found herself someone special to share her life with. All I had was my show, and although I loved it, I realized that it could never take the place of human love, togetherness, and children.

Burnt Out

The term *burnout* means someone is just ready to quit. You're worn out from head to toe from trying so hard to get somewhere or to accomplish things in life, and no matter how hard you try or how much progress you make, it feels like you're standing still. No matter what you do, you can't seem to find that peace of mind that would put your nerves at ease. Even with head starts, it seems like you're always finishing last. Your candle is out, and your wax is melted down to the plate. You're exhausted and too weak in spirit to even look for a new source of energy to get yourself started again. You're hurt and depleted of creativity and your soul feels displaced, as if it has left your very body. You don't even have the energy to scream, curse, or yell anymore. The energy that used to fill your muscles has worn thin, replaced by a dry, unmovable numbness. You just feel like lying down and never getting up again. But since you're still alive, and dedicated to the task called life, your family, your job, your community, and your God, you get up again anyway.

I decided I was overdue for a vacation, and I wanted to get as far away from things as I could, so at the end of 1994, I flew all the way to Brazil.

•

Brazil was a beautiful, scenic place, filled with millions of brown people. They even had paintings and sculptures of brown saints at their churches. I *never* saw that in America!

I was ridiculously rich in Brazil. The value of the American dollar in Rio de Janeiro made me practically a millionaire, and the people were so openly affectionate that it made me sick. I guess it might have been okay if I had someone of my own that I cared enough about to be with.

I was down there for five days, and every night I thought about picking up a woman, but I didn't. I didn't have the energy for it. There were brown women walking around on the beaches of Brazil who could easily make a family man jump in the water and cheat on his wife. I was a single man with plenty of money, yet I didn't even attempt to get wet. Something had to be wrong with me. I was burnt out. The only thing I got out of the trip to Brazil was a deep, dark suntan.

•

Big Bill had jazzed up his establishment by the end of the year. He said he wanted to bring 1995 in right, so Scotty's was no longer incognito. It had a new neon sign outside and flashy disco lights with more space for a dance floor. In fact, the place was getting too crowded for me.

"You ever think about getting married, Bobby?" Mark Bishop asked me. It was a Thursday night in late January, a week after my thirty-first birthday. We had been sitting at the bar for an hour and a half already. I had downed two tall drinks and was working on my third.

"Yeah, I just ain't asked nobody yet," I responded to Mark's marriage question.

"I'm thinking about making that move, man," he said.

I let out some strong alcohol fumes, rumbling like hot steam through my chest. "BLUURRP! . . . 'Scuse me." I didn't feel like hearing any marriage talk from Mark. I dozed off and began daydreaming about Pearl Davis and New York City again. Once I realized I had drifted off, Mark was frowning at me and shaking his head, pitying me. I took another sip of my drink, a screwdriver, heavy on the vodka.

"You know why you're lonely, Bobby?" Mark asked me. "You're afraid of taking a chance with a sister and falling in love. I mean, how are you gonna have a radio show that tries to inform and uplift black people, and behind closed doors, you can't give your total trust to a sister?"

I simply smiled at him. Mark had no idea what I had been through with women. I said, "Mark, Hecht's is having a sale on the men's style of *Wizard of Oz*, click-your-heels-three-times-for-a-black-woman shoes. Why don't you go down there and buy me a pair and I'll pay you for them when you get back? Sale ends Saturday."

Mark looked at me and laughed. "I'm convinced, man. You're thrown the hell off."

I had nothing better to do with myself. My jokes had become my salvation. I slammed the last of my drink to the back of my throat, feeling it burn as it went down. By your third drink, it burns much less.

"Where are you going?" Mark asked me.

I balanced my head and torso on two unsteady legs. "I'm going to Hecht's," I told him.

Mark grinned and shook his head.

I carefully swerved through the glittery bouncing crowd of suits, ties, boots, and skirts all attached to brown faces. Before I could make it to the staircase, I was sideswiped off balance and then quickly held upright again.

"Hey, Bobby Dallas! How you doin', brother? When are you gonna have me on that show of yours?"

My hands flew up to my head, attempting to soothe a zapping headache. "Talk to my producers," I mumbled.

"Come on, man. Every time I call they say you're booked."

I kept moving toward the staircase, protecting my head. "I am."

Jerry Willis, a D.C. government employee, faded from my blurred vision and melted into the background as I made it to the stairway. Each descending step sent shock waves into the eggshell that had replaced my skull. *Shit! My head is killing me!* I remember thinking.

"Bobby Dallas!" an anonymous voice yelled at me once I reached the bottom floor.

I waved without looking and continued on my way out the exit door, where the January wind threw open my unbuttoned sports jacket. I looked south and then north on Eighth Street to find my car.

"You got any extra change on you, brother?"

Still not looking, I painfully tossed my head in the direction of the bar and lied. "Big Bill got my last."

"Oh, okay. You gon' make it, brother?"

"Yeah, I'm all right. I just need a jumbo bag of ice and some Tylenol."

I remember a squeal of laughter that scrambled my eggs for brains even more. "I know exactly what you mean."

I squeezed my six-foot-four frame into my convertible BMW and reclined my bucket seat as far back as it would go. Elephants were stomping on my brain, refusing to let me drive. They let me smoke, though. I took out my pack of Marlboros and started to sing that crazy song I made up about Pearl:

"Pearrrll Day-vis. What have you been up tooo, girrrl?"

I knew I was in no condition to drive. I folded my hands behind my head and listened to the cars drive up and down Eighth Street.

Pearl Davis, pregnant! I thought. *And she was happy about it, and thinking about marriage and family!* It was too much for me to take. When I was with her, Pearl talked about kids like they were a curse rather than a blessing. She never had a strong sense of family like I had. Men were used for entertainment, to further her career or for sexual gratification. So with even the Wicked Witch of the Northeast being able to find a lifetime partner before I could, despite all of my recent successes, I felt like a caveman without a club.

•

I drove back to my new apartment complex in Takoma Park, Maryland, once my head had cleared. I would have surely gone to jail if I had gotten pulled over, because I was still very much loaded.

I had moved out of the Adams Morgan area for a change of scenery. My new place was as elegant as I was willing to pay for at the time. It was another single-bedroom with hardwood floors on the eighth level of a fourteen-story building. It was more spacious than my Adams Morgan apartment. I figured the next move I made would be into a private house.

I checked my answering machine from the night before. I had twelve new messages. A lot of them I ignored. My mother called and reminded me of the family get-together in North Carolina for Black History Month. I smiled, feeling delighted about another opportunity to see my niece and nephew. They were always a bright spot in my life.

While in the shower that morning, I began to think about the beginning of my roller-coaster ride. I thought about my good friend Faye Butler and my initial infatuation for Pearl while at Howard University. It was nearly a decade ago, but you never forget the decisions you make early on that affect your entire life. It makes it even harder to forget when you don't have anything to take the place of those old memories. I began to wish that I could go back and start all over again, with me still winding up with my show, of course.

By the time I got out of the shower, I didn't even feel like going to work. Yusef had been doing a good job on the show whenever he substituted for me, so I decided to give him another opportunity to make himself known.

"Yusef, you feel like doing the show today?" I called and asked him. I caught him right before it was time for him to head out the door. Yusef lived in Hyattsville, Maryland, just five minutes away from Takoma Park. It took him forty-five minutes to get to the station on the Metro system. Most of the time I gave him a ride.

"You're not gonna make it today?" he asked me.

"It doesn't look like it. I had a little too much to drink last night, and something that I ate didn't agree with me too well," I fibbed. I didn't want to give Yusef the impression that I was getting lazy or anything. I rarely called in sick for work because I loved my show, I just needed a longer weekend to regroup.

"All right then," Yusef said. "Did you let the station know already?"

"I'm about to do that now." I hung up with Yusef and informed someone at the station. It was no problem with management. Yusef could hold his own as long as I wasn't quitting on them.

I sat up in bed, thirty-one years old, and wearing nothing but my boxers, thinking back to the beginning of my career. Then I listened to Yusef pull off my show that morning. He had a style of his own. He wasn't quite as on edge as I was, but that kind of thing comes through life experiences. Yusef hadn't been through much yet. He was still pretty patient and happy with himself while seeing his one girl. I even got him a seven-thousand-dollar raise. I knew I wouldn't be able to keep him too much longer, though. Yusef had big dreams, he was focused, confident, and very driven—successful characteristics that had taken me *years* to develop. My strong points had been persistence, loyalty, humility, and hard work.

After my show, I turned my radio dial to Howard University's WHUR-FM and caught the beginning of an old Aretha Franklin song, "Do Right Woman, Do Right Man." WHUR's format was for the older black crowd who loved the classic stuff. They had done away with most of the lust-filled contemporary music teenagers preferred.

I listened to that Aretha Franklin song and smiled. I had been trying to be a "Do Right Man," it seemed, for years, and I just wasn't succeeding at it. I was a busy scientist mixing different chemicals in my secluded laboratory and never coming up with the right formula.

I spent my thirty-first birthday alone with my thoughts. That's when I first began to think of my radio career as a metaphor for my life, the roller-coaster ride of ups and downs, twists and turns, climbs and rapid free falls of my days, nights, and weekends. "The Bobby Dallas Whirl." And it was no sense in dragging any more sisters on that unpredictable ride with me. It would only make both of us sick.

Unbelievable!

I was climbing up another incline on my coaster. Once I got to the top, though, I planned on staying there. In 1995, my syndication rights had doubled my initial contract value. To have your salary double in one year would re-ignite anyone's fire. I was set to pull in close to two hundred fifty thousand dollars, and my next contract was going to be a whopper! I had already found myself a new agent. I wanted to land a multimillion-dollar contract like the other big names in syndicated radio: Rush Limbaugh, Don Imus, Howard Stern, Tom Joyner, etc. Just like Gene Carlton had said, as a black man, Tom Joyner had paved the way for me.

There were a lot of jealous employees at the station, but it was nothing they could do to dull my shine. I was the big man at WLRG-FM. "The Radioman" was a national hit. Frank Watts said before my introduction that every motherfucker on the radio was a "Radioman," but after 1994, I was the *official* Radioman, Bobby Dallas, in Washington D.C.! I even won five radio awards, two of which were national.

I got calls from Mona Freeman in Detroit, and my old basketball buddy Gary Mitchell in California. I had even heard from Angel Thompson and Gene. Gene called me at the station to congratulate me on my success. It was his success, too, even though he didn't like my "new ideas." Management at WLRG couldn't thank him enough for bringing me to the station. Michael Hines got a healthy bonus himself for his part in my success. He had shown a lot of faith in me.

I owed a lot of my good fortune to Brother Abu for bringing me in out of limbo and giving me that first opportunity to become a host, so I decided to take him out to dinner at B. Smith's restaurant inside Union Station to show my gratitude. I handed him a blank envelope over the table. It was the middle of March.

"What's this?" he asked me.

"It's a little something for getting me started."

He opened it up and looked inside. When he saw the fifteen-thousand-dollar check he smiled. "This is a lot more than 'a little something,' Bobby."

"That was my average salary in radio before I bumped into you," I told him. "I figured it would help you out in what you're doing."

Brother Abu nodded and said, "Thanks. It'll help out a lot.

"You've come a long way, Bobby," he told me. "And you're still doing good work for the community. Just don't let them change you when you get to that next level."

"It's my love for the community that got me here, and it's also what's gonna keep me," I responded. I had no plans on changing my winning format no matter how much my next contract would be worth.

After a waitress took our orders, I confided in Brother Abu that I hadn't been having much success in my love life. He had been happily married for years, so I figured he was a good person to talk to about it.

He grinned with his drink in hand. "Finding that perfect mate ain't as easy as it used to be, brother. It's too much confusion going on nowadays," he said. "Young people today automatically consider themselves men and women without wanting to do the things that *make* a man or a woman. Just because you have a job doesn't necessarily make you a man, and just because you can have a child doesn't automatically make you a mature woman. You have to grow into these roles like a pair of shoes."

He said, "The problem today is that everyone wants to keep buying new pairs. Every time something ain't quite right, people are jumping up and saying, 'Aw, man, I need a new pair of shoes! These shoes ain't fittin' my feet right!' But if you spent enough time in the selection process before buying, you would have *found out* which shoes are comfortable for you and which ones are not. And every shoe is not comfortable for every person."

I smiled and took a sip of my water. "You got that right," I told him.

He said, "Everybody wants a pair of shoes that ain't right for 'em. You go out and buy a pair of *turquoise* shoes because you just *had* to have 'em, right? Then you take them bad boys home and find out you don't have a damn thing in your closet to match them. But you *knew* that before you bought 'em. And you end up wearing them shoes *three times* in your life!

"We can't have lasting relationships like that, Bobby. But some of us will actually go out and buy an *entire* wardrobe to match these *turquoise* shoes when we *know* we ain't right!"

I broke out laughing.

Brother Abu continued: "Another thing is that everybody seems to be waiting for something. I mean, we have people walking around today in *no* shoes or wearing a pair of shoes that are too small for them, and then they're looking in the store window talking about, 'I'm gonna buy me a pair of them when I get ready.'

"When you get *ready* for what? Because once you *think* that you're ready, those shoes aren't there anymore, right? Now you're all upset about it," he said. "Half of these brothers and sisters are just plain scared of each other, Bobby. They're scared of having to work, scared of their emotions, scared of being hurt, and scared of making that committed bond to each other. And it's *definitely* more *boys* afraid than *girls*. Because a lot of you have *yet* to become men and women. Now which one are you?"

I grinned and thought good and hard about it. "I was scared once," I said, thinking back to Faye Butler and my senior year at Howard. "I had a good pair of shoes right in front of me, and I went for the turquoise," I admitted. "But with that being said and done, what do I do now?"

Brother Abu said, "The next time you're out with that young lady friend who fits, you take your time, get to know her—and that means the good *and* the bad, because some people try to ignore the bad, which is ridiculous—and then you *make* the commitment to this sister, realizing that you're gonna have to work at things. But don't go out there and rush into something. Take your time, because you have to feel comfortable about yourself first. So, in other words, if you don't like the size or shape of your feet, then don't go out there expecting to find a pair of shoes to cover up your shame, you have to accept *who* and *what* you are and learn to feel good about it. Only then can you find those comfortable shoes."

With all that talk about shoes, the waitress probably thought that we were shoe salesmen. When our food arrived, Brother Abu looked at me and said, "I wouldn't worry about it too much, Bobby. You're exactly what most of these sisters are looking for, a mature and good-looking man with a nice career who's serious about settling down."

"So how come they haven't found me yet?" I asked him with a smile. It wasn't as if I would have chosen to be with anyone. You don't just go out and buy a pair of shoes because they're there.

"Sometimes it takes time, that's all. Good guys may finish last, but they also finish good," Brother Abu responded.

I chuckled and said, "I hope so, because I'm wearing out my soles over here and the stitching is falling out."

Brother Abu broke out laughing. "Well, at least you still have your sense of humor."

I said, "I'm glad I do, because if I ever lost that, then I'd *really* be in trouble."

•

I took Brother Abu's advice and decided that I would take another trip out of the country to enjoy my own company. I wanted to take it at the beginning of the summer. I figured I would wear down again by then. I wanted to vacation in Italy.

A week before my scheduled vacation in June, I had lunch after work inside The Shops on F Street. I was really hungry that day. I ordered two slices of vegetarian pizza and a large Coke. I was sitting on the food court level, stuffing my face and looking around at people, when I noticed a middle-aged white man on a lunch date with a sister. She had her head turned to me, but I could tell that she was black. Sisters have obvious features that stand out, like their entertaining hairstyles and the voluptuous bodies that white women seem to lack. I doubted if it was "Jungle Fever," though. They were both dressed in business attire. I figured they worked together.

I continued people-watching as I ate. When the sister got up with the white man, I peeked in their direction again just to see what she looked like. I was stuck with a big chunk of pizza in my mouth when I noticed that it was Faye Butler.

"Oh shit!" I mumbled. It was unbelievable! One year I see Pearl Davis back in D.C., and the following year it was Faye!

I spit the pizza out into a napkin and quickly sipped on my Coke for my breath. I didn't want to say anything to Faye for the first time in years with my breath smelling like cheese and cooked vegetables.

I took my large Coke with me and went to chase them down. They were walking pretty fast. I guess they were on a tight schedule. "Faye Butler!" I yelled as they reached the escalators. I didn't care about the white guy, nor about drawing so much attention to myself. I was just happy to see her.

Faye was stepping onto the escalator when she spotted me. "Bobby!" she said. She seemed happy to see me, too. She had a busload of people behind her, though, so she was stuck on the way down.

"I'm coming right behind you," I told her.

I met them on the ground level and Faye introduced me to her friend.

"Bobby, this is William Reader at Channel Seven News. And Bill, this is Bobby Dallas. We went to school at Howard together."

We shook hands. Mr. Reader said, "Bobby Dallas. That name sounds very familiar. Do you have a radio program?"

Mr. Reader knew his stuff. I said, "Yeah, I have a syndicated show on WLRG-FM."

"Oh, yeah, you're 'The Radioman'!" he said excitedly.

I was impressed. "You guys listen to my show over at Channel Seven?" I asked him.

He grinned and said, "Hey, we're always looking to steal new ideas. That's the business that we're in. A lot of people *love* your show."

He was embarrassing me and stroking my ego at the same time. I wouldn't have to tell Faye about the show after his excitement, she would automatically ask me.

She pulled out a business card and said, "Bobby, I'm in a rush right now. I have a plane to catch in a few hours, but call me up in Atlanta." She reminded me of a too-busy-to-talk white woman. Most sisters, no matter how busy they were, could usually *find* time to chat.

"Love your show, man," Mr. Reader told me as they disappeared out the door.

I had mixed emotions about it. I wondered if Faye had given me a polite brush-off. She didn't even write down her home number on the back of her business card. I was in turmoil for the rest of that day. I called her job at a television station in Atlanta and left her a message to call me. Despite Brother Abu's good advice, my insecurity was starting all over again. I ran around for the next few days like a chicken with his head chopped off, waiting on Faye to call me back.

Faye finally made the call the Thursday before my vacation in Italy. "Bobby, I'm sorry it took me a few days to get back to you, but I've been really busy interviewing this week," she told me.

"That's why you were in Washington?" I asked her.

"Yup."

"Where else have you interviewed?"

"Dallas and Miami."

"Which one are you most excited about?" I asked her. I was hoping she'd say Washington.

"Dallas," she answered. "I really liked the people and the atmosphere there."

"What about Channel Seven?"

"Well, they invited me up, but I think they were just going through the motions. They were really eyeing this sister from New York."

When she said "sister from New York," a chill shot up my spine as I remembered once again the stupid decision I had made years ago to leave Faye and venture to New York with Pearl. "So, how's life been treating you?" I decided to ask.

"Fine, but I'm just ready to move on. I've been in Atlanta since the beginning of my career."

"You don't want to stay there at least for the Olympics next year?" I asked her. I was sure that the news people in Atlanta would have a field day covering the 1996 Summer Games.

Faye said, "Bobby, wherever I decide to go, they're gonna know how long I've been in this market, so they may send me back to Atlanta to cover the Olympics anyway. And that would be just fine with me.

"But what about you, Mr. Big-time Radioman?" she asked me. "I asked William Reader about your show, and I searched the radio for it down here the next day.

"Congratulations, Bobby! I'm proud of you! People know your voice all over the country now!"

Faye sounded totally professional. The conversation was going the wrong way for me. I wanted to ask her if she was married, who she was seeing, when was her next vacation, and things of a more social nature.

"Yeah, I worked hard enough for it," I said. I wondered how I could redirect things into a less career-oriented phone call. "I'm going on vacation next week. I'm flying to Italy," I told her.

"Oh, Italy," she responded. "I wish it was me. I don't have another vacation until the end of the year."

"Where are you planning on going, the Islands or somewhere?" I asked her. I wouldn't have minded going to the Islands with her myself.

"No, I'll probably fly west, out to California or something. I hear San Francisco's a nice place to visit," she said.

I couldn't take it anymore. I had to know some things about her personal life. I said, "You know, I'm thirty-one years old now, and I still haven't been married."

"Well, it takes some people time before they find their soul mates," she responded.

"What if they let their soul mates get away from them?"

"Mmm," Faye grunted. "That sounds like a good show to do."

"Good idea," I said.

"Yeah, let me produce it," she suggested.

"On camera?"

"Are you afraid of the camera?"

"I don't think so. How hard could it be?"

We laughed. Faye and I used to be such a great call-and-response team. I really missed that. "You know, I miss having a comfort level with a woman where you could just say anything and be yourself."

"And have bad breath and they can tell you about it without feeling embarrassed?"

"Yeah, and even take a dump with the bathroom door open."

"Ah, I don't know about all of that," Faye said.

We laughed again. I was having such a good time with the conversation that it was beginning to get a little scary. What if I could do no more than talk? What if she already had a family of her own, and was a sold pair of shoes?

"Yup, I never married, and I don't have any kids," I said.

"Is there something you would like to know, Bobby?" Faye asked me with a chuckle. It didn't take her long to catch on to my game. I was listening extra hard to see if I could hear a baby crying in the background or something. After the event with Pearl, I figured anything was possible. I thought of Faye as my last hope. She should have been my first choice, but I couldn't change the past, I could only hope to prepare for a better future.

I stalled and asked, "Remember we talked a couple nights before your graduation?"

"Yeah, I remember."

"Why were you so uptight then? I couldn't understand that."

Faye paused for a second again. "The guy that I was dating got locked up for selling drugs like two days before that."

"You're kidding me!"

"No I'm not. I was very upset about that. You know how I felt about drug dealers."

Faye wanted to give drug dealers a dose of their own medicine as a punishment. She wrote a commentary that was published in Howard University's *The Hilltop* newspaper. She got a heavy response from that article.

"He hid it from me very well," she continued. "I had no idea. I felt like a real fool, especially after that article I wrote."

"Yeah, I could imagine," I said.

"So, you know, my head wasn't on straight at all," she told me. "That damn boy even had the nerve to try and call me collect from jail and explain shit to me!"

"He said that he would stop it, and go out and get a real job?"

"Of course he did. And I didn't want to hear that. That's why I was screening my calls."

"I'm sorry to hear that, Faye," I told her. "I went through some trying times myself over the years, that's why I'm still not tied down yet."

"Is that what you call it, 'tied down'?"

"What do you call it, 'in love forever with your soul mate'?" I joked.

"That's the way it *should* be. But that's why so many people are unhappy, because they don't have their soul mates."

I chuckled. "You know, you're starting to sound like you went to a seminar on the subject."

"Maybe I have," Faye responded.

"So, what's your status right now?" I finally asked her.

"My status?" she repeated. She was going to make me sweat for it.

"Faye, you know what I'm getting at."

"Why not come right out and say it then? Isn't that what you do on your radio program? No holds barred, right?"

She had a point. "Okay, who are you seeing now? Are you married? Did you have any biscuits? What's your status?"

Faye chuckled. "No, I don't have any *biscuits*. I was married for two years. It was a mistake, though. It was with a man who didn't take my career as seriously as I did. He wanted to have kids right in the middle of things."

I thought about my sister-in-law, Brenda. She didn't let a career stop her from having kids. "Is there ever a right time for a woman to have kids, especially a career woman?" I asked Faye.

"Yeah, once you've established yourself," she answered. "And I really wasn't ready to have kids then. My husband had a fit about it, too. I knew we wouldn't be married long after he blew up on me. We couldn't even look each other in the face anymore. I figured we'd go ahead and get divorced before it got worse, because I wasn't giving up my career. I worked *too* hard for it."

My coproducer, Yusef Green, was right on the money with Faye. Marrying young was getting a lot more complicated with a two-career household.

"Did you discuss it before you got married?" I asked her.

"Well, we did, but I wasn't thinking about kids any time soon. I was thinking further down the line, like in five or six years, but I guess he was thinking a lot sooner than that. I mean, he was already picking out names and stuff. I thought he was crazy."

"When were you married?"

"It's been three years now since the divorce."

I started counting. If I was thirty-one, that made Faye twenty-nine. Twenty-nine minus three was twenty-six, minus two was twenty-four. "You got married almost right out of school then," I said.

"I thought I needed someone to anchor me. I didn't want to be floating around in the dating scene. I mean, you *do* realize that I didn't have much experience with serious relationships. My husband was only the third man I had ever been with."

I didn't care to hear that information. I could have been Faye's one and only man for life. I felt that I had done her wrong. "I'm sorry about that, Faye," I told her.

"Sorry for what?"

"You know, for not being there for you. You did reach out to me in that way, and I failed to answer your call."

Faye paused. "I thought about us a few times." She laughed and added, "A lot, actually. But I figured the time had passed us by."

"Why, because you thought I would be married with kids and living in the suburbs by now?" I asked her.

"Well, yeah. You were always the mature type, Bobby."

I chuckled and thought about the shock I went through during my brother's marriage. "You know my little brother got married before me," I told her.

"Get out of here! Brad got married?" Faye screamed. Brad didn't know that much about her, but I had told Faye enough about him. They met once during Howard's homecoming. Brad was running around like a sailor on an island full of virgins. He didn't even remember Faye.

"It shocked me, too," I told her. "My niece, Aminah, is turning six, and my nephew, Anthony, is two."

"He did it right out of school, too, then."

"Yeah, and they have a wonderful marriage," I said. "I get jealous every time I see them. They have a beautiful house in Charlotte, and they're both career people with master's degrees. They're living quite comfortably."

"I guess marriage still works for *some* people," Faye responded. "It is pitiful, isn't it? You feel that you need to be with someone to fulfill your life? The reality, though, is that it's not going to happen for everyone."

It was an open invitation for me. My gut feeling told me to go for it and dive all the way into love. "It'll happen for you," I told her.

"What makes you so sure?"

"Because Bobby's back."

Faye broke out laughing.

"I'm serious," I said. "I mean, sure, you don't want to feel that you *need* anyone, but isn't it beautiful when you have them anyway?"

"Oh, yeah, you know that."

I thought of my short stint with Kathy Teals as my cohost. I said, "I hosted a radio show in D.C. with this woman once who said that she didn't *need* a man, but that she may *want* one. Her name is Kathy Teals, and she wrote a few romance novels. Have you ever heard of her?"

"Ah, no, I can't say that I have," Faye answered.

"Well, anyway, in the middle of one of our shows—in fact, it was on Thanksgiving Day—right there on the air she tells this guy who asked her to marry him that she would do it. It shocked the hell out of me, because she was one of those superindependent sisters."

"So, what are you getting at, Bobby?" Faye asked me. I guess she was growing weary of all the beating around the bush that I was doing.

"If Kathy Teals can get married again, then I know you can," I told her. "Kathy's well into her thirties. You're not turning thirty until next year. So, who are you dating now?" I asked again.

"Bobby, every brother who's interested in me knows that I'm getting out of here soon, so what would be the point?"

"Maybe they might go with you," I told her.

"I don't think so," Faye responded. "Women up and leave everything for the man, but men rarely leave everything for the woman." Faye got a call on her other line and told me to hold on. When she came back on the line, she had to go. "Bobby, I have some running to do, but you have a good time in Italy and call me when you get back, okay? Who are you going with?" she asked me all of a sudden.

"I'm going by myself."

"Yeah, right. You don't have to tell me if you don't want to, Bobby. But don't lie about it."

"I'm serious," I told her. "I went to Vegas by myself."

Faye chuckled and said, "I can see going to Vegas by yourself."

"I went to Brazil by myself last year," I said.

"You've been to Brazil?"

"Yup."

"Was it nice?"

"Yeah, but I was too busy thinking about other things in my life to really enjoy it."

"And you went by yourself?"

"Faye, I don't have anyone to plan a vacation with, unless me and you go somewhere later on this year," I suggested. My heart was pounding like I stole something. *Please don't reject me again,* I thought to myself. I was trying to come on to Faye as smoothly as I could.

"Yeah, we never did get a chance to go on vacation together at Howard," she responded to me.

I was trying my hardest to forget that Virginia Beach thing, but Faye obviously hadn't.

"Well, it's up to you," I said. "I could take another vacation after Thanksgiving. I'll even pay for both of us."

Faye was hesitant. I didn't want to come off too desperate, but I *was* desperate. I felt like Denzel Washington's trumpet player at the end of Spike Lee's film *Mo' Better Blues*. I needed Faye to save my life.

"I'll have to see, Bobby," she told me. "But I really have to go now, okay?"

"All right, I'll call you when I get back," I said. "And Faye?"

"Yeah."

"Thanks for talking to me again. You just don't know how much it means to me."

Faye was smiling when she paused that time. I could feel it, and I could hear it in her vibrant voice when she said, " 'Bye, Bobby."

" 'Bye," I told her. I hung up the phone with a smile bigger than a kid's on his birthday. Having Faye Butler back was better than receiving any dirt bike. It was just unbelievable!

•

I enjoyed myself in Italy a lot more than I had in Brazil, not because Italy was a more lively place or anything, I just had a more positive outlook on my life. I noticed the Italian women eyeing me more than the Brazilians had, though. It made sense, too, because there weren't that many black faces in Italy. A tall, American black man with money could easily be considered a sex symbol there, especially if he happened to be athletic, which I was not.

Anyway, I visited Milan just to see what the fashion capital of the world looked like and ended up buying four suits, two pairs of shoes, socks, ties, and a brown leather briefcase. I went out on a limb and bought Faye a pair of leather boots and a briefcase, too. Those Italian women were really eyeing me with all of those bags in my hands. I was talked into taking a few friendly pictures with some of them.

I stayed in Milan, Florence, and Rome and skipped over to Sicily to see what that historical place looked like. It was the land of the *extra* brown Italians. I visited Venice too, but I didn't like that place much. It was like living in a maze. The buildings were all bunched together and there was water everywhere. I wasn't used to that. I liked it in Florence, though. Florence was very lively with vendors, open-window shops, and plenty of pedestrian traffic. I spent a lot of my time there sitting back on my hotel balcony with my feet up, enjoying the view, as if I was a member of La Cosa Nostra.

I had big plans for when I got back to the U.S. Instead of producing one show on soul mates, I wanted to have a "Soul Mates Week." Faye Butler was the girl for me all the time and I wasn't going to let her get away from me again. I re-evaluated the thought of my radio career as a metaphor for my life, and just like in radio, I had to be willing to do all I could to make a new relationship work with Faye. The second time around, I knew that I couldn't hold anything back.

Putting yourself on the line over and over again was something women had been doing for years, but men, on the other hand, were very reluctant to follow down that same hurtful road. Brother Abu was absolutely right about the fear that many brothers had. We feared having to humble ourselves for love. That was the predicament we were in, surrendering our nomadic pride, what we considered to be our social freedom, our rightful independence, our manhood.

We had gotten spoiled, out on the hunt, recklessly chasing bigger prey, greener grass, and cooler water. However, like the other males of the animal kingdom, we seldom achieved our lofty territorial goals and ended up talking loud and saying nothing. But I was *more* than ready to throw down my spear, chill out, plant my seeds, and share berries from the tree of life with a woman. I had had enough of aimless freedom and wandering. I wanted to be connected to someone. I wanted to be connected to my soul mate. Faye Butler.

Soul Mates

It was mid-July, and I had been talking to Faye at least three times a week since getting back from Italy. More than a few of the phone calls turned into all-nighters, so I knew that we were back to where we were as friends years ago. I also knew that my phone bill was going to be extra high for that month.

I planned to visit Faye in Atlanta the weekend after airing "Soul Mates Week." I told her she didn't have to listen if she was busy. I wanted to tape all of the shows for her. In fact, I thought it would have been better if she didn't listen that week so we could have a fresh discussion on soul mates ourselves, before I filled her in on what everyone else had to say about it. Faye said it wouldn't be fair because I would already know everything. Then I challenged her to produce a television commentary on the subject and see what she could come up with on her end.

"That still wouldn't be fair," Faye argued.

"Why wouldn't it be?" I asked. I knew why, though.

Faye said, "Bobby, you have an entire 'Soul Mates Week.' The most that I would be able to do is two days. And you have two hours a show, compared to my what—two, three minutes?"

"You need to produce a whole hour program then," I suggested.

"I've already been there and done that at a smaller station, and I wasn't making the kind of money I wanted to make. That's why I'm trying to move up in the market now."

"Well, that's on you," I told her. "I have nothing to do with that. I've already done my moving up in the market."

Faye sighed and said, "Fine, Bobby, rub it in."

I laughed and said, "Don't worry about it, it'll happen for you. Like you told me years ago, women have more patience than men."

"Yeah, and it's a good thing that we do," she snapped. "Because if we didn't, there would be hell to pay all over this country."

"Or, then again, a lot more women would be unemployed," I joked.

Faye grumbled, "Mmm, just like a man; if you can't beat them, fire them."

I laughed again, but I felt a lot more uneasy about that comment. I thought that I had been more of a friend to women and not the macho man type. "Hey, Faye, do you think I've changed any?"

"Yeah, Bobby, I told you that already. I have to tell you things two and three times now."

"Why do you think that's happening?" I asked her.

"Because you have a lot more responsibilities on your mind."

"Is that why most men don't remember things?"

"No, they remember what they *want* to remember," she said. "Most men can tell you how many points Michael Jordan averages a game in basketball, or how many touchdown passes Steve Young threw last year, but then they can't remember that their wives told them to take out the trash just three minutes ago."

I could tell that Faye had been paying a lot of attention to her news broadcasts, including sports. I chuckled. "I guess I should do a whole week on that, too," I responded. "I'd call it 'The Mind of a Man Week.'"

"Yeah, you should. I think it would make some good shows. I mean, look at all the interest that this Million Man March thing is getting," she told me. "It's all about the black man, but unless you're a criminal or an athlete, nobody knows you. There should be a book or a movie or something on brothers like you."

"You really think my life is that important?" I asked her.

"Yeah! Hell yeah, Bobby!" Faye answered enthusiastically. "I mean, you have a syndicated radio show as a black man, without playing R&B music or even talking about sports every day. I don't think you even realize how big of a deal that is."

"Yeah, because I've paid so much to get here."

"That's exactly what I'm talking about. People need to know about it."

"All right then, I'll put that on my list of shows to do," I said, getting ready to hang up. We had been on the phone for two hours already. "I'll call you up next week before Friday."

"Okay."

"And remember, you can't listen to the show."

"Yeah, well, I'll have to see about that, Bobby. In the meantime, you think about what I told you. You are definitely somebody."

I hung up the phone and smiled. *Now* that's *a soul mate,* I told myself. Then I called Faye right back.

"Hello," she answered.

"It's Bobby," I said. "I'm just calling back to say 'Thank you.' "

" 'Thank you' for what?"

"For making me feel so special."

Faye sighed and said, "You are still so modest about everything. I can't believe you. I mean, Bobby, how many black men do you think get a chance to vacation in Italy and Brazil? You *are* special."

I was grinning from ear to ear. "Yeah, I guess you're right. And you know what?"

"What?"

"You're somebody, too, and you're *very* special to me."

I could feel Faye's warm smile through the phone again. "I'll see you when you get here, Bobby," she told me.

"Yeah, I'll see you, too."

We shared a giggle like two high schoolers in love, and hung up. I felt so tingly inside that I was compelled to smoke a cigarette to calm down. Then I stared at my pack of Marlboros and mumbled, "Damn, I gotta stop smoking these things."

•

I started that Monday morning's show by reading the dictionary meanings for the words *soul* and *mate* to my listeners:

"In other words, a *soul mate* would be that perfect and equal match between a man and a woman where their spirits, emotions, and morale are either similar or complementary, forming a blissful and fulfilling bond between the two life energies," I concluded, with a little ad-libbing. "Wow, that sounds powerful, people! No wonder everyone is looking for this soul mate, including me, 'The Radioman,' because I want you all to continue being my soul-mate listeners," I said.

I had asked my listeners to write in their opinions on the subject a week in advance so I could begin the show by reading and discussing letters like an on-air Ann Landers or Dear Abby column. I then had my coproducer, Tamika Hill, book Kathy Teals for that Wednesday's "Trouble in the Kitchen."

I went on to read letter after letter, from southern California to Boston. The common denominator in most of the happy couples seemed to be good conversation, similar interests in life, and a general respect for each other. Our call-ins on Tuesday confirmed the same, and on Wednesday I introduced the listeners to my past cohost, Kathy Teals.

Kathy and I were back on good speaking terms, and I knew that "Soul Mates Week" would be right up her alley. She and her husband, Harold, were expecting a child before Christmas. I told her I was happy for her. Pearl had delivered her child in New York somewhere by then. I never did call her back to find out what she had. I was too busy feeling lonesome at that time.

Anyway, Kathy was much more technical and less emotional than what she used to be, which was excellent. She talked about the importance of making preparations for togetherness, shared family values, the organization of household economics, knowing your strengths and weaknesses, not being afraid to seek counseling, and last but not least, unity, commitment, and purpose with your partner under God, which she emphasized.

I was impressed! Kathy blew the show away that day! Then she swiftly announced that she would begin writing a nonfiction book on the subject, hopefully to be published sometime in 1996. She just couldn't help herself, I guess. I didn't mind, though. Everyone had to make a living somehow. And since Kathy had been so thorough with her information, I promised to have her back on when the book came out. I was certain that she would get her work published. Kathy was like Mona, she didn't believe in failure.

On Thursday, I called up "The Barbershop," and Mr. Joe told me I was blowing the whole soul-mate thing out of proportion.

"I think people are putting more into this soul-mate stuff and less into plain responsibilities," he said. "It's plenty of good women out here, and plenty of good men, but all I hear is young people walking around talking about, 'Oh, I ain't found the right one yet,' and in the meantime, they got three babies by three different people."

I could hear the other guys wailing with laughter in the background as usual.

"When I was coming up, Bobby, if you spilled some milk while messing around on the farm, then you bought the cow," Mr. Joe continued. "Nobody was running around talking about no soul mates, it was just plain responsibility."

Mr. Joe went on to tell me that he had been married to his wife for thirty-two years, and had five kids. He said she had lived right around the corner from him in the Cardoza section of D.C.

"I was walking to the corner store one day—when black people owned it—to buy a half gallon of milk for my mother. On the way back I saw this beautiful girl just sitting out on her steps. Well, I went up there and asked her her name and stuff and started talking to her until her father called her in. And I did that for a whole *year* until he finally let me in the house. Then it took almost *another* year before the man let me take his daughter out to a movie."

I started to giggle and couldn't stop myself. Things always got hilarious when I called The Barbershop.

"Well, maybe she was your soul mate," I said.

"Bobby, my wife was a beautiful woman who I wanted to be with, and I did everything I had to do to stay with her and make her my wife. Now what does this soul-mate thing have to do with that?"

"Well, you two obviously liked each other," I said.

"You never liked a woman before, Bobby, and she liked you?"

"Yeah, sure."

"And what happened?"

I chuckled to myself, already knowing that he had set me up. "Ah, I went north and she went south," I said.

"Exactly," Mr. Joe responded. "You quit on each other."

"What about your kids? Are they married?" I asked him.

"Some are, some are not. They all have kids, though, and you know what they tell me, Bobby?"

"What's that?"

" 'Dad, you just don't understand. Times have changed. It's a lot harder to stay together nowadays.' And you know why it's a lot harder to stay together now, Bobby?"

"No, why is that?" I asked him.

"Because people have turned into quitters. That's why everybody's talking about some *soul mate*. It's easy for you to quit and say it's because you were supposed to be doing something else. I was *really* supposed to be a doctor, Bobby, but since I own a barbershop, then I'm gonna be the best *barber* that I can be. That's how people *need* to think. But everybody's making excuses now and blaming one another. Why? Because so-and-so ain't my soul mate."

"You don't think that having a soul mate is a beautiful thing?" I asked him.

"Bobby, having a wife and a family is a beautiful thing. And black people had soul ever since we got off the boat, we just gotta find it with each other again."

When Friday finally came, I was ready to just fly to Atlanta and be with Faye for the weekend. My flight was boarding at 1:35, so I took a cab to work and had my bags with me.

At the station that morning, Yusef smiled and said, "You going somewhere, Bobby?"

I had to carry a few extra bags for the leather boots and the briefcase that I bought for Faye in Italy. I hadn't told her that I bought something for her. I wanted it to be surprise. I grinned and said, "Yusef, despite what Mr. Joe said yesterday, *I* believe in soul mates and I'm going to be with mine right after I leave from work today."

Yusef laughed. "Is that why you wanted a whole 'Soul Mates Week'?"

I looked at him and answered, "You damn right! I deserve a soul mate. And when you get your own show one day, then you can have any *week* that you want."

•

Faye took a half day off from work so she could pick me up from Atlanta's Hartsfield International Airport. I would have been satisfied with getting a hotel room to stay in, but she insisted that I stay with her at her northside apartment.

I was filled with anticipation until we got ready to land. Then I got unbelievably nervous. *What if everything doesn't go right? What if this turns out to be a better phone relationship than it is face-to-face? What if I put too much into this and end up being disappointed again?* I was asking myself a lot of paranoid questions, and since I flew first-class, I didn't have time to calm my nerves before getting off the plane.

I walked slowly through the flight bridge, trying to convince myself that everything was going to be just fine. When I stepped out, Faye was sitting in a chair to the left with her legs crossed, wearing a navy blue skirt suit and a mustard silk blouse. She was browner and more gorgeous than I ever remembered her being at Howard. She looked even better than when I saw her in D.C. in June. I was glad to be the guy she was waiting on!

We didn't even speak to each other at first. Faye stood up, and I walked over, dropped my bags, and held her like a real old friend. Then we couldn't seem to let go of each other. Faye began to gently rub the nape of my neck right there inside the airport, and I returned the favor by stroking her back. We must have stood there like that for two whole minutes, 120 seconds of public affection, which is a long time. It reminded me of the lovers in Brazil.

"I brought something for you," I told her once we disengaged.

"You mean other than yourself?" she asked me with a grin.

I smiled and handed her the bags from Italy. Faye sat back down and looked inside them. I sat down beside her, knowing that she would love her gifts.

"Oh my God, you bought me boots from Italy!" she said. "And look at this beautiful briefcase!" Faye wanted to stand up and hug me again. I was embarrassed. "You don't have to shower me with gifts, Bobby," she whispered to me.

I leaned back from her so that I could look her in the eyes. "I just wanted to bring back a few things for you, that's all."

"Well, thank you," she told me. "Thank you *very* much."

The Atlanta airport was huge, and designed like a sample of the future with a lower-level monorail service to take you to the different terminals and to the parking area.

"This new airport is nice, isn't it?" Faye asked me while we rode the monorail.

"Yeah, and big, too," I answered her.

We walked out to Faye's car in the parking lot, a white '91 BMW.

"I see you were able to afford style long before I could," I told her with a grin.

Faye opened her trunk and said, "You have to do a lot of driving in Atlanta, so the less problems you have with your car, the better." She smiled at me and added, "I heard a long time ago that BMWs were one of the most reliable cars to buy."

I climbed inside of her Beemer and joked, "So are Hondas and Toyotas."

Faye looked at me and said, "Bobby, after my divorce, I needed something to pick me up, and Hondas and Toyotas wouldn't have done it. Besides, I got this car in a great deal. It was used, with only twelve thousand miles on it."

I nodded. "Yeah, that *was* a great deal," I told her. "I wonder who that person was."

"The dealership owner's wife," Faye answered. "She decided that she *had* to have a darker color, so I said, 'Fine, I'll take this one off your hands for a few thousand less.' "

I shook my head and grinned. "Lifestyles of the rich and famous," I said.

Faye smirked. "Well, as long as they helped me out."

When we arrived at her building, she pulled out a security card and entered a code to drive through an outside gate. This place was as fancy as you could get, with extra-large balconies.

After Faye had parked the car inside a basement garage, I walked into the elevator with her and immediately began to wonder how much money she made on her job and if she had won some kind of expensive divorce settlement despite having no children.

"Faye, you're living a little high on the hog here," I said to her as I walked into her luxurious, fully carpeted two-bedroom apartment. She was using her second bedroom as a computer station. I was amazed like a kid at the circus. You would have thought that Faye was making much more money than what I was making.

"This was all after the divorce," she told me. She began to strip out of her clothes and said, "I'll tell you about it later. Did you bring any jeans, Bobby, you know, just casual stuff?" she asked me.

I smirked and said, "I thought I *was* dressed casually." I had on my usual uniform of a sports jacket, shirt, slacks, and a nice pair of shoes. I had taken my tie off during the plane ride.

"Well, do you have any kick-around clothes then, Bobby? I mean, I just want to go out tonight and act like we're both young again."

"We are young," I told her.

"Well, younger then," she huffed at me with a smile. Then she said, "Actually, you're over thirty, Bobby. I wouldn't call that 'young.' "

I didn't have a comeback for that, plus I was preoccupied with trying to look away from Faye as she revealed more of her flesh than I thought she would before leaving the room. She was treating me like a girlfriend. Or a husband. I was beginning to get comfortable with the husband idea.

Since I didn't bring any jeans with me, the first thing Faye did was take me out to a mall to buy me a pair. I don't know why I didn't think to bring any. I guess I had in mind that Faye and I would do more grown-up things that required the proper attire. I did bring a pair of comfortable dockside shoes, though.

"So, where are we going, looking all young and casual?" I joked with her. We were both in jeans and designer T-shirts like two incognito celebrities.

"Well, first things first. I'm hungry," Faye answered me.

I nodded and said, "Okay, I can agree with that. Let's get some chow."

We stopped inside Ruby Tuesday's and got ourselves a booth. After giving the waitress our sandwich, drink, and side orders, Faye sipped her water and said, "Bobby, my life has been through *so* many changes."

"You're not saying anything that I haven't been through," I told her.

"Have you ever been married?" she asked me.

"Ah, now you *are* saying something I haven't been through," I answered with a laugh.

"In my divorce settlement, my ex-husband decided to give me a load of money over a two-year period, since I was *so much* into my career," Faye said, mocking him. "He said that since money was more important to me than family, he would let me have what I wanted and he would get what he wanted. So, he goes out and finds himself a new woman to start his family with, and I end up with all this extra money and no man, right? So, I started helping my sisters and my family out with things.

"The next thing I know, I get used to having money, and the two years are over with. Then my only uncle dies, and he didn't have any children, so in his life insurance policy he had a couple hundred thousand dollars for me and my two sisters."

That didn't sound like problems to me. It sounded more like Faye had hit the lottery a couple of times. "What did you say your ex-husband did again?" I asked her. She had never told me.

"He's an investment broker," she said. Then she explained, "Bobby, I didn't start off wanting to live like this. I went to school for four years because I wanted to be able to use what I learned to make a living. But my ex-husband, he didn't care if I worked or not. He just wanted some kids and for me to be a mother."

"You two didn't discuss that before you got married?" We still hadn't covered the topic completely. Faye had given me a few pages but never the entire story.

"That's the craziest thing about it, Bobby. When I first married him, he didn't make the kind of money that he makes now, so it was okay for me to work. But once he got this gigantic raise and started pulling in more expensive clients, all of a sudden it was, 'Let's have a family and you don't have to work anymore.' "

"So you're saying that he changed?"

"He changed big-time. And now *I've* changed. That's why I'm trying to get out of here and start over modestly."

"But you're not looking for a modest salary," I reminded her.

"Oh, I paid my *dues* for my salary increases just like you. I've been working *hard*, Bobby," she argued. "I like what I do in television and I *want* to work, but I also expect to be paid what I'm worth. I mean, Bobby, this is the *nineties*, not the *fifties*, and I'm not a minimum-wage woman."

Faye was dropping some heavy dosages of finances on me. I wasn't sure if I could afford her anymore. *Maybe Faye isn't my soul mate after all*, I thought. I was panicking. *What if I lost my job again? Would she kick me to the curb? Would I lose my mind and end up a street person? Would I start to rob banks to support her high expenses?*

We received our food, and Faye tore into it like I remember Kathy Teals doing the first time we ate together in Adams Morgan. That scared me, too. What if Faye had turned into a tigress like so many other successful sisters?

I smiled nervously and asked, "Did you listen to the show at all this week?"

"No, you told me not to listen. I was really busy this week. I wanted to get most of my work done before today," she said.

I wondered what Faye thought about the sharing of household responsibilities and finances that Kathy had discussed on the show. I started to wish that Faye *had* listened.

"I mean, you did tape them for me, right?" she asked me.

"Yeah, I taped them."

She smiled and asked, "What did you find out?"

"I found out that most soul mates either meet or miss each other early on in life," I told her. Of course, I had found out a lot more than that, but that was one of the key points I wanted to make with Faye.

Faye nodded her head and rushed to finish chewing a bite of her sandwich. "If Magic Johnson would have married his wife, Cookie, a long time ago, he probably would have never gotten HIV."

I was stunned by it, but she had a point. Basketball star Magic Johnson and his lovely wife had known each other a long time before finally tying the knot. Just like we had.

"Have you been tested?" I asked Faye. The question just slid right out of my mouth.

"Yes," she said without flinching. "Have you?"

I nodded while chewing my food. I sipped my water and said, "I had to take a test for my health and life insurance policies."

"Same here," she told me with a smile.

"Are we both negative?" I joked, nervously again.

"I am. Are you?" Faye asked me.

I nodded to her, chewing another bite of my sandwich. "What do you think about kids now?" I asked, changing the subject. "We're not getting any younger," I said to her. I definitely wanted children. I wanted to make no mistakes about it.

"Well, once I get this next position in Dallas, Miami, or D.C., then I'm basically set for a while. But when my ex-husband wanted to have children, I was just getting my foot in the door. I mean, don't get me wrong, Bobby, I want to have kids, but it has to be at the right period in my life and with the right daddy," she said with a wink and a smile.

I grinned and asked, "What was all of that extra stuff for?"

"What extra stuff?" she joked with me.

Faye was giving me a hard-on, and it was still early in the day. We went to a movie after that for old times' sake. Faye propped her legs up on mine until my legs fell asleep from the weight.

"You know what that means?" she asked me.

"What?"

"That means you haven't been getting enough exercise."

"You're right about that," I told her.

For exercise that night, Faye drove us to Peachtree Street, downtown, and parked several blocks away from the traffic, so we could walk and enjoy the sights and sounds of Atlanta.

"Is it like this every weekend?" I asked her. Cars were backed up on Peachtree Street for six or seven blocks.

"Friday and Saturday nights," she answered me.

After a while, with all of the young guys eyeing us from their cars and whatnot, Faye decided to hold my hand. "Remember you used to just let anyone talk to me because I was your friend?" she asked me with a smirk. She was rubbing the palm of my hand with her fingers. "I used to hate that," she said.

"How come you never told me then?"

She looked at me and said, "I never told you a lot of things. Like your senior year, when you decided not to go to Virginia Beach, I wanted to lose my virginity to you. I thought that it would have been romantic to do it away from school and everything."

I took a deep breath and swallowed hard. Faye wouldn't let me loosen up, though. She squeezed my hand tighter, holding me hostage. Obviously, she wasn't going to let me get away again either.

"Do you think that we're soul mates?" I suddenly asked her. We were walking in the middle of the sidewalk with at least fifty other people, not to mention all the Atlantans who were in their cars, blasting their style of homegrown bass music.

"We've always been that to each other, Bobby. You were just looking past me all the time," Faye answered me. "And I don't know why. I've never been ugly or anything. I guess it was because I was younger than you. But most women are younger than their guys. My ex-husband was *six* years older than me. You're only *two* years older. I mean, I just didn't get it."

"It was because we were friends. I didn't want to take advantage of you," I responded.

Faye stopped us right there in the middle of the sidewalk, and I swear, it was like no one else existed to us. "Bobby, you wouldn't have taken advantage of me if I was your friend. It would have been consensual. I trusted you more than I trusted any other guy in my life."

"How come you were so cold to me when I came back to you then?" I wanted to know.

"Because you made that a rebound thing after whatever you had with Pearl. And I *hated* her ass!" she ranted. "I mean, every time I thought of that picture of her in your room, I wanted to just *break* something!"

"So how come you didn't break the picture when you had it in your hands?" I asked her. It was an unfair question. I didn't break anything of Pearl's when she left me stranded up in New York. Faye and I were so much alike. If *she* wasn't my soul mate, then nobody was.

Faye finally yanked her hand away from me. "Because I was in fuckin' shock, Bobby!" she yelled at me. "I couldn't believe that you had done that shit to me! With *Pearl Davis* of all people! And your ass was talking all that innocent shit like you didn't *need* sex from anybody, right! You fuckin' lied to me, Bobby!"

Faye was pissed! She was finally letting it all out on me in the middle of the crowded sidewalk. She shook her head and walked away from me, heading for a side street. All of a sudden, I noticed every couple and every carload of people on Peachtree Street, staring at me. It was as if I had parachuted on the field in the middle of a football game.

"I don't know what you said wrong, player, but you better chase after that ho before I jump out and get her! That ho was *tight!*" someone shouted from a car. I turned around and noticed a young teen hanging out of the passenger side of a burgundy Cadillac with gold rims. He looked barely eighteen.

I snapped and said, "Hey, man, what the hell is wrong with you? You don't know how to refer to a woman? She's nobody's fuckin' ho! You learn some goddamn respect before you open your mouth to somebody!" I yelled at him.

That young punk looked like a deer caught in the headlights. I guess no one had ever bothered to tell him a thing or two before. I heard a few people clapping and cheering me on in the background, but I didn't have time for that. I went after Faye.

"Faye!" I yelled down the side street. Faye kept on walking. Instead of screaming down the street and causing more unnecessary attention, I jogged down after her. When I caught up to her, she was wiping tears from her face. I couldn't believe it! She made *me* feel like crying. I just grabbed her into my arms. She tried to fight it, but I wouldn't let her go.

A black police officer gave me a look of concern from his cruiser.

"She's all right," I told him.

Faye lifted her head and nodded to him with a sniffle.

The brother drove off and went on about his business.

I held Faye's face up to mine and said, "Look, Faye, I'm sorry about that whole thing ever even happening between us. It was a big mistake that I made, and we both ended up suffering for it. But I came down here to see you this weekend so that we could start all over again."

I said, "Faye, you were the only woman I ever said the words *I love you* to, and I meant it," I told her. "I know that I sounded a little desperate the night I said it, but I still meant it."

Faye shook her head and smiled at me, still trying to wipe away her eruption of emotions. She said, "I wouldn't let myself call you back that night. I felt . . . disrespected, Bobby."

"I'm sorry," I told her again. It occurred to me at that moment that I had never even kissed Faye before.

Instead of kissing me, Faye looked up at me and just started to laugh. "This seems so damn awkward," she said. "Let's go back to the car." She grabbed my hand and led me down another side street. We crossed over Peachtree two blocks down and made our way back to the car.

Before we climbed inside, Faye moved in close to me and said, "I wanna take you home with me now, Bobby. Is that okay with you?"

She had a valid point. I had shied away from her sexually so many times before that any woman would have been unsure about it. "I want to go home with you and stay until you *make* me leave," I responded to her.

Then she kissed me, slow, and with an experienced twist of the tongue, just enough to tease me into insanity. We drove back to her apartment, and when we got off the elevator and walked through her door, I wasted no time at all. I grabbed Faye by two of the belt loops on her jeans and pulled her into me to kiss her back.

"I dreamed about this night so many times that I thought I was crazy," she said as she unzipped her jeans and went for mine.

"You wasn't the one that was crazy, I was," I responded. I slid my hand under her T-shirt and unfastened her bra to caress her.

We undressed each other, piece by piece, right there in the living room, with the efficiency of two surgeons. Then I lifted Faye's naked body in my arms and took her to the bedroom. As I carried her, Faye rubbed my chest with her left hand, the nape of my neck with her right, and kissed the side of my neck with her lips.

"Don't hold back, Bobby," she whispered to me.

I was afraid that if we didn't do something in a hurry, I might have wasted myself. Then I fumbled with the protection as if my life depended on getting it open in two seconds flat.

Faye said, "You don't have to use that if you don't want to."

I looked at her to make sure. Faye was dead serious, so I climbed into bed with her without it.

She rubbed my lower back and wrapped every body part around me that she could. "I wanted to wait until we did this to tell you that I loved you back," she said into my ear. Then she pulled my earlobe with her teeth as she told me again, "I love you, baby."

I slid deep into Faye and lost myself. "I love you, too," I mumbled. I had her hair in between my fingers, caressing her scalp, and then she attacked my neck and sucked hard. Talk about a soul mate! Faye gave me the best sexual experience I had had in years! I released everything to her, and in turn, she released everything to me as we made an earthquake in Atlanta. If we could have been on audiotape, we would have sounded like two safari animals. It was just *that* good! We were two eleven-year-old volcanoes filled with burning lava for each other that had never been released. And boy, did we melt each other!

When the ashes had settled and we were exhausted and resting in bed, I looked over at Faye and asked, "Will you marry me?" I was serious, too. I forgot about all my inhibitions. I thought of it all as plain nervousness.

Faye looked at me and just stared for a moment. "You know, we've never even met each other's parents before," she responded.

"We're representations of our parents, so it's like we know them already," I told her. "My father's a hardworking southern man with dignity just like your father. And my mother's a strong, ride-your-back-sometimes black woman just like your mother."

Faye laughed. "You say the craziest things sometimes."

"That's why I'm 'The Radioman,' " I told her.

She leaned over and caressed me. "Yeah, but are you finally *my* man, and more than just my friend?"

I looked into her eyes and said, "Definitely. And I'm sorry I waited so long."

"But what are we gonna do, though, have a long-distance thing? I mean, we really have to think this all through," she told me.

"Did you hear from your interviews yet?" I asked her.

"They were just preliminary interviews," she answered. "I probably won't get called again until they finish seeing everyone. That may take a few more weeks or a month."

"Well, in the meantime, we can meet each other's family and stuff, and introduce ourselves as friends."

Faye grinned. "That won't work. My sisters know who you are, *and* what you meant to me. We talked about you *plenty* of times."

"Well, now they'll get to meet me."

"And they'll know that we're in love the second they see us together," she said with a grin.

"Is that a bad thing?" I asked her.

She kissed me and said, "No. Of course not."

"Well, we'll just have to make the arrangements over the next few months to get our families used to us. I mean, we *are* grown now, aren't we?"

Faye smiled and said, "Yes, we are. We're all grown up now and still thinking about our parents. They must have done a damn good job on us, Bobby."

I chuckled. "That's respect. That's the way it should be. But at the same time, we're the ones that have to make things work, it's just a whole lot easier with your family's support."

"Amen to that," Faye told me.

I excused myself to use the bathroom and thought hard about smoking a cigarette. I was dying for one, but I wouldn't do it. I *couldn't* do it. Faye didn't even know that I smoked. It was a terrible habit that I had picked up from Pearl.

I walked into the bedroom, cigarette free, and asked, "Faye, why is it that you seemed to hate Pearl so much? Did something happen between you two that I didn't know about or something?" I just had to know. Faye hated Pearl long before she knew about my relationship with her, and I never understood why.

Faye looked at me evil-eyed and took a deep breath. She said, "To tell you the truth, it was nothing that she really did to me, it was just the way that she was. I mean, I just hated being in the same room with that girl because she was just so into herself, and what she had, and what she wanted to do, and who she knew . . .

"I just *hated* her! And I guess my intuition was telling me that something was going to happen between me and her, and I just didn't know what it was. So whenever she was around, I made sure to remind myself not to bother with her. It was like I just *knew* something.

"And sure enough, you see what happened. She ended up taking the only guy that I wanted to be with away from me."

I hugged Faye as tightly as I could and said, "Never again will that happen. Women like her give all sisters a bad name. I know that now, but I had to go through it to find out."

I *had* forgiven Pearl, but Faye didn't need to know. I figured we would discuss the entire situation in time. And I wasn't planning on rushing it.

Faye hugged me back and we cuddled. When we were good and rested, we made love again, and then once more when we woke up Saturday morning. We shared a huge breakfast in bed and spent another twenty-eight hours together before Faye drove me back to the airport and kissed me good-bye.

I sat through that entire two-hour flight with a grin on my face. It was the best getaway that I could have. And I wanted it to last forever, like Keith Sweat sang.

Guess What?

"Well, it's about time!" my mother said with a big smile. "Bobby hasn't brought a young woman home for us to meet in years." I sat at my parents' table with Faye, Brad, Brenda, and my niece and nephew. My father was grinning as well. In fact, everyone at the table was grinning, including Faye and me.

"All it takes is one," my father said with a wink. "The important one."

I felt like a big kid again at that table. It was as if we had already announced a wedding date, and we hadn't. I was simply bringing Faye home for a visit. Nevertheless, I guess everyone realized that my clock was ticking.

"So, you're from Macon, Georgia?" my mother asked Faye. I hadn't seen her that excited about anything I had done in a while.

"Born and raised," Faye answered.

My mother nodded to her. I could tell that Faye had Mom's full approval just from how she looked at her. Faye was from the South, and she was nowhere near skinny. She had the Venus frame and a good, southern heart. I should have brought her home a long time ago.

After dinner, Mom and Brenda took Faye hostage and had her help put away the food and dishes. I ended up outside on the lawn with Dad, Brad, and the kids. It was a beautiful summer evening.

"Are you gonna go ahead and marry this girl, Bobby?" Dad asked me.

Brad looked at me and smiled.

"Uncle Bobby's getting married?" Aminah asked him. She was nosy just like a keen girl would be.

"I don't know. You have to ask Uncle Bobby," Brad told his daughter.

"Are you getting married, Uncle Bobby?" my niece asked me with a smile. They were all waiting for me to answer. Even little Anthony seemed interested.

"Look, I'll let all of you guys know when the time comes," I responded, embarrassed.

My father said, "Well, this is what life is about, Bobby, taking care of business and building a family. Now you've done everything else, so it's nothing left but a couple more things on the list for you to do. So whenever you make that big decision, you just let us know.

"We're all very proud of you, Bobby. *Very* proud!"

I felt all bubbly inside. I didn't know what to do with myself. I went ahead and picked up Anthony just to release some of the energy I felt. Aminah wanted me to lift her up, too, so I ended up with both of the kids in my arms.

Then Brad said, "Everybody's talking about your show down in Charlotte, man. They're always asking me, 'Is he related to you?' I say, 'Yeah, that's my big brother! He grew up in the same house with me! That's my daughter's voice on his show! His niece!' And you know Aminah went ahead and told everybody at her school about you. All of the teachers in her building know."

"That's my uncle Bobby!" Brad said, mocking her.

Aminah and Anthony both laughed in my arms.

I just couldn't take it. I was feeling dizzy. Even my brother Brad was looking up to me. The next thing I knew, Brenda was outside with the camera. Faye and Mom were right on her heels.

"Smile!" she told me and the kids. We must have all taken thirty different pictures that night. Before we all went to bed, Mom made sure she got a word alone with me.

"Bobby, I know that I've been very hard on you, and I want to apologize for that, but I knew that I couldn't let you slack off," she told me. "Now I've been teaching *many* different kids all of my life, and I know which ones are gonna need that extra push. That's why I was never easy on you," she said.

"It's a very hard world out there for black men, Bobby, and you just can't allow your boys to settle for anything. But you *are* my son, and I *do* love you. And I'm very proud of you. You made this radio career work, and you did it on your own. Now you're ready to become a family man."

All of a sudden, my mother got all choked up and her eyes began to water.

"Aw, Mom, don't do this to me," I told her with a hug. You have to understand that I had rarely ever seen my mother getting all choked up about anything. I couldn't stand to see it.

"You just can't give up on your boys, Bobby," she said with a sniff.

"But I knew you could do it. I *always* knew that you could. I just had to make sure that you never stopped trying."

I was up all that night, staring at the ceiling. Faye was exhausted and knocked out, but I couldn't sleep. I had done all right for myself, I had to admit it. Things had gotten tough for me over the years, but I just kept on going like that little pink rabbit of Energizer batteries.

I realized that persistence was the key to success in life. No matter how bad things seem to get, if you're still living and thinking, you can never give up. Success could be right around the corner for you. And no matter how tired you *think* you are, you have to buckle up and make that sixteenth, seventeenth, and eighteenth turn, and then keep right on going.

•

After visiting Faye's family in Macon, we had the "okay" sign from both sides. All we had to do next was figure out how we would pull it off. I was willing to move if I needed to.

It took a couple of weeks before I could get all the guys together at Scotty's. I had filled them all in on the recent events of my love life. I was sitting at my stool having a light drink, and that was all I planned to have. I was just there to celebrate and gloat. All of the gang was there that night: Frank Watts, Mark Bishop, Big Bill, Yusef Green, and even Brother Abu. I invited Gene Carlton, too, but I guess that he was busy that night.

"So, you want us to throw you a bachelor party or a farewell party?" Frank asked me. Then he laughed and said, "I guess either way it's gonna be both, because you're not gonna be able to hang out around this place anymore."

Big Bill said, "Whenever you decide, Bobby, we can have the bachelor party right here."

"So when are you planning on doing it?" Mark asked me.

I shook my head and was grinning away. Faye and I hadn't announced any official marriage plans to our parents. We wanted to ease them into it. However, we still didn't know where we would live. Faye hadn't gotten any callbacks from her interviews yet.

"We haven't figured all of that out," I answered Mark.

Yusef and Brother Abu were just looking on. Scotty's was new territory for them.

Brother Abu asked, "How many years do you have left on your contract?"

"One more after this one." I looked at Yusef and said, "If I leave, maybe they'll let you take over my spot."

Yusef was baffled. "You're not really thinking about leaving, are you?" We all chuckled at the panic on his face.

"That's the name of the game, youngster," Frank told him. He looked at me and asked, "You didn't tell him how the radio game works, Bobby? You can't count on nothin', son. You picked the wrong business to go into if you want a security blanket. If you're in radio, you might as well be an artist like this guy over here, selling his art on street corners," he added, referring to Mark.

"I've never sold my art from a street corner," Mark responded.

"Would you do it if you had to?" Big Bill asked him.

Mark smiled. "I'm not gonna starve. I got a wedding coming up, too, now. So if I *must* go outside on the street corner, then that's what I gotta do. But I wouldn't count on having to do that. I've been doing pretty good lately."

"So when is your wedding?" Brother Abu asked him. Mark had told me that he asked the girl he met through my show to marry him a while back, but I had blocked it out of my mind.

"September sixteenth," Mark answered.

"You still want me to be in it?" I asked him. I hadn't given him an answer before. It didn't bother me anymore now that I had Faye.

Mark looked at me confused. "Well, I got somebody else now. I didn't think you wanted to be in it."

"Yeah, he'll do it now. He's in love now. He'll go out there and try to catch the garter," Frank said, laughing with a drink in his hand. They all laughed at me.

I joked around with the guys until midnight. Brother Abu, the family man, had left before then, and I gave Yusef a ride home when I left.

Yusef was extra quiet during the car ride.

"Hey, man, what are you thinking about over there?" I asked him. "If you're worried about me leaving the station, don't be. I'll get your job secured somehow. I'll even try to give you a year's pay if I have to," I said. Maybe I was a little tipsy, but I *was* sincere about trying to help him. I didn't want to do Yusef like Frank had done me years ago.

Yusef shook his head and said, "Naw, I'm not worried about that." Then he corrected himself. "Well, it does concern me, but I was thinking about my girl and all this marriage stuff that everybody was talking about tonight."

I smiled. "You're turning twenty-five this year, right?"

"I already did," he said.

"How old is she? It's the same girl you've been dating for a while now, right?"

"Yeah. She's twenty-three."

"What does she do?"

"She's a legal secretary right now. But she has a degree in journalism," he told me.

"So she can type fast, edit, and all that stuff?"

"Yeah."

I nodded. "She can get a job anywhere with those skills. Is she computer literate?"

"Yeah, she's on that Internet thing."

I nodded again. "I told you not to leave that girl. Now it's up to you to decide what you're gonna do with her. She sounds extra smart, willing to work, she's skilled, and does she tell you that she loves you?"

Yusef chuckled and said, "All the time. She's real emotional and affectionate and all that."

"In other words, she can be the mushy type?"

Yusef was still smiling. "Yeah," he told me.

"Well, I'll put it to you this way; you can put this thing off if you want to, talking about money problems and your career, and all this other stuff, but a good woman will stick it out with you. So I'm gonna tell you like my *little* brother told me years ago. And he's been happily married for seven years now. He said, 'It's nothing out there in them streets, Bobby. So if you find somebody that you really care for, and she cares about you, then you take her to the altar.'"

As usual, I added a few things, but I had the essence of what Brad had told me. Brother Abu had essentially said the same thing—you never let a good pair of shoes pass you by.

Yusef shook his head with a grin. "I knew I was in trouble as soon as we started that 'Soul Mates Week.' That's her favorite word now."

I broke out laughing. I said, "Well, to each his own, Yusef. I learned my lesson the hard way, and since you're your own man, I guess you have to learn your lesson the way you have to learn it."

I pulled up in front of Yusef's building.

He looked at me and said, "Good luck, man."

"So what are you going to do about this girl?" I asked. I was curious to see if Yusef would be as hardheaded as most young men in the nineties were. Including myself.

Yusef smiled. "I've been thinking about that for two weeks now. She wants us to get an apartment together. But I figure, if we're gonna move in together, then I might as well marry her."

I nodded my head and smiled at him. "Good idea." Maybe Yusef had been listening to his elders after all.

I got back home in Takoma Park and found that Faye had left me a message to call her.

"Hey, baby," I said to her. It sounded unusual to me, too, but that's how I began to refer to her.

"Guess what, Bobby?" she said.

"What?" I asked her. My heart started to race. Was it a good what or a bad what?

"The girl in Dallas decided not to leave, so their position isn't open anymore. I called Miami back, and they're not trying to give me the money that I want."

I was breathing real slowly. "What about Channel Seven in D.C.?" I asked her.

"Well, they called me today and left me a message."

"And?" She was torturing me.

"Bobby, they don't want to give me the money that I want either."

"So you didn't take it?" I was getting ready for an argument. She said she wanted to start over modestly. I could understand that she had gotten used to living a certain way, and that she expected to earn a certain salary, but I was ready to explode anyway. I wasn't exactly poor. How much money did she need?

Faye said, "Well, I decided that I wanted to be happy. And I know that I can be happy with you, no matter what I make. So tomorrow, I'll call them up and tell them I'll be back in Washington in three weeks, after I give the station in Atlanta my two weeks' notice."

"YES! COME ON BACK TO DADDY, BABY!" I shouted into the phone. It was the best damn news of my life.

Faye laughed and said, "Guess what else?"

I calmed down and took another deep breath. I said, "Ah, Faye, I don't want to be a sour sport or anything, but I don't think I want to play these guessing games anymore. One round of this is all that I can take in one phone call."

Faye sighed and said, "Okay, I'll tell you when I see you then."

I didn't like that idea either. I said, "Well, if you don't mind, how 'bout you tell me now." I had my fingers crossed. What could it possibly be?

"I'm pregnant," she said.

My mouth dropped open and my chest felt ready to cave in. Then my cheeks rose on my face and my teeth popped out. I took a deep breath and said . . . nothing at all.

Faye asked, "Well, are you gonna say something or what?"

"I can't breathe, and my head feels kind of light. But I'm smiling, I guess that's a good thing, right?" I said to her.

Faye started to laugh. "I'm smiling, too."

"Okay," I responded. "So what do we do next?"

Faye started to laugh even harder. "I don't know, Bobby. I'm not experienced at this."

I had spilled the milk while messing around on the farm, so it was time for me to get my wallet out. I said, "Faye, you never answered me before. . . . Will you marry me?"

There was a long pause on the phone. Then I heard Faye sniffling. "Yes, Bobby. Of course I'll marry you . . . Daddy."

Talk about feeling tingles all over! I couldn't think straight, breathe straight, or sit up straight! I was just a mess, like egg yolk spilled all over the floor. "Ah, Faye, I'm gonna have to call you back, ah, in a few minutes. All right?" My words didn't even come out straight.

Faye cracked up and continued to sniffle. The next thing I knew, my eyes were watering.

"Okay, well, call me back then," she said.

I gingerly hung up the phone and stood on unsteady legs. It was close to one o'clock in the morning. I went straight for my cigarettes. Then I caught myself.

"Dammit, I gotta stop smoking!" I hollered. I put the cigarette in my mouth and smoked it anyway. When I was finished, I smoked another one. I smiled and shook my head. "I'm just gonna have to work on this thing." Then I called Faye back.

"Faye," I said.

"Yes," she told me.

"I'm ready to talk now."

She started to laugh again.

I said, "And you know what?"

"What, Bobby?" she asked me through her laughter.

"We *are* soul mates, right?"

"Yes we are."

"And that means we can help each other through anything, right?"

"Yes we can."

"Well, baby . . . you're gonna have to help me stop smoking cigarettes."

Even though I was serious, and cancer was a serious issue, we both started to laugh and couldn't help ourselves. We laughed and laughed, and the wetness continued to swell up in my eyes and drip from my face. I didn't even bother to wipe them.

I had everything I ever wanted. *Angel Thomas, eat your heart out! Girl finds boy in real life, too!*

I sat back in my La-Z-Boy chair with my feet up and talked to Faye all night long. We had a lot of plans to make. And we had a lot of years ahead to love each other.

Special Thanks

To Patrick Peterson, Barry Murray, Chris Hollis, Bill Reed, John Rodriguez, Charles Ford, Malcolm Beech, Stephen Monroe, Ike Kendrick (RIP), Amos Drummond, Kevin Johnson, Tony and Daniel McNeill, Randy Crumpton, Mr. Harold Bell, Steve Thompson, Nathaniel Sollis, Gary Fields, Charles "Mann" Werts, Scott and Corey Hilton, James-Chris and Michael Bucknor, Charles Hutchinson, Ricky Burks, Jamil Hamilton, Danny McQueen, Isaac Taggert, Aubrey Watkins, Levan and John White Jr., Jay Debow, Wayne Brewer, Joseph McLeod, Shamir Simpson, Bodie Essient, Calvin Moore, Craig McBride, Tracy Hunter, Shawn Sollars, Keith Young, Eric "Killer" Young, Doug Bell III, James Caldwell, Walter Pearson, Malik Azeez, Vance-Parrish-Lou and Marvin DeBose, Jason and Carlin Warley, Kevin MacMillan, Andre and Perry Thomas, Charles Powell, Greg Green, Robert Collins, Richard, Melvin and Eton, Gill and Benny, Mark Butler, Che and Todd Mitchell, Greg Bell, Chris White, Chris Williams, John-John and Anthony, Terrence Peters, Shawn-Shang-Shannon and Stacy Reed, Steve and Nate Hill, "Smiley," Wayne and Brian Davis Jr. and Sr., Mark and Barry Jones, Roberto Bradley (RIP), "Poppy," Marc and Mike Hamilton, Chris Owens, "Chucky" Brunson, Mark "Burns" (Harris), Brian and Byron Bailey, Andre Hayes and Desmond (RIP), Charles Wise, Bruce McCall, Robert Black, Durell DuPree, Darryl Cephas, John Ashford, Kwame Alexander, D. Knowledge, Gene Roberson, Mark Alexander, Fred Thomas, Ray Mahari, Ray Llanos, Leslie Ali and Rico, Warren Sledge, Rick Medina, Brother Wadud, Brother Oba, Keith Robinson, J. R. Fenwick, Q. Jones, Ronnie M. Friday, Hakeem Rushdan and sons, Mamadi Nyasuma, Chris Downing, Grant Holly, "Tungee," Darin "Buck" Williams, cousin "Reece" (Reuben Simmons) and uncle Gary (RIP), cousin "Meatball" (David Crawford), cousin Kevin Tolbert and Alvin-Anthony-Keith (RIP), uncle Joe-Jose-Andre-Montaque-George and Dennis McLaurin and Grandpop Everidge (RIP), cousin Dennis Jr., cousin Steve-Henry-Bill-Shawn-Sammy-James-

Michael and George Briggs and uncle George (RIP), cousin Carl Tyree and sons, uncle Emerson Alston, Kenny Butts, Larry Frazier, William and Sean Brown, Ira Henderson, cousin Levonne Johnson, Tom and Anthony Robinson, Joe and Steven Carvalho, Joe Sr., and Joe Jr. Ballard, Randy Stribling and sons, Allen Ho and son, "T." and Dr. Otelio Randall, Kala Threat, Ernest and Keita Cooper, Sanfre DuBose, Michael "Teenager" Coates, Cornell Belcher, cousin "Bockey" (Bernard Wilkes), Li'l Jose, "Boo" (Shawn) and Wayne, L. J., Marcus, Jarriel, Andre, Jason, Maurice, Demetrius, Dominique, Li'l Larry and Will, Li'l brothers Mel Jr. and Phillip Alston, nephews Damaar, Antonio and Kahlil, Robert Tyree (Daddy, Love, MIA), my strong father figure and role model Melvin A. Alston Sr., The West Oak Lane Youth Association (The Wildcats of Philadelphia, PA), Central High School #246, 247, and 248, authors James Pritchett, Clarence Nero, Mikell Davis, Brother Akil, Kevin Clark, William A. Simms, Nelson George, E. Lynn Harris, and Terry McMillan, and all the postcollege and noncollege black men out there going through many changes in America and abroad, you were *all* my inspirations for this storyline.

To Mercedes Allen, who was like a writing manager impelling me to produce during times when I was frustrated and clueless. To Pamela Artis for your important suggestions. To my agent Denise Stinson for coming up with the marketable title (*A Do Right Man,* originally titled *Burned Out*). My editor Dawn Daniels for waiting for this rarely written about "good black man" book to arrive. To all the radio people who allowed me to pull on their ears for insider information, Paul Turner (Dallas, KKDA), Tamlin Henry (Philly, WDAS), Tamika Artist (Philly, WHYY), Mary Mason (Philly, WHAT), John Arnold (Detroit, WCHB), Bob Jones (Oak-town, KDIA), Mark Heimberger (Chi-town, WDWS), Mechell Jetter-Burgette (Philly, WNWR), and Kristance Coates, thank you for the 4-1-1.

To all the sisters and general readers who bought, read, and loved *FLYY GIRL, Capital City,* or *BattleZone.* To those few brothers who *do* read fiction, it's always a pleasure to see you guys with a novel in your hands. And last but not least, to Karintha and my son, Ameer, for putting up with Daddy while he nailed out his next book.

The next one is for my loving grandmothers, Geraldine Briggs McLaurin, Mercyle Tyree Simmons, Betty Alston (RIP), my sisters "Dee-Dee" (Deidra) and Darlene Adams, Cydnee and Paula Randall, and to all of my aunts and extended family of strong black women.

Peace & Love
Sincerely yours
Omar Tyree